The Slip

Katie Smith Matison

ISBN: 1502442876
ISBN 13: 9781502442871
Library of Congress Control Number: 2014917061
CreateSpace Independent Publishing Platform
North Charleston, South Carolina

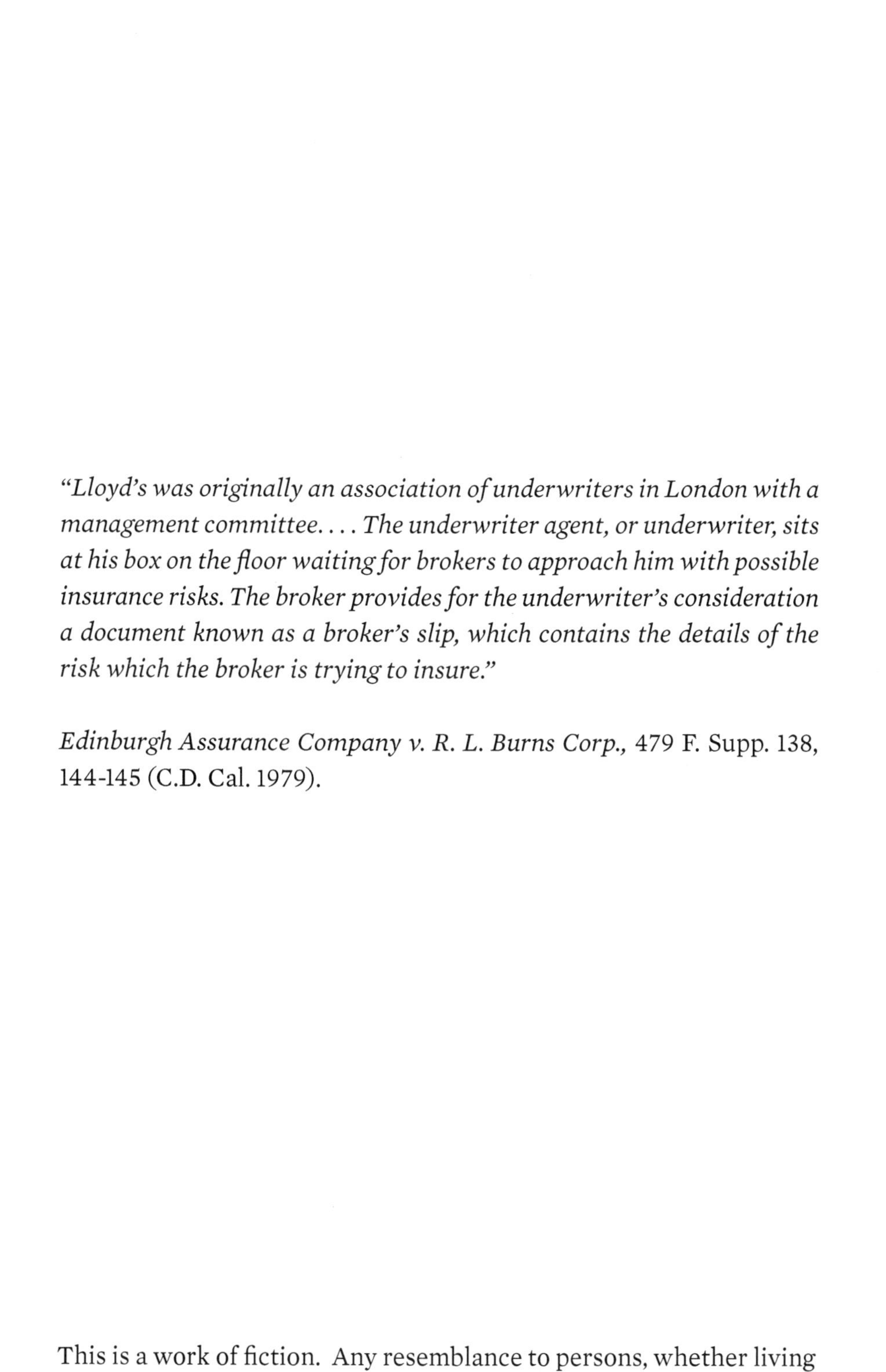

"Lloyd's was originally an association of underwriters in London with a management committee. . . . The underwriter agent, or underwriter, sits at his box on the floor waiting for brokers to approach him with possible insurance risks. The broker provides for the underwriter's consideration a document known as a broker's slip, which contains the details of the risk which the broker is trying to insure."

Edinburgh Assurance Company v. R. L. Burns Corp., 479 F. Supp. 138, 144-145 (C.D. Cal. 1979).

This is a work of fiction. Any resemblance to persons, whether living or dead, or to any event, is purely coincidental.

For Davey
and in loving memory of my mother, Vivienne

Prologue

JULY 15, 1920

The scrivener made the latest entry in the ledger with broad, fastidious strokes of the quill shortly after the bell rang to announce the disaster. When he completed the task, he leaned back in the scarred chair which was pulled against the partner's desk and shoved in the corner, waiting patiently for the ink to dry. Intent on his work, he was oblivious to the frenetic late morning activity of the underwriting floor of Lloyd's of London. Satisfied that his daily entry was finally complete, he reverently lifted the heavy ledger and returned it to its customary shelf on the rostrum in the center of the underwriting room. Following strict protocol, he opened the ledger to the current morning's entry. The older volume propped against the rostrum, which chronicled the known maritime disasters over the last 150 years, was carefully aligned with the newer book on the podium.

The pages of the older book contained the same meticulous calligraphy detailing the loss of the *TRIUMPH*, a fully rigged brig loaded with Greek antiquities that sank off the coast of Kithira while en route to London on July 18, 1820. The monumental disaster was legendary in underwriting circles. Three Lloyd's syndicates insuring both the vessel and its priceless cargo had been driven to insolvency by the event.

He returned his attention to the entry in the new ledger and gently smoothed the pages, silently offering a prayer for the lost souls aboard the *BYZANTIUM.* The screw-propelled iron steamer had been caught in a hurricane while sailing en route from Rio de Janeiro to New York. *BYZANTIUM* had carried one hundred four passengers and a crew of thirty-five, none of whom had survived. The ship and its cargo of emeralds valued at three million GBP had disappeared somewhere in the Eastern Caribbean. The hull, protection and indemnity, and cargo insurance policies were all subscribed by Lloyd's syndicates. The tragedy would undoubtedly extract a heavy toll from the underwriting syndicates who had insured the venture. Of course, he thought, the underwriters were paid to accept the risk. Underwriting was a lucrative business, and unprecedented fortunes had been made speculating on the maritime trade at Lloyd's over the last 250 years. The institution that had its humble origins in a London coffee shop in 1688 now dominated the world's marine insurance market.

The scrivener studied the script critically and aligned the books carefully one last time. He shivered involuntarily as he envisioned the stark terror of the passengers and crew as the howling winds and marauding seas capsized the *BYZANTIUM*, plunging the vessel into the green depths of the Caribbean. He could only imagine the horror of their final moments, struggling to survive and save one another, before the raging current ripped them apart and robbed them of their last breath. He heard the talk at the pubs that drowning was a peaceful way to die once a man finally stopped struggling and inhaled the water, giving into his fate. The scrivener had decided that these stories were just bloody old wives tales perpetuated by fools. He could never imagine his own beautiful young wife and baby suffering such a tragedy. Peaceful, indeed!

Catastrophic disasters of such magnitude had occurred on only a handful of occasions during his ten-year term of employment. At least two of the other losses before the Great War had been directly linked to pilfering pirates who absconded with valuable cargo, murdering the crew and burning the abandoned vessels. The *MAGENTA*, an Argentine vessel, had broken on the rocks off of Cape Cod on the American Coast. Only the *TITANIC* sinking on April 14, 1912, had involved the deaths of women and innocent children. Like the *TITANIC* disaster, the *BYZANTIUM* sinking was a tragedy of the worst proportion.

As he walked away from the rostrum, the scrivener noticed a small band of brokers discussing the casualty with a man he recognized as a hull underwriters' representative. He could hear the nervous tenor in their voices as they discussed the *BYZANTIUM* and he realized that at least one of them must have placed the risk. Across the room, he caught sight of the lead underwriter on the slip for cargo insurance for the *BYZANTIUM* in animated conversation with his claims manager. Still moved by the news of the travesty, he said another prayer for the passengers aboard the *BYZANTIUM* and their families as he returned to the telegraph room.

JULY 18, 1949

Gerald Morris sat with the grim assembly of onlookers seated behind the plate glass partition in the adjoining room. Although it was nearly midnight, the glaring cones of light illuminated the execution chamber as brilliantly as a midsummer Alabama afternoon. He sat transfixed with the spectacle of the prison guards as they smeared conductive salve and strategically positioned the electrodes on the condemned man's arms, chest, and legs under his thin cotton prison-issued pants and shirt. The prisoner took a deep breath as the Alabama prison guard slipped the death hood over his head, fastening it behind his neck.

Gerald stared at the hooded figure struggling against the leather restraints holding him in the electric chair. Alan Carter had been barely nineteen years old when he had murdered Gerald's five-year-old-granddaughter, Jenny. Gerald closed his eyes briefly and again mentally replayed the events of that spring evening two years ago. It had been a clear bluebird day and the azaleas were still in magnificent bloom. Jenny was sitting on the front counter playing with a new doll as Gerald closed down the business for the day. He recalled how Jenny's silken strawberry blonde curls cascaded down her back and framed her innocent face. Suddenly, Carter burst through the front door, brandishing a shotgun at Gerald, who was standing behind the counter. After Gerald surrendered the contents of the cash register, Carter had simply smirked before he raised the shotgun and pulled the trigger. Instinctively, Gerald ducked at the last minute. The shot pierced Jenny's skull, killing her instantly, before it exited and lodged in Gerald's left lung.

Gerald had somehow managed to crawl on his knees cradling Jenny in his arms through the smoke and out the rear entry as the flames erupted from the fire Carter had started. The front of Gerald's shirt was coated in copper-smelling blood and brain matter. Gasping for air, he took refuge in the grass lawn behind the station before he lost consciousness with Jenny in his arms. The two of them were found by a passing trucker who stopped when he saw the fire.

Jenny had been his Gerald's only relative in the world. *If only he could have saved her*! *Gerald would have gladly died in her place if Jenny could have lived. She had her entire life in front of her! If only he had not ducked, she might have been alive today.*

Gerald had testified on behalf of the prosecution at the trial of Alan Carter. He had broken down on the witness stand as he recounted the events of that evening and identified Jenny's killer who was sitting complacently at the defense table. He had gone to every appellate argument made by Carter's attorney seeking to overturn the conviction. Gerald had *lived* to see the man punished. Tonight, however, he felt an eerie sense of loss as he looked at the young man strapped in the chair.

There were only a few spectators in the somber room. He noticed two members of the press, sitting quietly in the back row with the

Baptist minister. Alan Carter's defense attorney was conspicuously absent. The prosecutor, prison physician, and the warden stood in the corner, intently discussing the upcoming University of Alabama football season.

A hush settled over the onlookers at midnight. The warden nodded and someone behind a curtain threw the switch to activate the electric chair. Gerald was transfixed in horror as Alan Carter's body gyrated with involuntary spasms with the current. Even behind the glass partition, there was a distinct odor of burning flesh and hair. After what seemed to be an interminable time, Carter's body was limp. The prison physician put the stethoscope to Alan's chest and then nodded, pronouncing him dead. Out of the corner of his eye, he noticed the district attorney shake the prison warden's hand.

Gerald waited to feel relief after witnessing justice dispensed for Jenny's murder. Instead, he felt only emptiness. A prison guard escorted him back to his car in the reserved lot. Gerald sat immobile in the driver's seat and cried for Jenny and everything he had lost.

If only he could have changed things!

He leaned forward and gripped the steering wheel as the fullness he had felt in the middle of his chest that evening intensified, replaced by a savage explosion. Suddenly his body was rigid from the post-cardiac arrest seizure from oxygen deprivation. He could hear the sound of the car door opening and the baritone voice of a prison guard promising him that he would get the doctor. The seizures stopped abruptly and Gerald was motionless, his pallor turning a lovely robin's egg blue from oxygen deprivation.

He was only vaguely aware of the voices around him as he floated on a peaceful sea. In the light above him, he could see Jenny extending her hand toward him lovingly. The golden corona at the end of the dark tunnel beckoned and he felt himself drawn toward the light, which bathed him in its soft, comforting glow. It was truly beautiful. Then the light faded, and he felt a profound sense of loss. The angel of death loomed overhead, suspended in the abyss. He was quite ordinary—the quintessential everyman. Gerald surrendered his soul before he fell into nothingness.

JULY 18, 2012

Ewan Donaldson reclined in the dilapidated aluminum deck chair trying unsuccessfully to shield his eyes with a folded towel from the noonday sun. For once, the usually noisy rundown apartment complex was relatively quiet, and he had some peace. The air was still and heavy with humidity and sweat poured down his torso. Despite the intensity of the heat, swimming was out of the question. The chlorine content in the swimming pool adjacent to the cracked concrete deck was low, and green slime was suspended in the cloudy water. He had decided that North Miami was a hell-hole since his move over a year earlier. On days like this, he longed for the soft sea breeze that he had loved in St. Thomas. A man could breathe in the Caribbean. The metropolitan sprawl of south Florida bothered a man like Ewan. He needed his space.

Ewan tried to doze in the sun. He did not have to report to work in the dive shop until 3:30 today. Thursdays were generally his day off, but today Ewan had agreed to cover for a coworker so he could attend his grandmother's funeral. Ewan had been glad to help. He was a team player and was eager for the income from the overtime. He was saving for the American dream. In his case, the dream would be a small cottage in Hawaii—maybe the Big Island or even the Waimea coast. He had heard that the diving in Hawaii was incredible and that the local women were beautiful. It would be paradise—maybe even better than St. Thomas.

He allowed himself to think about the money again. To date, he had saved almost $55,000. This time, he had decided to save this money instead of throwing it away as he had with the other jobs. Of course, most of it had been earned by snuffing out the diver, Harris Blake, who was trying to recover emeralds from the sunken ship, *BYZANTIUM*. He would have earned all $100,000 if he had not been compelled to split the money with Thornton. But of course, Thornton—the chicken-shit—had needed his help. Thornton had never had much backbone. It had been easy money. The diver had been using Nitrox I for the 130-foot wall dive. The diver had been very secretive about his destination, but Ewan speculated that the diver intended to go to the spectacular wall dive off of the coast of St. Croix. Typically, Nitrox I is specially prepared and measured because the safety of the dive could be compromised. It had been a simple matter for Ewan to radically manipulate the oxygen content in the tank and give the tanks back to Thornton, the diver's employee. Moreover, there was nothing to connect Ewan to the diver, other than Thornton. Predictably, the diver had drowned, and the Coast Guard had ruled his death accidental. It had been the perfect murder.

The diver's business partner had been happy with the results of Ewan's work. The man, however, had been visibly disappointed that Ewan could not pinpoint the dive location. Nevertheless, the man had even given them a small tip and promised that there could be other work in the future involving the diver's wife. Apparently, there was some unfinished business between them. Ewan had arranged to stay in touch. But after the accident, they had all agreed that it would be best for Thornton and Ewan to leave St. Thomas. Eventually, Ewan would have to deal with Thornton. Perhaps he could find a way to get Thornton's share of the money too before he killed him. After all, the more money he amassed, the quicker he could realize his dream.

Ewan checked his dive watch. It was high noon. He still had time to catch a quick nap before it was time to shower and go to work. He tried to relax, closed his eyes, and thought about Hawaii.

Chapter I

JUNE 9, 2012

The squirrel enjoyed his breakfast of cambium and acorns on the lowest branch of the live oak, which paralleled the expansive lawn for nearly eighty feet. The gnarled branches of the majestic oaks interlaced overhead, creating a shaded cathedral along the eastern path through the park. From the security of his perch on the tree, he could observe the early morning activity on the blacktop road below. For more than two decades, the road had been closed to automobiles and was now only accessible to pedestrians, bicyclists, and skaters. There were quite a few dogs out with their companions for a morning romp in the soft mist. The squirrel had learned to be wary of the dogs and cats in the vicinity. Although many of them were harmless, there were those who would like nothing better than to kill a squirrel. Over the last year, he had seen a nasty tempered Rottweiler kill a mallard hen and two baby squirrels. It had nothing to do with hunger. The killing had been merely for sport.

A tremendous marble fountain circled by wrought-iron benches gurgled behind the stone balustrade separating the front of Audubon Park from St. Charles Avenue. The branches of the oak trees along the edge of the park stretched over the median in an intricate network, allowing the squirrels and birds safe passage above the streetcar tracks below. A long, shallow lagoon inhabited by flocks of mallards and domestic geese ran through the center of the park. The lagoon was filled with water hyacinths and surrounded by tropical plants. Over a century and a half earlier, a lovely stone bridge had been erected over the lagoon near a stone waterfall. The squirrel had never once ventured beyond the bridge.

The park was dissected in the opposite direction by Magazine Street. The western half of the park had been enclosed and converted into zoological gardens. He had heard the occasional descriptions of the exotic creatures maintained in the zoo from those squirrels reckless enough to venture outside of their territory. None of the exotic animals held any interest for the squirrel. He had an acutely developed sense of danger and was content to remain in his territory. Neighboring squirrels, as well as the many predators inhabiting the area, strictly enforced their territorial claims.

The squirrel had staked a claim to approximately eight acres in the front of the park. His territory began at the bridge across the lagoon and extended to the oaks on the median of St. Charles Avenue. The grove of oak trees beyond the fountain marked the southern boundary. The northern perimeter extended through the expansive lawn of the stone mansion bordering the avenue and the park.

The squirrel sat on his haunches chewing the acorns and lazily tossing the empty shells onto the road below. The shells intermittently bounced onto a passing jogger or an unsuspecting dog. The gentle rain of the shells was generally unnoticed by the traffic below, and the squirrel's presence remained undetected. Occasionally, feeling mischievous, he would pelt a dog or cat with a shower of bark or acorn shells, taunting them from his perch high above the blacktop. Today, he did not make the effort. The squirrel did not have any scores to settle.

After breakfast, as was his habit, he set off to patrol his territory. He darted across the interlacing branches of the live oaks, leaping effortlessly across pencil limbs to adjacent trees. Despite the dizzying heights, his equilibrium remained intact as he scurried down the tree trunks, holding his position with his little claws.

It was still very early, and the streetcar stop was empty. The squirrel leaped down from a stately oak and ran across the concrete pad between two azalea bushes to a stash of acorns. He pawed the ground with his claws and pulled up three acorns he had seen a female squirrel who shared his territory bury three days ago. He consumed the acorns on the soft grass, still damp with the morning dew. He felt safe and secure. Dogs and cats, fearful of the traffic, rarely ventured onto the median without their owners.

As he finished the acorns, he heard the female scolding him from her perch in the tree overhead. He knew that at only a year, she was relatively young and inexperienced. He ignored her chatter and ascended a nearby oak on the median just as he heard the streetcar bell and felt the vibrations as the streetcar rounded the corner on the track.

The squirrel spent the rest of the morning searching for green acorns, which he buried at strategic intervals throughout his territory. Storing small caches of food was a driving instinct. In the winter, after the acorns had fallen and food was no longer plentiful, he could return to the caches he had buried and survive. Alternatively, he could pilfer the cache of another squirrel in the territory. Of course, there was never really a shortage of food in the park, and many of the caches remained undisturbed for years until small plants began to sprout and were removed by the park attendants.

As usual, he noticed the pedestrians gathering on the benches by the fountain as the sun was high overhead. Descending the trunk of a large oak, he cautiously scanned the area for predators. He noticed Rusty, an older retriever, lying comfortably at his owner's feet. Rusty and his man were regulars in the park, and the squirrel had learned that he was not a threat. There were a few young mothers with their strollers and prams enjoying the cool shade under the oaks as a welcome respite from the heat. A few students from the nearby schools joked and shared sandwiches. A pensive man with a goatee and wire-rimmed glasses read poetry from a paperback. None of them, except the old man, offered the promise of a snack.

The squirrel noticed that today Rusty's man had a clear plastic bag containing bread crumbs and peanuts resting on the bench. A small band of pigeons enthusiastically feasted on the litter of bread-crumbs on the cement. Gingerly, the squirrel approached the edge of the concrete perimeter of the fountain and waited patiently for the man to notice him. The young female squirrel who shared his territory nervously stood on the trunk of a tree a few feet behind him. She maintained her balance with her magnificent gray tail, which was tinged with hints of russet and cream fur.

The old man finally noticed the squirrel. "There you are! I am going to make you work for it today! What do you think, Rusty? Let's see if he will take it from my hand today." He held out a boiled peanut, waving it tantalizingly toward the squirrel. "Come on," he coaxed. "Rusty won't bother you."

The squirrel sat on his haunches, revealing his cream underside and assessed the situation. His finally honed instincts allowed him to sense danger in a myriad of circumstances. He had a peculiar ability to interpret human behavior and was the only squirrel he knew who could understand their language.

Rusty yawned, rested his chin on his paws, and closed his eyes. The squirrel moved a few feet closer and paused, standing on his haunches. The young female watched him intently.

He ignored her and scampered toward the man. As he approached, he could smell the overwhelming scent of the dog. Carefully, he took the peanut in his mouth and scampered a safe distance away to devour the contents. He returned again as the man held out another nut while Rusty snored softly beside him.

The young female was finally persuaded to abandon her perch on the trunk, although she refused to take the peanut from the man's hand. "You are a young one! In time, you and I can become friends," the man said as he tossed her a nut, which she voraciously consumed.

The man fed the squirrels the entire bag of nuts. Then, he folded the bag and stuffed it in his pocket. The squirrels and pigeons watched him as he ate a small sandwich before he and the dog slowly walked toward the avenue.

Their appetites sated, the squirrels chased each other playfully across the tree branches until they tired in the heat. The squirrel enjoyed these games. The young female he knew as Kiki was coming into season and would be ready to mate soon, in time to produce a litter in the late summer. As the dominant male of the territory, it was unquestionable that he would father Kiki's litter.

The squirrel spent the remainder of the afternoon safely resting in his nest, located in the spacious hollow of a sturdy live oak over fifty feet above the ground. The nest was a real find and offered sure protection from snakes and predatory birds. More than one squirrel over the last year had lost its life to an owl. Like all squirrels, he had constructed several dummy nests out of leaves and twigs in the crux of sturdy branches interspersed in the tree. These nests served as a foil against predators and aggressive squirrels and provided a safe haven in an emergency.

As the light dimmed and the soft air cooled, the squirrel emerged from the nest. Carefully, he scanned the area for predatory birds and cats before descending to the lowest branch of the oak that extended over a solid brick wall. The squirrel climbed down the wall onto the cool manicured lawn, pausing to drink from the reflection pool. He scampered lightly over to the brilliant white gazebo, delighted to find that she was waiting for him.

"There you are! It's late. I was afraid you were not coming tonight." The old woman sat in a wrought iron chair drinking an iced pink liquid out of a narrow glass. A plate of cheese, crackers, and sliced fruit rested on the table. The squirrel picked up a large slice of pear which he eagerly devoured, followed by an orange segment, an apple slice, and a thin piece of cheese. The woman ignored him as she set up the scrabble board and a checker board.

When the squirrel finished eating, he dipped his paws in the small water bowl the woman had laid out and washed his face, smoothing the hair on his cheeks. He was not bothered by the large Samoyed that slept peacefully at the feet of her mistress. The squirrel noticed that the dog's ears were still erect, nonetheless, and her frothy white coat shimmered in the early evening light.

"It's getting late. Brandy will be home soon. We should begin," she said, pushing a black checker diagonally onto the adjacent black square.

The squirrel studied her with interest. He loved the challenge of a good game. After a moment, he planted a forepaw in the center of the red checker on the far left of the board and shoved it forward to the next black square.

The game had begun.

Chapter II

JULY 19, 2012

At six thirty sharp, Brandy Blake programmed the burglar alarm securing the small antique shop before retiring to the crowded office located on the second floor. It took her over thirty minutes to enter all of the daily transactions on the new accounting software. Massenet was one of the smallest and the newest antique stores on Royal Street in the French Quarter. Since she had opened the doors three months ago, she had never shown a profit. Her advisors had assured her that it would take time and that things would pick up soon. She had her doubts. The shop was located at the foot of Royal near Esplanade, which was out-of-the-way for many tourists. Most of the carriage trade headed for the well-established shops like Manheim Galleries, whose glossy color ads graced the pages of many interior decorating magazines.

It was 7:30 by the time she turned off the computer and flipped the electronic thermostat to the evening setting to conserve electricity. The installation of central air-conditioning and heat in a 250 year-old building had been very expensive. But air-conditioning was a necessity in the sweltering heat of a late New Orleans summer, and Brandy had gladly made the investment.

Descending the small horseshoe staircase, she scanned the room to make sure everything was in order for the following day. She had acquired some lovely things in the inventory. There were two marble topped French commodes, a set of French Haviland china from the late 1800's, a number of paintings, gilded mirrors, armoires, and several small Persian carpets. Three glittering Waterford chandeliers were suspended over a French chaise lounge and two chairs. The Limoges, Baccarat and Lalique figurines were displayed in the magnificent bookcases lining the southern wall of the shop. She gazed at the collection appreciatively before switching the lights to the dimmed night setting, which softly illuminated the room for the benefit of evening window-shoppers.

She exited the building from a side door and walked three blocks to the small garage where she rented space for her car. A pale light cast long shadows down the busy street. Despite the darkening sky with threatening storm clouds, throngs of tourists strolled lazily through the French Quarter in the humid air. She heard the lively sounds of Dixieland jazz from the direction of Bourbon Street.

The festive atmosphere did very little to lift her spirits. Instead, it was only a painful reminder that Harris was gone. Before they were married, Harris loved to roam the Quarter, stopping for a beer and oysters in the Acme, a drink at the Napoleon House, and coffee and beignets at Café Du Monde in the early morning hours. The two of them loved the street musicians and Preservation Hall. As a doctoral candidate in marine biology, his funds had been limited, but they had enjoyed the inexpensive pleasures accessible to them.

The two of them had met when she had returned to New Orleans from Vassar to attend a debutant party. Harris had accompanied the older sister of a friend to a small gathering in the early morning hours after the party. Brandy immediately fell in love with his intellect and vitality despite the fact that she usually found that extremely good-looking men were annoyingly self-centered. They were married a year after Brandy finished college and moved to Coral Gables, Florida, where Harris secured a position as an associate professor at the University of Miami. Brandy found a job teaching art in the Florida public school system. They bought a tiny house in Coconut Grove and spent the weekends in the Florida Keys or the Bahamas scuba diving whenever possible. They were living their dreams. And money was certainly not a problem. Brandy's parents had died when she was seventeen in a plane crash in New Mexico. The real property, with the exception of the building in the French Quarter, had been sold and invested along with the sizable estate of her parents. Their future was secure.

Within the first two years of their arrival in Miami, Harris became fascinated with historic shipwrecks. As a result of his obsession, he failed to cultivate professional relationships in his department or play the political games necessary to survive in a competitive atmosphere. His interest in publishing articles in marine biology journals waned along with the promise of tenure. After five years at the University of Miami, he announced one day that he had lost all interest in marine biology and had given his notice to the university. He wanted to scour the Caribbean for historic shipwrecks. They sold their house for a sizable profit the year before the economic meltdown and moved to St. Thomas in the Virgin Islands.

Brandy found a job teaching art in a local primary school and spent her free time decorating their small hillside home they had purchased which had an enchanting view of the harbor. Their daughter, Rene, was born within a year, and Brandy then stayed at home to raise the baby. Engrossed in his work, Harris became increasingly distant. He developed a friendship with Thad Stuart, a local businessman who operated a small day sailing vessel for the tourists pouring into the area aboard the large pleasure ships. The two men quickly discovered that searching for shipwrecks was an expensive proposition. It was then that Harris prevailed upon Brandy to invest a substantial portion of her inheritance into their salvage operations. Harris purchased a magnetometer, differential global positioning system, Fathometer, side-scan sonar, sub-bottom profiler, and a forty-five-foot cabin cruiser built in

1960 that had been dry-docked, restored, and equipped with state-of-the-art equipment. It had been a huge expense and had strained Brandy's resources. Every evening, Harris dutifully chronicled their efforts in a Word file journal on his laptop.

Following several disappointments, their perseverance was rewarded after four years. Harris had surprised her one night with three uncut emeralds believed to be part of the cargo aboard a Panamanian-flagged cargo vessel, which was believed to have broken apart and lodged on a 160-foot-deep ridge about 13 miles off the coast of the United States Virgin Islands. Harris had discovered the emeralds scattered among the coral of a shelf during a shallow wall dive. They celebrated their success with a rare dinner and a bottle of French champagne in a posh dining room of one of the larger resort hotels. Harris worked feverishly over the next two months, remaining aboard the boat they had purchased instead of returning home. He seemed preoccupied, working for hours on the computer on the rare evening when he came home. Thereafter, he refused to discuss the project with Brandy, despite her persistent questions.

"I don't have anything new to tell you," he had snapped. "It may have all been a fluke."

They had argued several times about his secretiveness. Harris was paranoid that information about their small find could leak to some big-name operators who could use their data to locate the wreck and all of the emerald cargo believed to have a present-day value of $200 million and reap all of the profits. Brandy felt alone and shut out. Rene was growing up with a weekend father. Moreover, her assets had become alarmingly depleted over Harris's pipe-dreams. Brandy had Rene's future and education to think about now. Over time, she began to feel used and foolish. As the months wore on, she toyed with the idea of returning to New Orleans.

She retrieved the car from the secure garage and turned the car in the direction of Uptown. As she turned the car onto St. Charles Avenue, Brandy felt tears stinging her eyes as she relived the events of last October. Two Coast Guard officers had come to the door after ten o'clock one evening to somberly relate the news. There had been an inexplicable diving accident. Harris had become disoriented, ripping his regulator hose with his knife. His body was retrieved from the sandy floor of the Caribbean at a depth of less than forty feet. He was bloated, and his face was frozen in a permanent expression of horror. A large chunk of flesh had been ripped from his left thigh, presumably by one of the many tiger sharks in the vicinity. Later Thad had privately explained that Harris was trying to save money on their equipment and had purchased some used scuba gear a few weeks ago.

"He felt guilty about the money he had spent—especially since we don't have anything to show for it," he told her when she returned after the funeral to pack up their things and make arrangements for the sale of the house. "All we ever found were a handful of uncut, poor quality emeralds that we hoped were from the *BYZANTIUM*. But in months of searching, we have not found a trace of the ship." He paused and put his arm around her. "I would be happy to buy them from you. I could display them in our ticket office and create a lot of excitement and intrigue for the tourists."

She had thanked him, but in the end, declined his offer to purchase the emeralds and the computer equipment. They agreed upon a two-year time charter of the boat that Thad would use for snorkeling trips for the tourists. Eventually, they would find a buyer for the boat and split the proceeds. He assured her that he might be lucky enough to find a salvage operator eager to buy the salvage equipment. "It's a very narrow market, as you may imagine," he told her. "In time, we may get lucky. But I am through with the pipe-dream."

The two of them promised to stay in touch by email. She would miss Thad. He had become like a member of the family over the past few years.

Brandy and Rene returned to New Orleans and moved in with Brandy's grandmother. Ariel Massenet had always been a surrogate mother to Brandy. Now in her mid-eighties, she was delighted to have her granddaughters move into her imposing home during her twilight years. She had converted one of the guest-rooms into a lovely child's room with a single canopy bed, pastel walls, and a stencil of gold-winged fairies in flight below the crown molding. There was an adjoining playroom opening onto a second floor balcony, which was fitted with a flat-screen television, DVD player, bookshelves, and music station. Brandy took her old room that she had occupied after her parents' death.

Ariel was supportive during the first grief-stricken months after Harris's death. She allowed Brandy space and time to work through the initial shock of the loss. She was careful to shield Rene from her mother's sorrow and to provide as stable an environment as possible. In early February, she finally coaxed Brandy to think about the future.

"You need to stop punishing yourself for what happened. Harris was a wonderful man. You virtually gave up your life to allow him to pursue his dreams. He died doing what he loved. And he was doing something reckless—diving with substandard equipment. You nearly spent your entire inheritance on him. He is gone, and I wish I could bring him back. But you have Rene to think about now. She needs you and you need to start trying to live again. Besides, you are still a young woman—only thirty-three years old with your entire life ahead of you." Granny Ariel had counseled her as they sat under the gazebo admiring the pink azaleas in bloom.

During those conversations, the concept of Massenet was born. Brandy consulted with an architect and, along with a gift from her grandmother, bought and renovated the old building. The two of them traveled to the French and English country sides purchasing the inventory. Miraculously, Massenet opened three weeks before Memorial Day. And Ariel had been right. The activity had forced Brandy to focus upon something besides her grief and loneliness.

Brandy drove home in the waning daylight past all the stately homes on St. Charles Avenue toward Audubon Park. Things had changed drastically since Hurricane Katrina. She noticed every evening on the drive that many of the old landmarks had disappeared. The once bustling Uptown area now seemed unusually quiet. After a few minutes, she finally reached the red brick buildings of Loyola University, which bordered the three stone buildings at the front of Tulane undergraduate campus. Steering her Audi across the median she pulled into the long drive leading to a detached garage in the back which was connected to the main house by a colonnaded portico. The twenty-two-room house owned by her grandmother was one of the most beautiful homes in uptown New Orleans. The house had a prime location bordering Audubon Park and St. Charles Avenue. When Brandy had been younger, her grandmother had a staff of six people to cook, clean, and maintain the house and garden. Today, her grandmother hired a cleaning service that came three times a week and a gardening service to maintain the formal gardens and reflection pool behind the stucco walls.

Rene was visiting Harris's parents this weekend in North Carolina and would come home on Monday night. Tonight, she and Ariel would be alone. She cherished the time they spent together. Harris's death had forced her to realize how precious those moments were.

She found her grandmother in the gazebo by the reflection pool which had a small fountainhead shooting a delicate pillar of water into the air. The reflection pool was filled with water lilies and a few large koi. Ariel, who had been feeding one of the park squirrels, poured Brandy a glass of lemonade. The squirrel watched her with interest before scampering toward the stone balustrade at the edge of the patio.

Brandy gave her grandmother a kiss before sitting down at the table. Granny Ariel still had a bright expression in her blue eyes and a pleasant face, framed by the wisps of gray hair that she pulled into a thick bun at the nape of her neck. In her younger years, Granny Ariel's hair had been the color of cognac, resembling her granddaughter's hair. Brandy had loved to look at the old photos. It was undeniable that Granny Ariel had been a beauty in her day. Despite the loss of her only child, Brandy's father and her husband, Granny Ariel had retained an infectious enthusiasm for life. Brandy often wondered what would have become of them without the moral support of her grandmother.

Brandy nibbled on an orange slice between sips of lemonade as the squirrel stared at her watchfully from the capstone on the balustrade. He was an undeniably cute little animal, and it was amazing that he was not bothered by Chloe, the Samoyed. In fact, the two animals seemed to like one another. Brandy noticed, however, that the squirrel was wary of her.

"He seems ready to go," Brandy told her. "I do not think your little friend cares much for me."

"They are diurnal. It's time for him to return to his nest for the night. They need to be careful of predators," Ariel mused. She watched the squirrel scamper across the capstone, climb the stone wall over to the park, and disappear into the upper branches of a nearby oak. "I bought gumbo and French bread from Langenstein's for supper."

"I am starved. I had an apple for lunch. Aren't you going to eat tonight?" Brandy asked her grandmother.

"I ate a huge lunch at Commander's Palace today at the shelter meeting. I also had some fruit and cheese while I was waiting for you. But, I think I could eat a small bowl. I still have to watch my figure," the older woman laughed.

"Do you have a special someone you are thinking about?" Brandy teased.

Granny Ariel grinned. "Don't be silly! The last thing I need is another man in my life. At my age, I need to stay healthy!"

Brandy rolled her eyes in exaggeration. "Don't be coy! I have seen the way all the men look at you with adoration!"

Brandy gave her grandmother a hug and then helped her put all the dishes and the glass onto a large tray, which Brandy carried across the walkway into the house. As she rinsed the plates and loaded them into the dishwasher, her grandmother removed a green salad, rice, and a large tureen of gumbo from the Sub-Zero. Brandy ladled out just enough into a microwavable bowl and then reheated the gumbo and rice.

The two of them sat in the breakfast room to consume the salad, gumbo and a thin slice of French bread. Brandy was attempting to cut down on her carbohydrates, but she decided to allow herself this one luxury tonight in reward for her day of hard work.

While Granny Ariel rinsed the dishes, Brandy called Rene to say good night. It was one hour later in Charlotte, and Brandy's former mother-in-law coldly informed her that the child had already gone to sleep. Jenny Blake had never really connected with Brandy. She suspected that on some level, the woman blamed her for her son's death. Brandy chatted politely for a minute or two and then hung up the phone before returning back downstairs.

The two women retired to the study for a glass of merlot. Ariel listened as Brandy described the daily events at the shop. Brandy had reservations about the business. Granny Ariel had made a significant investment in the business, and Brandy was not sure that she was up to the task. Besides, working all day alone was lonely. Her grandmother insisted that Brandy already needed an assistant. As always, Granny Ariel gave her careful encouragement about the financial situation of Massenet. Thus far, she had been instrumental in encouraging her friends to patronize her little shop. The weekend after the shop opened, Granny Ariel had arranged and paid for a lovely catered champagne reception and a full page colored ad in *Traditional Home* to announce the opening of Massenet. That had given the little shop a real head start.

"Brandy, the shop is gorgeous. You just have to give it some time. I predict that with your taste and artistic ability, it will become one of the leading antique shops in New Orleans."

"Well, there is lots of competition, Granny Ariel," Brandy reminded her, thinking of the sleek galleries and well-known shops farther down the street with instant name recognition. The possibility of succeeding with yet one more antique shop in a city famous for myriads of antique shops seemed impossible most of the time.

"Damn the competition," her grandmother responded with a hearty laugh. "That is what free enterprise is all about. There is room for everyone. You will be a big success. You'll see. Honey, I believe in you."

Brandy gave a weak smile in reply. "You have been so incredibly generous and I appreciate everything you have done."

"Nonsense! I want what is best for you. The two of you have been through something awful. I am just trying to help you get things sorted out again. I remember what it is like to lose someone. Nothing hurts like that. At first, you think you will never live or laugh again. And, of course, you do. There are other people counting on you. In your case, it is Rene. I am thrilled that you two have been able to cope as well as you have. I believe in your ability, Brandy. You two are going to be happy again."

Brandy gave her grandmother a hug and then turned the conversation to inquire about her day. Ariel was on the board of directors of a non-profit corporation for a women's and children's homeless shelter. Earlier today, she had attended a committee planning meeting for the organization's auction, which was the major annual fund-raising event. Granny Ariel reported on the progress of the procurement of items for the black-tie event that would be held in early November. Brandy was amazed at her grandmother's energy and enthusiasm for helping others. Granny Ariel had amazing organizational skills and the tenacity to bring her ideas to fruition. With her numerous contacts in the city, she had been able to obtain incredible donations for the live auction. Her grandmother now estimated that the event would net nearly $1 million for homeless women and children.

At ten-thirty, Brandy washed the crystal wine glasses, leaving them on the marble counter to drain. Afterward, she went upstairs to wash her face and change for bed.

As always, she allowed herself those few moments when she was completely alone to think about Harris. It was still nearly impossible for her to believe that he was gone. She felt the familiar sting of tears that welled in her eyes. Crying was a luxury that she allowed herself only at night. She had an iron-clad rule now that she would never cry anymore in front of Rene about Harris. The child knew that her mother had grieved over Harris's death. But, Brandy needed to put on a brave face for her now because it was time to move forward. Together, they would get through this. For a few moments, she allowed herself to consider all the wonderful times she and Harris had shared during their early years. The tears were a welcome release. Finally, she wiped her eyes and tried to relax. She said a little prayer for Rene and Granny Ariel and closed her eyes. And then, she slept.

Chapter III

The squirrel sat on his haunches gnawing the orange crescent he held with his tiny forepaws. He barely noticed the cool juice, which splashed on his ivory chest and rolled down his belly. His fluffy tail was slightly longer than his body, and it allowed him to balance easily on his haunches when it was doubled up and curled behind him like a giant question mark.

Ariel nibbled on a plate of strawberries dipped in chocolate. She had placed two plain berries on the fruit plate for the squirrel, who detested chocolate. He had devoured his allotment of strawberries after their game of Hangman on the iPad. The squirrel had lost as usual. His spelling was deplorable, although it was improving with practice.

He washed his paws and face with the water from the tiny dish on the table. Afterward, he groomed his coat with his damp paws and reclined on the table. He had saved a large orange chunk that he planned to bring to Kiki before he retired to his nest for the evening. Kiki was nursing their litter of pups, and he had noticed that she had become ravenous of late. The little pups demanded all of her attention, and Raleigh was concerned for his mate. Right now, Kiki was extremely protective of the infants and instinctively chased him away from the nest because she was afraid that he might harm her pups. But he knew intuitively that the orange would lift her spirits, and she would regard the gift as a welcome gesture.

Kiki, of course, was not a special squirrel. She did not have the uncanny ability to communicate with humans and, in fact, her communication skills were limited. He enjoyed her company, nonetheless, during their exhilarating romps across the oak branches high above the lush grass of the park. For reasons that he could not explain, Kiki's company was very satisfying and comfortable.

"Let's talk," Ariel said to the squirrel as she erased the Hangman screen from the electronic tablet. Chloe snored softly at her feet dozing lazily in the late afternoon sun.

Raleigh sat up on his haunches again near the screen. He could smell the fresh scent of ozone from the thunderstorm earlier today. It was getting dark, and he would need to leave soon. There was only one week left in August, and he noticed that the days were getting shorter now. The weather was incredibly hot; and there were violent thunderstorms every afternoon. He knew from an innate sense that soon, the cooler weather would come.

The squirrel was glad for the opportunity to spend time with his old friend. Ariel had been very busy since the child and the young woman moved in with her almost a year ago. Of course, they did not know that he was a special squirrel. Ariel's granddaughter, Nevertheless, Rene, was quite fascinated with him, holding out her tiny hand filled with shelled pecans for him to take and eat. The child shrieked with delight when he rolled Chloe's ball toward her across the floor. Sometimes he even let Rene stroke his tail and ears with her tiny fingers. Ariel had told him that the child had recently suffered the loss of her father. The squirrel could feel the sting of the child's sadness and confusion. Unlike normal squirrels, Raleigh possessed a unique empathy for the suffering of others. It was another one of his special gifts.

The squirrel's relationship with Ariel had begun three years earlier. He had cautiously watched her for months, safely concealed in the oak branches overhead before he decided to approach her. In short order, he had determined that Chloe was harmless one day when he jumped down into the brick wall enclosure landing safely on the cool expanse of lawn. Chloe had eyed him with boredom from the loggia across the back of the house. Unlike many dogs, Chloe seemed disinterested in chasing the squirrel, preferring instead to doze on the porch. Her white fluffy coat gleamed in a shard of late afternoon sunlight that pierced the stately oaks. The squirrel had gathered acorns and juicy cambium, which he buried near the wall. In time he felt secure enough to enlarge his territory to include the walled garden behind the stone house.

Early on, the squirrel noticed Ariel sitting on the loggia under an array of ceiling fans drinking a cup of tea as he entered the walled enclosure. Cautiously, he maintained a watchful eye on Ariel as he sprang across the lawn gathering an errant acorn. He had learned to be vigilant. Many humans considered squirrels a nuisance. And sometimes the most elderly and seemingly innocuous humans presented the greatest threat. So, he kept his distance.

Over time, he studied and sensed her essence. It was one of his other special gifts that set him apart from other animals. He had a heightened sense of danger, love, pain, fear, anger and kindness. They all emitted a distinct smell and radiated an aura. He was lucky. This ability had saved his life on more than one occasion.

After a few months, he became satisfied that Ariel was a kind and gentle woman. He observed her kindness to other children and animals. One afternoon, the woman had thrown a party for underprivileged children living in a homeless shelter. There had been clowns, balloons, a little Shetland pony, games, and a virtual feast on long tables under the loggia. All of the children had received a new tee shirt and a matching baseball cap. The squirrel had watched her with the children, coaxing each one to smile and enjoy the afternoon. He could feel the aura of concern and generosity. Late that afternoon, after the party, the squirrel had approached Ariel as she sat reading in her gazebo and drinking a cup of tea. The iron tables still held the leftover vestiges of the party, including several board games. She fed him a few slivers of apple from her hand and spoke soothingly to him. He allowed her to stroke his underbelly softly with the back of her index finger and touch his tail.

"You are a sweet little thing" she cooed. "And you have such a lovely coat! Your tail is like a giant plume. It reminds me of the feathers worn by the Three Musketeers or Sir Walter Raleigh. You need a name, " Ariel mused. "I think I will call you Sir Raleigh, and we will call you plain Raleigh. And if only you could talk, you could call me Ariel."

The squirrel pondered the words. Raleigh and Ariel. They had a pretty sound. The two of them had a connection he could not explain. Spending time with Ariel made him feel safe. She was his friend, and she would never hurt him. He could feel it.

Reluctantly, he turned to leave as the darkness edged down from the eastern edge of the park. He scratched at the errant Scrabble pieces on the table left over from the party, arranging them to his satisfaction before he leapt down from the table. He glanced over his shoulder from the top of the fence toward the gazebo. Ariel's face registered surprise and amazement. The Scrabble pieces that Raleigh had arranged spelled "f-r-e-n-d." Raleigh gave her a knowing look as he gazed at him on the wall. He barked sharply before turning and running up the branch of a nearby oak toward his nest for the evening.

The next afternoon, Ariel was waiting for Raleigh under the gazebo. The air was heavy with humidity from the light rain, which puddled around the brick apron at the foot of the gazebo. The Scrabble pieces were organized on the glass table beside a tray of fruit and shelled pecans.

"I had hoped that you would come!" she said, smiling radiantly. "I have something for you to eat."

After Raleigh satiated his hunger, they turned their attention to the Scrabble pieces. Ariel kept her questions as simple as possible, requiring only one or two-word responses from the squirrel. In halting fragments and misspelled words, he explained that he lived in a nest in a nearby tree in the park. He was three and one-half years old, as best as he could tell. He had a mate almost two years ago who was killed by a stray cat before their pups were born. He told her about begging and foraging for food in the park and avoiding predatory birds, like the barn owl who lived by the fountain. It was a tedious process as he slowly selected the letters to spell each response. It was both frustrating and difficult because his ability to spell was limited. In order to speed up the process, Ariel set up three separate sections at the edge of the table. One section spelled "y-e-s" and the other section spelled "n-o." Another section spelled "don't know." She asked him a series of simple questions, and he could merely touch the proper answer with his paw. He could sense that Ariel wanted to keep him interested and minimize his discouragement.

"How long have you been able to understand what humans say?" she had asked.

He tapped 'don't know.'

"Has it been as long as you can remember?"

He planted his paw on the yes section.

"How did you learn to read? Did your mother teach you?"

"N-o."

"Then how do you know?" she persisted.

He tapped 'don't know' and sat back in frustration. He could not really explain to her.

Ariel looked at his answer thoughtfully, seeming to sense his discomfort. She changed the subject. "Can you talk with Chloe?"

He tapped yes.

His communication with Chloe was much more rudimentary. They could sense certain things about each other. He could attract her attention about something bad with a danger signal. He could feel Chloe's contentment, sadness, and excitement. There was a sense of friendship between them. But their communication was much more limited because the dog could not spell.

Ariel smiled in satisfaction. "This is a miracle! I am so lucky to have discovered you," she told him. "This is truly one of the most remarkable experiences of my life."

They spent the next year exploring their relationship. Because squirrels are diurnal, they met in the early morning and late afternoon. Sometimes she read simple children's stories to him about animals. *Charlotte's Webb* and *Peter Rabbit* were among his favorites. She bought a set of flash cards with large print and together they worked on his spelling and reading skills. Ariel always provided a generous supply of nuts, fruits, and vegetables at every meeting. She begged Raleigh to move into a small space in the attic.

"You will be safe there. And I could feed you," she coaxed.

Raleigh declined her offer. The attic seemed like a prison to him. He felt a compelling drive to forage for food and to live in his nest in the oak tree. He was a squirrel and he needed his freedom. But his time with Ariel made him happy and secure. He could sense the loneliness from her old age, and he relished basking in her affection.

Their routine changed, however, when Rene and the young woman moved in with Ariel. Raleigh could feel her focus shift to her grandchildren. Ariel seemed disconcerted and preoccupied. The two of them could find time to meet only once a day. Things improved when the young woman went to work. Ariel's spirits lifted and she began to find more time for him. Raleigh had learned to enjoy Rene's company. Of course, he was careful to conceal his special talents from her. Ariel had insisted that Rene would not understand.

Raleigh respected Ariel's wishes and he was careful to conceal his abilities from the rest of the world. As the years went on, he became more attached to Ariel.

As the darkness began fall that afternoon, Raleigh left for the park. He left the orange crescent at the opening of Kiki's nest. She barked and lunged at him furiously before dragging the orange inside the small nest. From his position on the branch, Raleigh could hear a soft squeaking and he smelled a strange odor coming from inside the nest.

Mindful of the risk of predators in the waning evening light, Raleigh returned to his nest with a trained eye scanning the surrounding branches. It was almost dark, and he was easy prey for a predator with night vision. Soon, he was enveloped in the safety of his nest. He arranged the leaves to conceal himself completely before curling into a ball. Exhausted but relaxed from his visit with his friend Ariel, he fell into a dreamless sleep.

Chapter IV

Ewan took a cold shower after his morning exercise routine of a five-mile run and thirty minutes lifting free weights in the run-down gym of the apartment building. The summer heat in Fort Lauderdale was oppressive, and the ice-cold fine spray of the shower was a welcome relief. He shaved and dressed in his uniform of pressed twill trousers and a bright blue tee shirt with the name of the waterfront restaurant where he now was bussing tables emblazoned on the front. The dive shop where he had been working had suddenly closed six weeks earlier. He had taken the restaurant job to pay the rent, but it was still necessary for him to dip into his savings. He still had most of the money left from the St. Thomas job safely in a safety-deposit box in a Chase branch, but he had not been able to increase his nest egg. The truth was that Ewan's skills were minimal, and the jobs available to him had lousy pay.

Ewan had enlisted in the Marine Corps when he was eighteen and spent two tours in Iraq, never advancing beyond the rank of private. After his discharge, he never returned home to Nebraska. College did not interest him. He had always hated school and knew that he would have very little in common with the frat boys after being in a war zone. Over the next three years, he lived a nomadic existence, migrating down the Florida coast and spending time in Jacksonville, Daytona and Key West until finally deciding to go to St. Thomas. He found a few menial jobs in resorts until he learned to dive and eventually found a job in a dive shop. Ewan would have stayed in the Islands indefinitely, but he knew that it was necessary to leave after he killed the diver.

Lately, Ewan had felt rather hopeless about the future and had been drinking heavily. The dream seemed more elusive than ever. Sometimes, he thought about re-enlisting in the Marine Corps. It was a certain paycheck, but he hated being controlled by the commanding officers. Ewan knew himself well. He was a real lone wolf and was never much of a team player. He had even hated organized sports in high school. Besides, at thirty-four, he was now old for the military and would be competing with young kids.

He answered his cell phone as he was leaving his apartment for work and was very surprised to see the Virgin Islands area code displayed on the screen. Ewan listened with interest as the man explained that he wanted him to go to New Orleans indefinitely to watch the diver's wife. Apparently, the woman had gone home and had some things that belonged to Thad. Ewan would need to keep an eye on the woman, Brandy Blake, and report back to him. Ultimately, Thad would need Ewan to recover his property from the woman. Thad said he would arrange for Ewan to pick up expenses from a Western Union office in South Miami. He had also arranged for a deposit in a Chase branch in Uptown New Orleans.

Ewan gave a huge sigh of relief when the call ended. This was a wonderful opportunity. Finally, we would be able to increase his nest egg and realize the dream.

When his shift ended, Ewan quit his job and collected his paltry wages and tips. Over the next weeks, he obtained a new Social Security card in the name of James Weeks, a twenty-one year old man who had been killed in an accident on the Sunshine Parkway five years earlier. He shaved his blonde hair and obtained a new Florida driver's license and debit card in the name of James Weeks. He sold his Harley and bought a used three-year old air-conditioned Camry with 65,000 miles on the odometer for the trip. Everything he owned fit into two small duffle bags in the Camry trunk. Before he left the following Saturday morning, he went by the office of the on-site manager to surrender the key. He had not bothered to clean the place before he left and forfeited his $500 deposit.

He steered the Camry north on the interstate, settling in to enjoy the drive with the satellite radio tuned to his favorite country music station. Traffic was heavy initially, and he lost two hours as he left the congestion of south Florida behind. He drove several hours through a line of summer thunderstorms before stopping to stretch and buy a sandwich at a Subway shop. By five o'clock., he had traveled more than 300 miles when he stopped at a Best Western. He paid cash for the room and went to the truck stop next door for a home style meal and a cold beer. He ate at a corner table by the window, trying his best to ignore the flirtatious behavior of the middle-aged waitress with dyed red hair. He left a good-sized tip and returned to his room to watch television. He would need a good night's sleep for the long trip ahead the following morning.

Ewan made it as far as Pensacola the following afternoon. After a fried seafood platter dinner, he crossed over to Santa Rosa Island and took a drive along the glistening water, enjoying the slower pace of the area. The following morning he went to a Walmart on the outskirts of town and purchased a prepaid cell phone and an inexpensive GPS in cash. He unwrapped the cell phone in the parking lot and sent Thad a text to a special number before heading east toward Alabama for the home-stretch. He stopped at a dumpster off Highway 90 in Biloxi and dumped the cell phone.

The traffic was still relatively light at four o'clock that afternoon as he finally reached the eastern edge of the city of New Orleans. The impact of Katrina was still very noticeable in this area of the city. Many commercial buildings, including a large mall, were damaged and appeared empty. It was a depressing site. The summer sky over the city was slate gray, and it began to rain. He headed over the towering bridge over the industrial canal and headed downtown.

The GPS guided him in the direction of the Super Dome and the downtown corridor. He took the Vieux Carre exit and followed the GPS across Canal Street with its palm trees and streetcar on the median before turning into the Quarter. Tonight he would treat himself to a hotel stay, a decent meal, and a few drinks. It had been a long hard trip, and he deserved to relax for a day or two. Tomorrow or the next day, he would find a cheap apartment and then get down to business.

~

Ewan checked into a recently renovated boutique hotel in the French Quarter. His room had an adjoining balcony on the fourth floor, nineteenth century period furniture and included a full breakfast in the brick courtyard in the center of the building. He ate dinner in a lively tourist bistro across from Jackson Square. Later, he explored the French Market, stopped into Café Du Monde for coffee and beignets, and spent a couple of hours in a strip joint on Bourbon Street before heading back to his hotel. He was surprised how much he enjoyed New Orleans. The old historic buildings in the Quarter had been lovingly restored, housing tourist shops, fancy restaurants, jazz clubs, bistros, expensive antique stores, and sleazy bars. He had always thought of the city as being seedy, but instead it was cauldron of vice, tourism, wealth, and hedonism that was appealing to someone like Ewan.

After he brushed his teeth, he caught sight of his reflection in the mirror. He was still slightly surprised at the real change in his appearance. He could not pass hard scrutiny, but most people who knew him would first look for his signature blonde hair. Even his casual acquaintances would simply pass him by on the street without a second look because of this change. He frowned at the light blonde stubble on his scalp and decided that tomorrow he would dye it black. James Weeks had been a brunette, and he did not need questions about his appearance. It might also be a good idea to grow a mustache.

He took a hot shower with the fragrant French hotel soap and sat on the balcony in the dark wrapped in the hotel terry-cloth robe before slipping into the antique bed by the windows. Despite the street noise from late night revelers, he fell into a dreamless sleep and awoke at seven thirty. He spent some time checking apartment listings before showering, shaving and going down to breakfast by ten. The breakfast buffet was impressive, with fresh fruit, eggs Sardou, steak, strawberry and cheese crepes, and strong coffee. He sat at a table in the corner by a gurgling fountain surrounded by well-heeled tourists.

So this was how the other half lived. Special soaps and towels with gourmet meals—he could get used to this life very quickly.

After checking out of the hotel and retrieving his car, he drove through the French Quarter across Canal Street in search of an apartment. He had located a couple of listings earlier in the Warehouse District that had been restored and gentrified into expensive condos, hotels and lofts. Ewan easily rejected the area because it did not seem to offer the privacy he knew that he would need over the next few months. Blending in with the locals was critical.

After a few hours he found an old duplex on Euterpe in the Lower Garden District toward the levee. A bored middle-aged rental agent, wearing too much makeup and a tight dress that emphasized her ample muffin top, gave him the tour. At one time, the house must have been a grand old building with heavy moldings and spacious rooms for the gracious life that some had once enjoyed in old New Orleans. It had been restored after Katrina with a few cosmetic, but inexpensive upgrades in the kitchen and refinished wooden floors and fresh paint. The house was simply but tastefully furnished with the basics. The bathroom on the second floor featured the original claw-foot bathtub which had been restored, beside a cheap toilet and sink cabinet from Home Depot. From Ewan's perspective, the best feature of the duplex was a private drive that led to a small fenced-in backyard and a detached garage that would allow him to enter the house from the backdoor directly into the kitchen. The large oak trees from the adjoining house to the right would shield him from the prying eyes of next-door neighbors. Moreover, the two houses directly across the street were vacant and in disrepair. He could easily come and go at will without attracting attention.

Rita, the leasing agent, gave him a winning smile. It was clear to him that Rita, like most women, found Ewan attractive. He noticed that her teeth were slightly yellowed from smoking and too much coffee. Rita, however, seemed oblivious to the fact that she was not a rival for Miss America.

"So?" Rita said expectantly with a pregnant pause.

He nodded. "Looks pretty good."

"I thought you would like it—two bedrooms, a large bath, living, dining with an eat-in kitchen. It is a steal for this price."

"What about the neighborhood?" Ewan asked.

A look of concern flashed over Rita's face and then was replaced by her perky confidence. She was obviously worried that the neighborhood would kill the deal. "It is not the most perfect neighborhood in the city. Where did you say you were from?"

"I didn't," he replied, aware that Rita was trying to deflect his attention. "I lived in Lubbock Texas, and was transferred down here for my job from Lake Wylie, South Carolina," he lied.

"Well, the Lower Garden District is one of the oldest parts of the city, and many people are restoring these houses. Many streets have been restored, but this area is in transition. For the most part, this is safe, but there are problems here as well as in the best areas of Uptown New Orleans. The owner has installed a burglar alarm, and you will need to be cautious at night. All utilities are included in the rent. And, of course, you get more bang for your buck in this area. If we moved this house to the fringe of the Garden District or closer to the St. Charles Avenue corridor, you would pay three times this much. But if you like, I can show you some other properties that we have, but none of them will be this cheap."

Ewan scanned the small backyard through the kitchen window, pleased that he had managed to find a place with so much privacy. A block in transition meant that most people would be inside or in their backyards, oblivious to his activities. Also, the other side of the duplex was empty and obviously had been empty for some time. Ewan knew that this was a good opportunity.

"I think you are right. I will take it." He gave Rita a big smile showcasing his perfect teeth.

Rita looked relieved. "Well, why don't you follow me back to my office and we can complete the paperwork."

After Rita locked up the house, Ewan followed her back to the small rental office eight blocks away on Prytania. He gave her his false drivers' license and Social Security card in the name of James Weeks and cash for the first and last month's rent. As expected, the credit check on James Weeks reflected a good credit score. Within twenty-five minutes, Ewan emerged with the keys to the duplex in his pocket.

He spent the remainder of the afternoon making a small withdrawal from his new bank account opened by his new employer at the Chase branch on St. Charles Avenue and familiarized himself with the city. He took a drive down St. Charles Avenue and, with the help of the portable GPS, located the house where the diver's wife now lived with her daughter and grandmother. He found a parking place down the street in front of Audubon Park and strolled through the park gradually heading over toward the palatial residence. The area was beautiful and green, with majestic oaks extending towering gnarled branches that interlocked over expansive green lawns. A magnificent fountain gurgled in the front of the park, separated by a lagoon with resident waterfowl. Despite the heat, the humid air was cool and pleasant under the shade of the oak branches. There were two universities across the avenue from the home of the diver's wife. The St. Charles Avenue streetcar rumbled past every few minutes on the median.

He pulled his baseball cap down and strolled in front of the three story stone house. By any measure, this house was a mansion, bordered on three sides by a large stone fence. A professional gardening service truck with a logo—IBIX—on the side was parked in the driveway. Ewan pulled up the IBIX website on his phone and continued his stroll until he ultimately crossed the street at the light and casually returned to his car. As he strolled down the avenue, he questioned Thad's unusual request that he come to New Orleans to watch the diver's widow. He assumed that it had something to do with the search for the *BYZANTIUM*, but whatever it was, Thad seemed almost desperate. Ewan would not be surprised if ultimately Thad asked him to kill the woman. Ewan would be willing to help, but this time, Thad would have to pay him handsomely to take such a risk. The diver's death had been ruled an accident, and no one suspected that Ewan had tampered with his tanks. On the other hand, harming the diver's wife would likely arouse suspicion that could ultimately lead to Ewan.

Ewan closed the car door and flipped on the air conditioner. He had a number of things he needed to do. First, he needed to find a grocery store to stock the kitchen. He would attract less attention by eating at home and keeping to himself. And he needed a job with IBIX so he could get close to the diver's wife without raising suspicion. He would work on that tomorrow. He turned the car around and headed back in the other direction. Rita had told him about a big grocery store at the foot of Napoleon Avenue near the levee. He programmed the address into the GPS and followed the directions.

Rene arrived home late Monday evening from North Carolina with a suitcase full of gifts from her paternal grandparents. The child was exhausted and fell asleep in front of the television shortly after supper. Thrilled to have her little friend at home once again, Chloe slept at the foot of Rene's bed all night.

The following morning, Rene was up early and was ready to go shopping with Ariel for her school clothes for kindergarten. The term was scheduled to begin in less than three weeks. The child was already seated at the breakfast room table playing an educational reading game when Brandy came downstairs. Rene was already learning to read. Brandy brightened immediately when she caught sight of the tousle of red curls that Ariel had neatly pulled into a ponytail. Like Chloe, Brandy was relieved to have her little girl back home. Rene and Granny Ariel were the only family that she had left now.

Over breakfast, Granny Ariel and Rene made their shopping plans. They planned to have a light lunch after shopping and then go to the zoo. The days of summer were waning, and Granny Ariel was obviously anxious to spend as much time with Rene as possible before the child returned to school. The three of them agreed that they would watch a Disney film on television after an early dinner. Rene's eyes sparkled as she discussed the plans for the day with her grandmother. Obviously she was glad to be home and back into the familiar routine.

Brandy slipped on a stylish polished cotton dress of soft coral, and bone-colored heels and pulled her long hair into a simple chignon. She wore the simple strand of pearls that Harris had given her as a wedding present. Fortunately, the traffic was light on St. Charles for a Friday morning, despite the light humid rain.

She arrived at the shop about nine and spent the rest of the morning at the shop awaiting delivery of several new pieces of inventory. She busied herself working on inventory files on the tablet near her desk in the front until the furniture was delivered. There was a new French commode and a lovely set of dining chairs and matching table from England. She met with her cabinetmaker and negotiated a price to restore the pieces. Things were beginning to pick up at Massenet. A new Waterford chandelier was delivered around noon that had been ordered by a customer restoring a home on Audubon Place. After she inspected the package for damage, she put a small stack of her own watercolors from the Caribbean in the corner. They were inexpensive, but they had sold nicely and served to draw people into the shop. She had learned that business always increased in the afternoon with lunchtime shoppers and browsers and tourists eager to escape from the oppressive heat.

The tourist season was active nearly year-round in New Orleans. The plentiful number of hotels catered to business meetings and conventions and, of course, Mardi Gras was a busy time. The Saints football season as well as the return of the university students, also unleashed a flood of visitors to the city. Brandy had begun to keep the shop open on Sunday from 11:00 a.m. to 6:00 p.m. to take advantage of the Sunday tourists and football fans. It was a necessary step to remain competitive. Ariel had been concerned that Brandy intended to work seven days a week. After many discussions, Granny Ariel had finally convinced Brandy to hire an assistant to work a minimum of five days a week. Brandy knew that it would be a burdensome but necessary expense. And Brandy realized that she was not willing to sacrifice her time with Rene for the shop. It would be impossible for her to work seven days a week. Rene needed her. In fact, they needed each other.

Brandy placed a discreet ad on Craig's List and contacted two employment agencies. Her resources were limited, but even a part-time student or a matronly woman who enjoyed antiques would be a great help. She wondered whether she would be able to find someone mature and reliable on her limited budget. Over the next few days, she interviewed several women for the position. None of them were acceptable.

Finally she interviewed Yvette Price, who was attending night school at the University of New Orleans. Divorced and the mother of a two-year-old at twenty-six, Yvette had returned to school to obtain a degree in art history and interior design. Despite her student loans and free child care from her sister-in-law, she was having a difficult time making ends meet. Brandy felt immediately drawn to the vivacious brunette, in part because of their similar circumstances. Yvette agreed to work Sunday through Thursday, allowing Brandy time with Rene and to perform many of the administrative tasks at the shop during business hours. Yvette proved to be dedicated and reliable. Within two weeks of her employment, Massenet's profits doubled.

On Fridays and Saturdays, Brandy manned the shop alone. Although it was an enormously hectic pace, she thrived on the excitement of each new sale. A handful of satisfied customers had even returned to peruse the new merchandise. Several women had approached her about specific items they were interested in purchasing from Europe. Brandy realized that she was developing a small clientele and felt a sense of accomplishment.

About five thirty one afternoon, a man in his mid-thirties entered the shop alone. He was dressed in a conservative black suit with a blue-and-gray tie.

"Brandy?" he said as he walked up to the counter. "I did not know you were living in New Orleans. Is this your shop? I was walking down to meet a client for a quick glass of wine, and I noticed that the building had been restored. It is really beautiful in here."

She gave him a radiant smile and shook his hand. Claude Parker had been an old friend from high school who had been two years older than Brandy. He had attended Princeton undergraduate and Yale Law School. Claude was a member of an extremely prominent New Orleans family. Ariel had mentioned recently that he was working in a large New Orleans firm. She had not been really interested. Since Harris's death, she had lost all interest in contacting any of her old friends. Brandy noticed that Claude had still retained his boyish good looks with sandy brown hair and brilliant teeth. Although most men his age were developing a paunch, Claude was still thin and radiated good health from years of playing tennis and sailing.

"I have only been open since mid-March. I never really thought of myself as a business woman, but here I am having the time of my life." She smiled, trying to project a confidence that she really did not feel. She steeled herself for the questions, that she knew, would be inevitable.

He laughed, putting her at ease. "Well, it's hard to imagine that any of us became real grown-ups, isn't it? Look at me in this somber strait-jacket. With the wind today, there is nothing more I would rather be doing than sailing on Lake Pontchartrain. But we all have to make a living." He gave her an appraising glance. "You look terrific! How long has it been? Ten or twelve years? You have not really changed a bit."

She smiled in spite of herself. "You still know what to say under all circumstances. My grandmother told me that you are working as a lawyer at D'Argent. Your clients must love you."

He laughed. "Unfortunately, I do not get an opportunity to see them very much. I work in the marine and energy department. Most of my work is assigned from the London insurance market. My instructions come by email and an occasional telephone call. Not much chance to be charming in an email."

They talked for a few moments catching up on the last few years. Claude had married a woman he had met in law school. They moved to Washington where she obtained a job in a senator's office on Capitol Hill, and he worked for the Justice Department. Connie had been killed in an automobile accident while commuting home from work one afternoon. Claude, devastated, had returned home to New Orleans after the funeral.

Brandy told him about Harris and Rene. Claude listened somberly without interrupting her. She was thankful that he did not try to offer her a lot of unsolicited advice about coping with the pain. It was the first time in months that she actually felt that someone could fully empathize with the pain of her loss.

"So, what brings you to my shop?" she asked finally, eager to change the subject.

"I bought a large condominium in the old Warehouse District a couple of years ago. It is convenient to the office, but it is nearly empty. I thought it was probably time that I began to furnish it."

"Well, I can help you with that, Claude. You've come to the right place," she smiled.

"Good. You at least need to see it and take some measurements. I would gradually like to furnish it with a few very nice things." He looked around the shop. "But Christ, at these prices, it's a cinch that I can't do it all at once."

Brandy grinned. Claude, of course, was being very humble. He was from one of the wealthier families in the city and could easily have purchased everything in the shop and the building it without making even a dent in his resources. “Well, I can help you start slowly, Claude.”

“Great. How about dinner? It’s nearly six o’clock now. Then you could swing by my condo, take a few measurements, and begin work.”

Brandy shook her head. “I am sorry, but I already have a date with my daughter, Rene, and Granny Ariel to watch a Disney movie tonight after work.”

“Well, tomorrow then?” he asked expectantly.

She hesitated. The last thing that she wanted was to give someone the impression that she was interested in a relationship. That part of her life had ended when Harris had died. “Claude, I would love to help you tomorrow. I can swing by after work and take a look at your apartment, but you do not need to take me to dinner.”

A look of understanding passed over his face. “No, Brandy, I am not asking you for a date. I was asking you for a simple meal because we are old friends. If anyone understands how you feel, I know how difficult the loss of a spouse can be.”

She smiled. Of course Claude knew how she felt. Surely he had experienced the same devastation and loneliness and the fear that life would never be the same.

“Tomorrow it is then,” she agreed. “But dinner is my treat. We may be friends, but this is a business transaction.”

Claude smiled. “That makes sense. It is a deal.”

She agreed to meet Claude for an early dinner at Galatoires on Bourbon Street. The popular restaurant was one of the oldest and most established in the city, serving wonderful fish dishes. She could easily walk from Massenet and it was close to Claude's office. She felt a twinge of excitement about her first business dinner. And, it would, of course, be nice to spend time with her old friend.

She closed the shop and finished the daily accounting ritual before heading home for the evening about seven. The streets were lively with tourists, and the air was humid from the summer thunderstorms.

Rene was already in her pajamas when Brandy arrived, nibbling on popcorn in the den before the flat screen television Ariel had bought a few months earlier. Brandy changed into a pair of lightweight slacks and a shirt, fixed a plate of chicken Caesar salad from the refrigerator, grabbed a bottle of Fiji Water, and sat on the sofa beside Rene, balancing the plate on her lap. The three of them chatted amiably while Brandy ate her salad before settling in to watch a movie. Rene predictably fell asleep within forty-five minutes, and Brandy carried her to bed. Of course, they would watch the movie again until the end. Brandy had memorized most of Rene's collection of Disney movies at this point.

Ariel was waiting for her in the kitchen when she came back downstairs. Brandy rinsed her plate and loaded it in the dishwasher while she told Ariel about her day and meeting with Claude.

"My first real business dinner," she told her grandmother. "I just hope that he is not trying to do me a favor and will not be pressed into buying anything he does not want."

Granny Ariel smiled. "I don't think you have to worry about that, but you can certainly be direct and tell him that you are looking for customers—not favors. I am sure he will understand."

Brandy was silent for a few minutes. "He seems to understand what I have been through since he lost his wife."

Granny Ariel nodded. "I am sure he *does* understand, and I am relieved that you have at least found a friend to help you work through your grief. You have shut yourself off since coming back, and you need friends your own age. Besides, I will not be here forever."

"Oh, Granny Ariel, please don't say that!"

"Hopefully, I have many years left—but after all, I am eighty-five years old now. Life passes very quickly, and I do not want to see you waste what will ultimately become the best years of your life."

Brandy shook her head. Granny Ariel was right. Her entire life was dedicated to the shop and Rene. She had rejected all social invitations to see old friends. Maybe she was punishing herself—if she had not complained about the money Harris had wasted, he might be alive today. She could not shake the feeling that perhaps his death was really her fault.

"I wonder every day if there was anything I could have done to have changed things." She felt her eyes welling with tears.

"Brandy, you have been through a terrible tragedy. Don't punish yourself by closeting yourself away. You need friends, and you need to start living again. I understand that you are not looking for romance, but it does appear to me that Claude understands that you are just friends. Frankly, I am so relieved that you will have an adult evening out."

Brandy dabbed her eyes. Of course, Granny Ariel was right. There was nothing romantic about the dinner—it was strictly a business dinner with a friend. She gave Ariel a big hug. "You are wonderful. Rene and I would be lost without you!"

Ariel hugged her granddaughter back. "You are a survivor, and you will be fine." She smiled. "Now get some rest. You have a big day tomorrow."

~

Brandy had a busy day at the shop with brisk sales of smaller items that she could ship back home to tourists. She brushed her shoulder-length dark-red hair and applied a light coat of powder and sheer lipstick. Her emerald green linen dress was slightly creased, but it would just have to work. The air was oppressively humid as she walked the seven blocks to meet Claude at the restaurant. Claude was already waiting for her at the table.

They talked about the adjustments they had been forced to make while enjoying a bottle of sauvignon blanc from the Marlborough region, trout almondine, and salad. Claude told her about the debilitating depression he had battled after Connie's death.

"I put up a great façade for a long time. But I was secretly living in hell. I buried myself in my work and, with time, I felt better. But the pain never goes away completely. It's been six years now. I am a partner at D'Argent. I have been trying to get on with my life."

She felt that she could understand. "Have you been able to see anyone else since then?" she asked.

He reflected momentarily and then took a long sip of wine. "There were lots of women. I am ashamed to say, too many to remember. It was my way, for a time, of trying to forget. I thought it was serious once or twice, but it never worked out."

Brandy smiled. "I think after you have been married for a while, you really have an understanding of what a real relationship is all about. It all seems so simple and easy when you are really young."

She sipped her wine. "I have a lot of anger and guilt about what happened. Harris had been working constantly. I think I resented his time away from us. And Rene was beginning to grow up. I am angry with him for taking absurd chances with his life. I am angry that we were all denied important time together. And I feel guilty about every argument that we ever had." Her eyes welled with tears. "I don't know if I could ever possibly get married again."

Claude put his hand over hers, giving it a short squeeze.

Brandy ran her fingers through her hair, pulling it back away from her forehead. "I'm sorry, Claude. I know that you are not a shrink. Obviously, I don't have it all together as much as I thought. And this was supposed to be a business dinner." She smiled weakly.

"No apologies are necessary," he said reassuringly. "Look, I've been there. I have a good sense of the hell you have gone through. As an old friend, I am willing to listen any time you like." He flashed his brilliant smile.

"Thank you," she replied soberly. "I appreciate this more than you know. But what I really need to do is to sell you some furniture. Shall we have the caramel custard and then you can show me your condo?"

The conversation was lighter over dessert and café au lait. Claude described his work and told her about the small sailboat he kept at the yacht club for sailing around Lake Pontchartrain. He talked briefly about his trips to London to visit clients in the insurance market and his latest trial. Brandy insisted on picking up the check. The two of them might be friends, but this was a business dinner, and she wanted to sell furniture. She did not want to mislead a ladies' man like Claude that she believed that it had been a date. Then she followed him in her car to his condo a few blocks away.

The condominium was on the top floor of an old warehouse building near Baronne. The first floor had been converted into a gated garage adjacent to a large indoor swimming pool surrounded by tropical plants and a fully-equipped gym. There was a small reception area paved with polished pink marble leading to a brass elevator. Claude explained that a large service elevator and a set of stairs were located behind the reception area.

"Pretty fancy" she said as they entered the elevator to the fifth floor.

The condominium was huge with vast open spaces. Brandy noticed that very little expense had been spared. A glistening polished marble foyer led into a spacious kitchen with top-of-the-line stainless steel appliances, mahogany cabinets, and black granite slab counter tops. The dark cherry floors had been stained and refinished with a high gloss throughout the condominium. There were two large marble baths with jetted tubs and six-foot stained-glass windows. A study was nestled between two bedrooms and a large living room and dining room area. Elaborate molding and paneled doors with butterfly handles had been installed. With the exception of three large Persian rugs, a battered sofa, a card table, a seventy inch flat-screen television mounted on the wall, a computer desk, an elaborate sound system, a scarred bed and matching dresser, it was empty. Claude explained that the Persian rugs had been inherited from his grandmother.

Brandy began laughing. "I'm sorry Claude. I don't mean to laugh. It's gorgeous. But, it is so much like a man with a bachelor pad. Put in a top-of-the-line television, a few rugs, and you don't really need anything else. Even the bedroom furniture is terrible."

Claude laughed. "I sold everything else in D.C. And for a long time, I could not afford anything. It has only been recently that I was even interested. I need to have a few people over—colleagues and clients. So, I need professional help."

Brandy took a few measurements. Then she told him about a dining room table and chairs she had ordered from England as well as a large four-poster bed. She agreed to prepare a list and present him with a quote the following week.

Claude kissed her chastely on the cheek beside her car in the garage. "It was great to see you again and to talk to someone who understands. Thanks for dinner."

Brandy grinned. "Don't thank me too much, Claude. I intend to drain your savings account. Talk to you next week."

She waved good-bye as she pulled into the street. Then she slipped a CD into the slot and drove home, feeling surprisingly warm and happy with the excitement of the day.

Chapter V

Raleigh spent the morning watching Kiki teach their young pups to forage for food at the base of the oak tree. The pups were playful and energetic, eagerly climbing down the trunk to race around in the warm grass. Every afternoon since their birth, Raleigh left a generous supply of food outside the nest for Kiki. The food had helped her stay strong until the pups were weaned. Afterward, she shared the treats with the pups to supplement their diet. All five of the pups had survived and were healthy with bright eyes, lustrous coats, and bobbed tails. Raleigh enjoyed watching them dart with incredible speed across the sprawling branches of the oak, down the trunk and onto the grass.

He felt a very strong attachment to Kiki and the pups. But he always maintained his distance. Kiki was still extremely protective, instinctively isolating the pups from all potential danger. Many adult male squirrels would kill a pup, given half a chance. So Raleigh was patient. He knew that very soon he would be able to play with the pups and Kiki again.

In the mid-afternoon, he crawled over the fence by the reflection pool. The days were slightly shorter now, and he often met Ariel about this time. Today, she was seated on the verandah with Rene, who was fastidiously writing on a large tablet while Chloe snored at her feet. Ariel had her tablet shoved over to one corner of the table. Raleigh and Ariel would not use them as long as Rene was present. They had an understanding about that.

"Rene is too young to understand or appreciate this miracle," Ariel had explained. "In time, things will change. For now, I think we should keep this our own secret."

Raleigh trusted Ariel. And he had always sensed that his special abilities could place him in danger. So, whenever Rene was around, he pretended to be extraordinarily tame for her entertainment and delight. He knew that this made Ariel happy.

"Oh, Granny Ariel, there is our little friend!" exclaimed Rene, looking over at Raleigh as he hopped onto the verandah and onto the seat of a chair. Raleigh sat up on his haunches with his paws in the air, looking intently at Rene.

I think little Raleigh wants you to feed him." Ariel gave Rene an apple slice. "Here, slowly hand him this. And remember, be very gentle."

Timidly, Rene accepted the apple, holding it in front of Raleigh. He took the apple with his teeth and held it between his paws until he had devoured the fruit. Then he hopped onto the table and gazed at Rene expectantly.

She laughed, tossing her auburn curls behind her shoulders and selected a slice of banana. "Look, Granny! He is not afraid or us or Chloe." Then she held the banana in front of the squirrel until he gently took the fruit from her hands and devoured it.

"I think you have a little friend, Rene," Ariel said, obviously pleased with Raleigh's performance.

After Raleigh's appetite was sated, he stretched out on the table and watched Rene playing with her Google tablet. She was doing very well identifying the letters in large print. Ariel praised her and gave her several pointers.

Raleigh hopped down on the verandah when Chloe stirred from her nap, stretching lazily as she lifted her head and scanned the lawn, watching the birds feeding in the grass. Raleigh studied her with interest. Everything about the dog fascinated him. She was the only dog he had ever been close enough to touch. He was overpowered by her strong scent and admired her long white coat fanning across the brick floor. Her luminous brown eyes held an intelligent and gentle expression. She was noble, alert, and tolerant. And Chloe had never appeared jealous of him.

He noticed the worn rubber ball by a porcelain garden stool. He had seen Chloe play with the ball occasionally. Sometimes, she brought the ball to Ariel for a quick toss in the yard. Chloe loved to fetch.

Bored with watching Rene, Raleigh scampered over to the garden stool near the ball. It was about one-third his height and clearly too heavy for him to lift. He batted it once with his paw and watched it roll a few inches. Playfully, he batted it hard toward Chloe. The ball rolled across the floor in between Chloe's paws. Stunned, Chloe gazed at the squirrel in silence. Their eyes met, and there was a connection between them. It was the rudimentary communication of animals, but Raleigh sensed a bonding and connection.

Rene giggled. "Did you see that Granny? The squirrel rolled the ball to Chloe!"

Chloe nosed the small ball back over toward Raleigh. He moved out of its path and waited for it to roll to a stop. Using all of his strength, he batted the ball back toward Chloe. Rene shrieked with delight and clapped her hands.

Chloe panted in the afternoon heat, studying the squirrel appreciatively. Raleigh marveled at her enormous white teeth and the long fur on her chest. With a coquettish glance toward the squirrel, she sprang to her feet, grabbed the ball, and plunged down from the porch onto the grass running in a large circle around the lawn. When she reached the other side of the reflection pool, she paused, peering over her shoulder toward Raleigh, and barked. Her message was implicit. He scurried down from the verandah and bounded toward Chloe. When he was within six feet of her tail, she raced off with the ball in her mouth. Raleigh chased her at top speed until she stopped and dropped the ball. Chloe's challenging gaze met his own. Slowly, Raleigh crept toward the ball, batting it quickly with both paws. The ball, wet with Chloe's saliva, rolled only a few feet across the grass before Chloe grabbed it again and ran toward the verandah. Raleigh continued to chase the dog and the ball until she finally collapsed in an exhausted heap on the verandah. Raleigh jumped on the porch and crept toward the panting dog. He noticed that she smelled of sweat and excitement, and he sensed that she had happily accepted him. Chloe returned his direct gaze and nosed him briefly before placing her chin on her paw. He stretched out beside her on the cool brick floor to cool off.

"They are friends now, Granny Ariel," Rene said soberly, putting her tablet away. "Chloe likes Raleigh, and they were playing a game."

"I think so, too," remarked Ariel. "It is very special. Most dogs would try to kill a squirrel. But I think that Chloe knows that Raleigh is our friend too."

Over the next week, Chloe seemed to anticipate his daily visits. When Ariel was involved with Rene, Raleigh would play with the dog in the back yard. It was not as fulfilling as his time with Ariel, but it was exhilarating nonetheless to engage in games with a predator. And he felt a real kinship with the dog.

Raleigh noticed that the pups became fascinated with the dog. When Kiki finally permitted him near the pups, he showed them his best foraging spots near Ariel's fence. Sometimes he observed the pups peering from the entrance of their nest watching him chase Chloe. He knew that Kiki disapproved of his relationship with Chloe. Whenever she caught the pups staring at Chloe, she clucked the danger sign, scolded the pups brutally, and nipped at their ears while shoving them into the nest. Kiki was afraid of the dog. She tried very hard to teach the pups to avoid all predators. Her driving instinct compelled her to fear all large animals that could inflict a mortal wound. Kiki, like all small wild animals was cautious, living with the recognition of the frailty of their existence.

Raleigh was enchanted with the pups, and he had been very happy when Kiki had finally allowed him to play with them. Since that day, Raleigh spent every morning foraging and playing with the pups and Kiki. The pups grew quickly and, within days, they had lost their ungainly quality and became miniatures of their parents. As the weather cooled the first two weeks in September, Kiki regained her lustrous coat, which she had shed after the birth of the pups. Raleigh helped her construct a larger nest for the growing family at the edge of the park. Every afternoon, he continued to leave a large parcel of food from his visits with Ariel at the entrance to the nest. He knew that without the extra food, at least two of the large litter probably would not have survived. He felt happiness and contentment. The little family, along with his relationship with Ariel, had made his life complete.

Soon, the acorns would fall. The pups would be large enough to store the food in large quantities for the winter. As adolescents, they would soon come into adulthood and move out on their own. They would become competitors with their parents for food and a good nest. They would all live in reasonable proximity in the park.

He taught two of the largest pups the art of begging by the fountain. He knew that Kiki disapproved of taking food from humans. On the other hand, Raleigh knew that this was a survival mechanism in years when the acorns were scarce. A large meal from a generous human could keep a starving squirrel alive in the cold winter. He introduced them to the old man first, who appeared daily at noon by the fountain.

The old man looked at the pups hanging timidly behind Raleigh. "So, you've been busy, old friend. I see you have a little family now."

He held out a nut for Raleigh and tossed a few nuts to the pups. They devoured the nuts greedily and crept closer. Raleigh barked at them to keep their distance. The little pups were still relatively fearless and needed to exercise caution.

Raleigh taught them to look for people eating a snack. He avoided mothers with prams and teenage boys, clucking the danger call. After a few days of begging, the pups became skilled solicitors, sitting up on their haunches in a praying position and staring directly into the human faces. The more brazen of the two even surprised Raleigh one afternoon when he tugged the pants leg of a young woman who sat reading while eating a bag of chips. She looked at the pup adoringly and fed him as many chip fragments as he cared to eat.

He was pleased with the pups' ingenuity. He knew that the park was safer than most places for a squirrel. But he knew that caution was still important. In order to survive the pups needed to be vigilant. Raleigh was eager to teach them everything that he knew to help them. He agreed with Ariel's sentiment. They were his most important accomplishment to date.

Raleigh felt deeply unsettled when the unseasonable cool air arrived during the second week of September. He had an overwhelming sense of foreboding and fear. There was a strange smell in the afternoon heat beneath a brilliant blue sky.

Ariel told him about the storm early that afternoon while Rene was still at school. She explained that she had been watching the weather forecast on television. Raleigh thought it strange that anyone would learn anything about the weather from a box. He felt and smelled the weather systems in advance. It was instinctive. But he trusted Ariel because he had never had this weather feeling before. Even Chloe was restless and agitated. She lost all interest in the ball and was reluctant to leave the house or the verandah.

"There is a hurricane coming from the Caribbean up the Gulf of Mexico. It is still nearly two hundred miles away, but it is heading toward New Orleans," she explained. "Tomorrow, the rain squalls will move into the area. If the storm hits, it will be here within two and a half days."

He tapped the letters on the electronic tablet. "S-t-o-r-m?"

"It is a terrible storm—more violent that anything you have ever seen. They are such devastating storms that the National Weather Service gives them a name. This one is called Hurricane Penny. If she hits, a lot of birds and squirrels will die. Big trees will fall down because of the wind. There will be snakes and floods." She looked at him earnestly. "I have told you about Hurricane Katrina. You will need to get Kiki and the pups and move into the attic until the storm is over. Otherwise, you will die."

Kiki was skeptical and refused to entertain the prospect of moving into a human house. She was convinced that it was a trap to kill her pups and feed them to Chloe. She was adamant that the weather was clear and warm, and Kiki refused to acknowledge the funny smell in the air or the unnatural stillness in the park. Raleigh was unsettled, fearful of the worst. He could not imagine life without Kiki and the pups.

Late the following afternoon, a brisk cool wind blew in from the south unnaturally chilling the humid air and plucking the still green acorns from the massive oaks. The acorns poured down on the cars and walkways like hail pellets. Sudden gusts of fierce wind rocked the tree branches, plunging one of Raleigh's dummy nests to the ground. Without warning, a line of tremendous thunderstorms unleashed a driving rain. The squirrel noticed that the nearby park grounds were littered with debris from the trees. He shivered with the primal instinct of fear.

This was Penny! He had to get Kiki! He would have to take them to Ariel's house. If the storm worsened, they could never survive in the leaf-and-twig nest high in the adjacent oak.

He peered out of the tree hollow, which provided an ideal refuge from the storm. He could see a drenched sparrow huddled on one of the lower branches seeking shelter. Raleigh realized that at least part of the debris on the ground had once been her nest. The wind shook the massive branches and whipped at the trunk. He knew that it was extremely dangerous to leave the safety of the nest. He could be blown out of the tree and hurled to the ground below. But he had a nagging sense that he could not wait.

Raleigh climbed out of the nest, clinging to the trunk against the fierce wind. The relentless rain blinded him as he crept toward the bottom. He was vulnerable to a predator now, although he suspected that the neighboring owls were uninterested in venturing out into the storm. It took nearly fifteen minutes for him to descend to the bottom of the trunk. To his horror, he realized that the surrounding lawn was submerged in water. From what he could determine, the water was over his head. A squirrel could swim for small distances, although Raleigh had never tested this skill. But this water was moving very quickly, and he knew instinctively that he could easily drown. He was trapped. It seemed that his only recourse was to return to his nest in the hollow of the trunk and hope for the best.

He crawled around to the opposing side of the trunk and studied the landscape. A large limb had been severed from the base of Kiki's tree. It was no more than twenty feet away. He could swim across the rushing water and climb across the branch. If he could only reach Kiki, they could crawl across the interlacing branches to Ariel's rear fence. It was their only hope. If the storm worsened, Kiki's twig-and-leaf nest would be destroyed, leaving her and the pups defenseless.

He plunged into the cold water, paddling furiously against the swift current with his feet and using his tail as a rudder, carefully keeping his nose and mouth above the water. He was blinded by the wind and rain as he swam toward the branch. It was more difficult than he ever imagined. The strong current swept him in a wide arc away from the branch. His heart pounded and his legs ached as he battled the current. It seemed impossible as he floated farther away from the branch. Finally, he reached a spot beside a small log where the current was less strong. His stomach lurched as he saw what appeared to be a small snake curled on the log. He paddled with all of his effort back toward the branch in the more placid waters by the log, trying to ignore the snake curled only a dozen feet away. Its triangular head was propped on its coils in readiness to strike. The squirrel instinctively knew that it was a pit viper and probably a copperhead.

Finally, he reached the branch, pulling himself onto the thin branches. Despite his exhaustion, he allowed himself to rest only momentarily. He had to reach Kiki. He raced across the limb away from the snake.

He heard a sharp bark the moment he crawled onto the trunk of Kiki's tree. The dog bounded to him and licked his face. *Chloe.* Through the rain he could see a human wearing rubber boots, a coat with a hood, and holding a gold umbrella that was buffeted by the wind. Raleigh noticed that the human held a large basket. It moved toward him. Then he recognized Ariel.

"Raleigh! Is that you?" She looked nervous, but her bright expression conveyed that she was glad to see him. She stroked

Chloe's coat. "We have been so worried. Are you going to get Kiki? I brought a basket to bring Kiki and your pups home. We have to hurry. This is only the squall. This will get worse. Penny is a Category 4 hurricane."

He twitched his tail and chattered, shaking his head in assent.

"We will wait here," she told him.

He started up the tree, blinded again by the heavy rain. As he reached the halfway point, he realized that he could not see her nest. Nearing the top, he noticed that the nest was gone! Kiki and the pups must have been blown out of the nest! There was no way that they could survive. He felt frozen with fear and grief.

He turned and slowly made his way down the other side of the trunk. It was then that he noticed them, huddled against a small hollow in the trunk and partially exposed. He could smell and feel their fear. As he neared them, he could see that the pups were trembling and cold. The remains of their nest were lying on the ground. Kiki looked resigned to their fate. The tiny hollow was the only protection they could find in the storm. She knew that death was near for the little family.

Raleigh convinced them to climb to the bottom. Reluctantly, Kiki followed the pups who eagerly followed their father down the trunk. It was a slow and dangerous process. The fierce wind threatened to sweep them from the trunk to the lawn below.

At the bottom, Ariel scooped the pups into the covered basket. Kiki climbed in, gingerly avoiding contact with the human or the dog. Raleigh crawled into the basket while Ariel trudged back across the park into the house. He noticed that the pups were shivering uncontrollably from the cold and exposure. They snuggled together in the basket and fell asleep. Kiki trembled from fear and wrapped herself around the ball of pups. She seemed completely exhausted from the ordeal.

Raleigh could hear Rene's excited voice from inside the basket. "Did you find him, Granny Ariel? Please tell me you found him!" she said, nearly hysterical.

"It was sheer luck. Chloe found him. He nearly drowned. And we have his little family. But they are not tame like Raleigh. You must not try to pet them or you may get bitten."

Ariel rested the basket on a table in the attic and flipped open the top that hinged in the middle. She had placed a tray of fruit, cheese, and vegetables near a large bowl of water. A nest of blankets had been placed on two old upholstered chairs. Chloe stood somberly beside her, eyeing the pups with interest.

"We will leave you alone to eat and get some rest. Whatever you do, don't try to leave the house. No one will bother you here. You are safe and sound. I will check on you later."

Raleigh went over to his chair and nestled in the blankets. The pups watched him over the rim of the basket. Chloe padded over to the chair and nosed Raleigh affectionately. Then Ariel and Chloe left and closed the door, shrouding the room in darkness. The only illumination was from the dormer windows on the front of the attic.

He watched as the pups scurried from the basket and devoured the food. Then, one by one, they crawled onto the blanket bed and fell asleep. In the half-light, he saw Kiki nibble some of the food before joining the pups. He could still smell her fear.

The branches scratched against the dormer windows, and the rain pelted the walls of the house. The attic was warm, dry, and cozy.

Raleigh felt content as he curled into a small furry ball to rest. They were finally safe.

The screech jolted him from a deep sleep. A large gray rat carried one of the pups by the scruff of the neck across the floor. Night had fallen outside, but he could clearly see the rat in the dark shadows. A few feet away, another large rat crouched in the corner by an old armoire. Kiki clucked the danger sign and raced after the rat. She caught his prehensile tail, biting it until she drew blood. Stunned, the rat abandoned his prey and turned on Kiki. The frightened pup raced back over to the chair. The angry rat turned and lunged at Kiki. Raleigh ran toward them and bit the rat on the flank. The rat retreated to the shadows, hissing and growling. Kiki returned to the chair standing vigil over the pups. She licked the pup that had been kidnapped by the rat. He was shaken, but unharmed.

Raleigh jumped up on the chair behind Kiki. He needed to rouse Ariel and Chloe, but the howling wind made that nearly impossible. He would have to defend them himself.

He felt a rush of adrenaline as he jumped onto a table studying the two rats. They became bolder now, circling the chair and table and studying the situation. They gave Raleigh a menacing glance and focused on the pups. Kiki clucked loudly, crouched over her brood. Raleigh could smell her fear and anger.

There were three stacks of old books on the table. Raleigh watched the circling rats carefully as they tried to confuse Kiki, rising up to inspect her brood. Kiki was beside herself, turning quickly to monitor the rat in front of her and behind the chair. Intent on the victims, the rats ignored Raleigh on the table. The pups clucked wildly, trembling at the sight of the large rats.

Raleigh waited patiently as the larger of the two rats slowly crawled around the chair and table, searching for the best vantage point to jump into the chair. It was clear that they intended to steal another pup, devouring it for a meal. Rats had notoriously voracious appetites, often preying upon infant birds and mammals.

He watched as the larger rat stood on his haunches with his fore-paws on the back of the chair, prepared to jump up and steal a pup. The squirrel summoned all of his strength, shoving the pile of heavy books directly onto the rat's head. The books knocked the rat unconscious, burying him beneath the rubble. Raleigh heaved a second stack off the table directly onto the rat hoping to ensure his death. The books made a tremendous clatter, frightening the smaller rat back into the shadows. The frightened rat emitted a deep growl and hissed at the squirrels.

"I think the big one is dead," Raleigh said finally.

Kiki trembled. "Maybe, but his mate is not going to give up!" she cried. She huddled over the pups, clucking furiously at the rat.

After a few minutes, the smaller rat emerged from the shadows. She cautiously inspected the rubble of books, peering through the crevices in search of her mate. She hissed up at Raleigh and began circling the chair, glaring at Kiki and the pups. They could sense her rage as she pawed at the upholstery, searching for a foothold.

Raleigh steeled himself to lunge onto the rat's back. She was nearly twice his size, but he knew that together he and Kiki could inflict serious wounds to deter her from harming the pups. He felt an anger course through his veins that he had never felt before.

Suddenly, he heard a loud bark outside the attic door. Chloe pawed the floor and barked furiously. The rat froze and crouched behind a chair leg. Momentarily, they heard footsteps on the stairs.

The door swung open, and Chloe bounded toward the squirrels in the chair, growling at the rat. Ariel and her granddaughter appeared and flipped on a light switch. A man Raleigh had never seen stood in the doorway. Chloe backed the rat in the corner, growling deep in her throat. The rat hissed and lunged toward Chloe's nose in an abortive attempt to bite her.

The man took a shiny shovel Raleigh had seen by the fireplace downstairs and brought it down sharply on the rat's back. He pounded the rat furiously until its bloody carcass lay motionless in the corner.

Chloe turned her attention to the pile of books by the chair. She snuffed and barked at the rubble. Ariel took the shovel from the man and pawed through the books until she uncovered the body of the dead rat.

"Oh my God! These rats were trying to eat the squirrel pups." She petted Chloe's head. "Aren't you the heroine for the second time today. Thank goodness you found them."

Brandy stood over the chair with the man. "These are the squirrels we told you about. Granny has made friends with the male. She and Chloe brought them here to ride out the storm."

Ariel picked up the basket and placed it by the chair. "They will have to stay in the basket downstairs. It is too risky to remain here. There are likely more rats that have somehow found their way into the house to avoid the storm. I will bring them down to the laundry room tonight. They will be safe."

Brandy shook her head. "Chloe can look after them. Rene would be devastated if anything happened to the squirrels."

It took a few minutes for Raleigh to coax Kiki and the pups into the basket. Finally, Ariel carried them downstairs to the laundry room. She placed some cheese and fruit in the corner of the basket. Chloe curled up beside the door and snored softly.

Restlessly, Kiki inspected her pups, licking their fur and curling her large tail around them. Raleigh crawled out of the basket and sprawled by Chloe on the cool floor. Finally satisfied that her pups were safe, Kiki and the pups fell asleep in the basket.

From his position on the floor, the squirrel maintained a watchful eye over them all for the rest of the night.

Chapter VI

Hurricane Penny's northern peripheral edge invaded the southern Louisiana shore at midnight. The eye of the hurricane was centered over New Orleans before seven the following morning, heralding a temporary calm. The storm that followed muddied the sky and ravaged the city with a frightening intensity and sustained winds over 100 miles per hour gusting at 150 miles per hour. The storm severed power lines, felled stately trees, and devastated homes. Areas immediately south of Lake Pontchartrain were protected by the complex levee systems constructed after Hurricane Katrina. The areas south of New Orleans toward Grand Isle were not so lucky.

The National Weather Service had forecast that the storm nearly packed the force and intensity of a Category 4 storm. Those residents who had endured Hurricane Katrina in 2005 evacuated the city. Troops of Uptown residents boarded up their homes and fled to the sprawling communities north of the lake with friends or to inland Mississippi. Temporary shelters were opened in schools and churches on higher ground north of the lake. Barges and large ships from the port traveled north up the Mississippi River to avoid the force of the storm. Yachts and small pleasure craft on the lake were towed inland or placed in covered moorage.

Brandy heated a pot of frozen gumbo on the gas stove in the kitchen for lunch. A deafening wind whistled and howled, pelting the driving rain and branches against the house. They had lost electricity shortly after midnight. Fortunately, Granny Ariel had several oil lamps she used for parties on the verandah and a generous supply of candles.

Brandy had been relieved when Claude had called that morning asking if they wanted company riding out the storm. He had spent the evening before looking after his parents' brick mansion two blocks away. Fortunately, Claude's parents were away in their second home in a small village in the south of France. Claude had hired one of the storm services to board the windows and remove several of the priceless antiques. He was confident that his condo would be safe. The doorman had been paid to stay in the building throughout the storm to protect the property and watch for looters. The exposed windows had been covered with plywood. Claude had left his car parked in the keyed garage of his building. Unless the building collapsed, it was probably safe.

In the three weeks since they had reconnected, Claude had proven to be a good friend and to date, one of Brandy's most profitable customers. She had begun to value their renewed friendship. Somehow it was comforting and less threatening to have someone other than a romantic relationship with a man. Claude was one of the only people who understood her grief and did not offer canned advice and platitudes about her loss. Instead, he just listened without being judgmental. It was remarkably therapeutic.

Claude had assisted them in filling water jugs and bottles. Residents were advised not to drink the water unless it had been bottled or boiled. Granny Ariel had purchased several cases of bottled Kentwood Spring water last week preparing for the possibility of such a storm. Most of the food in the defrosting freezer would spoil and be thrown out. They could prepare a few small meals before that time with bottled water on the gas stove. Brandy knew from past experience that the food in many grocery stores in the city without generators would also spoil from the lack of electricity. She dreaded the thought of the lack of air-conditioning in the muggy heat and the prospect of sponge or cold baths for the next few days.

Brandy was worried about the shop and her inventory. The stucco-and-brick building in the back of the French Quarter was nearly two hundred years old and certainly had endured its share of hurricanes. The Massenet building did not flood during Katrina and remained dry and intact, except for the roof repair. After Hurricane Katrina, a cottage industry of professional post-storm caretakers sprang up in the city. These services boarded up retail glass windows with plywood and stayed on-site during the storm to protect the property. The men were armed to guard against looters. Two days ago, when it had been a certainty that the storm was heading to New Orleans, the service had moved all items toward the back of the shop, out of the path of water and flying debris, and sent Brandy a text photo. After the storm, the service would immediately replace any broken windows, patch leaks, and remove any water. She made a mental note that she would install a generator in the shop and at home after the storm.

Rene sat with Ariel and Chloe in the dark hallway in the study playing old maid in the candlelight as the storm raged. Chloe lay against the wall by the basket containing Kiki and the pups. Raleigh sprawled over the top of the basket, maintaining a watchful eye. The study was the safest place during the storm, offering a safe haven from the wind, rain, tornadoes, and flying debris.

The raging storm had already caused substantial damage to the antebellum house. A tree branch from an adjacent oak in the park had fallen on the verandah, collapsing the roof and breaking several windows in the rear of the house. Earlier that morning, the wind had stripped away the shingles from the garage roof and ripped the garage door from its hinges. The lovely octagonal gazebo on the rear lawn had been lifted by the wind and carelessly tossed over the fence, shattering the sides. The tree where Kiki and her pups had their nest had toppled onto the park grounds, its roots exposed.

Brandy ladled the gumbo into large bowls and placed them on a tray with paper napkins. Claude opened a carton of lemonade and poured four glasses, which he carried into the study with two loaves of French bread and a plate heaped with Oreos.

He set the tray on a small table and sat in an adjacent chair. "Here we are—a picnic in the study. Our own little hurricane party."

Brandy followed him in with the gumbo. The four of them ate in silence.

"Mommy and I had a hurricane party before—at our old house," Rene announced. "Remember, Mommy?"

Brandy smiled and touched her daughter's face lightly. She had only been three and a half then. It was amazing that she could remember.

"I remember, sweetie," she said, placing her empty gumbo dish on the tray and pulling off a piece of French bread.

"It's fun to use candles in the daytime. It's so dark outside!" she marveled.

"It's the storm, baby. It has turned the sky black," Brandy said.

Rene studied Claude. "Have you been to a hurricane party before?"

"I was here for some of the smaller storms, but I probably haven't had the experience that you and your mother had in the Caribbean. Fortunately, I missed Hurricane Katrina. I was born a couple of years after Hurricane Betsy hit the city. It destroyed many homes and wrecked boats. But if we stay inside, we'll be safe."

Brandy brought the dishes to the kitchen and rinsed them in the half-light. When she returned, she coaxed Rene to take a nap on a pallet on the floor. She noticed that Granny Ariel looked tired but remarkably calm. She had probably seen a number of hurricanes in her day. Her grandmother had worked in the shelters continuously for the last three days helping those who were forced from their homes because of the approaching storm and providing survival packets for the homeless children. She was a truly selfless person.

"The noise from the wind is incredible," Ariel said finally. "This is a very bad storm. It will keep the painters, carpenters, and gardeners busy for quite some time." She looked sadly toward the living room. Plywood had been shoved over the broken crescent transoms and the windows to protect the house from the driving rain and wind. The silken drapes on one wall had been soaked and shredded. "Your grandfather loved that room. I bought those peach silk drapes because they were his favorite color. He said the color reminded him of my hair—or the way it used to be about a hundred years ago." She sighed. "Oh well, enough about that. What we really need to do tomorrow is worry about the people without a home. I am going to go through the attic and my closets tomorrow looking for clothes and items for people whose homes have been destroyed by the storm. I can't imagine how terrible that must be. Imagine—all of your memories and prized possessions destroyed in one fell swoop, leaving you with only the clothes on your back. Some people never recover financially from that, you know."

Brandy smiled. She had always admired her grandmother's willingness to help those in need. She was always thinking of others, including the ridiculous squirrel family in the laundry room. "We'll help you, Granny. And maybe we can bring some of this food that hasn't spoiled to the shelters—that is—if the streets are not blocked off and we can get out of the city."

The promise seemed to inject Ariel with new energy. "That's a wonderful idea! I will start this afternoon. It will give me something to do while the power is out."

Brandy and Claude made rounds throughout the house while Rene napped on the floor. She had been so excited and fearful about the storm that she had hardly slept. Ariel stayed behind to comfort and feed Chloe and the squirrels.

The storm dwindled in the late afternoon, trailing a squall line that chilled the air. After a dinner of thawed shrimp Creole and a crabmeat-and-Swiss cheese casserole, Brandy and Claude went out on the partially destroyed verandah to survey the damage. The usually manicured lawn and the park looked like a war zone with debris from plants, houses and cars littering the ground. Streetcar and power lines were strewn across the median like giant snakes. A tremendous oak limb had been sheared from its trunk, crushing the roofs of cars lining the left side of the street. A large tree had fallen across the middle of a neighboring house, piercing the roof and destroying the exterior wall of a third-floor bedroom, which was now visible from the street.

Claude and Brandy walked over to check on his parents' home in the early evening with a flashlight. The two of them donned rain gear and went out to survey the damage, carefully avoiding the power lines and downed limbs. A light from the interior of the house burned brightly from the generator, and the professional storm service was removing the plywood. Claude and Brandy quickly surveyed the interior. Only the slate roof seemed to have been damaged by the storm. Since it was the middle of the night in Europe, Claude sent his parents a text with a photo and the good news that the house had survived. He promised to contact the home insurer to have the roof repaired. The shingles had clearly been ripped from the roof by the forces of wind and not water damage. The loss would be covered.

They walked back down St. Charles toward Granny Ariel's home. The sidewalk was blocked in several places by severed oak limbs lying on the ground. Claude spotted a large copperhead curled next to the stone balustrade by the park. Carefully, he steered Brandy out of range of the snake. Storms often brought snakes and, on occasion, small alligators into the city.

Brandy felt a chill down her spine. "It is easy to forget that a poisonous snake is occasionally found in the city," she told him as they walked around the fountain, now littered with debris.

"Sometimes the storms bring them out. Watch your step," Claude told her. "If I had the shovel, I could probably kill it. I think it would be a good idea to watch Rene very closely until all of this mess is cleaned up."

Brandy shook her head. "This is incredibly depressing. It will take a couple of months to repair this damage. And my favorite climbing oaks from my childhood have been destroyed. What a shame. And to think that it is only the end of September."

"I think it is global warming—these terrible storms are generated by the heat off of Africa and pick up strength over the warmer waters of the Atlantic. According to the weather service, they are becoming more frequent," he said.

"Interesting and depressing. I have never seen such devastation. Everything here is usually so perfectly maintained. I have always loved this area," she mused.

He touched her arm lightly. "Tomorrow, we can try to go downtown to check on the shop. Maybe we can also deliver the food and clothing to the shelters. It all depends upon whether the roads are passable."

"That's a good idea," she said. "You know, I am really glad that I was back here. Can you imagine Granny going through this storm by herself with only the dog and squirrels for company?"

Claude flashed his brilliant smile. “If anyone could do it, she could. She is an amazing woman.”

“I guess you are right. She took me in after my parents were killed and treated me like her own special daughter. Her incredible wisdom has helped me through several tough times. I think the older you are, the less you get into a flap about things.”

They walked silently for a few moments. “You know, I worry. Granny is eighty-five. Do you think that she is losing it—I mean this squirrel fascination? Do you think that is something I should be concerned about?”

He grinned. “I think it is interesting. The male squirrel is more of a pet than anything else. That sort of thing doesn’t happen very often. I think you should be happy about it. It is harmless and she treats him like Chloe. You worry too much,” he teased.

“I am just afraid. I don’t think I could take losing someone else,” she admitted, realizing what it was that bothered her about the squirrel.

Claude lightly touched the arm of her rain slicker again, signaling that they should return to the house. “I had that fear too after Connie died. It never really goes away, but it lessens with time. It is the fear of suffering again. Counseling helped, but I really would not allow myself to be close to anyone—at least before I began spending time with you.” He turned to face her. “It has been really great talking through all of this with you over the past three weeks, Brandy. I think I have finally been able to put a few issues to rest.”

“Me, too.”

They walked in silence back to the house. Ariel had put out several more candles and had refilled the oil lamps in their absence. They spent the remainder of the evening playing cards in the candlelight. Despite the turmoil around them from the storm, Brandy felt safe and happy. It was a good sign. She was starting to live again.

The following morning was crystal clear, dry and warm. The weather was so perfect that the storm seemed like a dream until Brandy surveyed the wake of devastation in the harsh light. Blocked by trees and branches, many of the roads were not passable in the Uptown area for two days. She spent the time working in the house, pulling out old clothes for the shelters, and emptying the freezer and refrigerator. Granny Ariel's cleaning service would not be able to return until next week.

The electricity was restored on the third day after the storm. Rene's kindergarten was cancelled for the remainder of the week. The child spent her time with Granny Ariel, going to the shelters and playing with Chloe and the squirrels. Claude returned to work and life in his condo, and Brandy went downtown to check on Massenet. Remarkably, it was undamaged—as if the storm had never occurred. The storm service had removed the plywood, replaced a small window on the second floor, and moved the inventory to its proper place. Tourism and shopping had been interrupted by the storm, and Brandy decided to close the shop until Saturday.

As she was preparing to close and leave for the afternoon, two New York tourists attending a convention that was scheduled to open the following day came in to browse. One bought a lovely French commode and an eighteenth century painting. It was one of the more profitable afternoons since she had opened the shop. She stayed briefly working on the books and arranging for the shipment of the painting and commode. Then she went by the French Market and bought a supply of fresh fish, fruit, and vegetables for dinner and a newspaper.

She noticed that three men from the lawn service, IBIX, had cleared away the debris from the front lawn as she drove up. She waved and smiled, noticing a new man had joined the crew. He had a dark mustache, bald head, deep tan, and wore a baseball cap He waved to her absently and averted his gaze.

Inside, she noticed that for the first time in four days, the basket in the laundry room was empty. The squirrels had returned to the park to locate new homes and rebuild their nests. Chloe sat dismally by the basket, lonely without her friends.

Brandy fried the lightly breaded catfish strips in oil, prepared a large salad and arranged a fruit tray. Rene, Granny Ariel, and Brandy ate dinner in the breakfast room, chatting about the cleanup process. Rene told her about the new gazebo that Granny planned to purchase. Granny Ariel had made an insurance claim and contacted several contractors about repairing the damage to the house. She had also contacted an exterminator about the rats. He had agreed to set traps and utilize a method that would not pose a threat to the squirrels. After dinner, Brandy and Rene cleaned up the kitchen. Brandy had almost forgotten what a luxury it was to have a dishwasher. They played a few hands of old maid at the table before bathing Rene. Afterward, they retreated to the den to watch TV.

It was late when Brandy returned downstairs. Granny Ariel subscribed to the *New York Times*. Brandy grabbed the paper to read upstairs after she put Rene to bed. She did not often read the newspaper, but she was interested in the stories about the storm. She nearly missed the small story on the third page of the second section. She felt sharp pain in her stomach as she read the headline:

"*BYZANTIUM*! Salvors Find Sunken Ship with Treasure!

The article detailed the long efforts of Virgin Islands businessman Thad Stuart to locate the hull of the nineteenth century vessel in the Caribbean. The vessel had carried 104 passengers and a cargo of emeralds believed to have a present value of $400 million. Thad filed suit in federal court in St. Thomas, seeking title to the vessel and its treasure, or alternatively a salvage award and the exclusive right to salvage the vessel. He had recently formed an alliance with several prominent investors who were partially funding the venture. The Lloyd's syndicates who had insured the vessel and its cargo had been joined as defendants in the suit. Thad had presented the court with several emeralds that had been recovered from the wreck site last year.

Her breath caught in her throat. Harris was not even mentioned in the article. And the emeralds had been found at the wreck site! Thad had lied to her. He and Harris had actually found the *BYZANTIUM* before Harris died. *If only Harris had confided in her! And to think that she had lost faith in him.*

She dissolved into tears of anger and guilt. There was something strange about this situation. She needed legal advice. Checking the clock, she noted that it was only eleven o'clock. She picked up the phone and dialed Claude's number.

Ewan took a long hot shower after work, enjoying the hard spray and scented soap he had bought at the market. The electricity had been restored earlier in the day. The central air-conditioning system gradually cooled the warm musty air from the apartment. It had been a long day. That morning, in the cool hours of the early dawn, he had cleaned the debris from his porch and the small yard in front of the duplex. He had also raked the debris from the back and swept the porch. The old place had weathered the storm well, without sustaining even a small leak or a broken window.

He pulled on a tee shirt and shorts and headed to the kitchen to pan-fry a steak and toss a small salad. He grabbed a beer from the refrigerator to sip while he cooked and flipped on the television in the living room for background noise. His muscles were tight and sore. He had been working at IBIX now for two weeks, and he felt the familiar ache of heavy exertion. He had not engaged in such hard physical labor since the Marine Corps.

He had gotten soft working in the dive shop and waiting tables. This work was good for him—like a real man.

The IBIX team to which he had been assigned had been busy over the past two days cleaning up debris from the lawns and gardens surrounding the fancy houses in the Uptown area. Ewan had never been so close to such gorgeous properties in his life. Many of the mansions serviced by IBIX Lawn and Garden had sparkling fountains shooting a fine mist from garden ponds, gracious verandahs with flowering plants, brick patios, swimming pools, and elaborate parterre gardens.

Christ! It was amazing that people lived like this with so much fucking money!

Ewan had very humble origins, growing up in a Nebraska farm town of less than fifteen hundred people. It had been a hard-scrabble life without much joy. His father had been a drunk and a house painter, taking an occasional job when he was not drinking. They were always short of money. His mother had left with another man when he was only seven. The bank had foreclosed on their ramshackle house on the outskirts of town in the middle of his senior year of high school. The two of them had lived in his father's truck until Ewan had graduated from high school, working odd jobs in exchange for food. After graduation, Ewan had joined the Marine Corps and never looked back. Leaving his father, he finally felt free. He had lost track of his old man and really did not care. He was probably dead by now. The old bastard had a violent temper and was lazy. Ewan was determined to make something of himself. He had the dream.

He ate his steak and salad in the living room and watched a reality show. After loading the dishwasher, he grabbed another beer, savoring its cool flavor after a long day in the heat. Ewan's thoughts drifted from the television show to Brandy. He had seen her often from a distance, checking out her shop in the French Quarter and twice when she had met a male friend for dinner. One evening, he had seen her in the kitchen of her grandmother's house standing over the kitchen sink as he stood in the evening shadows of the park. Today, he had been a mere seven feet from her as she drove into the driveway and exited her car. He had felt his breath catch in his throat as she turned, facing him fully, and smiled. She was quite beautiful, with long red hair, porcelain skin and blue eyes. He had instinctively turned to avoid her gaze but then instantly regretted his decision. He knew that it was important to establish some rapport with her. That is what Thad would want. Next time, he resolved to engage her in a conversation, no matter how brief. He also learned that an old lady and little girl lived in the house with Brandy.

He would establish a rapport with the old lady and kid first—being helpful and friendly. That would immediately bring him closer to Brandy.

He smiled and went in to grab another beer from the refrigerator before settling in on the couch to watch more TV.

Chapter VII

Four days after the storm, Raleigh returned to his old nest in the hollow of the live oak. The tree had been prematurely stripped of its acorns and a number of small branches. Nonetheless, because it was situated in a protected grove surrounded by larger trees, it had weathered the storm quite well.

The tree that had held Kiki's nest had been uprooted like a weed and tossed carelessly on the ground. Raleigh assisted Kiki and the pups in locating a new nest in a nearby tree. They found an abandoned high hollow in a live oak bordering the avenue.

Apparently its former resident, a cardinal, had perished in the storm. It was a safer refuge than her former twig-and-leaf nest, with a deep crevasse offering protection from most predators living in the territory. After reestablishing their homesteads, the squirrels set about constructing their dummy nests to foil predators. This required a great deal of strategy and savvy. The dummy nests needed to be accessible to the squirrel's own path across the tree, but far enough away to avoid compromising the location of the real nest. It was a good learning experience for the pups.

Most of the acorns were too still too green to eat. The squirrels feasted on the ripe acorns, planting new caches of food for the winter. The high water had washed away many former burial sites, robbing them of their emergency food stashes for the winter. Raleigh knew that it would be a harsh winter, forcing Kiki and her brood to rely upon the generosity of park visitors and Ariel for their food.

The aftermath of the storm was a shock to them all. The high water, mud, and rotting debris filled the air with a pungent odor. There was a marked absence of birds and squirrels in the park. The geese and ducks that had inhabited the lagoon were gone. From their position in the trees, the squirrels noticed a number of small poisonous snakes writhing across the park grass. Even the old owl that had lived on the other side of the park had disappeared. With the exception of the crickets, it was now unusually quiet at night. They seemed to be alone in the park.

Raleigh felt a deep sense of fear when he saw the dead bodies of animals who had died in the storm. The rotting bodies of three cats, a large dog, several squirrels, birds, a raccoon, and a possum were visible in his territory. Many of them had a permanent expression he recognized as pain and fear. He watched in horror as a large snake devoured the bodies of a small female squirrel and two males by the fountain. He knew that they had probably been catapulted from the safety of their nests during the worst of the storm.

With the exception of the city gardeners, the park was relatively devoid of human activity for the following week. They slowly cleaned the debris clogging the lagoon and the once sparkling fountain by the park gate. Stray limbs and branches were loaded into large trucks. Bushes were pruned and flower beds were prepared for the spring. Whenever possible, the gardeners killed the numerous snakes and carried away the bodies of dead animals along with the debris filling the bed of the flatbed trucks.

The dreams returned and restful sleep evaded him over the next few days. His dreams were filled with death, destruction, and violence. He dreamed of the snakes and rotting bodies. Clucking and squealing with terror, he watched as Kiki and the pups were swept out of the tree in their small nest, plunging nearly one hundred feet to the ground only to be torn apart by a voracious family of rats. He dreamed that he was a human child being held under the swirling water of the storm until his lungs burst. Each morning when he awoke, his fur was damp, and he had soiled his nest. Kiki sensed that something was wrong, but he merely ignored her questioning looks. They were all anxious, having narrowly escaped death and returned to this strange new world.

When the streetcar lines were repaired, a few morning walkers and joggers with their children and dogs returned to the park. Once the fountain was cleaned and the debris was cleared away from the walkways, a handful of people returned to enjoy the late afternoon. Only a few of them were interested in sharing their food with the squirrels. It was as if everyone were still preoccupied with the death and destruction.

Every afternoon, Ariel and Chloe came down to the park to visit while the carpenters restored the verandah and repaired the damage to the house. Ariel brought fruit and nuts for Kiki and the pups as well, spreading it out onto the deserted bench. She laid out the electronic table to enable her to communicate with Raleigh. He told her about the new dummy nests they had constructed, the green acorns, and the depressing corpses. She told him about the ornate new gazebo she was ordering in addition to the playhouse for Rene.

"I have contacted an exterminator. They are going to kill the rats. Then, I am going to fix up a little place for you and Kiki in the attic—you could come and go. I would not expect you to live there, but it might be handy in another emergency."

He was not sure that it was necessary, but Ariel and Chloe had saved his life. He touched the "o" block on the keyboard, which was their shorthand for "ok."

"You are my special little miracle friend," she said. "And I have an obligation to make sure that you are safe." She stroked his cream chest with her finger. "You have added something miraculous to my life—in fact you restored my faith that there is more to the world than we can see. I think it is a gift from God she mused. "Promise me that you will use the attic hideaway."

He promised. He knew that he was different with special abilities. Neither he nor Ariel had an answer for his gift. But he was fulfilled by this friendship, and he trusted her. She had, after all, protected him and his family.

Sometimes, they silently played checkers on the game board she stowed in her basket. On other occasions, their conversations were limited to the mundane. She described the repairs to the house and the people she had been trying to help who were left without homes as a result of the storm. Raleigh told her about the death of the other animals in the park. He felt saddened and confused by the mass devastation and death.

Chloe seemed to sense his anxiety. She would place her nose on the squirrel's chest, giving him a swift lick with her tongue as if to comfort him. Ariel began bringing the dog's ball to allow the squirrel and Chloe to play chase around the fountain. Much to Kiki's dismay, the pups began playing with the dog, chasing her while she raced through the grass with the ball in her mouth. Kiki stood on the tree, scolding and nipping the pups when they returned home. Despite everything they had been through, she still did not trust the dog or Ariel.

The squirrels now spent all of their time in the park because of the construction on Ariel's house. Their normal activities were curbed during the brief period of time that the park workers cleaned their area of the park grounds. Kiki and the pups were extremely disturbed by the high-pitched squeal of the chain saws used by the work crew to sever the dead trees and the fleet of trucks parked on the road to haul away the debris. They spent most of the day quietly in their nests until the workers left the area each afternoon.

Four days after the storm, Raleigh noticed a young male squirrel in the lower quadrant of his territory, foraging on exposed cambium from the felled trees. He learned that the squirrel lived in the vicinity of the seal pool of the Audubon Zoo and had found shelter in one of the zoo buildings during the storm. Most of the squirrels in the park had perished in the storm, and the young male boldly expanded his territory without fear of reprisal. As the dominant male, Raleigh chased the squirrel away back toward his territory. Soon the pups would leave the nest, and they would need to find their own areas to live. Raleigh did not want them crowded out by the imposing new male. On the other hand, he did not want to discourage the male completely because Raleigh recognized that he was a likely mate for one of his female pups one day.

The late afternoon before twilight was still his favorite time. Without many of the tree predators, like the old owl, the squirrels enjoyed an unusual freedom to race across the branches without reprisal, basking in the cool air. Raleigh knew that it was only a matter of time, however, before the ecological gap was closed and new predators moved into the territory.

Early one morning a week after the storm, Raleigh saw a new female squirrel gliding across the concrete streetcar pad directly across from the university. Skillfully, she dodged an oncoming car and scurried across the cement walkway toward the fountain. Effortlessly, she hopped on a bench, gnawing on the bark from an errant branch that had fallen across the seat. He admired her lovely full coat and bushy curvaceous tail that arched toward the brilliant blue sky. Raleigh was entranced by her beauty and felt a stirring of his primal need to mate.

As he admired the female, he spotted a feral cat, probably left homeless by the storm, lurking behind the stone balustrade. The gray feline emerged from the shadows near the fountain, crouching silently in the late afternoon shadows intently studying the female squirrel. High overhead, Raleigh began clucking the danger signal to warn the young female of the approaching danger. Engrossed in her meal, she did not notice the call at first. Then she paused and looked toward the cat. Startled, the female squirrel sprang from the bench, springing toward a nearby tree.

Raleigh's heart pounded as watched the female below him bounding across the muddy grass toward a large live oak. She was incredibly fast.

She was going to make it!

The female squirrel reached the trunk of the tree, springing onto the base and heading for the top. Propelled by hunger, the voracious cat climbed up the tree in determination after the female squirrel. With lightning speed, the cat caught the tip of the squirrel's tail prying her from her hold on the trunk and pitching her ten feet to the ground. The female squirrel landed on her head, temporarily disorienting her and affecting her quick reflexes. As she sprang to her feet and turned to run, the cat fearlessly pounced from the tree onto the squirrel's back, repeatedly biting her hard behind the neck until he drew blood. The young squirrel shrieked in pain until the cat's final vicious bite severed a carotid artery and crushed her windpipe. Helpless and mesmerized by the drama unfolding below him, Raleigh watched in stunned silence as the young female squirrel died.

The cat seemed irritated that the squirrel had died so quickly. The predator ran back and sat a few feet from the squirrel, prepared to pounce again when she moved. Like all cats, the feline seemed to enjoy torturing its victims. Riveted on his perch on the branch overhead, Raleigh watched the feline predator bat the dead squirrel a few times with its paw and roll her onto her back. With a heavy heart,

Raleigh watched as the cat finally carried the female into a stand of azalea bushes over by the edge of the park.

Devastated, he returned to his nest for the remainder of the evening. Raleigh fell asleep and was plagued by the dreams again. Around midnight, he was jolted awake by a traffic accident on the avenue below. Sirens howled and were eventually followed by a series of revolving lights visible on the street below. It was an event he associated with human death. He ducked back inside the tree hollow set behind his nest and tried to ignore the noise.

Usually a meticulously clean animal, Raleigh was disconcerted that his fur was damp and emitted a sour odor. He recognized that it was the smell of fear. There had been so much death over the last few days. He closed his eyes and tried very hard to wipe the horrific image of the young squirrel's death from his mind. It was yet another reminder of the fragility of life for small animals in the park. He needed to protect the pups and Kiki from the same fate. He resolved that he would encourage them to utilize the attic accommodations offered by Ariel in an emergency.

He willed the image of the struggling female squirrel from his mind and tried to rest. Despite his best efforts, sleep evaded him for the remainder of the night.

~

Claude sat across the small table from Brandy while she reviewed a photocopy of the *BYZANTIUM* complaint. The librarian in his office had obtained a copy of the pending lawsuit filed in federal court in St. Thomas through PACER. Federal court pleadings were filed electronically now and were available instantly. Claude had emailed the complaint to Brandy at her store a few hours ago.

Brandy propped her arms on the table in the open-air seating area of the small restaurant, finishing her gumbo and studying the pleadings. Before they had ordered lunch, Brandy had surrendered the envelope of emeralds to Claude in a large manila envelope. He had instructed her to put them into a safety deposit box before she returned to work that morning.

The café was situated in one of the two original Eighteenth century French market buildings. From their table, they had a view of the Mississippi River levee and Jackson Square flanked by the Pontalba Buildings, the St. Louis Cathedral, the Cabildo, and the Presbytere. The square, with its classically French buildings, was considered one of the most beautiful areas in the city. Usually, it was one of Brandy's favorite spots. This morning, she was so upset that she barely noticed her surroundings.

"Thad is a liar! This is incredible!" she said finally, systematically folding the paper. Thad and a large salvage operator, Recov, had filed the vessel arrest action jointly as plaintiffs. The complaint essentially asked the court to take jurisdiction over the vessel until title was resolved, as well as the disposition of the cargo. The complaint contained claims for both "a salvage award" and "title pursuant to the law of finds." Brandy recognized Recov as the same large operator that had approached Thad and Harris before his death. The complaint alleged that the *BYZANTIUM* had been located in early November of the previous year.

This was merely a month after Harris's death. It was a lie.

Thad's attorney claimed that a seam in the hull had split at impact, spilling a portion of the emeralds onto the seabed near a diving wall. The gems had been systematically collected and stored in a warehouse in St. Thomas. The *BYZANTIUM*, the emerald cargo and the hull insurers who paid the claim, including the Lloyd's, London syndicates and London Market companies, were named as defendants. She felt a pounding in her chest when she noticed that Harris's name was never even mentioned. It was outrageous, since Harris, and not

Thad, had in fact discovered the vessel at least eleven months before his death.

It was all an outrageous lie, and she was helpless to do anything about it.

Claude patted her arm gently. "It is a shock, I know. Sometimes I hear the lawyer's version on the other side of a case and I wonder if we are even talking about the same thing."

She put the complaint down on the table and finished her beignet silently. She and Harris had dreamed about what would happen if they located the *BYZANTIUM* and its cargo. But, she had never quite understood the legal ramifications. "What is the difference between salvage and finds?" she asked finally.

"Recov and Thad are trying to get what is known as a 'salvage award' from the owners of the ship and cargo. In other words, they are trying to get the court to award them a substantial sum of money for the recovery of the boat and emeralds. A salvage award is based upon a lot of factors. They are called the Blackwall factors. For example, the court will consider how difficult it was to find the boat and recover the cargo, the value and expense of the equipment and technology used to find the boat, the length of time that was required for recovery, and the value of the cargo and vessel. Here, we have a fairly old boat with some historical interest and a cargo of emeralds conservatively worth more than $400 million in today's market. So, the salvage award could be astronomical," he explained.

"How high?" she asked.

"At least half and possibly more. In the Fourth Circuit about fifteen years ago, the court awarded a salvage operator 90 percent of the value of the gold recovered aboard the *S.S.CENTRAL AMERICA*, which sank in a hurricane off of the east coast of the United States.

The gold was a couple of hundred years old and had a high value. The court ordered that the gold should be sold and that the salvors should be awarded ninety percent. The cargo owners, who were the London market insurers, were awarded 10 percent of the value of the cargo and the vessel, which was substantial. The case still spawned a lot of litigation."

Brandy shook her head in disbelief. "Ninety percent. That is incredible! It hardly seems fair."

"I know that it seems strange, but you have to think about how much the value of the cargo and the vessel appreciated. The London insurers paid the claim and, of course, they lost the use value of that money over time. They were subrogated to the rights of their insured. In other words, the underwriters owned the property on the sea floor, but, they could not get to it. A court will evaluate this from the perspective that if it had not been for the efforts of the salvors, the insurers might never have recovered their property. Also, the insurers were not making any effort to recover the cargo. So, the salvors were offered something substantial for their efforts. It is, in part, to encourage operations of this type."

She sipped her café au lait, mulling his explanation over in her head momentarily. "Well, if you put it that way, I seem to remember Harris was always talking about an award. I have to admit that I never really understood what he was talking about."

"If the court orders the salvage award, the insurers can then market the emeralds and still make a recovery."

"It seems very odd," she said pensively.

"It is a very ancient doctrine. There is volunteer salvage—like this, when someone decides to recover a ship or cargo. Then, there is contract salvage—when the boat owner signs a contract to tow his vessel or Recover it. Think about the *COSTA CONCORDIA*. That is actually contract salvage."

"So, Harris must have understood these things," she replied pensively.

"He must have," Claude replied.

"So, what is 'finds'?

"The term 'finds' is slightly different. A court can determine that property was abandoned by the owner and can award the finder title to everything. So, that would mean that Recov and Thad would get everything." He looked at her soberly and leaned back in his chair, studying the bands of tourists strolling around Jackson Square.

"So, that would leave out the insurers and us entirely."

"Exactly. But it is an extremely remote possibility."

'She knew that she should feel reassured, but she did not. Brandy hated dealing with legal matters and legalese. "Where do the insurers fit into all of this? How does it work?"

"Well, the London insurance market is fairly complex. If someone wants to insure something, he or she must use a Lloyd's broker to place the risk. The broker goes around to various London syndicates and/or London Market companies at what was formerly known as the Institute of London Underwriters. He is a type of salesman or middleman. The broker must disclose the important factors of the transaction, even if they are unfavorable. First he isolates and finds one or two 'leaders.' Those leaders are the syndicates or companies who will assume the greatest percentage of a risk. Each underwriter will sign the 'slip' for a percentage of the risk. These risks are often less than 15 percent, but occasionally they may be 20 percent or greater. Once the broker has obtained 100 percent subscriptions on the slip, the policy is prepared. This usually takes a great deal of time—maybe even a year or two for the Lloyd's Policy Signing Office to prepare the policies. In the meantime, the broker's office prepares the cover note, or a memorandum of the policy." He looked at her and smiled. "Clear so far?"

"As clear as mud," she laughed. "I am an artist, remember, all of this is way out of the realm of my experience. So, tell me, exactly what is a syndicate?"

"In the Lloyd's of London market, the various insuring groups are called syndicates. They are often numbered or have the name of the principal underwriter. For example, some of them are called things like 'Syndicate 999' or the 'Brandy Blake Syndicate.'

"I like the sound of that. Catchy!" she said, trying to project an enthusiasm that she did not feel.

"Each syndicate has a box or station on the Lloyd's floor, and the primary underwriter and claims personnel are in attendance at various times. They are the people who are approached by the broker. They assess the risk and calculate a reasonable premium. These people are highly sophisticated. Twenty years ago, each box had some notes and a card catalog system. Today, things are computerized." He paused as if to assure himself that she understood before he continued. "Each syndicate has many investors called 'Names.. Those names, or participants, include people with wealth who wish to invest all over the word, including many famous people. Each one of those investors gets a return by earning money on the premiums. They are counting on their underwriter to only agree to take risks that will not result in a loss. When a casualty occurs, like the sinking of the *BYZANTIUM*, each name has to cough up enough money to fulfill his or her obligation on the risk and to pay the claim. So, the whole thing is like gambling. It is a calculated risk. Sometimes, it is a bad risk."

"Are there records about what insurers were on the slip for the *BYZANTIUM*?"

Claude turned to the back page of a document marked as "Exhibit A". "Here is the slip. You can see all of these percentages and abbreviations. These are the companies and syndicates subscribing to the risk. Many of them exist today or were purchased or acquired by other companies or syndicates."

"So, what happens in the market when a ship like the *BYZANTIUM* is lost at sea?"

"The broker presents a claim, and each syndicate or company is responsible only for its percentage of the risk."

"Do the companies or syndicates ever go out of business?"

"Yes, many do and have, just like many of the insurers in Louisiana. And in the late eighties and early nineties, it was becoming more frequent because of the huge expense of asbestos and pollution claims. All of the old pre-1992 claims were organized and handled by Equitas, which has since been acquired by Resolute, a Warren Buffet company."

"What happens to the insured if a company went bankrupt or went out of business?"

"It is called 'going bare.' For example, if a company who has agreed to insure 15 percent of the risk goes out of business or is 'wound up' because of an insolvency, that portion of the risk is uninsured. The other companies and syndicates do not kick in any contribution."

"Isn't there anything that can be done for the person who has paid all of those premiums? Can't they sue or something?"

"Well, a person can file a claim with the administrator of the winding-up proceedings, which is very much like filing a claim in a bankruptcy action. Generally, the insurer only recovers a small percentage of the syndicate's percent because there is not much to go around."

"I don't think that Harris ever considered these insurance issues in all of those years he was desperately looking for *BYZANTIUM*. And of course, I was too ignorant about the circumstances to ask." She sighed with exhaustion. "Love is really blind, you know." She brushed her hair away from her face. The September weather was still quite warm and humid. She suddenly felt tired and confused. Harris had just been chasing a wild pipedream. "So, what you are telling me is that some insurers in London own the *BYZANTIUM* remains and all of the emeralds. Recov and Thad will likely get a giant salvage award, or title to everything and that all of Harris's work and his death was for nothing!" She fished in her large purse for a Kleenex and dabbed her eyes which were stinging with tears. Brandy looked off in the distance for a long time, trying to calm down.

Claude patted her on the arm and drank his coffee, waiting for her to settle down. Brandy could see that her tears had attracted the attention of some of the patrons at a nearby table.

Finally, she pulled herself together enough to speak. "I bankrolled the expedition for about eleven months from my trust fund and inheritance from my parents," she said finally. "I was practically hemorrhaging money to finance the expedition, and I started to worry that I would spend it all and compromise Rene's future. Harris was so secretive, and things were not really good before he died. I actually had considered coming back home with Rene. If only he had just trusted me! Why did he conceal this from me?"

Claude nodded. "Clearly, he was foolish not to say anything, but there was so much money at stake, he probably wanted to be careful.

People kill other people for less money than is at stake here. Maybe he was concerned about your welfare, and maybe he stopped trusting Thad. It is hard to know what he was thinking at the time."

"Things did seem strained with Harris and Thad before he died. Thad wanted Harris to invest with Recov. Harris was cutting corners with expenses." Tears streamed down her face again. "It was all for nothing," she said with resignation. "And it kills me that Thad and Recov are going to become fabulously wealthy from all of Harris's hard work."

"Not necessarily," Claude said.

"What do you mean?"

"Well, you were the principal investor before Recov. Thad and Harris utilized equipment you purchased and your capital. Harris spent all his time for five years looking for the *BYZANTIUM* and you funded the endeavor. You are claiming that the vessel was located a few months before his death. Even if you assume the truth of their position, I think you have a claim to a percentage of the salvage award."

She brightened. Maybe not all was lost. "Really? How much?"

"I do not know. But the fact that we have some of the emeralds is circumstantial evidence that Harris found the vessel before he died. And Harris died trying to recover more cargo. A court will look favorably at your claim for no other reason."

"So that explains why Thad was so anxious to charter the boat and take Harris's share of the emeralds! He knew that if he had possession of everything, there would not be any way I could prove that Harris had found *BYZANTIUM*. He had been trying to cheat us even after Harris's death!"

Claude shook his head in disgust. "It looks that way. Greed causes people to do a lot of incredible things."

"It is not much consolation for losing my husband, but it would be what Harris would want. And I do need the money. Between Harris's salvage expedition and the shop, I have now spent almost everything I inherited from my parents. And I have Rene and her college to think about."

Claude looked pensive for a moment. "Do you think that Harris had other emeralds that he did not tell you about?"

That had never really occurred to her before.

"I really do not know. He kept some boxes in one of the spare bedrooms that he kept locked. They were really just plastic totes, but I know that there was a small locked strong-box in one of them. Harris kept an ongoing journal on his laptop. After he died, I did not look through anything, but I did not throw it out because it was all so important to Harris. We boxed everything up in moving boxes and shipped it with our things to New Orleans. We did not bring much back—just our clothes, dishes, sentimental things, and Rene's toys. I sold our house with the furniture to a couple from New York looking for a second home and used the money to open Massenet."

"Now that this lawsuit has been filed, you probably should go through his things. If it is too painful for you, I can help, or I am sure that your grandmother would be willing to help as well."

"I will," she said resolutely. "I need to know. I could not deal with it initially, but maybe it is time that I understand what Claude was doing with his time. He sacrificed his life for those stupid emeralds, and I cannot let it be for nothing."

Claude nodded. "Probably the most important thing is the laptop. Hopefully, the hard drive has not been damaged by the heat in the attic."

"Tomorrow is Monday. It is traditionally a slow day at the shop. I can have my assistant come in and cover so I can spend the day looking through his things."

"Once we find the laptop, we need to have it forensically evaluated and copied. Don't modify anything. Let's just find it and give it to the experts. I do not want anyone saying that we created documents or erased critical entries. Dealing with electronic evidence is different than paper documents."

"What is this going to mean? Should I sue Thad? I have never sued anyone in my life."

"I think you should seriously consider it, Brandy. But first, we need to know what physical evidence we have. This is why you need to look through the boxes."

"I will give you a full report tomorrow. If I find the laptop, can we have someone come by Granny Ariel's house to pick it up?"

"I will arrange it," Claude promised.

"I can hardly believe this has happened. Thad must have had this planned for months," she mused.

Claude patted her hand gently and looked at her soberly. "I will make a further investigation and then we can talk about what you need to do to proceed. But you have to understand that you would have to file suit or intervene in the existing lawsuit in St. Thomas and go through litigation for several years. We are talking about real money here, so you are going to have an incredible fight on your hands. Thad and Recov are going to fight you tooth and nail, not to mention the London insurers. And they will spend a fortune on attorneys. I am not trying to discourage you. In fact, I would think it would be very foolish for you to pass up this opportunity. You and your daughter have a right to part of that recovery. Both of you could be set for life!"

"I only want what is fair," she replied.

"I understand."

"Will you represent me? I trust you," she said, looking at him levelly.

"I would be flattered. But we would need to discuss the terms. I suppose we could work it on a contingency fee, but I would have to have that approved by the powers that be at D'Argent. You would want to think about it."

"I do not want to think about it. Who better than you? I trust you," she insisted.

"I would be honored and I would love to represent you. It would be a high profile case—a real recognition maker. But the D'Argent firm is closely tied to the London Market. I would have to sell it to the management committee. You may want someone else, and if that is the case, I can help you identify the best attorney for this suit. You may want someone in Miami. The federal court in St. Thomas would require you to retain local counsel if you hire someone who is not a member of that bar. Let me see what other information I can find out about *BYZANTIUM* on the Internet and about the suit. Then we can make a decision about what attorney and strategy would be best."

She smiled. "Sounds like a plan. Thanks for meeting me."

He kissed her chastely on the cheek and stood to leave, leaving two tens on the table for the tip and refreshments. "Well, back to the salt mines. I have a brief to file tomorrow. Take care. Send me a text when you locate the computer."

Brandy watched him walk down near the Jax Brewery as she sipped her café au lait. She perused the complaint again before folding it in half and stuffing it into the side pocket of her purse. She could not allow Thad to get away with it. She would sue him and join in the suit. It was what was best for Rene, and it would be her way of vindicating Harris. With Claude's help, she was sure she would win.

With a new resolve, she picked up her purse, smoothed her hair, and began the short walk to the bank before she returned to the shop. She needed to call her assistant to work for her tomorrow. She would discuss the matter with Granny Ariel tonight. She was certain that her grandmother would agree that she could not walk away from what rightfully belonged to her and Rene. Thad had thrown down the gauntlet, and she was determined to pick it up. First thing tomorrow, she needed to find Harris's laptop.

Chapter VIII

Massenet was extremely busy for the rest of the afternoon. Brandy made a number of smaller sales—old oil paintings, a curio case, and a pair of matching Limoges vases. Today was a home game for the Saints, and the tourist trade always picked up before and after the game. She barely had time to think about her conversation with Claude as she sent emails to the carrier to make arrangements to pack and ship the items she had sold. Also, she managed to spend a couple of hours on the computer after the shop closed at 5:00 o'clock.

Granny Ariel was on her way out to dinner by the time Brandy arrived home. Brandy had not had time to even tell her about her conversation with Claude that morning.

Brandy and Rene sat in the breakfast room for their dinner of sliced broiled lemon chicken paired with a small salad, followed by a small cup of raspberry sorbet. Rene's hair was slightly damp from her bath, and she wore her SpongeBob pajamas. Afterward, they watched an animated movie until Rene fell asleep on the couch. Brandy carried her sleeping child upstairs and tucked her in bed before coming back downstairs to clean the kitchen.

She felt restless and returned upstairs to pull on an old tee shirt and thin pair of slacks. She was wired after her conversation with Claude that morning and knew that it was pointless to try to go to sleep. The attic space in Granny Ariel's house was not air-conditioned but it would be cooler at night. She checked on Rene to be certain that she was sleeping soundly and then climbed the stairs to the attic.

She felt the wall of intense heat before she even opened the door. It was sweltering and the air smelled of pesticide. She flipped on the light and located the boxes containing Harris's things shoved in the back corner of the attic. They were enormously heavy, but she managed to rock one of the smaller boxes across the floor. She found a box cutter and slipped open the packaging tape, retrieving four totes from the interior. She dragged the totes near the attic door. It probably would be easiest to unload the boxes and bring the totes to the second-floor study where she could review the contents in the comfort of air-conditioning.

It took her nearly three hours to bring the totes down to the study. She took the old packing boxes and stacked them neatly in the utility room for the recycling service later that week. After stacking the boxes, she closed the attic and took a cool shower. It was a miserable experience, but she was exhausted. Granny Ariel had returned home while she was in the shower and was already in her suite getting ready for bed.

Brandy quietly returned to the study and began examining the contents of the totes. There was a tote filled with invoices, receipts, and lists neatly organized in manila folders. There were written journals as well and three digital underwater cameras she recognized that Harris had used. She recalled how expensive the newest camera with the large lenses had been, but Harris had been adamant that it was necessary. It had been one of their last arguments. Harris's laptop was in the last box she searched along with two small metal strongboxes. Each strongbox had a metal loop and was closed with a padlock. They were the size of a very large, deep, and long safety deposit box. She also found Harris's cell phone and charging cord. By the time she had finished, it was 1:30 a.m.

Brandy sent Claude a text. "Found laptop/ camera/ call tomorrow when up."

Then she organized the file folders, the GPS, an underwater digital camera with a small container of memory cards, and the laptop in the corner of her bedroom, resisting the urge to turn any of them on. They had been subjected to oppressive heat, but hopefully the contents could be recovered.

Although she was exhausted, sleep evaded her. What in the world could be in the locked metal boxes?

It was nearly 3:00 a.m. when she went down to the laundry room to find a pair of pliers. After nearly thirty minutes, she finally managed to pry the loop holding the lock away from the side of the smaller of the two boxes. After a few minutes, the lock finally slid off, and she lifted the box cover. A thin layer of cotton batting covered the contents. It was yellowing from age and slightly dusty.

Brandy drew in a sharp breath as she removed the batting. The contents of the box danced and glistened with a green glow from the overhead light. Brandy scooped her hand into the box and lifted a handful of the polished emeralds recovered from the *BYZANTIUM*.

She secured the boxes in the back of the safe in her closet and then sent Claude another text.

Wayne, the forensic computer specialist from Preserve Your Data, met Brandy and Claude at 2:00 o'clock the following afternoon. Brandy guessed that Wayne was only about twenty-six years old. Claude had worked with Wayne on several occasions to assist with collecting and preserving electronic data for discovery in federal court. The recovered data would be collected, searched and installed into a database for later use in litigation. According to Claude, Wayne was working on his Ph.D. in electronic engineering. Wayne wore a navy shirt with the Preserve Your Data logo and a pair of tan slacks. His unruly dishwater blonde hair was pulled into a small ponytail with a rubber band. Brandy and Claude sat in the leather chairs in the library of Granny Ariel's house as Wayne fastidiously photographed the equipment and prepared a catalog that he provided to Brandy and Claude.

"How was this equipment transported from St. Thomas?" Wayne asked Brandy.

"We kept it in a spare bedroom in St. Thomas. We lived in the hills, so the salt corrosion was not as much of a problem as it would have been if we had lived by the water. When we moved, it was packed into boxes and loaded into a shipping container. For the last eleven months, it has been in the attic here."

Wayne nodded silently and continued to load the equipment into a tote to bring back to Preserve Your Data to download and retrieve the data in the lab.

"Do you think this equipment and data were damaged by the heat in the attic and humidity?" Brandy asked him nervously to bridge the silence. It would have been a terrible thing if the electronic data was no longer available because of her neglect. This had been Harris's life work. How could she have been so careless?

"I can't make any promises, but hardware like this is fairly hardy. We have been able to clean up hardware from devices that were underwater for a year. Of course, that was quite the project. We will know more once we get this baby back to the lab to download, preserve and do any cleanup necessary." Wayne replied. "I can't wait to see some of this underwater footage."

"Well, my fingers are crossed," she said ruefully. "I was so upset after Harris died that I almost threw all of this away. But then I realized that this had been Harris's life and one day, Rene might want some of these things to remember her father."

"Do you have a personal computer, laptop or tablet?" Wayne asked her as he slipped Harris' phone into the box.

"Yes," she replied, wondering why in the world he would need her electronic devices. Brandy had an old laptop in her closet upstairs and an old Windows telephone she bought in St. Thomas before Harris died.

"Are these the same devices you had in St. Thomas?"

"Yes."

"I need to take them as well. We will dump the phone and image the laptop. Can you get to them now? Wayne asked.

"Sure, but what about my private matters?" She had personal emails with friends and Granny Ariel, her electronic banking data, photos of Rene and occasional emails with Harris on the laptop. There were some old photos Harris sent her from his dive sites on the Windows phone and loads of text messages. Harris had always hated it that Brandy never erased her text messages.

"We simply image and preserve everything, including all text messages. Later, we can pull out anything that you tell us is relevant. If you have some private information, it will remain private," he explained.

Claude put his hand gently on Brandy's arm. "Your attorney will file a motion for a protective order to prevent anyone from looking at your private data," he told her.

Brandy noticed that he emphasized the words "your attorney." She had asked him repeatedly to take the case, but he had explained that his law firm likely would have a conflict. A significant percentage of the firm's work was generated by underwriters at Lloyd's, London and some of the syndicates might have insured either the cargo or the ship and, therefore, would be adverse to Brandy. Claude had assured her that he would help her find competent counsel. But Brandy trusted Claude and had known him nearly her entire life. She was not sure that she would be able to trust a stranger.

"Alright," she said. "I don't have anything to hide, but it feels somehow invasive."

"Everyone says the same thing," Wayne told her. "It is a common complaint."

Brandy went upstairs long enough to grab her laptop and old telephone from her closet before coming down and surrendering them to Wayne. He examined the two devices, and then catalogued and photographed them.

As Wayne worked Claude explained that it was critical to download the data in sterile conditions and to carefully document all work of Preserve Your Data. The camera footage and all electronic files would become evidence in the lawsuit for Brandy to assert her claim. Some of the text messages from Harris to Brandy and Thad might contain important information. For that reason, Claude explained, it was critical to preserve the information. The data would be downloaded and preserved in a forensic lab to avoid the allegations that the electronic data had been fabricated. Preserve Your Data would be able to document when the files were created and that they had not been modified by collecting the metadata. They would also collect and preserve the slack space to establish that the files had not been deleted or overwritten by disk defragmentation. The electronic devices would remain in the custody and control of Preserve Your Data until the dispute with Thad was concluded.

Wayne closed both storage boxes and handed Claude and Brandy a receipt in triplicate for Brandy to sign. Afterward, he provided Brandy with the Preserve Your Data invoice for professional services. The cost of the collection of electronic data was staggering—more than $10,000. Fortunately, Claude had already given her the estimate earlier that morning. Brandy had called her private banker and arranged to transfer those funds into her checking account two hours earlier. Reluctantly, she handed Wayne the check, which was more than her profit from Massenet last month.

Brandy slipped her copy of the receipt into a manila folder and gave the other copy to Claude. The two of them walked Wayne to his Subaru parked in the drive. She noticed that three of the IBIX crew were trimming shrubs, weeding flower beds, and fertilizing the flawless carpet of grass. The hot pink vincas damaged by Penny had been replaced with copious masses of purple, gold, and white pansies for the winter. Brandy waved and smiled at the crew absently as Claude and Wayne loaded the boxes into the back of Wayne's Outback.

Wayne shook their hands. "I'll call you later today after I am in the lab and let you know how it goes," he promised as he closed the Subaru car door and drove onto St. Charles Avenue.

"You have my cell number," Claude told Wayne. "Let me know as soon as you find out anything."

Claude and Brandy went back into the house after Wayne left. Granny Ariel was attending an afternoon tea, and Rene was spending the day at a friend's house, so they had the house to themselves. The cleaning service had spent the entire day there the prior day, and the house still smelled faintly of lemon furniture polish.

Brandy had organized Claude's leather-bound ledgers which included cryptic details about each dive, on the corner of the library table. Most of the entries simply listed dates, coordinates, weather, and depth. Claude planned to provide copies of the ledgers and other documents relating to the recovery to an expert in the field of Gulf of Mexico oil exploration for review. Until then, they would be locked safely away in a safe-deposit box at the bank.

Earlier that morning, Brandy had also assembled a box of cancelled checks, bank statements, fuel invoices, and equipment receipts for the funds she had spent through the years helping Harris with his project. Tomorrow morning, she and Claude had an appointment with a forensic accountant, who would review the documents and compile a report. First, the legal copying service would electronically scan, copy, and number the documents for authenticity. The originals would be locked in a safety-deposit box.

"Are you ready to go by the banks?" Claude asked as they entered the library. They had made arrangements with two different banking institutions to rent large safety-deposit boxes to temporarily store the emeralds. Ultimately, they would need to be evaluated by a gemologist who could establish the value and provenance of the stones based on their cut and quality. The cut emeralds clearly had an old-fashioned cut that was not always used today.

"Yes! It makes me nervous to have these stones in the house," she said anxiously.

The two strong-boxes were very heavy. Earlier that morning, Claude had picked up some very small plastic storage boxes and cotton batting. The small storage boxes would easily slip into the safety-deposit boxes they had reserved. Together, they gently transferred the emeralds into the plastic boxes between layers of cotton batting to prevent scratches and chips. The stones easily filled sixteen plastic containers. Brandy and Claude had reserved 6 safety-deposit boxes.

Claude transferred the stones into two large wheeled litigation bags. They loaded the bags into the trunk of his BMW. Brandy felt a sigh of relief that the IBIX crew truck was already gone. She felt strangely paranoid about wheeling a briefcase loaded with emeralds in plain view of the yard crew as she headed toward the BMW.

Claude steered the car in the direction of the Chase branch on St. Charles. They brought both briefcases into the bank for safe-keeping. Within an hour, Brandy had rented three large boxes, paid the advance fee for one year, and transferred the plastic boxes from one briefcase into the three boxes. The next stop was Bank of America, where they unloaded the last litigation bag. Finally, they stopped at Regents Bank. Brandy rented a small safety-deposit box where she stored all of the safety-deposit box keys from Chase and Bank of America, as well as the small ledgers. Ultimately, she might need to find a better solution, but for now, she felt a sense of relief that the emeralds and ledgers had been safety stowed in bank vaults.

It was nearly six o'clock when they finished their tasks. Brandy was famished and exhausted from the excitement of the day. She realized that she had not given one thought to Massenet the entire day. Rene and Ariel would not be home for dinner.

"Hungry?" Claude asked her.

"Famished. Let me treat you to a sandwich," she replied. "You have taken the entire day off to help me, and I owe you that."

"Sounds good. What about Camellia Grill?"

"Perfect," she replied.

Claude found a parking place in front of the small restaurant located in the bend of St. Charles and Carrollton Avenues. Camellia

Grill was a graceful old white building. The interior was painted a lovely hot pink. The restaurant had not yet filled since it was midweek, and they quickly found two seats at the counter. Brandy indulged herself with a large burger and chocolate freeze. Service was quick and efficient, and they were back in the car in less than forty minutes.

The air was heavy with humidity, and it began to sprinkle as Claude drove them back to Granny Ariel's house. As Claude pulled into the garage, his phone rang.

It was Wayne from Preserve Your Data and Claude put him on the speakerphone. "Good news! The data from the laptop, the digital camera memory cards, and the old cell phones are in good shape. We are going to work late and preserve the data. The underwater photos are incredible. I will give you a report tomorrow."

∽

Ewan stopped at a small bar on Magazine Street just as it started raining in earnest. He had gone home to shower and change after his shift at IBIX. He noticed that he was bulking up, and the heavy labor bothered him less these days. He ordered a cold beer and oyster po'boy sandwich from the overweight barmaid with the major cleavage display. He sat at the far end of the bar and noticed in his peripheral vision that he had caught the attention of two younger women obviously just off work from their office jobs. He casually looked over, noticing that they were both peroxide blondes, approximately twenty-four years old. From their appearance, he guessed that they were receptionists in boring office jobs out spending money they really did not have to spend.

The barmaid set the second round of pink martinis with a catchy name in front of the young women. The taller of the two tittered loudly and furtively glanced in Ewan's direction. He ignored her for now and concentrated on his sandwich.

Ewan caught his reflection in the old mirror opposite the bar. He had let his hair grow slightly and had dyed it black. He also had grown a mustache that he tinted with a brush-on color. The effect was dramatic and, with his new dark tan, he looked almost Hispanic. He noticed that the tan made his teeth look almost unnaturally white. He smiled at the barmaid when she set another beer in front of him.

"You looked thirsty," she said matter-of-factly.

"Thanks. I am," he said.

"Work outside? You've got a great tan."

"Offshore," he lied. "Just finished my shift—three weeks on and five days off. No alcohol when I am working."

"No wonder you are thirsty, honey," she said before turning to help another customer.

Ewan mulled over the events of the day. He would need to contact Thad. The crew had switched the order of jobs for the day and he had just happened to be at the widow's house as she came outside with a man from Preserve Your Data. The Subaru he drove had the logo painted on the side. He had looked the service up on his smart phone and determined it was some computer specialist. Her rich lawyer friend was there talking to the fellow with the ponytail. Later after work, he happened to see them both rolling heavy briefcases into a branch of Bank of America. If he had not glanced over as he drove past, he would have missed them. This was the type of unusual event Thad would want to know about. Of course, it might be nothing, but his gut told him that what he had seen was significant.

He finished his sandwich, French fries and beer before sending Thad a quick text: "She and lawyer gave boxes to Preserve Your Data today. Brought suitcases to BOA. Update soon."

He put the throw-away phone into his pocket just as the two women next to him were draining their third round of pink martinis. He left a ten dollar tip for the barmaid. Time for some fun. He walked up behind them and embraced them both with his arms in a gentlemanly fashion. They turned and looked at Ewan adoringly.

"Hello, lovely ladies," he cooed. "What do you saw we blow this joint and have some fun?"

~

Rene arrived a few minutes after Brandy returned home. Brandy gave Rene a bath before tucking her in bed. Together, they read Rene's favorite short story about a baby kangaroo. Rene fell asleep before Brandy reached the last page. She left the night light on and closed the door to Rene's bedroom halfway.

Afterward, Brandy took a long hot bath scented with jasmine and honeysuckle bath salts in the jetted tub. Refreshed, she changed into a short gown and Japanese floral robe and poured herself a glass of Columbia Crest cabernet. She spent the rest of the evening combing through all her accounting records to be sure that she had not missed any documents. She was asleep before Granny Ariel came home.

Brandy and Claude met with the forensic accountant at his Poydras Avenue office at seven thirty the following morning. Mick James's office spanned half of the twentieth floor of the building and offered spectacular views of the Port of New Orleans and the Mississippi

River. Mick was in his 50s, was bald, and wore thick glasses. Mick was yet another of Claude's many litigation experts.

Mick embraced Brandy's hand firmly and gave her a warm smile. "Brandy, I am Mick James. It is a pleasure to meet you. Thank you for coming in so early this morning."

"Thank you for seeing us today," Brandy said as she sat in one of the two leather chairs positioned by the Chippendale sofa.

Claude sat across from Brandy and set the Bankers Box of financial documents on the floor. "These are copies, Mick," Claude told him. We had the originals copied and numbered yesterday."

Mick smiled. "Thank you, Claude. You have made my job easier." Then he turned to Brandy. "Claude emailed me a copy of the federal court complaint in St. Thomas yesterday. This is an amazing case. Your husband must have been an incredible fellow."

She felt her eyes welling with tears. "He was. This became his life's work. He was a professor who decided to pursue his passion. Unfortunately, it cost him his life."

Mick waited patiently as she regained her composure. "It was tragic, and I am sure it was a terrible loss."

"It was very tragic. I cannot let Thad and Recov profit from all of his work. I have a daughter to think about and her future."

"Claude explained that you invested a great deal of your personal funds in this venture. I will reconstruct your expenditures initially. I am assuming that later we will have the advantage of reviewing the documents relied upon by the other parties to support their expenditures. Then we can create charts and graphs establishing who shouldered what proportion of the expenses."

The three of them continued to discuss strategy. Brandy signed a retention letter with Mick and agreed on an hourly rate. He would bill her monthly. Mick promised to have a preliminary report for them in no less than three weeks.

The meeting with Mick was over in less than an hour. Brandy retrieved her car from the parking garage and arrived at the shop before 9:00 o'clock. She was relieved and encouraged that she and Claude had made so much progress in developing her case over the last two days. Claude had promised to stay in touch with her about locating an attorney to represent her. He advised that he had several suggestions that he would present to her later in the week.

The next two days, Brandy was very busy with the shop. The intense heat had abated temporarily, which was a sure sign that fall would arrive soon. The milder weather enticed more foot traffic in the French Quarter, and Brandy made several large sales, including an armoire, a Waterford chandelier, and a marble-topped eighteenth century Bombay chest. Her assistant, Natalie, sold three antique oil paintings of European farm scenes. At Granny Ariel's urging, Brandy also had retained a website designer. The service sent periodic email reminders to past customers, and slowly Brandy was building a customer base. The website had been a good investment. Two customers had purchased a few antique pieces of occasional furniture just that week from the website.

Claude contacted Brandy again on Thursday afternoon with a report from Wayne at Preserve Your Data. All of the data had been recovered from the computer, GPS, and digital camera. Wayne had imaged Harris' cell phone and Brandy's old phone as well as her laptop. Apparently, the underwater shots were amazing, documenting Harris's recovery of the emeralds. They arranged to meet for dinner on Friday to discuss prospective attorneys to handle the lawsuit on Brandy's behalf.

Brandy met Claude for an early dinner at Arnaud's on Friday night. Rene had been invited to a birthday party, and the hostess was taking the girls to a Disney movie for the evening. Ariel had promised to pick up Rene after the event and Brandy had the evening free.

The air had turned delightfully cool, and she was refreshed during the six-block walk to the restaurant. Throngs of tourists meandered down Bourbon Street in search of food, hotels, a drink, or a strip bar. The restaurant foyer was crowded with patrons sipping wine and waiting for an available table.

Claude was sipping a glass of Marlborough region sauvignon blanc at a table on the first floor. He was still wearing his black suit, silver tie and crisp white shirt. He waved to her and stood as the waiter pulled out her chair and hung up her jacket. Underneath, she wore a simple black wool crepe dress with a Kelly green Hermes scarf fastened with a Tiffany gold dolphin pin.

"You look great," he remarked as Harold, Claude's customary waiter, poured her a glass of wine. "Very chic."

She smiled. "Thanks. I always feel a little dowdy at the end of the day. It is almost strange to wear wool in the fall again. The most I ever needed in St. Thomas was a sweater or light jacket."

"You look radiant tonight. Big day today?" he asked as Harold set the plate of oysters Rockefeller before him.

"I sold a beautiful buffet to a woman from Pennsylvania and an armoire to a couple from Denver. Both were big-ticket items. So, I can at least keep the electricity on for another month."

He clinked her glass. "Congratulations."

"I hate to admit it, but I still am a little surprised with every sale. I guess that I still cannot believe that I am a shop owner."

"And a very good saleswoman. Before you know it, you will be giving all of the big names a run for their money."

She smiled warmly. "Well, it is a worthy but ambitious goal."

Harold refilled their glasses and they chatted lightly over soup, French bread, a crab dish, and caramel custard. He told her about his plans to participate in a sailing race on Lake Pontchartrain the next day.

"There has been an interesting development," he said over dessert. "Our firm was approached this morning about representing the London underwriters in the salvage action filed by Thad and Recov."

Obviously, the underwriters were very good clients. What could she have expected in such a big case? "So I guess its final then—I actually need to hire someone else." she said finally.

"It means that the firm has a conflict of interest, and our office cannot represent you. Of course, my representation of your interests was never really official at D'Argent. Because this would have been a contingency case and not an hourly rate, I would have needed the authority of the managing committee to proceed on that basis."

She studied her hands momentarily. His firm was one of the largest and most prestigious in the state with offices in London, South America, and throughout the southeastern United States. He was certainly in a tight spot. One of their premier clients needed help. This was a big case, and no one needed to explain to her that this meant truckloads of legal fees to the D'Argent firm. Now she understood his sudden invitation to dinner. She smiled wanly, trying desperately to hide her disappointment. "Well, I appreciate everything you have done, Claude. I understand your position. I am sure that Granny Ariel's law firm can help me find a lawyer to represent me in this suit if your friend does not work out."

Claude had recommended a smaller boutique maritime firm, Wilson Crutcher, consisting of approximately twenty-five attorneys. He had assured Brandy that these attorneys could competently handle the case on a contingency fee basis.

"Well, if it is not too late, I would like to represent you if you are still interested," he said, looking at her earnestly.

"How? I thought that you just said that your office could not represent me because you were representing the syndicates."

"Well, technically there could be a real issue with the firm because I have been unofficially consulting you about this. In fact, under those circumstances, you could potentially claim that the firm could not represent our Lloyd's clients. I did not think that would really be in your best interests. So, I resigned from the equity partnership yesterday afternoon when I heard through the office grapevine that there was an expectation that the firm might get the case. We do a lot of work for the lead underwriters on the hull and cargo slips for *BYZANTIUM*. The management committee would never have agreed to allow me to handle your case because they would have been concerned that we were foreclosing a potential fee from one of our regular clients. It would have been an impossible sell because the management is very conservative. A contingency fee is a risk. I wanted to represent you because I think you were cheated."

She looked at him incredulously. "You walked away from your job? Claude, I can hardly pay you what you would ordinarily charge an hour. The D'Argent firm is one of the most prominent firms in the south. Hopefully, you can undo this."

He grinned. "It's not as serious as all that. The truth is that I have been slightly unhappy there for some time. It is a grind, and I am not really paid what I can earn in a smaller boutique firm. D'Argent is a large impressive place. The overhead from the combined expense of the salaries of attorneys, secretaries, and paralegals, along with the cost of the fancy office space, is tremendous. Then, there are the client development expenses and the large accounts receivable. A few alums that left a couple of years ago approached me two months ago to come in with them. I have been toying with the idea for some time. It is a small boutique firm with about fifteen attorneys on Magazine Street named Boudreaux Banks. They have a good business and handle the runoff from D'Argent and other large firms caused by conflicts of interest. I will know in a couple of weeks how many clients I can take with me. There is a specific procedure that we have to follow. In the meantime, since I technically had not opened a file on your case, you can come with me, if you are still interested. I can certainly cut a deal on the fees and am willing to represent you on a contingency fee basis."

"What does that mean?"

"It's lawyer talk for—I don't get a fee unless you recover something. You would have to pay the legal expenses, though, like court reporting fees."

"So, you would be taking the gamble with me?"

"Exactly." He smiled and leaned back in his chair. "I won't mislead you, Brandy. I am not a complete altruist, and there is more than just friendship at stake here. This is an incredibly high-profile case and that is just as intriguing to me as it would be to any attorney. Sooner or later, lawyers will be coming out of the woodwork soliciting this case. This case is a once-in-a-lifetime case for me. My reputation will be made by this case. As I have been telling you for days, once the word is out, you could probably have your pick of plaintiff's lawyers who would associate an insurance attorney like me experienced in maritime matters and the London insurance market. So don't labor under the false impression that I am your only hope." He paused, giving her a direct look before he continued. "But on the other hand, I really feel that you were cheated. There is something very wrong here. And I have the knowledge and experience with the market to provide stellar legal services. And the new office has six really good maritime attorneys whose practice is limited to representing the London Market."

"Claude, this is definitely what I want. I trust you, and I have known you for years."

He held up his hand. "This is a business deal, Brandy. I have some concerns about representing a friend, but I have talked with the senior partners at Boudreaux Banks, and they are anxious to work on the file as well. Chris Banks will probably be the lead attorney. He is over fifty, a very seasoned and respected trial attorney. You need to meet him before you make any decisions. Also, I want you to at least talk to John Crutcher at Wilson Crutcher before you decide. There are many good attorneys in the world. Again, this is about business, and there is more at stake than just business. So, think about it. Talk it over with your grandmother. And you can let me know what you decide in a week or two."

There really was no decision to be made. Claude would represent her interests well. There was no question about that. Some might say that she should find someone more objective than a friend. But given the circumstances and the amount of money at stake, her instincts told her that she would need someone she could trust.

"Claude, I feel relieved that you want to take my case. I really do not need to think about it, but as you suggested, I will talk to Granny Ariel about it. If you want me to meet other attorneys, I will set it up next week."

He drained his cup. "You need to consider this carefully and meet other attorneys. You may think differently about it, and your grandmother may encourage you to think about other options.

"I need you because I can trust you. I need to get those bastards for cheating Harris, Rene and me."

He patted her hand. "Whomever you hire will give them a real run for their money. I promise you that."

They finished their meal, and Claude walked Brandy back to her car. Her mind was racing after her conversation with Claude as she headed home. She needed Granny Ariel's advice.

∾

The carpenters installed a magnificent new gazebo on the rear lawn to replace the structure destroyed by the hurricane. The new gazebo was equipped with outdoor heat lamps. The rear verandah had been restored and furnished with comfortable cushioned wrought iron lounges, tables, and chairs. On mild afternoons, Raleigh sat with Ariel under the new gazebo playing checkers, while Chloe sprawled comfortably underneath the table. Sometimes, the dog allowed the pups to nestle beside her, enclosed in her luscious white fur as Raleigh fed her small pieces of cheese. She accepted the pieces gingerly, mindful of his tiny frame. They did not share the same communication that he had with Ariel. Chloe was very intuitive, though, and they communicated by smell and feelings of emotions.

Ariel had the workmen install a small trap door on tiny hinges for Raleigh, Kiki, and the pups that led into a small area that had been walled off from the rear of the attic. The room adjoined the attic stairwell and allowed the squirrels access to the house. There was a tiny latch that the squirrels could squeeze between their teeth. This precaution prevented predators from intruding into the security of the attic. An exterminator dispensed with the rat population, and the premises were now safe for the little family. Two straw baskets filled with soft blankets were in the corner. When the temperatures plunged in the fall, the squirrels would have the option of sleeping indoors, enjoying the warmth and security of the attic and feasting on a tray of fruit and nuts.

The groundskeepers had long since cleaned the debris from the park. But the park remained depressingly devoid of its former inhabitants. The little band of cottontail rabbits had disappeared. Gradually, a few predators expanded their territory into the park. A small owl sometimes hunted from one of the trees that abutted the avenue, and a few feral cats patrolled the perimeter of the park beyond the bridge. A small flock of geese and mallards replaced the inhabitants of the lagoon. The new birds had been farm raised and were extremely aloof and skittish. A few neighborhood squirrels began encroaching into the territory. The squirrels could hear the zoo animals from the other end of the park in the quiet evenings and the seals barking for food at their daily feedings in the morning and late afternoon. The delicate equilibrium of the park destroyed by Penny's wrath was gradually restoring itself.

One Saturday morning shortly after dawn, Raleigh met Ariel and Chloe on the verandah. Rene and Brandy were still sleeping upstairs. The mild air was deliciously fresh. He noticed that despite the early hour, Ariel had already showered and dressed in casual slacks and was sipping a cup of steaming hot chicory coffee when he arrived. The floral fragrance she wore today reminded him of the gardenia bushes at the edge of his territory.

"When you are as old as I am, you sleep less," she told him while he ate breakfast. "And I do not want to waste the time that I have left."

Raleigh finished the nuts and fruit she left for him on the tiny doll's saucer and drank the fresh, cool water. He was tired this morning. The nightmares had returned leaving him exhausted. When he awoke this morning, to his horror, he had soiled his nest, and his fur was saturated with perspiration. He had only a vague recollection of the dreams. He had been a baby seal that had been ripped from a tiny breathing hole and devoured by a voracious polar bear. Then he had been a tiny mouse that had been bitten by a large rattlesnake and paralyzed by the poison before being swallowed by the enormous creature. Suddenly, he had been a jackrabbit ripped apart by a pack of hyenas. The pain he had felt as his muscles ripped and his bones were crushed by the wild animals was excruciating and haunted him still as he sat safely on Ariel's porch. He had never seen those animals, but somehow the dream had a feeling of reality. This morning, he felt overcome with a bone-crushing fear and depression that somehow seemed oddly familiar. Chloe sensed his fear and became restless and apprehensive.

"You don't seem yourself this morning and your coat is rather a mess," she remarked gently. "Would you let me tidy you up?" She gently dampened her napkin in a glass of water and dabbed the squirrel's coat lightly. Then she brushed the fur lightly with her fingers. "There," she said. "That's better."

He told her what he could about the dreams. Using the tablet to communicate was cumbersome and he could not adequately convey how he felt.

'It's anxiety brought on again by the storm—all the fear and loss have taken their toll on everyone," Ariel told him.

The squirrel sat on the table and relaxed a bit. He had no one else with whom to share his fear. Kiki and the pups did not have such dreams. Kiki only dreamed about racing across graceful tree limbs and gorging on acorns. He could not explain the vividness and reality of the dreams that provoked such fear.

"I had terrible nightmares after my husband, Carlton, died. He lingered for a year with debilitating cancer—just a shadow of himself really.

I thought I would never get over the pain after his death. Then my son died. He was my only child. He and his wife were killed in a plane crash over the Colorado Rockies on the return home from a ski trip to Vail. I had to be strong for Brandy, though. She got me through some of the darkest hours of my life. But I was terribly anxious. After a while, I was afraid for her to go out—afraid that I would lose her, too. The nights were the worst. Now, I have tried very hard to be there for Brandy and Rene—to pull them back into the land of the living." She took another sip of coffee in the silence. "We all get through those things, with God's help. And I promise you, my little friend that you will too."

He tapped the tablet."T-r-y-i-n-g. H-a-r-d."

She stroked the fur on his chest softly with her finger. "I know. It will pass. You'll see. You and your little family are safe now."

He leaned back and allowed her to stroke his chest. It was almost hypnotic and felt wonderful. He could sense her affection, and it made him feel safe.

"You know," she said finally, putting her finger back into her lap. "I think of you as a little angel, sent to me by God. Knowing you has been one of the greatest privileges in my life. I think a younger person might have exploited you for his own gain. But I know that you need to live freely and anonymously. I don't want you to be unhappy because you are so special."

She began placing the dishes on a tray. "Well, it's getting late—almost seven thirty. The cleaning service will be here soon, and Brandy and Rene are probably getting up." She touched his head lightly. "Have a good day, little angel."

He sprang off the table and scaled the brick wall, sailing through the air and landing on an overhanging branch. He could smell the cambium near a broken branch. Feasting on a sliver of chewy cambium, he watched the morning joggers on the tarmac below. He could see Kiki and the pups beside their nearby tree searching through the rotting acorns for a meal. After an hour or so, he saw Ariel's granddaughter leave for work in her car.

Feeling overwhelmed with exhaustion, he returned to his nest intending to take a short nap. He planned to get up again in the early afternoon. The weather was mild enough to draw walkers and people simply out enjoying the weather. Rusty and his man would certainly come to the fountain today feeding the squirrels.

Sleep overtook him very quickly in the security of his nest. It was a deep sleep, and thankfully, he did not dream.

A shrill scream pierced the silence, jolting him from his sleep. It was the sound of pain and fear. He knew that the voice belonged to a squirrel.

His heart pounding, he bolted from his nest, scurrying down the tree in the direction of the sound. It was now late afternoon. He had slept most of the day. Through the branches high above, he had a filtered view of Rene on the verandah, working intently on her tablet. Ariel was nowhere to be seen.

He felt a surge of fear coursing through his veins.

Danger.

He continued to descend the tree toward the sound. As he neared the bottom, he saw the torso of one of his pups lying lifelessly on the grass. She had been decapitated. As he looked toward the perpetual screaming, he was frozen in horror.

The transient owl had grabbed Kiki.

Chapter IX

Riveted by the horrific scene a few feet away from him, Raleigh's heart pounded furiously in his tiny chest. Obviously, Kiki had tried to intervene in the struggle between the owl and her pup. The predator's large talons gripped Kiki's tail as he relentlessly tried to grab her back with his deadly beak. Kiki shrieked with fear, desperately trying to wrench her tail from the owl's ironclad grasp. The pups watched from above in a knothole of the tree, frozen in terror at the hopeless plight of their mother.

Raleigh's thoughts raced. He needed to stop the owl, but he knew that it was impossible by himself. He was far too small to stave off the owl. He would be dead in less than a minute. He would have to act fast. He needed help. If only Ariel were here.

He heard Chloe barking insistently behind the garden wall. Then he remembered Rene on the verandah. He would have to get her to let Chloe out. Chloe would kill the owl and save Kiki.

With lightning speed, he raced across the grass, ascended the wall, and ran over to the verandah. Chloe, frightened by the smells and sounds of fear and death, turned and followed him, barking excitedly.

Rene looked at Raleigh questioningly and then smiled as he jumped on top of the table in front of her. "Oh hello Raleigh. I can't play now. I am writing for school. She held her hand out to proudly display her work. "See?" she said, holding up the tablet.

Raleigh raced around the table and sprang down to the grass trying to get her to follow him. Rene giggled and turned her head down to her work. "Not now! And Chloe, hush up! You are going to disturb the neighbors."

The squirrel heard Kiki's bloodcurdling scream over Chloe's bark. Time was running out! The child was ignoring him.

He would have to use the electronic tablet. Ariel might be angry. She thought Rene was too young to understand. He had to protect Kiki. There was no other choice. The child would have to learn the secret.

He hopped to the edge of the tablet and in record time, he spelled h-e-l-p. He stood next to the tablet scolding Rene.

The child stared at him in amazement. "Raleigh! You can spell!"

As Raleigh continued to scold her, he dashed out onto the grass by the gate. Chloe followed him. He retraced his steps and then ran to the gate.

"Do you need help? I am coming," she said as she jumped down from the verandah and ran toward the gate.

The small child could barely reach the latch. On her third try, she opened the latch and the door swung open. Chloe and Raleigh bounded through the gate toward the owl and Kiki. The huge bird flapped its wings to lift in flight. Kiki, limp and bloody, hung from its beak. Although she was silent now, Raleigh could detect a glimmer of life in her glazed stare.

Chloe growled and sprang into the air, grabbing the owl as it spread its wings to fly away. The force of the dog's fierce jaws across the bird's rib cage caused the owl to open its beak in a shriek, dropping Kiki to the ground. Chloe shook the bird furiously, biting it relentlessly as it squealed and sprayed blood across the grass. When the owl was finally dead, Chloe dropped it onto the ground, planting a giant white paw across its chest as if to establish her victory. Her luscious white coat and muzzle were drenched with blood and covered with gray feathers.

Kiki's breathing was ragged. Her lovely coat had been viciously torn, exposing deep wounds down her side. Her tail was nearly severed and both of her rear legs were broken, lying haphazardly on the ground. Raleigh stood by Kiki as Rene scooped her up into the front of her shirt. "She's hurt bad," she told Raleigh solemnly. "We need to get her to a vet."

A few runners from the park had gathered at the commotion. "Don't touch the squirrel," chided a thin woman in her thirties, her hair drenched in sweat from her run. "It might bite you."

Rene looked at the woman defiantly. "My grandmother feeds this squirrel family every day. They are our pets and they would never hurt us. I need to bring them to the vet."

A younger man stared disapprovingly at Chloe. "Is that your dog? It should not be allowed to kill an owl in the park. Owls keep the rodent population down. The squirrels are a nuisance, and they carry diseases. Besides, there is a leash law. I am going to complain to your parents."

"You can't tell my father. He's dead! And Chloe saved the squirrel!" Rene replied defiantly as she turned to walk toward the house. "Come on, Chloe," she called over her shoulder.

Raleigh and Chloe followed closely behind as Rene raced back to the house with Kiki in her arms in search of Granny Ariel. Chloe barked at Ariel, running toward her excitedly.

Ariel screamed when she saw the blood spattered across Chloe and Rene. "Oh my God, Rene! What happened to you? Are you alright?"

Rene held out the front of her shirt, exposing Kiki's bleeding body. "I'm fine. It's the squirrel. We need to take her to the doctor, now. The owl tried to kill her. Chloe and Raleigh got me and Chloe killed the owl and saved the squirrel. And the man outside said that he was going to tell on Chloe because she was not on a leash," Rene explained in a voice breathless from her run. Her small face was flushed with concern for Kiki.

Ariel examined Rene. "You didn't touch the owl, did you Rene?"

"No, Granny Ariel. I'm fine," she persisted with tears in her eyes. "But Kiki is hurt! We need to take her to the vet now before she dies!"

Ariel kneeled down to look at Kiki. She stroked Chloe's ears and scooped Raleigh into her open purse. He stood on Ariel's wallet, peering over the leather brim at Kiki's battered body.

"It's such a shame. She's barely alive. I am going to take them all to the vet. We don't have much time to spare," Ariel said as she continued to inspect Kiki.

Ariel folded a dish-towel into a small cardboard box. Gingerly, they transferred Kiki's limp body into the box before calling the emergency number for the vet. Rene told them about the pup's body that still lay in the park. They would bury the pup when they came back. The on-call vet was waiting for them at the Carrollton Street clinic.

Ariel loaded the child, dog, and the squirrels into her Mercedes sedan. As the vehicle roared to life, Raleigh felt a deep uneasiness. He had never before left his territory or traveled in an automobile. He was filled with a vague fear by the strange vibrations of the engine and the gentle rocking of the car as it pulled across the median and headed down the avenue toward the clinic.

Traffic was still moderately heavy with morning traffic. Raleigh hopped out of Ariel's purse and stood over the cardboard box, watching Kiki breathe. He took his paw and softly stroked her behind her ear. Her look briefly registered recognition before she closed her eyes. She was slipping away. He could feel it.

"Granny Ariel," Rene said as they neared the clinic. "Did you know that Raleigh can spell?"

"How do you know that, honey?" Ariel asked as she maneuvered in and out of the traffic.

"He spelled 'h-e-l-p.' He and Chloe came to me, and they were barking and racing around. When I did not pay attention, Raleigh spelled 'h-e-l-p.' He can spell. I promise that I did not imagine it," the child said earnestly.

Ariel was silent momentarily. She turned to Rene as she stopped at the light. "Rene, I know that. But it has to be a secret from everyone. Raleigh is special—like an angel."

"An angel?"

"Yes. He is very special—like a gift from God. But it is important that we not tell anyone about him. Not even your mother or the vet. You and I will talk as long as you want about this later." She searched the child's eyes. "Can I trust you with this secret?"

The child nodded solemnly. "You can trust me Granny Ariel. I know he's special. Not even Chloe can spell."

Ariel nodded. "Good. Now remember, this is our secret. We will go inside and have the doctor fix up Kiki. I want him to look at Chloe and Raleigh too. Then, tomorrow, you and I will go someplace special and talk about Raleigh's special talent."

Rene looked at Raleigh and Ariel reassuringly. "I promise. We will talk tomorrow."

Ariel called the clinic again from her cell phone, and two staff members came out to meet them when Ariel pulled the car in front of the clinic. They took Kiki, Raleigh and Chloe inside. Rene went with them while Ariel parked her automobile.

A young vet was waiting in the examining room to have a look at Kiki. She was barely thirty, although she exuded an air of confidence. She patted Rene's head. "I'm Dr. Greene."

Rene looked at her stoically. "I'm Rene and this is Kiki, my grandmother's squirrel. This is Raleigh and Chloe. The owl tried to take Kiki away, and Chloe killed the owl."

Dr. Greene looked over toward the blood-soaked ruff of the Samoyed, who leaned protectively against Rene. Chloe's eyes were bright and alert. "So, you are the protector of the squirrels, Chloe," she smiled as she began to examine Kiki. Raleigh peered over Rene's arms to watch the examination. Kiki's eyes were still glazed, and her shallow breathing was labored. Raleigh trembled with fear. Kiki was dying. He could feel it. And the smell of death was everywhere.

"She is in pretty bad shape," Dr. Greene said as Ariel joined them in the examining room. "I probably can't save her, but we can try."

“I want you to do everything you can. I am not concerned about the cost,” Ariel said.

Dr. Greene shook her head. “Alright. I think you should wait here. We need to take this squirrel into surgery. Her lung may be punctured and I need to set the legs and insert pins. She will never be able to run or climb trees again. She appears to have some internal trauma. If she lives, chances are that she will just be a house pet. While you wait here, Dr. Miller will examine the other squirrel and the hero dog. I think the dog should also have a medicated bath. We need to keep an eye on her for disease. Will the squirrel bite?” she said, looking at Raleigh.

Ariel stroked Raleigh with her fingers. “No. He knows that you are trying to help him. He is completely tame.”

“Good, but we will have to put him into a carrier while he is in the clinic. Now that he has escaped from an owl, I do not want a cat or dog in the waiting room to try to grab him.” She lifted Kiki up on the small pallet and disappeared through a rear examining room door.

Dr. Miller joined them momentarily after Kiki was taken to surgery. Raleigh leaned against Rene, his thoughts solely focused on Kiki. He allowed the Dr. Miller to perform a complete examination upon him, pronouncing him fit. She advised that Raleigh she be given a set of vaccinations, including rabies. He barely seemed to notice the injections and submitted to a medicated grooming by one of the staff.

Two hours later, Raleigh and Chloe rejoined Ariel and Rene in the waiting room. Kiki was still in surgery. Raleigh sat in the corner of a small pet carrier, looking stoically at Ariel. The carrier smelled vaguely like a cat. Ariel slipped her ancient fingers through the bars and stroked his coat. “Still no news.”

After what seemed an eternity, they were ushered back into an examining room, where Dr. Greene waited for them in her blood-stained green scrub suit. Her clear eyes were somber, and Raleigh understood the situation immediately.

"I'm sorry. We did everything we could, but she was just too far gone."

Rene sobbed loudly, and Ariel brushed the tears from her soft, paper-thin cheeks. Raleigh crouched down on the floor of the pet carrier, overcome with a sense of loss he had never previously experienced.

Kiki was gone.

Chapter X

That night, Raleigh slept on the fireplace hearth beside the velvet box holding Kiki. Ariel had received the ornate box as part of a fragrance promotional at Saks. A strong floral smell emanated from the makeshift coffin. Ariel had cradled Kiki's tiny body in satin and placed a velvet sachet underneath her head and closed the lid. The dead pup's body had been mangled beyond recognition. She was inside a closed decorative box on the mantle.

When Raleigh awoke before dawn, he noticed that one of the pups had lifted the lid and crawled inside the box, curling up beside his mother. The two remaining pups lay close to Raleigh, touching his tail. They were incapable of understanding why their mother did not get up. They were his responsibility now. Careful not to wake them, he stood and stretched his rear legs. His body ached from sleeping on the hard marble hearth, and his fur reeked from the medicated bath.

Chloe lay in the foyer, her side positioned against the cool air coming underneath the front door. She had the strange scent of antibiotics that the vet had prescribed. Her clean fur glistened in the shaft of light from the foyer chandelier, which had burned through the night. Because of her enormously thick coat, Chloe always sought the coolest places in the house, like the marble-and-granite bath off the study on the main floor. She raised her head and gave him a look of concern before padding softly to lie in the living room by the fire with the pups and Kiki. Raleigh pushed open the latch of the dog door and ran out onto the cool grass to relieve himself. A soft mist fell, and the air was heavy with humidity. He gnawed the cambium of a small branch that had fallen during the night before returning inside. Despite his access to fresh fruits and vegetables, he still craved cambium and bark. It was very dark and still in the hour before dawn. He noticed that the kitchen light cheerfully illuminated the rear of the house, signaling that Ariel was up.

When he returned to the house, Ariel was sipping a cup of hot tea in the breakfast room. She patted the arm of her flannel robe, signaling him to come over. He sprang into her lap and curled against the soft flannel. Gently, she stroked his head and ears with her long fingers. Within a few moments, he was overcome with the feeling of warmth and security. He could feel the love emanating from his friend.

She finally spoke. "I know you must feel devastated. One of the most terrible nights of my life was the night my husband, Carlton, died. The others were the deaths of my son and parents. It was awful. I cried continuously and stopped going out when my son died. You think that you can't go on, but we all do somehow. One day, you realize that you just can't bury yourself in your own pity. Others need you and depend upon you. In my case, it was Brandy. She was sixteen when her parents died. I was her only surviving family member. There was no one else."

She softly stroked Raleigh's chin and then lifted his eyes toward her down-turned face. He looked at her expectantly and gave her a soft bark.

"I know that you loved Kiki. But you have three pups left and they are not ready to survive on their own. All of us are going to have to help with them. It is what Kiki would want. You are going to have to put aside your grief as much as possible and go on with life. I can tell you from personal experience that you will become stronger, and the grief will lessen the more that you help the pups." She continued stroking his chin. "I know that you feel that the pain will never go away, but in time you will learn to overcome this."

He replied with a low bark to signal that he understood and stared miserably at the tiny beads of condensation on the bottom of Ariel's teacup. This morning, he was glad that she was not pressuring him to spell to communicate his feelings. He felt strangely debilitated and overcome with a grief that he never knew existed. It was worse than the dreams.

They sat in silence for a while as Ariel sipped her tea and stroked Raleigh's fur. Her flannel robe was soft and smelled deliciously clean. He admired the thin protruding veins and smattering of brown age spots marking the translucent skin on the back of her hands. Despite the fact that she was in her eighties, her silver hair was still lustrous and thick. Ariel kept it swept away from her face and pulled into a French roll at the back of her head. Her pale facial skin was only gently lined across her forehead and the corners of her mouth. Ariel's arresting blue eyes radiated warmth and intelligence. He had developed an appreciation of human characteristics and decidedly believed that Ariel had a kind and pleasing appearance.

"I talked to Rene last night about things. She was devastated about Kiki and the pup. It is very difficult to explain the miracle of your ability to communicate to a six-year-old child—it is like something out of a fairy tale. I explained to her that you were like an angel. That may have been a poor analogy because she believes that you can communicate with her father, Harris. At least, she understands that we cannot tell anyone about your ability—especially Brandy. I am concerned that she would never understand."

Raleigh nodded absently. Perhaps Kiki was an angel now—a guardian angel like the stories he and Ariel had read. She would like that—flying on silver gossamer wings over the clouds watching over him and the pups. It was comforting to think of her that way instead of inhabiting her cold, stiff body on the fireplace hearth.

Ariel looked at him seriously. “I hope you can help her. Knowing you will be the most magical experience of Rene’s entire life. She needs something special with the terrible loss she had. And Brandy is very distracted these days with her shop and the lawsuit seeking rights to the *BYZANTIUM* emeralds.” She met the squirrel’s gaze. His liquid brown eyes lacked their usual brightness this morning. “I want you to be her guardian angel. I am old now, and Kiki’s death reminds me of just how fragile life is. Get to know her. Can I count on you?”

He tapped his paw twice on her robe, signaling that he understood. It was shorthand that the two of them had developed when the tablet was not available. He really was not sure what he could do to help the child. She was very sweet and gentle, and she had tried her best to help him to stave off the owl. He would do what Ariel asked.

Ariel smiled warmly, evidencing relief. “Good. Between Rene and the pups, the two of us have our work cut out for us.”

The pups and Chloe awoke when Brandy came down at seven. She fixed the pups a small tray of sliced fruit and vegetables, which she placed in the corner. Chloe had a bowl of dog food, a few treats, and sliced cucumbers. She ate daintily, standing protectively by the pups, nudging them to eat. After breakfast, she cleaned each one with her tongue, chasing one recalcitrant pup up the front staircase. Raleigh watched the commotion from his perch on Ariel’s lap.

Brandy grinned. “They breathed new life into her.”

Ariel smiled. “Chloe is very maternal. I think she has decided to raise the pups herself.”

Certain that the pups were in Chloe's care, Raleigh returned to the living room to stay with Kiki until the late afternoon. He curled beside the box, inhaling the overpowering floral scent that partially masked the odor of death. He touched Kiki's face with his nose. Her body was ice-cold now and emitted a slightly sour and medicinal smell. He thought she looked remarkably as if she were sleeping.

Ariel and Rene came into the living room when they returned from church and their errands delivering food baskets to the homeless shelter. The sun was low on the horizon now and cast dark shadows from the casement windows. Raleigh was sitting up, leaning over the rim of the box, watching Kiki and trying to will her back to life.

"The rain has stopped," Ariel said softly, stroking the crown of Raleigh's head. "I had the gardeners dig a small hole in the rose garden. We even have a small piece of marble that we can use to mark the grave. I think it is time now."

Raleigh stared at Ariel. She was right, of course, but he did not feel that he could let her go yet.

Ariel seemed to sense his reluctance. "I know," she said softly. "I know you don't want to let her go. But think of the pups. It is best for them and best for Kiki."

He finally acquiesced and he, Rene, Ariel, Chloe, and the pups buried Kiki and the young female in a fresh hole in the rose garden. It was a very solemn occasion. Rene recited the Lord's Prayer, and Ariel read from the Bible as Raleigh sat beside the tiny grave and mourned. The confused pups watched with interest for a time, until their attention waned and they raced across the lawn and chased each other across the row of crepe myrtles, their flowers fading in the fall. Chloe eyed them laconically as she lay beside Raleigh, fully cognizant of the solemnity of the occasion. Finally, Ariel placed a four-inch white marble tile left over from the repair construction on top of the tiny grave. Afterward, Rene and Ariel put cut roses over the tiny graves and returned into the house.

Raleigh lay beside the tiny grave until dark, long after Ariel had shooed the pups and Chloe inside for the night. Although he still felt miserable, he felt a strange sense of relief after the little funeral. He decided that this was the beginning of what Ariel had described as 'closure.' He had never realized how much he would miss Kiki.

~

For the next three days, he felt strangely detached from the world. Sometimes he would go over to the park in the morning, half-expecting to see Kiki on the branches of their shared oak. Then the sickening memory of the horrible killing a few days earlier reminded him that she was gone forever. He passed the time repairing his dummy nests and looking for buried acorns that had survived Penny's floods.

The pups visited their old nests with him once or twice, although they spent much of their time now with Chloe, who had seemed to adopt them. Raleigh was both amused and concerned by Chloe's relationship with the pups. The little squirrels needed to establish a healthy fear of all dogs and predators, and Raleigh worried that by spending all of their time with a dog, they would become less vigilant. Also, Chloe was definitely earth bound and could not teach them anything about life high above. She spent some time demonstrating to the pups how to dig a decent hole and chasing them across the lawn. She consistently bathed them with her tongue, almost desperately trying to eradicate their squirrel smell. But Chloe seemed fiercely protective of her little brood, angrily chasing away a neighbor's cat that dared to stand on the fence. Chloe had killed for them and in her mind, the pups belonged to her as much as to Raleigh. He knew that for all intents and purposes, the pups would never have a normal life again. They would become domesticated house pets like Chloe if he did not take over some of the responsibility of the pups. Ariel was right. He could not ignore them. Kiki would want him to help the small squirrels.

By the end of September, Raleigh began adapting to the change in his daily life. Rene had returned to kindergarten, and the morning air was cool and brisk. Autumn colored fall wreaths graced the front and back doors. The air smelled different now with the scent that Raleigh recognized as the portent of cold weather. The days were becoming shorter, which meant that there was less time for him to forage for food and spend time outside.

About a week after the little funeral, Rene and Ariel brought the squirrels down to the study to spend the evening. The pups were tired, but Raleigh encouraged them to come. Ariel had a few treats for the squirrel pups, who snuggled with Chloe in the far corner of the room. Ariel, Rene and Raleigh played a word game on the electronic tablet. Rene watched Raleigh with rapt attention as he fastidiously spelled "k-i-t-c-h-e-n".

"He is amazing, Granny Ariel!" said Rene. "Raleigh can spell better than me."

"Better than I can," Ariel corrected her.

After a game of Scrabble, Rene and Raleigh played two rounds of checkers while Ariel sat beside them, an amused look on her face as she sipped her herbal tea. Ariel had explained to Raleigh that since Rene knew about his special abilities, she could spend more time with him now.

After the games, Ariel began reading them the first three chapters of *Alice in Wonderland*. Ariel and Rene had agreed that they would read the book at least five nights a week until they were finished. It was an unusual fantasy, but Raleigh was amused by the story. He enjoyed spending the time with Rene, snuggled against Ariel's wool sweater in the lamplight. Before Rene went to sleep, she kissed Raleigh on the head.

"Thank you, God, for bringing us this little angel. And please God bless my daddy."

For the first time in a few days, the feeling of overwhelming grief was temporarily alleviated. Raleigh was captivated by the child, and felt a sense of happiness that he would be spending so much time with her. Despite Kiki's death, he was not alone. He had the pups, Ariel, Rene, and Chloe. And he was safe, dry, and well fed. Despite his loss, he would go on.

∽

Mick, the forensic CPA, called a few days later with a brief report. Based upon his calculations, Brandy had invested almost $900,000 in Harris's salvage venture through the years. Mick estimated that Thad's contributions were less than $35,000, although he cautioned that this opinion could change once additional documents became available. Claude had explained that the ratio of the investment would be taken into account by the court in measuring a salvage award to Brandy and Thad.

Claude also made some discrete inquiries of jewelers in New York for an estimated value of the emeralds. The emeralds in the safety-deposit boxes could conservatively be valued at $70 million.

Finally Wayne had extracted all of the data that was transferred to memory sticks. The documents were also printed with Bates numbers. Duplicates were also made of the incredible underwater footage of fragments of *BYZANTIUM*. At some point, Brandy knew that she would need to review the documents, but it was a task that she hoped to put off as long as possible.

At Claude's insistence, Brandy met with two other law firms about handling her case against Thad. Her first appointment was with two senior attorneys at Simms Carthage, the largest firm in New Orleans which was located in a restored old building on Carondolet. The law firm had represented Ariel for years and had drafted the trust fund established for Brandy after her parents had been killed. The interview occurred in a cavernous conference room at a thirty-foot long conference room table topped with white granite slabs. The shiny wooden floors were covered generously with thick Persian carpets, and oil paintings hung on the walls. There were several antiques placed prominently along the walls that in Brandy's expert opinion were quite expensive. A woman in a uniform served Brandy a cup of tea in a china cup and saucer. Two men in expensive suits that she guessed were in their early fifties, joined her momentarily in the conference room, introducing themselves as the 'senior' partners. Two tired looking young associates and three paralegals solemnly introduced themselves and sat silently at a respectful distance from the senior partners. One of the young associates placed a large black reference book labeled *Benedict on Admiralty* on the table in front of him and opened his laptop, his fingers poised over the keyboard.

Brandy patiently engaged in the obligatory small talk until the attorneys signaled that they were ready to get down to business. The senior attorneys were enthusiastic about her case and the probability that she would prevail against Thad. Unfortunately, they explained, they would need to be compensated monthly at their substantial hourly rate. The firm, they told her, did not handle contingency fees. They promised to assign two associates and paralegals to the case full-time through the conclusion of the litigation. At those rates, Brandy knew that she could easily spend $500,000 through trial. It also made her slightly uncomfortable that the men had knowledge of Granny Ariel's net worth. Did this factor affect their fee? She could not be sure, but she felt wary.

Brandy had mentally eliminated the Simms firm before she finished her tea.

The second firm was located on the top two floors of an old building on Canal Street. The interior had been freshly remodeled and was inexpensively furnished in a sparse modern style. The boutique firm was filled with attorneys who had eschewed the grind of the big firm life and had decided to strike out on their own. Every single member of the firm was under the age of fifty. Claude had explained to Brandy that this was a 'lean-and-mean-shop' with low overhead and expenses. She met with a baby-faced attorney in his mid-forties in his spacious and orderly office. The only associate in the office was a young woman, who sat in the modern client chair beside her. Both of them were dressed in business casual attire with oxford cloth shirts and slacks. She noticed that a copy of the Virgin Islands complaint sat prominently on his desk. The more senior attorney was knowledgeable, and she felt comfortable in his presence. He listened silently as she detailed what had occurred. They discussed options, and he pointed out the potential problems that she might face in a legal battle with Thad. He readily admitted that her case was unusual and that they had never handled a similar matter. Overall, however, like the big firm, he was enthusiastic about her legal position. By the end of their two-hour meeting, she was willing to consider his firm if Claude's new firm decided not to take her case.

Any thoughts that Brandy had of hiring the maritime boutique firm disappeared as soon as Brandy met Chris Banks at the Boudreaux Banks firm that Claude had joined. The firm was situated on a single floor of a high-rise office building near the Fifth Circuit courthouse. Chris, who was originally from Baton Rouge, was a Harvard Law School graduate who had worked in a mega-firm on Wall Street for twenty years practicing securities litigation cases before returning to his Louisiana roots to open the Boudreaux Banks firm with a friend. Today, he represented at least two large oil companies and handled complex litigation for the oil field industry and other large corporate interests. Despite the fact that he was in his mid-fifties, he had retained a boyish charm and thin athletic build. He shook Brandy's hand firmly as he came into the reception area to meet her and usher her back to his office. He had a friendly, relaxed demeanor and immediately put her at ease.

"Please have a seat on the sofa," he said, motioning her to a comfortable tuxedo couch. "I have asked my assistant to bring us a couple of lattes. I splurged on a fancy machine for the office since I spend so much time here. You do drink coffee?"

"Absolutely! I could use a cup," she told him.

Brandy sat on the white damask, noting that the room was tastefully furnished without being ostentatious. Framed industrial photographs of the oil industry were hung on the walls. A Harvard diploma with the inscription 'Order of the Coif' was in a plain wooden frame in the corner.

Chris sat across from Brandy in a chair and put a legal pad and pen on the coffee table between them. Claude, by agreement with Brandy, would not be joining them. He had explained to her that it was important that she feel comfortable with Chris because he would be the lead counsel on her case.

"I have read the complaint and, of course, Claude has told me a bit about the case. It looks like you have documented your expenditures and contributions to the salvage venture," he told her as they sipped their lattes from two giant white mugs. "But I would like to hear your story and what you can recall."

"Where would you like for me to begin?" she asked.

"Start from the beginning," he told her. "I just want a general chronology about what occurred and what agreements you understand existed between Thad and Harris."

She hated telling the story again, but she began with Harris quitting his job at the University of Miami. They talked for more than two hours. Occasionally, Chris prompted her with short question, but he appeared to be truly interested in what she had to say. She did not have the same feeling that she had at the Simms firm that she was just another dollar in the door to be earned and exploited. Instead, they had a long, real conversation and during the entire discussion, Chris did not take a single note.

"Well, this is fascinating, and I understand why you felt cheated," Chris said pensively as the conversation lulled. "Have you ever heard from Thad over the last few months? For example, did he ever call you and discuss his intent to file this lawsuit and ask you to join?"

"Never," she replied with rancor. "I have not heard from Thad in nine months. At first I was hurt, but now I understand that he had a motive in avoiding me."

Chris placed his pen on the blank legal pad and folded his hands in his lap. "This is an amazing case. In the interest of full disclosure, though, I need to tell you that no lawyer that I know of in the State of Louisiana has experience in a treasure salvage case. These are unusual cases and there have been only a handful in the country over the last century. If any attorney tells you that he or she has significant experience in this area, you should ask the name of the case and for a copy of the legal opinion. This is a unique matter. I have never been involved in a treasure salvage/ finds dispute, so I want you to understand this very clearly."

"I understand. Claude has explained this to me."

"We do have a few attorneys here who have handled contract salvage cases. These generally involve a ship that breaks down and needs to be towed to safety. The dollar amount is negotiated generally up front, and the disputes generally center around whether the salvage was handled properly. This case is a case of volunteer salvage when a party voluntarily rescues an operating vessel in danger or brings up items from an old shipwreck. The court will have a great deal of discretion in creating the award. For a case like this, I wish we were in federal court in New Orleans. "

"Could we bring the lawsuit here?"

Chris leaned back in his chair, pensive for a moment. "Well, we would definitely need to intervene in the Virgin Islands case because we do not want to risk inconsistent rulings. The federal court in the Virgin Islands will be making a salvage award. But, since such large quantities of emeralds are located in Orleans Parish, we could file suit and ask the court to take jurisdiction over the *res*—or in this case the emeralds. Then, Thad and Underwriters would have to appear here as well to contest your right to those emeralds."

Brandy smiled. She liked the idea of filing suit locally as well. Neither of the other firms had suggested such a strategy. "I would feel comfortable bringing the suit here."

"Well, it does increase the expenses with dual lawsuits," he replied. "Also, there is always the possibility that one of the courts would stay the case while the other case proceeded to judgment. But it is worth a shot."

"I think I would like to try it."

"If you were to hire us, I would be the lead attorney on the case. I know that you have a friendship with Claude. He could work on the case, but I want you to consider that very carefully. This is a good case, but we cannot guarantee you a result. Many things in lawsuits go south and unexpected developments occur. For example, it is possible that Thad may claim that your husband assigned all of his rights to him, and the court or jury may buy that argument. There have been many friendships ruined because of bad results over lawsuits. I know that you have talked with other law firms. You need to consider your best interests here and not friendship."

Brandy met Chris's direct gaze openly. "Claude and I have talked about this, Chris. And of course, he wanted me to meet you to be certain that I was comfortable with you. I have also spoken with two other law firms. The most important thing to me is to feel comfortable and to trust the attorneys and firm that represent me. I trust Claude and know that he will not lie to me. And I feel comfortable with you. Claude speaks so highly of you."

"Claude is a fine lawyer and he is a good fit for our firm with his trial experience and the three years at the D'Argent firm. Our practice here is more of an industry practice, and we do not represent the London Market. I am very happy that he has decided to join us, but I am concerned about your friendship. I do not want you to hire us based upon some misguided feeling that you are obligated to hire your friend."

"I do not feel obligated at all," she told him. "I want to be represented by someone who is interested in my case, will tell me the truth, and not view me as just another case to handle."

Chris smiled. "Good. I have to ask, you understand, so we set the ground rules at the beginning. And you seem like an independent woman with a good head on her shoulders for business."

"I understand, and I have considered those issues carefully."

"Alright then. We are willing to take the case on a contingency, but you would need to pay the expenses, such as depositions, court costs, expert fees, discovery, and travel expenses. Also, we will need to associate a law firm in St. Thomas as local counsel to assist us in the lawsuit there. You would need to pay them directly. We will have double track expenses if we file suit in New Orleans. So, this is not a cheap pursuit."

"I pay the fees, but we are taking a risk together—correct? No recovery, no fee?"

"That is correct. I have to also tell you that this is the only contingency fee case that I have taken or ever will take. But, this is such a unique and fascinating case. Also, don't overlook the possibility that Thad and London Underwriters might settle the case with you. That would be the smart thing for them to do under the circumstances."

"That would be the fair thing, but my opinion of Thad has changed quite a bit over the last few weeks. I think he will fight until the end."

"Again, I cannot guarantee you a result, but chances are because of your investment, you will have a very decent recovery. I would not be surprised if you and your daughter and her children never had to work a day in your lives."

Brandy knew that the costs would be staggering. But Granny Ariel had already told her that she would be willing to loan her some money to fund the suit.

"So where do we begin?"

"First, we will need to prepare and execute a contingency fee agreement. Claude and I will also do our best to provide you with a monthly estimate of the expenses through the trial so you will not have any surprises. Next, we can make an appointment so you and I can go over the agreement. Then, I would like to wait a week before we both sign. Again, this is a big step, and I want to be sure that you have time to think about it."

"I appreciate that," she said simply.

"After we execute the agreement, I will need a deposit for the initial fees—court costs and the fees for the local counsel. Then we will draft a federal court complaint for the Eastern District of Louisiana to arrest the emeralds—or place them in the custody of the court. We will file that lawsuit first. Finally, after we have prepared our complaint for intervention, I will call Thad's attorney."

Brandy was pleased that Chris was so methodical and had a general plan. It all seemed very logical and fair. A sense of relief washed over her that she had finally found an attorney to represent her interest.

"I want to hire you and your firm, Chris," she told him. "Go ahead and draft the agreement."

~

Thad had seemed highly agitated about the widow during Ewan's last phone call with him. He had seemed particularly troubled about the fact that Ewan had seen Brandy and her male friend rolling suitcases into the bank together. He had also been concerned when he learned that Ewan had followed her downtown one Saturday morning to a meeting in the Simms Carthage law firm. He had been insistent that Ewan should double down his efforts to monitor her activities.

As the weather cooled, Ewan started walking in the French Quarter and passing by Massenet on a daily basis. He noticed that Brandy had an assistant, but sometimes Brandy was in the store alone. There was a control panel for a burglar alarm in plain sight near the cash stand in the corner. At night, a security service patrolled the area to guard against burglaries and vandalism. Ewan decided that it would be impossible—and unnecessary—to break into the shop.

On weekends, he occasionally went to Audubon Park to exercise on the walking path that ringed the front of the park. He sometimes heard the large Samoyed barking playfully at the little girl as they ran in the walled enclosure behind the house. It seemed that the old lady enjoyed sitting outside in the mild fall weather as well. He could hear their laughter and happy voices over the wall. It all seemed perfect and idyllic to Ewan. His home had never been a happy place. It had been a place of terror.

Brandy was rarely at home except in the evening. Sometimes at night, he waited by the old tree, smoking cigarettes in the dark as he watched Brandy in front of the kitchen sink, washing dishes. His position by the old tree gave him a good view of the landing at the top of the stairs as she went upstairs at night to tuck her little girl in bed.

Ewan felt that his surveillance was a waste of time and pointless. Nonetheless, he dutifully reported every development to Thad.

The fourth Monday in October, Ewan's shift ended early because of the torrential rain storms in the area. Of course, Ewan would not be paid for the three hours that he was unable to work. Ewan drove home in the driving rain at about two-thirty, took a shower, and sat on the couch with a beer channel surfing. He bought a new movie release from the cable company and settled in for a quiet afternoon. After the movie, he reheated the Vietnamese food left over from the evening before for dinner. He had broken a cardinal rule and brought a beautiful young woman he had met in a bar a few weeks ago home to his house. They had dined on take-out Vietnamese food before an evening of wild sex. Ewan knew that it was a risk. He needed to be invisible and a loner while he was in New Orleans, but occasionally he needed companionship. He would just be certain that Thad never knew.

He turned on the local news in time to catch the weather report for the rest of the week. Violent thunder storms were forecast through Wednesday, and the weatherman predicted as much as five inches of rain would fall in the city over the next three days. He continued to enjoy his dinner through the local news recap. He looked up suddenly when he heard the announcer mention the name Harris Blake.

Could it be the same Harris Blake that he had murdered?

He watched carefully as a large legal pleading filled the screen. The announcer described a lawsuit that had been filed in federal court that afternoon by the widow of Harris Blake seeking title or a reward because her husband had located emeralds worth nearly $75 million from an abandoned shipwreck *BYZANTIUM*. The ship had run aground on a reef in a storm ninety years ago as it steamed toward New York from Brazil.

No wonder Thad wanted the woman watched! There was a lot of money at stake. Obviously Thad wanted the diver killed because he wanted the jewels worth $75 million.

Ewan immediately decided that he would need to demand more money from Thad. Hell, with money like that at stake, Thad could easily spare a million or two. Ewan's dream would become a reality then. First, he needed to report the development.

Ewan picked up the cell phone and sent Thad a text. Within three minutes, Thad called him. They would need to figure out how to deal with the widow. She had become a real problem.

Chapter XI

The lawsuit filed by Boudreaux Banks seeking the maritime arrest of the emeralds in New Orleans federal district court unleashed a media firestorm. The following morning, the Virgin Islands firm associated by Chris filed a complaint in intervention on Brandy's behalf in Thad's federal Virgin Islands lawsuit. Thad's attorney had been furious and refused to speak to Chris when he called to alert him that Brandy would be filing a complaint in intervention.

Chris ultimately learned that Thad had a smaller stash of emeralds worth approximately $10 million that were in the custody of the Virgin Islands court. Thad's complaint argued that any and all emeralds recovered from the *BYZANTIUM* were his property. Thad alleged that Harris had never located any emeralds on any of his dives. Chris had explained to Brandy that this was a favorable development because the photographs taken by Harris documented his finds.

"Thad is digging a hole for himself," Chris explained when they read his answer to the Rule E complaint in intervention. "The evidence we have contradicts his position," he assured her.

Boudreaux Banks, at its own expense, had hired a publicist to assist them in drafting media statements and dealing with media inquiries. CNN, Fox News, and the other major networks interviewed Chris, who also appeared on several morning television shows. Thad's attorney, Quinn Beazley, was also interviewed as Thad sat silently next to him on the sofa.

Brandy was unable to go to the shop for nearly a week because news crews camped in front of Massenet. Granny Ariel hired a guard service to keep the news crews away from her home. They stopped answering their land-line telephone. Thankfully, by early November, the public interest waned, and the media storm finally abated. Life gradually began to return to normal.

Chris and Claude were extremely busy with the two lawsuits and worked seven days a week. Claude had not had an occasion to properly move into his new office and worked on a cheap rented desk until he could take time to buy furniture. Litigation expenses mounted rapidly. Brandy felt as if she were hemorrhaging money.

The New Orleans lawsuit was assigned to Judge Harry Christian, who had been appointed to the federal bench by Ronald Reagan when Christian was only thirty-three years of age. Judge Christian signed an order arresting the emeralds and placing them into the custody of the United States Marshal. The jewels were divided among various bank vaults and services in the city, and were technically under court custody and control. The jewels could not be moved without a court order.

As expected, Thad hired local counsel and filed a complaint in intervention seeking title to the emeralds under the doctrine of finds or alternatively a large salvage award. Thad's complaint alleged that Harris had stolen the emeralds from Thad, and that Brandy, who was complicit, unlawfully removed the stones from the jurisdiction of the Virgin Islands. Remarkably, Thad's complaint denied that the stones were the former cargo aboard the *BYZANTIUM*. Instead, his attorney argued that the provenance was unknown and that the stones were abandoned.

The London underwriters filed a complaint in intervention in both actions. They claimed that they had paid the cargo owner in full for the loss. Technically, the emeralds belonged to them, and they wanted to recover their investment. Underwriters argued that a reasonable salvage award to Harris Blake's widow should be less than $500,000. They argued that Thad's recovery should be only $250,000.

All parties exchanged their initial disclosures and began preparing a flurry of discovery requests. Chris served London Underwriters and Thad's counsel with a litigation hold letter requiring that they preserve all electronically stored information relating to the lawsuit. Thad's counsel filed a motion to stay the New Orleans litigation until a resolution of the Virgin Islands case. Judge Christian denied the motion after a lengthy oral argument.

All parties had thrown the gauntlet down, and their respective legal positions had been etched in stone. Chris prepared Brandy for the worst.

"Thad and his attorney are taking ridiculous positions. If a settlement can be reached, it will be months away. We are in for the long haul," Chris told her.

Brandy had simply nodded stoically. She resolved to focus on her child and Massenet. The worst had already occurred when Harris had died. She knew that she could tolerate the unpleasantness of the litigation because she could not let Thad wrongfully profit from Harris' s life work. She wanted justice, and she was determined to get it.

~

By the second week in November, Brandy had helped Claude select new furniture for his office at Boudreaux Banks. The D'Argent firm had owned the furniture in Claude's old office, and he needed the bare essentials. They arranged for a moving company to make the move on a Sunday afternoon so it would be the least disruptive to Claude's daily routine.

Brandy supervised the movers as they maneuvered the antique desk and ornate bookcase into Claude's new office at Boudreaux Banks. The antiques looked nice even inside a modern office building. When the three men finished, Claude tipped them generously for working after hours. Humming softly to herself, Brandy worked alone, hanging the framed diplomas and a pair of oil paintings of nineteenth century sailing ships which Claude had acquired on one of his trips to London, next to the black-and-white photographs of his small sailboat.

Claude came in to survey her work as she arranged the lamps and side chairs. "Looks great," he said enthusiastically. "There are some real perks having an antique shop owner for a client."

She grinned. "Wait until you get my bill. It will knock your socks off."

"Touché," he replied, handing her a cold, sparkling ICE drink from the refrigerator in the small office kitchen and leaning back in his desk chair.

The afternoon light was waning and evening was approaching. A sharp brisk wind edged from the north and buffeted the flags hanging from the wrought iron balconies across the street.

Brandy looked around the room as she accepted the drink. It had a real elegance now, and she was pleased with the effect. The furniture, with its inlaid parquetry and polished wood was expensive. Other than the antique bed and marble-topped chest she had sold Claude in September, his condo remained virtually empty. It would have to be a work in progress now until he was able to build his practice. He had explained to her that initially there would be some lean months. She knew that Claude would not starve. He was the beneficiary of a large trust fund, and his future was secure, whether or not he worked. But, she admired the fact that Claude did not rely on his independent wealth and had a very strong work ethic. It was one of the things she admired most about him.

They had begun spending a fair amount of time with each other, time permitting, and their friendship had grown over the past two months. Claude had taken Rene and Brandy sailing twice on his small sailboat in the mild fall afternoons when the temperature hovered in the mid-seventies. They had gone to dinner and a movie a few times, and last week they had even attended a casual party together. Every Wednesday night, Claude ate a late dinner with Ariel, Brandy and Rene. It really pleased Brandy that Rene and Ariel were so fond of Claude. Initially, she had been concerned that Rene would find Claude's presence threatening after losing her father. Much to her surprise, he seemed to fill some void in Rene. Brandy decided that the child could probably sense that they were only friends and that there was no romantic involvement. She had learned that children were very intuitive about these things and that an involvement of that nature would have been impossible to disguise from Rene.

The two of them had reached an understanding early on that their relationship was strictly platonic. Although Brandy enjoyed spending time with Claude and found him enormously attractive, she was not ready for a relationship or another deep emotional commitment that she sensed Claude would want. Commitment meant the possibility of loss, and she was still protecting herself from the pain of losing Harris. Then there were the ethical considerations arising out of the fact that Claude was now one of her attorneys. He had explained to her that the American Bar Association had adopted rules prohibiting either a romantic or sexual relationship with a client. Brandy was relieved about this because her relationship with Claude was now safe.

Brandy suspected that Claude saw other women, and it was a relief to her. Friendship was the most fulfilling thing to her now. Claude understood her pain because of his own loss. Sometimes she felt extremely guilty confiding to him about her grief, but he always seemed willing and even eager to listen to her feelings. Their friendship had seemed to take away a lot of the loneliness she had felt after Harris's death and helped her move forward.

Claude handed her a legal document after she sat in one of the chairs across from him. "It is the answer filed by Thad and Recov to our motion to intervene in the Virgin Islands action."

She reviewed the documents with the Virgin Islands caption with interest. It was all fairly complex legal jargon, but she understood the general drift. Brandy's pleading had alleged that she as Harris's widow and representative of his estate, had the right to recover a salvage award. Thad and Recov claimed that they—and not Harris—had located BYZANTIUM and recovered cargo and part of the vessel while Harris was alive. Thad and Recov denied that Brandy was entitled to recover any award for the salvage operation.

Brandy set the papers on his desk, feeling a deep disappointment in the pit of her stomach. "So, they did not respond to our demand?" She had harbored a very childish hope that the matter would be resolved outside of court. All she wanted was a fair settlement. Nothing more.

"The attorney for Thad and Recov sent us this letter, so they currently are not interested in settlement. They are seeking the entire Recovery. I think one of the motivations is that Recov's predecessor was on very hard financial times a few years ago. The company was discharged in Chapter 7 under the Bankruptcy Code and ultimately the corporation was dissolved. The major shareholders formed Recov, which has never really been very successful because of the economic crisis. The treasure salvage business is expensive, time-consuming, and the rewards are few and far between. Chris and I, along with our team, will need to fight hard initially."

He gave her a two-page letter on legal stationary. Thad and Recov had hired a prominent and very large law firm in Miami to represent their interests. "I have not had a chance to show it to you since it came in Friday, although my secretary mailed you a copy that afternoon. I am sure that you will receive your copy in the mail tomorrow. But, we should talk about it now. Given the content of this letter, it is highly unlikely that Thad will want to settle."

The letter from the attorney representing Thad and Recov was very brief: "We understand that as a grieving widow, Mrs. Blake is bitterly disappointed that her husband's efforts in locating *BYZANTIUM* were unsuccessful. While it is true that Mrs. Blake chartered a small vessel to Thad Stuart in October of last year, this vessel was never used thereafter by either Mr. Stuart or to Recov in the salvage operation. The business arrangement between Mr. Blake and our clients dissolved long before his tragic death. Mr. Blake declined Recov's invitation to form a partnership before his death. Recov, a world-renowned international salvor, utilized some of the most sophisticated salvage equipment available to date to locate to *BYZANTIUM.* All of this equipment was exclusively the property of Recov. While Mr. Stuart and Mr. Jennings, the president of Recov, are sympathetic to Mrs. Blake's loss, they do not have any duty to pay her any portion of a salvage award. Moreover, the emeralds in her possession were stolen by Harris Blake. She has no right to possession of any of the emeralds, and we request that she return them promptly. Please be advised that we are in contact with the FBI about the stolen emeralds and will be in talks with the United States Attorney. We will vigorously oppose Mrs. Blake's motion to intervene. We also will be filing a motion to dismiss the groundless lawsuit she filed in federal court in New Orleans. Moreover, if you and Mrs. Blake persist in this groundless claim, we will seek all remedies available to our clients pursuant to Rule 11, including but not limited to, sanctions and attorneys' fees."

She felt her face flush a deep rose, and her heart pounded wildly in her chest. Angrily, Brandy tossed the letter over to Claude. "Groundless? Those bastards!" she cried bitterly, getting up from her chair and walking over to the casement window. I bought the boat strictly for the salvage operation. Thad was on the boat as much as Harris. Of course I did not steal the emeralds! We have proof that Harris found the cargo and the boat."

Hot tears spilled onto her cheeks and burned her throat. How dare Thad treat her like this. He had been like a member of the family. He had betrayed her and Harris. The bastard!

Claude returned the letter to the out basket and shuffled the pleadings he intended to file in the lawsuit, giving her a minute to regain her control.

"I am sorry that the letter upset you Brandy, but ethically, I have to share the communications from the other side. Most of this letter is petty blustering to assert a bad legal position. He is just representing his clients, and he is attempting to use intimidating litigation tactics which are sleazy and unnecessary. Most of the time, hard edged threats are asserted because that party has a lesser bargaining position. You have more emeralds than they have and your investment was substantial."

She wiped her eyes. "Are they threatening me with a criminal prosecution? Harris never stole those emeralds, and Thad knows it."

"Those are just empty threats. I worked for the Justice Department. There is no basis for anyone to prosecute you. We have proof of your investments. Any investigation by the FBI would very quickly focus on Thad and Recov. No United States attorney will touch a case like this. It is a civil dispute and nothing more."

She finally felt composed. "Of course, you are right. There is something about seeing these false and horrible allegations against Harris and me in writing that is so upsetting. How in the world could we ever have believed that Thad was our friend?"

"There is a lot of money involved, Brandy. Real money—not just chump change. As Chris explained to you, you would have a fight on your hands. These people are serious about this and we're in it for the long haul. But there will be many opportunities to settle along the way. I am sure we will have a court ordered mediation, and we may be shuttled off to a federal settlement judge. "

She wiped her face and pulled herself together. She was just being childish. *BYZANTIUM* was one of the most important shipwreck finds to date. She would just make things harder on herself if she assumed that they would just settle the case without a fight. She had to steel herself for this unpleasant thing ahead. That was what Harris would have wanted.

"I guess I just deluded myself into believing that they would settle. I thought that because of our friendship with Thad—."

Claude cut her off. "Large sums of money have gotten in the way of a lot of friendships."

"Alright. What do we need to do at this point?"

He held up the pleadings. "We will serve a set of interrogatories, requests for production of documents and requests for admission. Then we wait for them to respond. It is a long process. You, Chris and our team will probably be working together for some time."

She shook her head. How could Harris have gotten her into this mess? They had everything together—a wonderful life in paradise with a beautiful child. But it was never enough for Harris. And now she was going into war with a large corporation without any guarantee that she would win. "When will you serve the discovery?" she said finally.

"When Chris returns on Wednesday, we will FedEx it down to St. Thomas to our local counsel. This will progress just like all lawsuits. Also, we will be serving them with discovery in the New Orleans suit. Things will be busy for a while."

"I trust you and Chris implicitly. I do not really need to see every pleading or letter if it will upset me. I need to focus on my shop, my daughter, and my life."

"Well, how would you like to handle things?"

"I will call Chris when he returns and explain how I feel. Maybe we could just set up occasional appointments to go through the status. I just do not want the stress of opening the mail and seeing such upsetting documents."

"I understand," he replied. "We need to discuss one more thing. Chris and I believe that we should have the emeralds tested. Ultimately, we will have them compared to any other emeralds obtained from the site. As you know, we have been speaking to an expert in New York who I think we should use and who is trustworthy. We will have to obtain court approval."

She picked up her jacket. "Whatever you think, Claude. The emeralds are our real proof that Harris found *BYZANTIUM.* And to think that Thad wanted to buy them from me for a novelty for the tourists within three days of Harris's death! Now I understand that he believed that without the emeralds, I would never have any proof that Harris found the ship. within. It convinces me that he had something to hide then," she replied angrily.

"Good. I will start on that next week." He flashed his brilliant smile. "Have time to grab a quick bite after all of your hard labor?"

She smiled. Ordinarily, she would have gone, but she had some shopping to do. Christmas was bearing down on them in less than seven weeks. "Let me take a rain check. I need to buy a few things to get started."

He smiled. "Have fun. And don't worry about this case. Everything will be fine."

Grinning, she gave him a playful tap on the arm. "I'm going to hold you to that promise, counselor."

She stopped by Saks on the way home. The Saints were not playing and the usual weekend throngs were visibly absent. The mall was an impressive glass-and-marble structure wedged at the foot of Canal Street. Brandy parked in the garage and shopped for nearly two hours. She bought a lovely dress, nightgown, and silk robe for Granny Ariel. It was a good start. This year, Christmas needed to be special for Rene. She also bought several children's books and some new clothes for Rene. She would wrap everything tonight after everyone else was asleep.

The aroma of hot mulling spices emanated from the kitchen as she arrived home. The nursery had decorated the mantles in the living room and study with unique dried arrangements for Thanksgiving. The Thanksgiving Spode china was stacked on the dining room table that had been decorated elaborately for Thanksgiving. Granny Ariel always had a large gathering of friends for a champagne dinner celebration late on Thanksgiving afternoon. Rene, her reddish hair pulled in a long ponytail, wore a bright green sweater and matching socks. Her face flushed with excitement, she rushed up to her mother.

"Mommy! Look at how beautiful everything is. Look at the beautiful decorations!"

"It is gorgeous," Brandy replied, looking in wonderment at the virtual fairyland. Last year, she had been almost oblivious to the holidays. She had forgotten how beautiful the house was during this season. Granny Ariel made sure that her house was a fairyland for Christmas and Thanksgiving season. Brandy inspected all of the decorations. Chloe lay in the corner with the adolescent squirrel pups, who amused themselves hiding in her enormous coat. Brandy noticed that Chloe had a large green-and orange-bow around her neck.

"Granny is making us mulling cider and hot chocolate for after dinner."

Brandy put her coat into the foyer closet. "Hot chocolate would taste good. It is very cold. The humidity goes right through your clothes."

She found Granny Ariel in the breakfast room stirring the mulling spices. Brandy noticed that Granny Ariel's tablet was on the counter, and the large male squirrel that Granny had named Raleigh, seemed to be inspecting it carefully. Brandy eyed them with curiosity. She had begun to accept the squirrel over the last few weeks. Raleigh and the pups had been vaccinated by the vet, who had assured Brandy and Ariel that the squirrels did not pose any real threat to anyone. Granny obviously loved the little animal, and after she had lost her fear that the squirrel would bite Rene, Brandy had to admit that he was very cute. And he seemed truly attached to Granny and intuitive about her moods.

Brandy kissed Granny Ariel on the cheek and sat across from her. Raleigh gazed at Ariel expectantly and then quietly accepted a wedge of apple from her hand.

"Everything smells divine," Brandy said. "You don't think the squirrel pups will try to jump up on the mantle and knock anything over?"

Granny Ariel laughed. "One already tried this afternoon. Chloe disciplined him soundly and since then, they have all avoided the decorations."

Brandy laughed. "I think Chloe should be in *Guinness World Records.* There could not have been too many times that a Samoyed has adopted a bunch of adolescent squirrels."

"Unlikely, but it is very cute. If I had known Chloe was so maternal, I never would have had her fixed."

"Well, she has her own little brood now. We'll take pictures tonight for our descendants. No one would believe it without them." She stretched. "I am going to take a quick shower and freshen up. See you in about twenty minutes."

Brandy stowed her packages in the bedroom closet until she could wrap them later. She really needed a shower. The large bathroom she shared with Rene had been renovated several times since the house had been constructed in the 1830's, but the ball and claw foot tub had been preserved. Today, white marble tiles covered the floor and a large white marble-and glass-shower had been wedged into the corner next to an elaborately painted Sherle Wagner sink. All of the dentil molding had been painted white and the walls were painted a light gray.

Brandy wrapped her hair in a shower cap and took a hot shower before repairing her light coat of makeup and slipping into a pair of black slacks and aqua sweater. She tried not to think about Harris and the unpleasantness with Thad. Tonight was going to be special.

Refreshed, she grabbed her digital camera and went down to the breakfast room for dinner.

They had a crabmeat dish delivered by the food service Granny Ariel used with a large salad with a generous supply of fresh fruit. The three of them sat by the fire and admired the ornaments, drinking hot spiced cider after dinner. Rene finally fell asleep. Brandy carried her upstairs and tucked her in, while Granny let Chloe and the pups out for the last trip of the evening.

When Brandy returned, Chloe was in her little bed in the laundry room with the pups. Granny Ariel was in the living room with Raleigh, sitting on the sofa. The squirrel had curled up in the skirt folds of Granny's black wool dress, sleeping soundly. Brandy stirred the fire with a poker and then sat on the sofa across from her grandmother, who had poured them each a glass of sherry.

"I thought you could use a little drink to relax after your meeting today with Claude."

"It is unpleasant because I feel we were all betrayed," she replied, sipping the sherry and drawing her stockinged feet underneath her and tucking them behind the silk pillows. "But this was such a wonderful evening. Thank you very much."

"It's me who should be thanking you. Both of you have been such a joy to have around. I am a very lucky old woman with my family and little friends. So many people have nothing in the world. I thank God every day."

"Granny, if it had not been for you, I would have still been moping around in St. Thomas instead of here, carrying on with my life. You have had to take me in twice in my life, and I will never forget it."

Granny Ariel waved her hand. "Nonsense. I just wanted someone young enough to enjoy the holidays. Children like Rene make the holidays."

Brandy smiled. "You are right. I do not want to lose sight of what is important."

They discussed Granny's shelter drive over the next two weeks. Her organization had raised almost $1million this season for the largest homeless shelter in Orleans Parish. Granny had spearheaded a toy drive for the homeless children and a large clothing donation providing decent work clothes for those individuals going out to find a job. It amazed Brandy that her grandmother, at eighty-five, was still so incredibly active and concerned about those less fortunate. Granny had organized a legion of volunteers and carefully delegated many of the tasks to various committees. She was a person who was determined to make a difference.

They also discussed their social commitments and schedules over the next two months of the holiday season. Granny Ariel, still the society matriarch, had a myriad of party and dinner invitations before New Year's Day. Brandy had been included in the invitations to some of the larger parties. Although she would have been content to remain at home with Rene reading by the fire every night, because she knew that it was important to her grandmother to resume her social status, she had agreed to attend. Also, Granny was hosting a large open house on Christmas Eve. They also had plans to attend a performance of the *Nutcracker* the following Sunday afternoon. It would be an incredibly hectic time.

Fortunately, business at the shop had picked up by about 20 percent during the season. Every month, the shop had begun to show a small profit, and Brandy was pleased with the progress. It had also given her a new confidence about abilities that she had not even known she possessed. She was surviving and enjoying life beyond her marriage with Harris, despite how impossible that had once seemed.

“How was Claude today?” Granny asked as she placed her empty sherry glass on the coffee table in front of her, taking great care not to disturb the sleeping squirrel in her lap.

Brandy described his new office and the pieces she had sold him. Granny Ariel admired Claude and enjoyed his visits immensely. Brandy knew that she was pleased that she and Claude had renewed their friendship.

“It is perfectly healthy and natural for a beautiful woman like you to have male friends,” Granny assured her. “It does not mean that you have to get married or that you take things to the next level. You should just enjoy the moment.”

“As long as he represents me, there could never be a romantic relationship,” she replied. “I do not want to do anything to jeopardize his career. I just want the companionship. Nothing more.”

Granny Ariel patted her on the arm. “I think that is perfect for now. There will ultimately be someone else. You will see.”

“Or not. I may never be ready.”

Granny Ariel smiled. “Life does a lot of strange things. Only time will tell.”

Inevitably, the conversation turned to *BYZANTIUM*, Thad, Recov, and Harris. Brandy related the events of the morning, describing the letter from Thad’s attorney. She fought the urge to cry, not wanting to distress her grandmother. Ariel listened quietly.

“I am glad that you are going to fight them. It is what Harris would have wanted. And money like that is worth fighting for. You sunk a fortune into Harris’s dream. And now, you should be entitled to get it back, with interest.”

"I guess I wanted to believe that they would just settle. I did not want it to go this far. I just hope I have enough spunk to do it."

"Honey, they will fight you until they don't have any choice. If anyone can do it, I think you, Chris Banks, and Claude can win. I am counting on it."

Granny Ariel was quiet for a moment as she watched the squirrel stir, yawn, and sit up on the sofa. Granny stroked him behind the ears softly before she got up and came over beside her granddaughter. She leaned over and patted Brandy's hand. "Good night, angel. Remember that you are a fighter. Now, go up and get some rest. Tomorrow is a work day." She kissed Brandy on her forehead.

Brandy yawned. She had not realized it, but she was very tired. "I think you should get some rest too, Granny."

Granny smiled, putting her hands on her hips. "Brandy, I am an old woman. We never really sleep. One day, you'll find that out, I suppose. That is why I have my little friend here to entertain me. We'll put the glasses away and get the lights. See you in the morning."

Brandy gave her another hug. "Night, Granny. It was a wonderful evening."

"Say your prayers. You're never too old."

Brandy watched her carry the sherry glasses toward the kitchen, followed by the little squirrel. Brandy stretched again, checked the fire, and went upstairs. Before she fell asleep, she remembered her grandmother's admonition. For the first time in almost a year, she said a silent prayer of thanks.

Chapter XII

Ewan spent Thanksgiving with a young brunette in her small apartment a few blocks off Louisiana Avenue. He had met Lola when she waited on his table in a diner on Prytania Street. She was a workout fanatic and spent a minimum of an hour and a half at the gym every afternoon after work. Lola was not really even pretty, but she was thin and in good shape. She had a salty vocabulary and never took anything too seriously. Ewan had taken Lola to dinner in a bistro not far from Lee Circle one evening. He made it a point never to see a woman more than two or three times. He knew that Thad would be angry that he was making even casual acquaintances, but Ewan was lonely and decided not to deprive himself of companionship.

He had been surprised, but pleased, when Lola had asked him to Thanksgiving dinner as they finished their meal. At least he would not have to spend the day alone at home. Ewan had always hated the holidays. His family had been poor, and their meager attempt to celebrate the holidays had always reminded him of how little they had. Later, when they had lost their home, Thanksgiving had been spent in a food line at the Salvation Army. It had been his only hot meal in a month. During his service in the Marine Corps and later when he lived in St. Thomas, he never really celebrated the holidays. He had no family. To him, Thanksgiving was just another day.

He arrived at Lola's small apartment at about two carrying three cheap bottles of wine and a flimsy bouquet of flowers he had bought at the grocery store the night before. The air was unseasonably humid and a soft rain began to fall as he parked his Toyota.

Lola had invited two other waitresses from the diner to the small celebration. The two women worked with her in the small galley kitchen. The pervasive scent of poultry spices, thyme, and sage filled the small apartment. The central room was clean and tidy with a long sofa and small table covered with a patterned gold tablecloth. Lola was delighted to get the flowers and wine. She introduced Ewan to her friends, Kirsten and Sally.

The three of them drank wine and played cards as the fragrant turkey continued to roast. They had opened the third bottle of wine by the time dinner was ready. Kirsten expertly carved the turkey and brought a large platter to the table. The meal was delicious, with cornbread dressing, fresh green beans and pecans, sweet potato casserole with marshmallows, cranberry sauce and pecan pie with praline ice cream. It was the best Thanksgiving dinner Ewan had ever had in his life.

He helped the three women clean up the kitchen after dinner. Afterward, they watched a chick flick on Lola's small LCD flat-screen television. Bored with the plot and satiated from dinner, Ewan snored softly on the sofa.

Kirsten and Sally left shortly after eight. By nine, Ewan and Lola made a small plate of leftover turkey and dressing to share and bowls of ice cream.

"This ice cream is good," he told her. It had a nutty, sugary taste.

"It is my favorite," Lola told him. "But tomorrow, I need to hit the gym tomorrow for two hours after this. I don't want to be fat like my momma."

"Is she heavy?" Evan asked absently, still enjoying every spoonful of the decadent ice cream.

"Like a house. I don't want to be like that. I want something different."

"As much as you work out, I don't think it will be a problem."

"Well, there is more than just her weight. She's fat and ignorant and an alcoholic. I am going to make something of myself," she announced with conviction. "I am going to college at night school at UNO. It's a real school—not just one of those online universities. I have finished two years and have three more to go. I am going to be a nurse. I just work at the diner to pay for my expenses. I am going to get another job after the holidays so I can save up and go full-time."

Ewan was continually surprised by Lola. He had never even considered college. Higher education had been a mystery to him. Of course, his options had been limited. His family had barely had enough money to survive.

"That sounds good. Whatever makes you happy," he told her.

"I am going to be something and not just a waitress. I am going to do it myself."

He smiled, put his ice cream dish down on the coffee table, and gave Lola a deep kiss. He decided that he would stay another hour or two and enjoy her company. But he resolved that it would be the last time he would see her. He had misjudged Lola. He had believed that she was a free spirit. Instead, she was a planner. He had learned the hard way that women who were planners always had a long term agenda for a commitment. He was not interested in anything but casual entertainment. He had a job to do and needed to be reasonably anonymous.

He left after eleven with promises to call Lola in a day or two. He was relieved that he had never brought her to his apartment or given her his cell number. It would be easy enough to avoid her. All that would be necessary would be to avoid the diner where she worked.

Traffic was nearly nonexistent as he drove back to his apartment on Euterpe. He tossed his clothes in the hamper, slipped on an old tee shirt, and flipped on the TV. Within five minutes, the throw away cell phone rang displaying Thad's telephone number. He noticed that the phone showed that he had missed four telephone calls from Thad since he had been at Lola's apartment.

It was two hours later in the Virgin Islands—the middle of the night. Thad had obviously been drinking heavily, and his speech was slurred. He was clearly irritated that he had not been able to reach Ewan.

"I have been trying to reach you all day. Where the hell were you?"

"Down in the French Quarter getting a bite to eat." Ewan easily evaded the remainder of Thad's questions about his whereabouts for the day and waited patiently for Thad to get to the point.

"I pay you to be available. Unless I call when you are at work, answer the goddamn phone."

"I took a long nap this afternoon. Sorry I missed you."

Thad seemed slightly mollified by Ewan's halfhearted apology.

"The widow is causing me too many problems. I am going to need your help. It is finally time for you to pay your keep."

"Is there a plan?"

"I am going to make that bitch regret the day she ever crossed me. She is costing me a fortune in legal fees. She has an Achilles' heel like everyone else, and I know what it is. She will do anything to protect that kid."

"What does that have to do with me?"

"You—asshole—are going to kidnap that kid. That will force the bitch to drop the lawsuits and settle for a pittance."

Ewan listened in stunned silence. Killing Harris Blake had been easy enough. He had simply altered the Nitrox, and it had been easy money. There had been nothing to connect him to Blake's death. He had not been required to touch Harris physically. Sometimes he could actually convince himself that it had not really been his fault that the diver had been killed. Ewan had always been good at self-deception. Hurting a kid was another matter. Kidnapping a kid might be a federal crime, and the last thing he needed was the FBI on his tail. Ewan would be taking a huge risk. Thad had suddenly raised the stakes. But Ewan had to be practical. Thad would have to pay Ewan handsomely to kidnap a little girl. He would need to plan everything meticulously so he would not get caught. He promised himself that he would not hurt the kid. It was a good thing that he had never really spoken with the widow's family. After the job was done, Ewan could leave the country and change identities. He had heard great things about the Philippines, with its beautiful beaches and willing underage women. A man could live like a king in the Philippines. With enough money, he would be set for life.

He had been reluctant to raise the subject of more money over the past three weeks. But now, he had the upper hand. If Thad wanted him to kidnap the widow's kid, he had to pay handsomely for it.

The dream was even closer than he imagined.

Finally Ewan spoke. "Thad, that's a big fucking deal. We need to talk about money. What you are paying me is not nearly enough for me to take a risk like that."

Thad's voice had an angry edge. "How much?"

Ewan chose his words carefully. He did not want to make Thad angry. "Thad, you are going to be a multimillionaire with the lawsuit. If I were caught, chances are that I would go to prison for the rest of my life. I won't take a risk like this for less than three million. Afterward, I will need to leave the country and I need to have enough to last me the rest of my life."

Ewan waited for Thad's response in the uncomfortable silence. Finally after nearly a minute he responded.

Thad sighed audibly. "Alright asshole. Start making plans," he barked as he disconnected the phone.

~

Massenet was extremely busy after Thanksgiving. Brandy had decorated the shop with a flocked tree covered in antique and crystal ornaments, and garlands of gold and silver artificial flowers were draped over the windows. Several poinsettias were strategically placed in several large urns. Granny Ariel helped her organize a large eggnog and wine open house one Sunday afternoon in the shop two weeks before Christmas. Much to Brandy's surprise, nearly one hundred customers came by over the course of four hours, and she made several significant sales. A woman from Michigan visiting New Orleans relatives purchased all of the Christmas ornaments on the tree. Brandy promised to ship them to her at her home in Michigan after New Year's Day.

Fortunately, the lawsuits had required very little of her attention during the holiday season. She had two long conversations with Chris about upcoming strategy. All parties had served written discovery on other parties, although by agreement, the responses were not due until the third week of January.

"Things slow down over the holidays," Chris told her. "Lawyers are like anyone else. They need downtime and there is no reason for everyone not to cooperate during the holidays."

Brandy had been relieved. She wanted to enjoy this time with her daughter and grandmother. The Christmas season was her favorite time of year, and she wanted the holidays to be memorable. After losing Harris, she was all too aware that anything could happen in life. Granny Ariel was in good health, but she was unquestionably getting older. Brandy resolved to live every day as if it were her last. She wanted no more regrets.

Christmas Eve was cold and windy with afternoon temperatures in the mid-thirties. The house had been transformed with Christmas splendor. A twelve-foot tree graced the elegant foyer of the old house. Equally magnificent trees adorned with elegant ornaments and garlands were placed in the living room and study. Garlands, crystal ornaments, and fresh flowers adorned all of the gracious archways and surfaces of the house. Antique stockings hung from the mantle over a roaring fire. It was a whimsical, spectacular Christmas display.

Granny Ariel hosted a formal catered buffet dinner and champagne reception for forty people early that evening. The squirrels and Chloe were banished into the pantry and laundry room area for the evening with a plate of hard corn, sliced apples, and pears.

Brandy thought Rene looked beautiful in her new green velvet dress with the lace collar which Brandy had ordered from Neiman Marcus. Brandy wore a simple black silk sheath with pearls. Claude had told her that she looked like a Madonna. In keeping with family tradition, everyone was allowed to open one present before the guests arrived. Rene squealed with delight as she opened the complete set of the Harry Potter series and a new electronic reader. Granny Ariel loved the red satin robe Brandy had bought for her a few weeks ago. Claude gave Brandy a lovely green scarf and a complex fresh water pearl ponytail cover. He was pleased with the antique maritime print she gave him.

After the guests left, Claude stayed to help Ariel and Brandy put out the Santa Claus presents for Rene. They stacked the gifts near the sofa by the tree. Brandy had selected several video games, a new bicycle, a Minnie Mouse telephone, in-line skates, CDs, and a new tablet and computer. Ariel went upstairs after they finished.

Claude surveyed the pile of gifts and laughed. "You are spoiling this child rotten, you know. Not that she doesn't deserve it. She is a great kid."

Brandy put her hand to her throat in mock horror. "Oh, certainly you don't think I am spoiling her, Mr. Parker. Let's get this straight. Santa Claus is the frivolous one here. She is just getting the boring stuff from her mother—pajamas, jeans, a sweater and a new computer and tablet she can use for school. Although some of her kindergarten friends already have a cell phone, I resisted the urge to buy one for Rene."

"You are right. That sounds completely boring," he laughed, nibbling at one of the cookies left for Santa Claus. "Well, I think Santa is on the right track here."

Brandy sat on the sofa and finished her glass of champagne. "I admit, I went a little over the top. But last year I was so devastated, that I barely even remember Christmas. I wanted to make it up to Rene—to give her the best Christmas imaginable this year."

He sat down across from her. "I think you have succeeded. How well I remember the first Christmas after Connie died. I went down to the office and wrote a brief. That was my way of ignoring the holiday and trying to forget about all the memories. It was two years before I could bring myself to even celebrate Christmas without her."

Brandy leaned over and squeezed his arm. "Do you think about getting married again and maybe having a couple of kids? I can see you with kids. You are such a big kid yourself."

He looked at her rather strangely, and she was immediately sorry that she had brought the subject up. It was innocent enough, but she knew that he might have construed it as a not-so-subtle invitation to become involved with her after the suit was over. On the other hand, he might decide that she was being just plain nosy. They never really discussed his romantic life, and that was fine with her. She knew intuitively that a man as handsome and successful as Claude must have a string of admirers.

She held up her hand, feeling her face flush. "I'm sorry Claude. I am not trying to pry, really, and I am not trying to drop any hints or come on to you. It was a natural question from a friend—really," she said before he could answer.

He grinned. "I am not offended. My mother asks me the same question day after day and year after year. I am sure tomorrow that I will be barraged with the same litany. She wants grandchildren, and she feels that I am letting her down on that score so far."

"So, what do you tell her?"

"That no decent, self-respecting woman, would ever have me. And I know that she would not want me consorting with riffraff."

"Touché."

"It doesn't always work. She always wants to introduce me to some airhead or fix me up with a friend's homely daughter."

"Well, if you ever decide to take the plunge, you will find out what an incredibly rewarding experience it is. Rene is really my whole life."

"And she is a lucky kid to have such a devoted mother," he said rather pensively.

He drained his champagne glass and checked his watch. "God, it's after midnight. Technically, it is Christmas morning, and Rene will be up with the chickens."

"Yes, and there are so many chickens in Uptown New Orleans."

"With the park geese then and your brood of squirrels," he laughed.

"Oh, yes, the squirrels. They are literally taking over. Granny Ariel, Rene, and Chloe dote on them. I have to admit that at first, I was concerned about rabies and other diseases. But they have all been inspected and vaccinated by the vet. And, they are very cute. It is a rare thing to have a relationship with a wild animal."

She walked him to the door.

"Don't forget about the New Year's Eve party. I'll pick you up at eight for dinner."

He was referring to the large soiree at the Orleans Club and dinner at Commander's Palace. It promised to be a wonderful evening. She smiled. "I wouldn't miss it."

He leaned over and kissed her lightly on the cheek. "Merry Christmas, Mrs. Santa. Have a great day with the toys."

She felt a warm glow wash over her as she watched him walk toward his car. For a fleeting instant, she realized that Christmas Eve had never been so perfect when Harris was alive. He was always preoccupied with the next dive searching for BYZANTIUM. Quickly, she dismissed the dull ache as she locked the front door. Then she turned off the Christmas tree, rinsed out the champagne glasses, and went to bed. Tomorrow would be a big day.

Rene woke her a few minutes before six. It was still pitch-dark outside. Groggily, Brandy pulled on her robe and followed her little girl downstairs. Granny Ariel was already having tea in the kitchen with Raleigh while Chloe and the pups ate breakfast. Brandy grabbed a coffee pod and made herself a strong cup of Italian coffee.

Granny Ariel had already turned on the Christmas tree and had dumped out the glass of milk for Santa resting on the coffee table. Rene ran over and inspected each new gift as Brandy sipped her coffee on the sofa. For some reason that she could not understand, Rene seemed particularly enthralled with the tablet. When Rene had picked up the new electronic tablet, she observed a momentary knowing glance exchanged between the child and Granny Ariel. Of course, she decided, Granny loved her tablet, and she had noticed lately that she and Rene had been with it frequently.

She was thrilled to hear Rene exclaim: "Santa knew just what I wanted!"

"I think it had something to do with the letter you wrote him," she said, wondering how much longer the child would believe in Santa.

"Of course, I forgot! But he got me everything on my list. Nobody ever gets everything on their list!"

"Well, it's probably because you are such a sweet girl," she assured her. "And that pays off in the end," she laughed, stealing a conspiratorial smirk at her grandmother.

After breakfast, they dressed and opened the gifts under the tree before church. Brandy surprised Granny Ariel with an antique doll canopy bed for her pet squirrel. The bed was constructed from polished mahogany and was fitted with a down pillow for a mattress with a chintz coverlet and canopy. She also found a new cedar-lined basket for the pups and a larger matching size for Chloe.

"I hope that they will use these. Since they are practically living inside now, I thought they would need a proper bed—especially Raleigh."

Ariel's eyes shined with happiness. "Honey, thank you very much. It is just perfect."

"I got the chintz because I thought we could wash it from time to time. I found this from a dealer in Atlanta, and I was afraid that it would not come before Christmas. I hope he likes it."

"He will love it," her grandmother assured her.

She noticed that Rene was particularly excited about the laptop computer. She had explained to Rene about email. The child could email her friends, her mother at the shop, or on her cell phone. "That way, during the day, I will always be close by," she had explained.

The software, including the latest version from Microsoft, had already been installed. Brandy watched as her daughter play with the mouse with Raleigh on her lap. She seemed to be explaining the computer operation to the squirrel. “See, we use these in school,” she said, pretending to demonstrate each function to the squirrel and encouraging him to touch the mouse and keys.

Brandy laughed, marveling at the imagination of a child. “I don’t think you can teach a squirrel to use the computer.”

Rene started and looked guiltily at her mother. “We are just playing school, Mommy. Raleigh won’t hurt anything. He is just curious.”

“I remember you playing school as a little girl,” Ariel said, her eyes misting over. “Once, you and one of your friends rearranged all of the furniture in your grandfather’s study to resemble a classroom.”

Brandy smiled remembering the hours as a child that she had played school with her little friends. She chided herself for saying anything. It was completely harmless, and the squirrel was incredibly cooperative. She did not want to do anything to make the child self-conscious.

She leaned over and gave her daughter a hug. “You and Raleigh can play school as much as you want. He almost seems to comprehend what you are telling him. It is funny that a wild animal will sit here and tolerate that.”

“He is really special, Mommy. He knows everything.”

“Good. Then you will have to give him all “A’s”, she replied. “But you need to call a recess for a while, because we need to go to church soon and out to dinner.”

She checked her makeup and exchanged her flat-heeled slippers for black suede low heels, matching her bright green suede dress and scarf. The ensemble contrasted beautifully with her red hair and blue eyes. She wore the pearl hair cover Claude had selected for her. Grabbing jackets for herself and Rene, she went downstairs.

The three of them went to a late church service and then over to dinner with Ariel's nephew, Richard Etienne, his wife, children and grandchildren. Richard and his wife lived in an imposing stone structure on First Street in the Garden District. The house, which was listed on the *National Register of Historic Places*, had been lovingly restored, and was elaborately decorated for the holidays. Fortuitously, several of Richard's grandchildren were close to Rene's age, and she was immediately entertained. They ate a scrumptious dinner in the grand dining room that had a capacity for twenty people. Afterwards, the adults drank champagne and visited in the living room while the children went upstairs to play with their new toys.

It was nearly eight when they returned home. "Are you hungry? There is a pot of shrimp Creole, and there are plenty of cookies and petit fours left from last night," Granny Ariel asked.

Brandy patted her stomach. "I couldn't eat another thing. I will have to diet for six months after these holidays."

"Alright then. Why don't we read the first chapter of the Harry Potter series?" She flipped on the rear light and let Chloe and the pups out for their last romp. Since the yard was so well lit at night, she did not think there was much danger of a predator taking one of the pups away—at least with Chloe around to protect them.

"Sounds great. I think I will change first."

Brandy and Rene went upstairs and changed. A mild front had come through during the afternoon, chilling the air into the low twenties. Brandy lit the fire in the living room, burning up the wrapping paper along with the logs. They returned to sit in the room with the big tree; drinking hot spiced apple cider and taking turns reading aloud. She carried Rene upstairs after she fell asleep and tried to organize the toys in the living room.

Granny had placed the canopy bed on top of a marble-topped chest in her room. When Brandy had gone in to wish her grandmother good night, the squirrel was sitting on the bed watching Granny Ariel as she hung up her clothes.

Claude called to wish her a Merry Christmas after she washed her face. He told her about the day with the family. He and his brother had gone sailing for an hour or two in the afternoon during a blustering wind. She promised to call him later in the week to discuss her case.

She climbed into bed, relieved to have some time to herself. She opened the shopping icon on the new Kindle that Granny Ariel had given her for Christmas and downloaded a popular novel. Satisfied and content, she settled into read.

Chapter XIII

Strains of the lively tune played by the Dixieland jazz band floated from the Orleans Club as Claude and Brandy strolled down the block to the car. The warm mist shrouded the iron streetlights, forming a soft corona. She adjusted the green tulle shawl that perfectly matched her emerald satin gown studded with rhinestones. The air was mild again and she had not bothered with a coat.

"It is hard to believe that last year is over," she said dreamily.

"And we are advancing into yet another year into the twenty-first century," he said, taking her arm. "Just think. One day, you will be able to tell Rene's kids that you were actually born in the Twentieth Century."

"No doubt, they will think I am as old as the dinosaurs."

"Oh no. They won't believe for a second that you are older than the last Ice Age."

"Now that is the kind of compliment a girl lives for," she laughed, standing back for him to open the passenger door of his sedan.

"Feeling up to making an appearance at one more party," he asked her after shutting the driver's door.

"God, you're a party animal," she laughed. They had been to three parties that evening and she was exhausted.

"It's only twelve thirty. What happened to the old Brandy who was never too tired to go to another party?"

"She grew up and has a child. And she is getting older—maybe not as old as the Ice Age as you implied, but she has responsibilities now. And I feel tired and haggard."

"Just a quick drink at a friend's house," he replied, cranking the engine. "Besides, you look beautiful. "

"Well, at least you are trying to atone for the Ice Age compliment."

"It's true. I have been the envy of every man we have seen tonight. Anyway, I need to put in a brief appearance now that I am working at Boudreaux Banks."

She knew it would be unreasonable to refuse. Mike was one of the senior partners at Boudreaux Banks. Rene was safely at home with Granny Ariel. No doubt, they had spent the evening playing computer games and reading Harry Potter. Besides, it was New Year's Eve, and she was still enjoying the fabulous dress she had found at the after-Christmas sale at Saks. It set off her red hair perfectly and was beautiful with the elegant emerald-and-diamond necklace and bracelet belonging to Granny Ariel. She rarely wore the lovely pieces anymore and had insisted that Brandy wear them that evening. "The pieces are gorgeous with your dress. Anyway, they will be yours one day, and you might as well enjoy them while you are young and beautiful," she had told her. Because she knew that it meant so much to her grandmother, she had agreed to wear the jewelry. Wearing something so extravagant and expensive, however, had made her slightly nervous. The jewelry was worth more than most people earned in a year.

She held up her finger. "One drink and then I turn into a pumpkin."

"It's a deal. A quick glass of champagne, and we will call it a night," he grinned, heading the car toward the University area.

Mike Reynaud and his wife, Maureen, lived in a lovely Greek revival house three blocks from Freret on State Street. Maureen was from a prominent old family, and the house had been a wedding present from her parents. It had been beautifully restored with a fabulous kitchen, palatial baths, and a gleaming marble foyer and staircase. Despite the late hour, the house was packed with revelers welcoming in the New Year.

Mike Reynaud gazed at Brandy appreciatively as he shook her hand. "Welcome and Happy New Year to you both," he said warmly.

Mike was in his late forties. Despite his graying temples, he still held his boyish good looks. He had been a poor boy, who, through scholarships, had managed to acquire a law school education and marry into one of New Orleans's finest families. Maureen, mousy and graying, greeted them with her usual vivacious manner.

"I have been meaning to come by your shop," Maureen assured Brandy. "Everyone says it is simply wonderful! I don't shop much anymore, though. The kids keep me running all of the time."

"I would love to have you come by sometime," Brandy told her. She looked around the room, admiring all of Maureen's beautiful antiques. "You have really beautiful things. This room is exquisite," she told her.

"Thank you," she replied dismissively. "I really love what you did with Claude's office. He is completely smitten with you," she whispered conspiratorially. "I have known him since he first worked with

Mike at the D'Argent firm, and he had women chasing him all the time. I don't think he ever really noticed any of them."

Maureen's assumptions that Brandy was just another one of Claude's countless girlfriends made her feel awkward and angry. Coming to the party with him obviously had been a mistake. If things had been different, she could easily have fallen in love with Claude. He was certainly charming and handsome—even more so than Harris. And they had such fun together. But, she was not going to let it go further because she did not want the pain of another loss.

"We're old friends from high school. He was two years ahead of me in school. Besides, he is my lawyer, and this is strictly platonic. I am a client of the firm, and Claude is representing me now in a case. And I think the fact that we both lost our spouses has given us a real bond." She paused, shoving her hair back from her face, deciding that she had sounded too defensive. "Harris, my husband, was killed about fourteen and a half months ago. We have a little girl who is six now. I think it will be quite a while before I can think about anything other than friendship."

Maureen looked slightly embarrassed but recovered easily. She placed her hand over Brandy's, looking at her sympathetically. "I am very sorry about your loss. I can't begin to imagine how difficult that must be. But Claude does seem very fond of you. It's probably the long friendship that makes him appear so comfortable with you," she smiled sweetly.

Maureen artfully steered the conversation away from the Claude, discussing Granny Ariel's fundraising, the upcoming carnival season, and the vacation she and Mike planned to take to Antarctica in February. Before Maureen moved on to mingle with her other guests, she promised to drop by Massenet's one day soon.

Brandy chatted with several people she knew before locating Claude in the living room, cornered by two blonde women who were beautiful enough to have been models. He immediately made eye contact with Brandy and excused himself to rejoin Brandy. The women looked deeply disappointed as they watched him walk away.

"I hated to tear you away from the representatives of the Ford Modeling Agency, but it's nearly 2:00 a.m., and I need to call it a night," she told him.

"I thought you would never come and rescue me," he replied with mock helplessness.

"You didn't exactly look as if you needed rescuing," she quipped.

He rolled his eyes. "At one time, I would have agreed with you—when I was very young or after Connie's death when I was trying to avoid my pain with a lot of empty relationships. Women like that bore me silly now."

She laughed. "You did look terribly bored. Lucky I was here to pull you away. It is my first act of heroism of the year."

"You are much more beautiful than either of them," he assured her.

"Good answer."

He grinned and gave her a tight squeeze as they made their way through the dwindling crowd and out to the car. It was a short drive back to Granny Ariel's house. The beveled glass on the side-lights and transom glistened like diamonds from the chandeliers in the foyer. When Claude walked her to the door, they noticed that several of the beveled panes had been smashed and lay in shards on the stone porch. Claude shoved them away from the door with his shoe.

"Do you think it was an attempted break-in?" Brandy asked him, suddenly afraid.

He examined the hole, which was about five inches across. "No, because it is on the opposite side from the door knob. I think it is just a kid's prank." He touched the small half-brick lying near a planter. "This was probably the culprit."

She surveyed the damage. No doubt, he was right. The sidelight nearest the door had not been touched. Anyway, it would have been difficult for someone to break in through the front. The door had a dead-bolt that could only be opened from the inside with a key. The sidelights were too narrow to allow someone to pass through. They left the light on every night, which would certainly deter a burglar. Claude was right. It was probably just the work of a bunch of bored kids. The repair would be expensive, though.

"Oh, I am sure you are right. I will let Granny know tomorrow, and we will get it fixed after the holiday."

She opened the door with her key. Afterward, Claude gave her a quick kiss on the cheek.

"Happy New Year. I had a wonderful time tonight."

She smiled. "Me too. Happy New Year."

She went upstairs after locking the door to check on Rene. The child lay sleeping soundly in her room. She could see Chloe's silver fur in the night-light. The dog snored softly as she lay on her side on the cool bathroom floor. A light shone from under Granny Ariel's door. Brandy tapped lightly before opening it. Granny was propped up in bed. The iPad was on a tray opened to an electronic Scrabble game, and Raleigh sat beside her on the comforter, his luxurious tail curled over his back. Both of them looked alert. She had a fleeting thought it was rather strange that her grandmother was always playing this word game by herself. Brandy felt slightly guilty that it was so late. Obviously, Granny Ariel was waiting up for her.

"Hi, Granny," she said, coming over and sitting on the antique rocker near the bed. "Happy New Year."

"Happy New Year, darling. You look all flushed, beautiful, and happy. Tell me all about this evening."

She slipped off her heels and told her about the evening. While she talked, the squirrel hopped off Ariel's comforter and sprang up to his canopy bed, curling up to go to sleep.

Brandy looked over at the little animal, with his tail wrapped around him. "Does he bother you at night scurrying around the room?" she asked her grandmother.

"Oh no. He usually sleeps through the night, and he gets up early in the morning when I want to drink my tea. The bed is a perfect gift Brandy—really."

She really wasn't sure that it was such a good idea for her grandmother to keep a squirrel in the bedroom, but it was probably harmless. She had been concerned at first that the squirrel would be destructive. But actually, he had proven to be the perfect little houseguest. It was truly remarkable. She was glad to see that Raleigh actually used the little doll bed instead of sleeping in the closet.

She kissed her grandmother good night. "I am glad you like the bed. I am going to call it a night."

Before she left, she put the jewelry away in its case and locked it in the safe in her grandmother's bedroom. As she hung up her dress, washed her face, and changed for bed, she realized that she had forgotten to tell her grandmother about the broken sidelight.

~

Late the following afternoon, Brandy and Claude took Rene to the Sugar Bowl at the Superdome. It was Rene's first football game. One of Claude's friends had invited them to his private box on the fifty-yard line. It had its own private bath, a small reception room with a closed circuit TV, and a balcony with private seating. The catered food served at halftime was simple—jambalaya, shrimp Creole, gumbo, salad, French bread, and pecan pie.

Rene sat between Claude and Brandy on the front row of the balcony. Claude patiently explained each play to the child. Engrossed with the spectacle before her, she concentrated on the game. She was fascinated by the size of the dome and the thrill of the crowds.

"I think she is a real fan," Claude whispered as Rene cheered for her favorite team.

Brandy smiled, never really caring for football. Harris had never really cared for the game either. Living in the Virgin Islands had put them strangely out of touch with these things. "Looks like she is hooked," she agreed.

Brandy bought Rene both team pennants and a cap from the concession stand before they left.

"It was wonderful, Mommy. Can we come again next year? She asked.

Brandy picked up Rene and swung her around, as she had when the girl was much younger. She suddenly realized that Rene was much heavier. She was growing up. "Maybe so, Rene. We'll see."

The child beamed. "We'll see means probably," she told Claude on the way back to the car. "So, we should just plan on it."

"She has good advocacy skills already. She may want to consider law as a profession," he said to Brandy.

She smiled, not sure that she really liked the idea of her daughter working as a lawyer. Most of the women in Claude's office seemed to work harder than the men, looking tired and haggard, more often than not. The legal profession to her connoted conflict, and given her limited experience with the lawsuit, she was not sure that it was such a pleasant profession. "Well, she is only in kindergarten, but who knows? She only has another sixteen years or so to decide."

"I'll just have to start encouraging her then," he replied.

Claude did not come in when he dropped Rene and Brandy at home. Brandy had taped the sidelight earlier with cardboard and tape until the glazier could come later in the week. Tomorrow was a school day and she helped Rene with her bath. Then they ate a snack with Granny Ariel before reading another chapter of Harry Potter. Exhausted, she and Rene were in bed by nine thirty.

Rene was happy to see her old friends when Brandy dropped her at school early the next morning. Afterward, Brandy drove to Massenet. Her assistant Yvette had found another job at Macy's and Brandy had been forced to replace her. Natalie was a college student interested in becoming an interior decorator. Natalie had been a huge help over the holidays, working full time to earn extra income to pay for her tuition. Today was also Natalie's first day of class, and Brandy would have the shop all to herself.

The morning was surprisingly busy with holiday tourists. A woman from Omaha bought a lovely French secretary of polished beech wood and a man from Ontario promised to bring his wife back later that afternoon to look at eight dining chairs. Brandy, encouraged by the prospect of another large sale, promised to make him a good deal. The early afternoon was relatively quiet, and she spent the time making telephone calls about new inventory and reviewing the books. Massenet had shown another reasonable profit in December. She also made an appointment with her CPA for later in the month.

After four, she received a text message from Rene. The display read: "Mommy, home now. I luv you."

She smiled as she typed a reply. If she could not be at home as much as she liked, Rene could always get in touch with her.

The man from Ontario returned with his wife before closing. They purchased the chairs, and Brandy made arrangements for them to be shipped. They also purchased a set of antique Haviland china. It had been a profitable day.

She stayed an extra hour after closing to work on the books and pay bills. The time she had been away over the holidays had been a luxury, and she realized that a mountain of work awaited her.

Over the weeks after New Year's Day, she expanded her hours at the shop to work on the books and remove the Christmas decorations. When Natalie came in on Friday, she spent the entire day upstairs working on the books and organizing things for the year. She was glad for the routine, and when she could not be with Rene, she focused all of her energy in Massenet. Maybe Granny Ariel was right. Maybe the shop was their future. She was finally convinced that she would survive as a businesswoman, and she derived a lot of satisfaction from her accomplishment. Of course, she would never earn enough to repay all of the money she had invested in Harris's salvage operation. But even if she never recovered from Thad and Recov, she was now convinced that she had enough to support herself and Rene.

Gradually, Brandy, Rene, and Ariel settled into their old routines over the next two weeks as the vestiges of the holidays faded. The florist packed away the ornaments and removed the trees and garlands. Rene resumed her extracurricular activities, and Granny Ariel launched another charity drive for the homeless shelters.

January continued to be profitable. Fortunately, the New Orleans tourist industry funneled a fresh influx of tourists into Massenet every week, and Brandy sold several larger pieces of furniture. She was surprised to realize that she would need a serious infusion of inventory. She might need to go on a brief buying trip to Atlanta or New York for a few days very soon. Natalie could mind the shop, and Rene could stay with Ariel. She hated to be away from them, but it would be necessary.

Claude called one cold afternoon the third week in January. She had been so busy of late that she had not seen him since New Year's Day.

"Hey, stranger. I have some news about your case."

She felt a familiar clenching feeling in her chest. She was still angry about the letter from Thad's attorney. Sometimes, she was not sure that she had the emotional stamina to deal with a case of this magnitude. It was an unwelcome intrusion into her otherwise happy life. Damn Harris!

"We received an email from counsel representing the lead cargo underwriters that insured the emeralds. I have also heard from the hull underwriters. The long and the short of it is that they would like a meeting with us."

"Where? Will they come here?"

"No. We would need to go to London," he replied.

"When?"

"No later than the first week in February. I think they want to explore the possibility of a deal with you—or at least some sort of joint cooperation. It would be to their benefit and might reduce any salvage award payable to Thad and Recov. Technically, it is an opportunity for them to cap their damages."

"But I need to go on a buying trip for the shop," she insisted. "I need more inventory."

"Well, that's perfect. We'll make a side trip to Brighton."

She considered the proposal. Brighton had a lot of wonderful antiques, as did other areas of the English countryside, if one knew where to look. She could also go up to the Scottish Highlands. The trip would kill two birds with one stone.

"Well, alright," she heard herself reply.

"Great. This is actually good news, Brandy. I'll have my secretary call you about the arrangements," he said as he rang off. "Anyway, I am late for an appointment."

"Talk to you soon," she said. She was already mentally making a list of her purchases in the United Kingdom as she hung up the phone.

Chapter XIV

Ariel sat at the breakfast room sipping a cup of hot tea with Chloe at her feet. Rene had a piano lesson and ballet class after school and would return before dinner. Ariel had placed the chicken and artichoke dish delivered by the meal service she used in the refrigerator for dinner that evening.

Raleigh sat on a mat at the table, shelling walnuts with his powerful teeth. The meat was fresh and tasty. Like all rodents, his teeth grew perpetually to compensate for the wear caused by the constant gnawing tree bark and nutshells.

Raleigh noticed that the days were getting longer now. Outside, a crisp dry wind rustled the trees standing in the rear lawn and in the park adjacent to the brick wall. The new white gazebo was clearly visible in the reflection pool. From his perch on the table, he could see two of the three remaining pups raiding the bird feeders suspended from a wire beneath a live oak limb. He watched as they carefully gripped the wire like tightrope artists and hung from above by their rear legs, gnawing open the sack of birdseed. It was a game for them, and the pups had learned to gnaw the nylon line holding the sack of seed until it fell to the ground, spilling its contents on the grass. The pups had become highly competitive of late, and Raleigh watched as the larger male knocked the smaller female down from the line ten feet to the ground. Unharmed, she quickly began eating the birdseed before her brother climbed down to the grass.

Recently, the pups had become highly destructive and were now allowed only in the rear foyer of the house. Inquisitive and fearless, like all squirrels, they had mastered the art of opening the kitchen cabinets and canisters, devouring the contents, and spilling them onto the floor. One of the pups had even learned to open the child-proof locks Ariel had installed on the cabinets. The smallest female had recently developed a penchant for sitting on the rack hanging from the ceiling that held the copper pots and shelling walnuts, throwing the hulls on the floor. Chloe watched the pups' antics with interest, barking excitedly and demanding that they return to the ground.

When Brandy complained repeatedly about the mess, Ariel finally decided to bar the pups from the house with the exception of the small room off the rear foyer. As a compromise, the room adjoining the foyer was now always stocked with seeds, nuts, fruit, and hard corn for the pups. Now that the pups were asserting their independence from each other as well as from Raleigh, Ariel fixed small converted cat beds for each squirrel in separate shelves of the room.

Raleigh understood that the pups could not combat their feral instincts and that these actions were necessary. The pups remained friendly, however, and would gladly allow Ariel and Rene to hand-feed them. The young pups loved to sit on Rene's shoulder while she fed them hard corn and stroked their ears. They still loved Chloe and enjoyed playing chase with her and snuggling down for a nap after breakfast and a romp in the morning. Raleigh realized with a little sadness that the pups were not living like normal park squirrels, but were partially domesticated house pets. It was obvious, however, that they were happy and that was really all that was important.

He knew that by the end of the year, the two females would come into season and perhaps have pups of their own. All of the pups had been spending more and more time in the park, scurrying like acrobats over the magnificent live oak limbs.

One of the pups had disappeared within the last three weeks. The largest pup, a magnificent male, had probably moved into another territory beyond the stone bridge. He had been an independent sort, preferring to explore the park alone rather than spending time with his siblings. Raleigh felt certain that the pup was safe. He was nearing adulthood and it was only natural that he had given into his instincts to begin an independent existence. Besides, he knew that it was a matter of time before the rest of the brood began living independently.

The smallest of the remaining pups, a tiny female, had mysteriously disappeared last week. Chloe had been depressed and agitated, waiting for the little pup to return. The little squirrel had clearly been her favorite of the brood. Instinctively, Raleigh knew that something was very wrong. Perhaps because of her size, the little pup had been the most sedentary and tame of the litter, preferring a good romp with Chloe on the ground to sailing across the tree branches. It was likely that she had fallen prey to a stray cat or to the large hawk that lived at the other end of the park. She had been weak and was at the greatest risk. Chloe had been grieving since her disappearance, listlessly lying at her mistress's feet with a glazed expression.

Raleigh knew that these changes were natural and part of the circle of life. At the same time, the pups were all that remained of Kiki, and he would be sad when they ultimately moved away.

Raleigh stared at the checkerboard set up on the kitchen island. He watched his old friend wipe her eyes behind her glasses. Today, she looked tired and he could feel that her energy level was lower than usual. His instincts told him that she felt tired and weak. It made him feel slightly alarmed, fearing that his friend was ill. Ariel and Rene had become his whole life. He was not a normal squirrel. He would be devastated by the loss of Ariel.

"I need to wash my cup and saucer, and then we can play checkers," she told him.

The squirrel waited patiently on the island. Today, Ariel had turned off the air-conditioning system and opened the windows to take advantage of the cool breeze. The air felt luscious. Raleigh had never really become accustomed to air-conditioning.

Ariel's expression suddenly brightened. "Well, I have enjoyed spending time with you and Chloe today. The three of us are alone together so infrequently now."

She leaned over and pulled out the checkerboard toward the squirrel. "Your choice. Are you red or black today?"

Raleigh felt relieved to see Ariel return to her old self. He swiped at a red checker with his paw, sliding it over to him. Red checkers were his favorite.

Chapter XV

Brandy met Claude downstairs in the lobby of the Royal Horseguards Hotel in London's fashionable West End. The hotel was located strategically along the Thames embankment approximately two blocks from Trafalgar Square.

Chris and Claude decided that Claude would be a better choice to handle the meetings with the London underwriters. Claude, unlike Chris had a history with the London market. He also had a history with the Miami attorneys and the D'Argent attorneys that the underwriters had hired to represent their interests. Additionally, it would be more economical for Brandy if only one attorney attended to represent her. Claude intended to contact a few clients on other matters while they were in London and because of that, the Boudreaux Banks firm paid his plane ticket and hotel stay. The final consideration for the trip was that the London insurance market is a relationship business. Claude and Brandy would be more likely to forge an alliance with the underwriters against Thad and Recov if they made the effort to come to London.

As they waited for a taxi, Claude explained that during his business trips, he generally stayed in an array of flats at Calico House on Bow Lane or on Pepe Street in Central London, located only a very few blocks away from the Lloyd's building. This saved him the taxi ride into town every day and, if necessary between appointments, he could return to the flat. The Bow Lane flats, however, were also in close proximity to the D'Argent London office and the trendy bars patronized by the underwriters, brokers, and claims handlers after work. Since Brandy did not visit London very often, Claude had recommended that they stay in the West End, which was close to a number of wonderful restaurants and elegant shops. Thus far, she enjoyed the ambiance of the hotel and was thoroughly delighted with his selection.

Brandy had a full English breakfast and two strong cups of coffee. She had slept well, with the assistance of melatonin and had awakened refreshed and acclimated to the time change. She had been thoroughly exhausted the evening before, willing herself to stay awake until nearly ten. She had been concerned that the red wine and drinks they had consumed with the rich dinner at the Stafford Hotel would have kept her awake once she had returned to her flat. Instead, she had slept like an infant. After a warm shower, she applied a light coat of makeup and selected wool slacks, a heavy sweater and coat for their trip to Bath. The February weather in London was extremely cold and damp, and the chill in the air pierced through her bones in comparison to the subtropical New Orleans winters.

They planned to spend Monday and Tuesday in meetings with the lead underwriters who had subscribed to the insurance policies covering the *BYZANTIUM*. Claude had explained to her that the vessel's hull and cargo of emeralds had been insured under separate policies. Moreover, Claude had retained a world-renowned salvage expert in London and the United States. They had a meeting scheduled later in the week about her case. On Thursday, she was off to the south of France and then a few days in the Scottish Highlands, searching for suitable inventory for her shop. Her return ticket was not until the following Thursday.

As she exited the elevator, she noticed Claude by the front door, chatting amiably with a deeply tanned, handsome man she guessed was about forty. Despite the threat of rain, the man was dressed for a day of golf. Claude introduced him to her as Greg Connor from Charleston, North Carolina. He explained that Greg represented the London insurance market in a number of matters relating to his major client, a well-known cruise line. It surprised Brandy to learn that he was familiar with her case.

"The dispute over the find of *BYZANTIUM* has caused quite a lot of speculation in the market as well as maritime legal circles in the U.S.," he told her. "It is fascinating what technology can do." He turned back to Claude. "First, there was the fight over the gold from the *SS CENTRAL AMERICA* and then the *BROTHER JONATHAN*. And I am sure that you have read the Fourth Circuit decision about the recent salvor's claim to the wreckage of the *TITANIC*. It is a few years old now. I read that the fellow Ballard, who located the *TITANIC*, claims that now he has aspirations of locating Cleopatra's navy and Ernest Shackleton's *ENDEAVOUR* near the Antarctic ice cap. At least Cleopatra's navy was not insured," he laughed.

Claude smiled. "At least that we know of."

"I never really thought I would see someone like you take on the market in a case like this. Have you jumped over to the plaintiff's side of the fence now," he asked, not really bothering to disguise his curiosity.

Claude smiled, ostensibly ignoring the jibe. "No, actually, we are cooperating with the underwriters on this case and trying to reach an accord jointly against Recov. We see ourselves as more aligned with the market's position. I have joined Boudreaux Banks now, and it is more of a commercial law firm." But I am sure I will continue to handle London work in the future.

Greg nodded with interest and acknowledged the doorman who came to announce the arrival of his taxi. "I have heard of Chris

Banks. He is a well-respected fellow. Good luck with your case." They shook hands, and Greg assured Brandy that it was wonderful to meet her as the doorman loaded his golf clubs into the black London taxi.

"Smug and officious," Brandy remarked to Claude when they were finally seated comfortably in their black taxi in route to Paddington Station.

"Claude grinned. "That is what I really love about you Brandy. You always cut through the bullshit."

"Always," she laughed, settling back in her seat for a few minutes of silence to take in the scenery.

"So, will this case affect your old business relationships?" she asked a few minutes later. It bothered her to think that her case could cause Claude any difficulty in his professional life. On the other hand, she knew that his involvement was not a matter of altruism. This was a high-profile maritime case, and recovery would make them both extremely wealthy beyond their wildest dreams.

He was pensive for a moment before he answered. "It may affect some of my former relationships. But I opened two new London files this week. And as you know, I am meeting several clients in other cases. Overall, it may actually increase my business opportunities in another area. As Greg mentioned, the recovery of shipwrecks is becoming more frequent. It is an opportunity for me to become an expert in another field."

She brushed her cognac-tinted hair back from her face with her left hand. "That makes me feel better. Your acquaintance made me spiral into a real guilt-trip."

He smiled reassuringly, revealing his perfect white teeth. “Don’t feel guilty, Brandy. If we win this case, or even reach a decent settlement, the future for both of us is very bright.”

“And if we don’t?” she asked as the driver pulled into the drive leading to Paddington Station.

“Our evidence is very strong. We have a good case.”

“They do not seem to recognize our position,” she replied.

“They love to use bullying litigation tactics. They are underhanded people—maybe even a little sinister,” said Claude after he paid the taxi driver.

She mulled over his comment. An uneasy feeling gnawed at her stomach. Surely Thad had not had anything to do with Harris’s death. She dismissed the thought. Thad was dishonest, but surely he was not a killer.

Despite the early hour, Paddington Station was alive with echoes from the throngs of bustling train passengers. Several of the station shops were already doing a brisk business. She noticed a few errant pigeons searching for food as she and Claude walked across the cavernous room toward their train.

They sat in the first class compartment of the train headed for Bath. Soon, the London urban sprawl gave way to emerald fields, lightly doused with a misting rain from the sky. Brandy pulled a deck of cards from her purse, and she and Claude played gin rummy until the train arrived in Bath shortly before eleven.

They squeezed into the rear of the cathedral a few minutes after eleven. It was a gorgeous old structure steeped in history. Afterward, they took a tour around the city in an open-air bus before returning to the Pump Room for a late lunch. They toured the old Roman baths and strolled lazily through the cobblestone streets of the city. Then, they had a glass of wine in a pub before returning to London on the train. Before returning to the hotel, they had a light dinner in a small intimate restaurant in Soho.

Brandy felt that it had been a nearly perfect day. The trip had been a pleasant diversion, allowing her to forget the real purpose of her presence in London. Sleep came easily.

About nine-fifteen the following morning, the black taxi dropped them on Lime Street in front of the new Lloyd's building. Constructed in the late eighties, the building was a futuristic metallic-and-glass structure that soared between the surrounding Georgian buildings. An external elevator shaft encased a glass cage in curved shiny ribs. Brandy fell in love with the building instantly.

"It's gorgeous!" she told Claude.

"I think so, too. It evokes strong reactions, though. People either love it or they hate it. It is called inside out because everything you would expect to see concealed is on the outside of the building."

They took a short walk down the cobblestone streets of the Leadenhall Market wedged behind the Lloyd's building and other buildings in Central London. Brandy recognized the spot instantly.

"This Market was in a Harry Potter movie," she said, staring at the ornate canopy overhead. A number of restaurants and trendy shops lining the interior had not yet opened for the day.

"Yes, that's right. Later, we will walk down to Minster Court. You might recognize it from the family movie about the Dalmatians."

"What an amazing place to work with all of this history!"

Claude smiled. "I never tire of coming to London on business. I have made a number of good friends in the London insurance market.

They obtained their Lloyd's passes from the receptionist. Brandy noticed that everyone was dressed in black, navy, or charcoal gray with black shoes according to the Lloyd's dress code. Despite their somber dress, many of the men wore beautifully colored silk ties. She felt that she blended in perfectly in her simple black fitted dress with a gold broach.

Claude had explained to her that the dress code is mandatory. "They bar entrance to those who are not dressed appropriately," he had told her. "Brown or cordovan shoes or suits are forbidden."

Claude gave her a quick tour of the bottom and first floor of the building. Downstairs was a beautiful library with traditional paneling, a balcony, and a spiral staircase. Claude explained that the library had been removed from the older Lloyd's building, and reassembled in the new structure.

The main floor had a soaring atrium. Underwriting boxes for various marine and aviation syndicates were located throughout the room on this level. Claude pointed out the rostrum erected in the front of the room.

"They ring the bell after a significant casualty," he explained.

He also showed her a glass case containing information about the loss of the *TITANIC*. A podium held two large books. Each ledger contained neat calligraphic writing. The first one was opened to the losses on the same date one hundred years ago. The adjacent ledger was used for present-day losses. Several nearby racks held notices of recent losses throughout the world insured in the London Market.

After a quick visit to the Lloyd's coffee shop, they walked down St. Mary Axe to the Silverton Syndicate for their ten o'clock appointment. Brandy gasped as they entered the lovely old Georgian Building. The interior was a maze of glass and chrome with lighted glass catwalks and glass elevators. They showed their Lloyd's passes to the receptionist, who asked them to take a seat.

Momentarily, a man who Brandy estimated was about thirty-five introduced himself to them as Gary Richfield. His dark blonde hair was thinning on top, and he had a prominent paunch. He guided them upstairs to a glass conference room.

"We are going to be joined this morning with two leads from the company market," he told them. "I thought it would be easier if everyone just came here."

The four men in the conference room rose to greet them. Claude was already acquainted with Hardy Williams from the Excelsior and Michael Temple from CMT. Both men also appeared to be in their mid to late thirties. Two attorneys from D'Argent and Miami, Dick Simpson and Jeff Hastings, were also present along with a representative from Resolute. Brandy estimated that these men were at least fifty-five. They greeted Brandy with gracious civility. After they were seated, they made small talk before the tea, coffee, and biscuits were served.

Gary was the first to broach the issue of business. "Brandy, I am the claims handler for the lead syndicate for the Lloyd's syndicates for this loss. Since this claim is pre-1992, it is automatically handled through this office. As I am sure Claude has explained to you, Hardy and Michael are the company leads. From the Lloyd's market side, there is only one insolvency for a percentage of 5.623479. Accordingly, any potential claim for your recovery will be reduced by that amount." He looked over at Hardy and Michael. "Any insolvencies from your side?"

Michael shook his head. "Miraculously, no. Amazing for a one hundred-year-old loss."

Claude set his cup into the saucer and lifted his pen over his legal pad. "We really appreciate the opportunity to meet with you today. I think that we have a mutual interest with underwriters in the partial resolution of this matter. Brandy, as the widow of Harris Blake, does not contend that she owns the vessel and jewels according to the law of finds. One thing that appears to be clear here is that underwriters paid this loss for the hull and cargo at the time of the casualty. We take that as a given fact. Under the circumstances, we think it would be unreasonable to assert that underwriters intended to abandon their interests in *BYZANTIUM*. This was only a 100-year-old casualty. If the loss had occurred 400 years ago before the inception of the market, our argument would be different. Unlike the Recov interests, we do not claim an ownership interest. We think that position is without merit and have not asserted this claim in our complaint for intervention either in the New Orleans or Virgin Islands case."

As Claude paused Brandy noticed the men nod and smile in satisfaction. Claude was very smooth and the fact that he was acquainted with these people and had inherent credibility was helpful. She sipped her tea, watching the reactions of the men at the table with interest.

"Instead," he continued, "we are asserting only a salvage award. Harris Blake conceived this salvage operation, salvaged some of the jewels and hull fragments.

"What about your client's affiliation with Recov?" interrupted Jeff Hastings. There was an obvious tension in his voice.

"My client's husband died before Recov's participation in this venture. But there is no question that Recov and Thad Stuart have used some of the Blake assets. We are asserting this right against Recov for a sizable proportion of any salvage award they obtain. Stuart and Harris Blake had a written contract, drafted by an American lawyer in St. Thomas. Brandy and her daughter, Rene, are entitled to assert a claim for the use of these assets against Recov."

"And the emeralds?" Hastings asked. "Do you have any idea of the value of the stones in your client's possession that were recovered to date?"

Claude leaned back in his chair. "They are now under the control of the registry of the United States District Court and not in my client's possession. The gemologists that have looked at them to date have estimated their worth at about $400 million. Also, the hull fragments now have value."

"And Recov also has some stones, don't they?" Hardy Williams asked.

"Yes. Recov's discovery responses indicate that they are in possession of approximately $10 million worth of emeralds."

Hardy Williams grinned sheepishly and sipped his coffee. "Underwriters will like the sound of that. Quite a good return on a one hundred-year investment." There was a ripple of soft laughter from the others present.

Claude smiled. "Yes, it is quite a return, even after paying a hefty salvage award."

Williams' pen hovered over his legal pad. "What do you consider a hefty award?"

"Well, in the *SS CENTRAL AMERICA*, the Fourth Circuit awarded the salvors 90 percent of the value of the hull and cargo," Hastings interrupted. "So, don't let him convince you that we are all on the same side. He has his client's interest at heart here."

Claude seemed unfazed by Hastings's intentional jab. "There were other considerations in the *SS CENTRAL AMERICA*. The vessel was significantly older than the *BYZANTIUM* and in deeper waters. The fight between the underwriters and the salvors was much more contentious. We are here trying to work toward a common goal. Obviously, my client is entitled to something for her husband's efforts. But for Harris Blake, the vessel and its cargo could have remained at rest for another fifty or one hundred years. Significant assets have been recovered to date, including segments of the hull that have historic and intrinsic value." Claude stared at Jeff Hastings coldly. "And do not forget the sacrifices made during the salvage operation. Harris Blake lost his life."

Claude stared at the attorneys representing the underwriters. Hastings, coloring with embarrassment, looked down at his legal pad to avoid looking at Brandy. Claude had made a good point. London underwriters would profit from the recovery with an unexpected windfall. But Harris, Brandy, and Rene had made the ultimate sacrifice. Their lives had been changed forever.

Confident that he had everyone's attention, Claude continued. "But before Harris died, he recovered over $400 million worth of assets. It is estimated that another $40 million of emeralds may be in the seabed. But, finding them will be difficult. Several of the wooden containers seem to be missing. There is some indication that the cargo was pitched overboard during the storm after the vessel grounded on the reef. The storm is believed to have lasted at least twenty-four hours. The vessel had been detained and it was believed by everyone that she sank off of the Bahamas. Today we know that *BYZANTIUM* seemed to be headed toward St. Thomas at the time that she sank. The additional cases, if they are intact, could be anywhere within a five hundred square-mile radius. So, it is unlikely, in the foreseeable future, that additional emeralds will be recovered."

"That is one theory, of course," injected Hastings, still unable to stymie his nasty side.

"Absolutely," agreed Claude. "It is a theory."

Gary Richfield exchanged a knowing look with Brian Johnson, the chairman of the Roche Syndicate, and folded his hands over his legal pad. He was a very experienced claims handler with an impressive reputation in the market. Claude had explained to Brandy before their arrival that Richfield, and not the Miami attorneys, would actually be in control at the meeting. Richfield, always the pragmatist, along with Johnson, was the real decision maker in the room. Their attorneys would be compelled to follow their instructions to the letter.

"Everyone here is deeply sympathetic to your client's terrible loss," said Richfield, looking directly at Brandy. "And we recognize that this salvage operation will be very beneficial to all concerned. I think that we all believe that it will be to our mutual interest to cooperate here in discovery and litigation strategy. Recov, after all, seems to be our common nemesis, and we can reach a better resolution by working together."

Brandy watched the two Florida attorneys shift in their seat. They were being told to cooperate. Claude was right. Gary Richfield was in control.

"We could not agree more," smiled Claude. "I have known Jeff and Dick for several years now. There are not any attorneys around that I respect more. I think our mutual cooperation will be very productive."

"Certainly," chimed in Hastings, in his most convincing tone. "We have slain dragons together, as they say."

Richfield watched the exchange with interest before resuming control again. "Have you and your client given any thought to the amount of the salvage award that would be reasonable in this case?"

"The total percentage for all salvors, including Recov?"

"Yes. We would like some sense of where we will be with this thing at the end of the day," he replied.

"Obviously, the cargo is the most valuable asset recovered to date in the salvage operation. The total recovery is about $410 million. There are purportedly additional artifacts that may have some historic value, including the hull fragments. Without binding myself, I think a court could easily grant a salvage award of at least $200 million on the bottom end and a higher range of $350 million. The court will obviously also weigh underwriters' investment over the last one hundred years and determine the amount that would have been recovered if their money on the cargo claim had been prudently invested."

Claude looked over at Brandy and smiled. She returned his gaze and refolded her hands in her lap as she turned to watch Richfield's response. The figures were staggering. She and Rene would never want for anything again. In a strange way, Harris had taken care of their future.

Richfield furrowed his brow. "So, despite the Fourth Circuit opinion in the *SS CENTRAL AMERICA* and other authorities, you think that under these circumstances, that Underwriters should recover no less than one sixth and no more than one-third of the Recovery?"

"Exactly," replied Claude. "We are meeting with our salvage expert on Wednesday and we can refine our numbers. But I suggest that it may behoove us to present a joint equitable recommendation to the court over the division of the assets. Obviously, this is not something we can do today, but we could ultimately reach a decision."

Williams laughed. "You mean blindside Recov and Thad obviously."

"Exactly. Also, underwriters may want to give some consideration to conceding the issue of salvage and allowing the court to determine only the amount of the salvage award. That is something that we may wish to explore over the next few months. Additionally, to avoid legal fees, we might want to agree upon a range of the award. No one wants to keep this case in litigation for years. We all know that cases of this nature can go on for years. My client wants to get on with her life, and I am sure that underwriters would enjoy a cash infusion in this instance. The British Museum may want part of the hull fragments and a few of the smaller emeralds."

Brandy caught the knowing look pass between Richfield and Williams. The men seemed to have reached a tacit agreement.

Johnson nodded. "We can look into that. We want to streamline the handling of this matter without spending a fortune on costs and fees." Johnson was an American attorney, working in the United Kingdom. With a background working for American domestic insurers, Johnson had a reputation for being extremely cost-conscious. Claude had explained before the meeting that because this would essentially be a windfall to the syndicates on the slip, Johnson would have a special interest in the case.

"How long will you be in town?" injected Richfield. Obviously, the group wanted to wrap up their meeting to give them an opportunity to discuss the matter privately before lunch. Richfield was subtlety dismissing them.

"I leave on Thursday night," said Claude. "Brandy is off to the south of France on Thursday and then to the Highlands to shop for antiques for her shop."

"Ah, the Scottish Highlands! What a gorgeous place in the summer but not my choice in the dead of winter. You have a store?" inquired Johnson.

"Yes. It is called Massenet—that is my maiden name. The shop is very small and is in the French Quarter at the foot of Royal a couple of blocks from St. Louis Cathedral. I sell English and country French antiques, rugs, porcelain, and other wonderful things."

"Are you a designer?"

Brandy smiled. "No, just an artist with a love of beautiful things."

Johnson extended his hand toward her as he rose from his seat. Brandy noticed that he was short and portly. "I have a conference in New Orleans in April. Perhaps my wife and I will drop in to see what you have. We love the city."

"I will look forward to seeing you then," smiled Brandy, as she shook his hand.

They bantered pleasantries with the other insurance representatives before taking their leave. Gary Richfield escorted them to the lobby where he gave them a warm farewell.

"We'll talk again later in the week before you leave," he told Claude.

The sky had darkened, and there was a steady drizzle as they headed back down toward Leadenhall Street for their luncheon meeting. Brandy was glad that she had had the foresight to carry an umbrella.

"It went very well," Claude told her on the way to the restaurant. "With our assistance, both parties can cooperate in putting a ceiling on the salvage award to minimize Recov's judgment. We can help each other."

They had a drink in the bar of Caravaggio as they waited for Michael Trevor, an internationally known salvage expert. Trevor was a Queens Counsel with an impressive reputation. He taught a short salvage course at Tulane Law School every year at the Admiralty Law Institute. He had agreed to consult on the case for a small fee and to assist them with retention of the appropriate experts. Trevor had written several books on salvage, and his assistance would be invaluable.

Trevor was early, and the threesome was shown to their table. Brandy instantly liked the thin grandfatherly man with silver hair. His affable and gentle manner instantly put her at ease. He seemed fascinated with Harris and their life in St. Thomas.

"Your husband did something incredible," he remarked. "It is rare that a man follows his dreams against convention and succeeds. It is a truly wonderful story and probably will be one of the most exciting cases of my life," he told Brandy.

She smiled appreciatively. If only you were here, Harris, to enjoy all of this.

The fish and pasta dishes were delicious, followed by an array of incredible desserts. Brandy noticed that business lunches in London were a leisurely affair, often accompanied by wine. The restaurant patrons lingered over coffee, and by three, the crowd had dissipated. Claude, Trevor, and Brandy were the last stragglers as they left at three-thirty.

The lunch meeting was tremendously productive. Trevor had lined up several potential salvage experts to testify concerning the sea conditions in the area, the methodology used in the recovery, necessary equipment, and the difficulty of the salvage operation. They would need to prove that Harris had done the lion's share of the work in locating *BYZANTIUM* and recovering significant assets. Thad and Recov were just trading on his information. Additionally, Trevor had armed them with a list of appraisers for the cargo, as well as the hull fragments and other artifacts. Claude and Trevor arranged to meet the following morning before he and Brandy took a black taxi down to the West End.

They spent an hour at The National Gallery before returning to the hotel to freshen up before dinner. Claude had invited clients to meet them Oblix in The Shard at seven o'clock. Brandy perused a few shops on Piccadilly before her shower.

They took a taxi to The Shard. The rain had stopped and a brisk wind stirred the hem of her coat. Oblix was located on the midway up the 72 story glass tower. The walls were sheets of glass, and the lighted London embankment was at their feet. Brandy could see the dome of St. Paul's Cathedral in the cityscape of London below them.

"It's beautiful," remarked Brandy as she surveyed their surroundings. "This courtyard must be more than an entire city block." She smiled at him. "Exciting life you have, Claude. I want to be a lawyer when I grow up."

"It is also a very posh and expensive place."

"Anything to impress your clients, right?"

"It is only necessary to impress those with discriminating taste."

Brandy giggled. The stressful part of the day was over, and now she was determined to enjoy the evening.

Chapter XVI

Brandy and Claude spent the next two days working with a myriad of experts at Trevor's London office. The evenings were consumed with West End theatre productions and fashionable dinners at the OXO Tower and Butler's Wharf. Overall, it had been a highly productive visit.

As she wheeled her stackable suitcases into the elevator on Thursday morning, she realized that she was exhausted. The meetings and work on the case had dredged up her old feelings about Harris's death. She decided that complete immersion into her work for the remaining week in England and Scotland would be a welcome change.

Brandy had called Granny Ariel and Rene every afternoon that week. Things were going well at home, and Rene was happy at school. As usual, Granny Ariel had things well in hand. Natalie and another part-time employee, Pam, were watching the shop. Tourism was still strong in New Orleans, partly due to the upcoming Mardi Gras season, and Massenet was still showing a profit. Their inventory was low, and Brandy needed to make a number of purchases.

Claude was waiting for her in the lobby. The two of them were sharing a car that would drop her at the London City Airport and carry Claude on to Heathrow for his British Airways flight back to the States.

"How are you this morning?" Claude asked, looking up from his paper.

Brandy noticed that he looked remarkably refreshed, despite their hectic schedule. "Tired but still ready to go shopping," she replied. She planned to stay in Marseille and then leave for the Scottish Highlands early Sunday afternoon. Brandy and Granny Ariel had traveled to France, Ireland and Eastern Europe to purchase inventory for the shop before it opened. This was Brandy's first foreign shopping trip for Massenet, however, since the store had opened. Up to this point, she had purchased items from wholesalers or while attending regional sales.

"We have had a productive few days," he said, stuffing his paper into the briefcase along with a stack of legal documents. "We have allies, credible experts, and tangible evidence. Things are going our way." He gave her his biggest grin which usually put her at ease. Today, she was a bundle of nerves, and it did not create its usual magic.

"When will you tell Thad and Recov about the emeralds hidden in the boxes Rene and Granny Ariel discovered in the attic?"

Claude absently brushed his hair back from his forehead. "We have prepared updated discovery responses to send to Thad and RECOV for your signature when you return disclosing their discovery and explaining the circumstances. I am sure they will not be pleased. Of course, the Underwriters are very pleased that you have such a large share in your possession, because now they have a friendly adverse party. "

"I suppose that Thad's attorneys believed that we only had the handful of rough-cut emeralds that Harris had shown them at the time he died. But, judging from the journals, Harris did not confide in Thad about the remainder of the jewels. It appears that the only person who may have had any idea about their existence was Jimmy Thornton, Harris's part-time employee."

The journals had been pretty clear about that point. Thad primarily ran his day sailing business ferrying tourists between St. John and St. Thomas. Until his death, Harris had primarily handled the salvage business alone. According to the entries in Harris's journals, after discovery of the initial seven or eight emeralds, Thad attempted to convince him to team up with several unsavory investors. Harris had resisted, speculating that these men had potentially organized crime connections. This opposition had seriously strained his relationship with Thad, and at the time of his death, Harris was attempting to sever their business ties. He had become distant from Brandy to insulate her from the problem.

"Clearly, they had some suspicion that you had more stones. I think Thad was testing you when he asked you to turn over the emeralds. He obviously did not know whether you were aware of the falling out between him and Harris. Since you were not and did not appear to have any stones for over a year, he obviously became very confident. But I think the journals will concern them as much as anything else. It completely destroys their theory that Recov was solely responsible for locating and salvaging the vessel and jewels. That is why the original journals are locked away in a bank vault, and we have made copies that have been numbered."

"I will try to come in next Friday afternoon. Why don't you have your secretary call and leave me a time, and I can ask Natalie to cover the shop. The morning is certain to be very hectic—first day back and everything."

"We could have lunch first if you like."

She rolled her eyes. "In your dreams. I will have to diet until eternity to shed all this fat from these elaborate meals on this trip. I am sure that I will just grab a sandwich or salad near the shop on that day."

He smiled. "You are still as thin as a rail. Besides, you cannot blame this on me. Remember that you are heading deeper to the most dangerous food capital of the world—France."

"Well, hopefully without your bad influence, I can exercise some self-control," she grinned.

"Ok, but remember, my lunch invitation still stands," he said as the car drove up.

The driver quickly loaded their luggage. Traffic this morning was relatively light, and they were shortly at the airport for her trip to Marseille. Claude gave her hand a squeeze as the driver unloaded the luggage. She waved and went inside to check her luggage.

The flight to Marseille was only about two hours. The city was warmer than London with the distinct odor of sea air. She found a taxi and checked into a small stylish hotel recommended by a friend and had a light dinner in a small restaurant nearby. The next morning, she hired a driver who drove her through the nearby countryside where she purchased an armoire, two lamps, an eighteenth century bed, two oil paintings, a seventeenth century sideboard, a French trestle table and several miscellaneous pieces of antique copper cookware. She arranged for the shipping and insurance back to the United States. She was pleased that the venture had been so highly successful. The following day she traveled to Aix-in-Provence. She passionately loved the French countryside dotted with medieval castles and villages.

Brandy felt an excitement welling up inside her just anticipating the wonderful items she was sure to find for her shop. The trip to London and the problems with Thad and Recov seemed far away now. She spent the next three days busily immersing herself in purchasing items for her shop. Provence was a gold-mine for antiques if one knew where to look. She found two incredible Louis XVI beds, a country French commode, and a carved dining table and eight chairs. Also, she located two Louis XV occasional living room chairs with the original fabric, and a nine-foot beveled mirror with a gilded frame. The items exceeded her budget, but she purchased them anyway. She was certain to be able to sell them at a hefty profit. If not, she could always sell them for her basis to another antique dealer in town. She reasoned that if she suffered a loss, she would have a good tax deduction.

During her last afternoon, she hired a car and toured the countryside and the Abbaye de Senanque founded in 1148 in Aix. It was a welcome respite from her hectic schedule over the last few days. That evening, she had a quiet dinner at the hotel and then strolled around Aix before returning to the warmth of the lobby fireplace. She took a seat by the fire, enjoying the soft, heartwarming scent of smoke. She felt peaceful and relaxed, as she reflected on the events of the last few days. Despite the pain of Harris's loss, she realized, rather guiltily, that life over the last year had been much more exciting than teaching art in St. Thomas. Harris had been consumed with locating the wreckage and *BYZANTIUM* cargo, and she and Rene had been left to their own devices. Most of their close friends were really friends that she had cultivated. She had met the majority of them through Rene's activities. She would have given anything if Harris had just stuck to his teaching in Florida. She regretted being deprived of a more mainstream married life while Harris pursued his dreams. Harris had truly accomplished his dreams but had paid the ultimate price. It was a tragedy of the greatest proportion.

Her thoughts turned to Claude. How did she really feel about him? Thankfully, it was impossible for them to have anything more than a platonic relationship while he represented her. That relieved her of the obligation to make a decision of any kind in the near future. Claude was incredibly handsome and a lot of fun. His stability was a marked contrast to the excitement that had seemed to emanate from Harris. In life, Harris had an incredibly high energy level that supercharged everyone around him. It was exactly that quality that had initially attracted her to him twelve years earlier and that had ultimately resulted in his death.

She finally went upstairs at ten o'clock to call Rene and Ariel. Tomorrow, she would fly to Inverness, rent a car, and explore some of the small shops for the next day and a half before returning to New Orleans. Rene would be at home from kindergarten by now and they could chat. She talked to Granny Ariel first about her latest acquisitions for the shop before Granny Ariel turned the phone over to Rene.

"Hi, Mommy!" Rene said brightly as she answered the phone.

"What are you doing, sweetheart?"

"Granny Ariel, Chloe, Raleigh and I are watching *Animal Planet*. Today, they have something on about squirrels, so we are watching it for Raleigh."

"Are you learning anything?" she asked. Despite her initial prejudice about the squirrel, she had to admit that it was an interesting pet for her daughter and a nice companion for Granny Ariel. Even Chloe seemed to like him. She had lived near the park for many years, but she had never known any squirrel like Raleigh. He was truly an anomaly.

"Yes, Mommy. Squirrels are real air robots. They can do everything."

"That's acrobats. Yes, they are amazing creatures."

Rene chattered on excitedly about an obstacle course an animal behaviorist in England had constructed that the squirrels had mastered. At least the child was learning something.

"So, can we build an obstacle course for Raleigh, Mommy?" Rene persisted.

"We'll see when I come home. How is school?"

"Fine. I brought three books home for someone to me read over the weekend. Granny Ariel and I might read one tonight."

Rene was enrolled in an advanced kindergarten class. She was already reading and writing at a level that exceeded the threshold of most first grade curriculums. "That's wonderful sweetie. Well, I should go now. This is an expensive call. I will be home in two days. I love you, sweetie."

"From here to Pluto and back?"

"Much more than that."

"How much?"

"More than from here to the end of the universe."

"The universe does not have an end, Mommy."

"Exactly. There is no end to how much I love you," she replied, slightly taken aback by her daughter's precociousness.

"I love you, Mommy," said Rene as she hung up.

"See you tomorrow." Then she rang off.

Brandy began packing her suitcases, leaving out a comfortable pair of slacks and sweater to wear on the trip home. She would need clothing that she could layer because it would likely be much warmer in New Orleans than London.

Talking to Rene and Granny Ariel had given her a real lift. She could not wait to get home.

~

Raleigh sat on the sofa in the den beside Ariel watching Rene finish her homework. She practiced her writing on a large pad. Soon, the three of them could play on the computer. Or maybe they would play a board game like Candy Land or the new Harry Potter game. Raleigh was not really interested in Monopoly. He could not understand the point of acquiring property and constructing houses. Monopoly was a game geared toward people. But Candy Land was a race. Squirrels could understand speed and competition.

Finally, Rene completed her task. Ariel's instructions had been firm. Under no circumstances was he to give the child the answer unless absolutely necessary. Ariel had explained that Rene needed to learn things at her own speed.

"It won't really help matters at all if you give her the answer. Then she will not have any incentive to work herself," she told him.

After dinner, Rene took a quick bath, and the three of them retired to the game table to play Candy Land. Knowing that red was his favorite color, Rene gave Raleigh the red game piece. Tonight, Ariel won by a landslide, leaving Rene and Raleigh stuck far behind. Afterward, Rene read them both a short story from a small book that she had checked out of the library while the employee of the cleaning service washed dishes in the kitchen. Chloe snored softly at the foot of the sofa. Then, they turned the television on for a few minutes until Rene's bedtime at eight thirty. Tonight, there was a nature show about wild horses. Raleigh studied the large screen with interest.

He had seen horses infrequently during his lifetime. There was an equestrian center at the far end of the park, and one Sunday morning, a brown quarter horse and rider had ventured to the front of the park. Raleigh had been mesmerized by the enormous size of the creature. The gelding had a magnificent mane and a tail that swung softly with each step. As the horse and rider had trotted under his tree, he inhaled the unique scent of sweat and horse hair along with leather. He felt that the horse was tired and was not interested in his rider. There was a slight stress in the air that he recognized as pain and fear. As the beautiful creature trotted off, he noticed that it favored its left front foot. It was an older gentle animal, he decided, and very bored. Sometime later, he had observed two other horses from a distance. Both of them were fitted with elaborately decorated reins and headdress and carried men in uniform. He heard one of the humans in the park say that they were stragglers from a Mardi Gras parade. These horses were younger than the gelding, but far less magnificent.

Rene gave Raleigh a kiss good night at bedtime. He waited downstairs for Ariel as she went upstairs to tuck the child into bed. Raleigh had already been out for the last time earlier in the evening. It was too dangerous for him to go outside after dark. The risk of predators was still too great. He might be an unusually intelligent animal, but he was still fair game for an owl, hawk, raccoon, or cat. As was his habit now, he would spend the night in the antique canopy bed on Ariel's dresser. The bed was lined with soft satin covered bedding. It was certainly preferable to sleeping on the hard branches of a tree, although instinctively he felt safer in a closed-in space. When he had haltingly explained this to Ariel with the Scrabble pieces, she had the small bed fitted with a set of drapes that could be closed at night.

Within the past week, the two female pups had finally moved into nests of their own. They seldom, if ever, came down to the house except to consume the cache of seeds and fruit that Ariel left them on the rear verandah. Occasionally, they romped around the yard with Chloe, jumping up onto her back and grabbing onto her tail. Usually their visits were of short duration. Neither squirrel had inherited Raleigh's unusual talents and intelligence. Instead, driven by instinct, they preferred to spend most of their time in the park, avoiding human contact.

The early spring marked breeding season for the squirrels again. Most litters were born in late fall or spring. Raleigh ignored his instinct to breed with any of the females. Kiki's death and the dissipation of the litter of their pups had left him uninterested in finding another mate. It was too painful. Instead, he found himself drawn more and more to stay inside with his friends, Ariel and Rene. Admittedly, he was no longer a wild animal. He was just a house pet—like Chloe.

Chloe had accepted him completely with a dog's undying loyalty. She had become fiercely protective of him as well as the surviving pups. She began accompanying him outside in the early morning and evening to guard him. Now, if he ventured outside of the enclosed rear yard, Chloe barked furiously until he returned. The two of them shared a real understanding that was beyond the appreciation of their human friends.

Chloe padded softly after Ariel as she returned to the den and curled up at her feet, snoozing quietly again. Chloe was beginning to slow down now. At nearly ten, she lacked the exuberance that she had shown even a year or two earlier. She slept more, and she carried the slight scent that he had smelled on the horse in the park. No one else seemed to notice but Raleigh. It frightened him. He knew that it was a matter of time before she was gone, but, he did not want to think about that. Death was like the terrible dreams that woke him at night. Sometimes he was a seal pup, trying to breathe through an ice hole. The dream was always the same. After taking a deep breath, he was suddenly ripped from the water by a large polar bear and savagely ripped apart. Sometimes, he was a tiny bird, swallowed by an enormous snake, or a beautiful mallard shot from the sky by a hunter. Other times, he was a laboratory chimp being taught sign language and letters, until he was euthanized when his body became wracked by disease. Death was ever present in his dreams.

Chloe's age also made him face his own mortality. He was not really sure how old he was. At least six. What was the life-span of a squirrel? It was at least eight, and in captivity, some of them were reported to have lived until fifteen, according to the television. He said a prayer with Ariel every night. He really did not understand spiritualism or religion. The concept of religion was too abstract—perhaps another human thing. But he could feel the sense of peace that settled over Ariel after she prayed in the evening, and it gave him an aura of security and happiness. Ariel told him about the angels and explained that he certainly had a soul. It was too abstract for him, but he listened patiently. The thought of human figures with huge wings bathed in a golden light was rather an interesting concept, though.

Ariel turned down the volume of the television. Raleigh was thankful. The nine o'clock show featured a man who always consorted with reptiles like crocodiles. He hated to think that such creatures existed. It was a frightening thought. Sometimes there were shows about the Louisiana swamps outside the city that were filled with alligators, which were very much like crocodiles. Areas like the swamp would be a death knell for a squirrel.

"She is finally asleep," Ariel told him. "She is so excited about her mother coming home in two days that it is difficult to get her to relax."

The shrill bell of the telephone interrupted them. Ariel went to answer it on the other side of the room.

Raleigh sat up and began munching on the tray of seeds on the coffee table, fastidiously placing each hull into a circular bowl. If he had been outside, he would have carelessly tossed the shell onto the ground. Such things were not permitted in the house though, and he curbed his sloppy instinct in respect for Ariel. He noticed that even Chloe carefully avoided spilling her food.

Ariel talked to a friend for a few minutes before hanging up the phone. "I am feeling lucky tonight," Ariel told him. "Are you up for a game of checkers? There is nothing really on television."

He jumped onto the game table in response. Checkers required strategy and knowledge of your opponent. He could use the stimulation.

With his four-fingered paws, he lifted the box top up. It was heavy, but the exercise was good for him. Ariel lifted the checker pieces out of the box and together they arranged them on the game table. They tossed a coin to see who would begin first.

Ariel won the bet with tails. As usual, she selected the black game pieces and began to play. They intently played six games until nearly midnight. The concentration had been good for both of them. As usual, they just enjoyed each other's company until it was time to sleep.

Raleigh woke at six thirty. Ariel was already in the bathroom bathing and getting dressed. She required less sleep than the squirrel. She had explained that she needed less sleep now than when she was younger.

"It's age. Older people stop sleeping as much at night," she told him.

He stretched, feeling slightly groggy. Later in the afternoon, he decided, he would take a long nap. That would make him feel refreshed.

The squirrel patted the satin comforter and little sachet pillows in his bed before jumping down from the dresser. Chloe was already in the kitchen waiting to go out. Ariel had installed a dog door with a sliding lock for the squirrels and the dog. Raleigh slid the lock, and he and Chloe went outside through the dog door to relieve themselves.

A strong front had blown through the area during the night, leaving behind clear fresh skies and a brisk wind. The ground was slightly damp with dew, but the morning held the promise that it would be a beautiful mild February day as only could be experienced in New Orleans. The early morning light still cast deep shadows across the manicured lawn. Most squirrels would not venture out so early until the morning was doused in full sunlight. Chloe's company, however, gave him additional security that he would not otherwise have enjoyed. Exhilarated by the cool wind, the animals bounded down the brick steps.

Chloe suddenly stopped and sniffed the air. Her sense of smell was much stronger than the squirrel's. She ran over to the brick pathway by the gate, stopped, and pawed the ground roughly, examining three white stubs of paper crushed on the pathway inside of the gate. He scampered over beside her. Raleigh recognized the stubs as cigarettes. They were human smoking things that smelled terrible. The animals bristled with the sense of danger. No one in their house ever smoked, and no one that they did not know was allowed in the backyard except the gardeners. The gate was generally locked with a key to keep out prowlers. Only the gardening service—IBIX—had a key to enter the back garden.

Someone had invaded their territory. These belonged to an intruder. Someone had been watching them.

Chloe looked at him soberly, her large slanted brown eyes unusually inquisitive. She pawed the ground again before losing interest and going over to relieve herself. Raleigh, slightly unnerved by the experience, inhaled the foul scent of the spent cigarette butts before going through his morning ritual. After relieving himself, he fastidiously groomed his tail and face while sitting upright on the porch. The early morning air felt deliciously cool, buffeting his tail fur slightly.

Ariel peeked outside just as the animals were again pawing the cigarette butts with interest.

"What is it?" she asked as she stood on the rear covered verandah.

Chloe barked furiously in reply.

"Chloe, shush! You'll wake up the whole neighborhood. It's early yet."

Chloe pawed the ground and Raleigh sat beside the butts to attract Ariel's attention. She needed to know about the intruder. His sense of danger was very strong this morning.

Ariel walked over beside the gate leading toward the park and kneeled down, picking up one of the butts. "Probably kids," she muttered. "I am sure that these belong to kids who scale the walls and do not have enough sense to quit smoking."

She collected the butts and wrapped them in a Kleenex from her purse. "I will tell the security service. They can watch the area for a few days." She patted Chloe lovingly on her fluffy white head. "Good dog. You don't let anybody get away with anything."

Raleigh watched as Chloe followed Ariel down the brick walk toward the rear verandah. The dog seemed reassured. But for reasons he could not explain, Raleigh still felt uneasy. There was something dangerous about the cigarette butts. Reluctantly, he followed Ariel and Chloe into the house.

Chapter XVII

Brandy's flight from New York was delayed, and she did not land in New Orleans until three hours after her scheduled arrival. Exhausted, she retrieved her car from the long-term parking lot and drove onto the freeway ramp heading toward the Uptown area. Her reflexes were slower than usual from sleep deprivation, but fortunately, traffic was almost non-existent at this time of night. She cracked the window, enjoying the deliciously cool air that tickled her face.

It was after midnight when she arrived at home. She parked in the garage and unloaded her suitcases as quietly as possible. Granny Ariel was waiting up for her inside, sitting by the fireplace in the den reading a book. Raleigh and Chloe were sleeping soundly on the Persian rug.

The older woman hugged her granddaughter. "It's so good to have you at home! I was getting worried, but I called the airport and found out that your flight was delayed. You look rested and refreshed! I think that the trip did you good."

"You should not have waited up for me. I could have let myself in."

"Nonsense. An old woman like me does not sleep very much anymore."

"How is Rene?"

"Upstairs sleeping like a baby. She wanted to wait up for you, but I finally insisted that she go upstairs to bed because tomorrow is a school day."

Brandy unzipped her carry-on bag and extracted a Harrods's teddy bear and nightgown for Rene and a cardboard box for her grandmother. "Open it."

Ariel pulled the lid off of the box and removed a delicate porcelain carriage clock. "It's beautiful."

"Versace. I did not think you had one for your collection. I have a few other small things in my suitcases for both of you. But locating them now will be difficult."

The older woman gave her granddaughter a hug. "Let's get your things upstairs now, and you can get some rest. I am sure that Rene will burst into your room at the crack of dawn."

"You are right. I am totally dead. I dozed for a while on the airplane, but my body is suffering from time-zone confusion."

Brandy carried her things upstairs followed by Granny Ariel and her companions. She hugged her grandmother good-night, washed her face, changed into a nightshirt, and fell into bed in a deep sleep.

It was almost seven-thirty when Rene woke her up. The child was already wearing her school uniform with a crisply starched white blouse.

"Hi, pumpkin! What time is it?"

"Time for my ride to take me to school. I wanted to kiss you hello."

Brandy opened her arms. "Well, give me a kiss."

The child embraced her warmly. "I love the teddy bear and the nightgown, Mommy."

"I have a few more things for you in my suitcase. I will give them to you tonight. We'll have a little celebration after dinner. Now, give me a kiss before you leave. You don't want to be late."

Brandy followed the child downstairs. After Rene left, she had a strong cup of chicory coffee, juice, and dry toast before returning upstairs to shower and get ready for work. She dressed in a jacket, black slacks, and a cashmere sweater and drove downtown, arriving at the shop by nine thirty. She still felt slightly dazed from jet lag, and her neck ached from the cramped seat on the plane the evening before.

It was an extremely busy morning. While Natalie handled the customers, Brandy worked upstairs in the office, revising the inventory lists, modifying the computer accounting ledgers and reviewing correspondence. She also paid the bills that had accrued and put a stack of information together for the CPA. Natalie brought both of them a sandwich from the Central Grocery for lunch. They spent the remainder of the afternoon working on the displays in the main showroom. Mardi Gras was three weeks away, but it was unlikely that any of Brandy's European purchases would arrive before that time. Over the next two weeks, the number of customers browsing through the shop was expected to increase exponentially because of increased tourist traffic.

Claude's secretary called after lunch, inquiring if Brandy could drop by the office about four thirty to sign their updated discovery responses. In the interim, she agreed to fax the responses to Brandy at the shop for her review.

Brandy dropped by Claude's office at the appointed time and signed the documents. Claude had a sudden court appearance, and she did not have an opportunity to talk with him. With a pang of guilt, she realized that she was relieved that Claude was gone. The litigation was very time-consuming, and she felt overwhelmed by the amount of work she needed to finish at the shop. Natalie and Pam, the new assistant she had hired, could certainly handle the day-to-day matters, but they did not have access to the bills and accounting information. That was strictly Brandy's domain, along with the assistance of her CPA. After signing the papers, she returned to the shop to work for another two hours before returning back home.

Ariel had purchased a container of shrimp Creole from the market earlier. The three of them ate a light dinner of shrimp Creole, salad, and French bread in the breakfast room. Rene had already taken her bath and was wearing her new Harrods' nightgown and matching robe. The new teddy bear sat in one of the empty chairs. After dinner, Brandy brought out the remainder of her small gifts. There were toys for Rene, and a pink cashmere cardigan from an upscale shop in Knightsbridge for Granny Ariel.

Granny Ariel had purchased a Disney movie On Demand for Rene for the evening. Brandy, still adjusting to the time change, fell asleep during the movie. She woke up in time to tuck Rene in before returning downstairs with her grandmother.

"Now, I am as wide awake as a night owl," she said, collapsing on the sofa. A small fire smoldered in the grate, but Brandy was still chilled. She pulled an angora blanket over her slacks. "I took a melatonin. Hopefully, I can sleep through the night."

Granny Ariel smiled. "That should do the trick. We can also microwave some milk and vanilla. That is a fail-safe remedy that my mother taught me. Anyway, it is always easier for me traveling west rather than east."

Brandy wrinkled her nose. "I think I will pass on the milk. We can use that trick as a last resort."

The older woman put her teacup down on the coffee table. "So, was the trip productive?"

"Absolutely!" She described all of her purchases for the shop again in great detail. Afterward, she told her about her meetings with underwriters and their attorneys. She generally described their meetings with Michael Trevor. "Now we are viewed by London as allies in the lawsuit. The bottom line is that there is something for everyone here. We want to cooperate with the underwriters to the greatest extent possible, and ultimately, we will be suggesting a division of the salvage award to the Court. Claude and the attorneys representing underwriters think that the court might adopt this position if the parties agree. Thad and Recov are going to hold out for everything. We probably are in this thing for the long haul. There is a lot at stake, and they are apparently really greedy."

"What does Claude think?"

"He thinks that we have a good shot and that we might be able to resolve this quickly."

Granny Ariel seemed pensive. "You know Brandy, you and Rene are my only heirs. When I die, you will inherit this house. I have a little stock and some money put away. You won't be rich, but the two of you will be comfortable, even without any money from this lawsuit."

"Granny, I—"

The older woman held up her hand. "I understand. No one likes to talk about death. But it is a fact of life. I thoroughly agree with what you are doing. Harris gave his life to find that ship, and all of you have suffered tremendously. I just want you to remember that you have the luxury of settlement if you like. Your life is secure, regardless of whether you get every dollar you want, although I am sure that you will. Just consider this the intermeddling of an old busybody who just doesn't want you to feel any more stressed than necessary. I only want what is best for you, and I don't want you to worry any more than necessary about all of this. It would be a terrible shame for this dispute to disrupt years of your life with aggravation over money."

Brandy leaned over and gave her grandmother a hug. "Thank you, Granny Ariel. I don't know what I would have done without all of your help and encouragement."

She smiled. "You would have done fine. You are strong—probably stronger than I am."

"So, tell me what exciting things have been going on here?"

Ariel told her about her recent fundraising-efforts for the shelter. Last week, Walmart had agreed to donate some new spring clothes and three new flat-screen televisions to the shelter, primarily due to Ariel's persistence. A large grocery store chain had also increased its monthly food supply that would enable the shelter to feed twenty-five more people each month.

"I was very happy, because traditionally, January and February are slow times for donations."

Brandy smiled. She loved her grandmother so much. She was always thinking about other people's needs. Charity work was her life.

"Oh, and we had a little excitement here yesterday. Chloe and Raleigh found some cigarette butts by the back fence leading toward the park. There were three of them on the brick walkway."

"An intruder?" The thought of an intruder coming into the enclosed back garden gave her a sick feeling in the pit of her stomach.

"I think that they belonged to kids sneaking out at night and going to the park. Only a kid could easily scale the brick wall. No one but IBIX has a key. They just wanted the thrill of coming to Audubon Park, which is a dangerous place now at night. Years ago, it was as safe as anyplace else. Your grandfather and I would go out for late evening walks down by the lagoon. Sometimes we walked as far down as the seal pool and Monkey Hill when we were feeling energetic and never thought anything about being mugged or robbed or worse. Those days are gone now." She took a sip of her tea. "Anyway, I don't think our intruder was doing anything sinister. Just kids trying to feel old and important."

"Did you call the security company?"

"Yes, they will keep tabs on things for us and promised to park nearby for the next two weeks."

"Well, as long as we set the alarm every night, I think we will be safe," she replied partially to placate her grandmother. It was unusual for anyone to ever go into the back garden without a key. Perhaps someone was actually casing the house for a burglary. She would have to be careful.

"I set it religiously. The city is not the same as it was years ago. Anyone breaking a window or coming inside would set off the alarm at night," Ariel replied. "It makes me feel safe."

Brandy made a mental note to check the alarm every night before supper. She changed the subject so that Granny Ariel would not worry. "I remember sneaking down to the park with my friends when we came to visit. Everyone else but me smoked then. I was a geek."

"Just a smart geek who really should go to bed."

Brandy hugged her grandmother good-night. "Thank you for taking care of Rene and everything else. I don't know what I would do without you."

She walked by the security alarm panel on the way upstairs. The electronic display reflected that it was armed. She could not stop thinking about the intruder as she walked upstairs.

∽

The next few mornings when Raleigh went outside, he and Chloe checked the vicinity of the brick walk for cigarette butts or other evidence of an intruder. Chloe sniffed the ground, patrolling her territory with the squirrel.

All clear.

Raleigh had heard Ariel's speculation that the cigarettes belonged to kids. But the area had not smelled like a group of people. There had only been the lingering scent of a single male. But after a week, when the incident did not recur, Raleigh and Chloe lost interest in this pursuit and confined their morning romp to their usual rituals.

At night, he began to hear the distant music again. He remembered the music and crowds from his days in the park. Ariel and Rene had explained that these were the Mardi Gras parades.

"I would like to bring you to see one, Raleigh," Rene told him one night as she was getting her jacket to attend the Freret Parade. Throngs of parade attendees had parked on St. Charles and would walk through the university campuses toward Freret Street to attend the parade.

Raleigh tapped his paw once forcefully on the table, which was their signal for "No." He did not like crowds and had only ventured away from the territory twice. The first time had been the day that Kiki had died. On the second occasion, he had traveled in Rene's backpack with Rene and Ariel to the Audubon Zoo, an unseasonably warm day the first weekend that Brandy had gone to Europe. He had peeked through the backpack at the animals confined in large fenced areas. The large cats and bears had been among the most frightening of the creatures in the zoo. The smell of carnage and death surrounding their territory had been incredibly frightening. They reminded him of the dreams. Then there had been the reptile center. He had almost fainted when he had seen the size of the snakes and the alligators piled in a shallow pool. The most interesting creatures had been the seals, swimming in a Palladian style colonnaded structure surrounded by a wrought iron fence. He felt their contentment with life. When he returned home, he had been overcome with relief. The zoo reminded him of death and his own vulnerability. He did not want to leave the territory again for the unfamiliar. Ariel had understood his fear completely.

"OK," replied Rene, with evident disappointment in her voice. But I will miss you, Raleigh. "Tell you what. I will catch some beads for you and Chloe! We can all dress up for Mardi Gras!"

Raleigh stayed at home with Chloe while Ariel went out to a cocktail party. Brandy also left to take Rene and several of her friends to the parade. They had planned to cut through the front segment of the Tulane campus to Freret Street, which bisected the university. It was a mere three-block walk, and they could avoid taking a car out. Parking was a nightmare during the parade season. Outside, he could hear increased street noise of parking cars and pre-Mardi Gras revelers. The noise and confusion bothered the squirrel. He preferred to remain in the tranquility of the house.

He could sense Chloe's heightened nervousness from the sound of the celebratory activities a few blocks away. She paced around the house and finally curled up in her favorite cool spot near the living room fireplace. Raleigh stayed in the den watching the Discovery Channel. When the din of the shrieking crowd and the marching band escalated, Chloe ran into the den howling like a wolf. Raleigh stroked her face and neck, trying to calm her. Soothed, the dog finally relaxed, putting her head between her paws on the cool floor, eyeing him miserably with her huge brown eyes. Raleigh hopped on the counter and retrieved a peanut butter dog treat from the pottery rabbit and brought it to the dog. She accepted it delicately, careful not to harm her friend as she devoured the treat. He sat back on his haunches, admiring the dog and her incredible white teeth. She panted appreciatively, and the squirrel retrieved two more treats that he tendered to Chloe. She devoured them eagerly. Pacified, she gave him a swift lick across the face. Anxious to keep Chloe mollified, Raleigh selected one of her squeaky toys from her basket. Most of them were too big for him to carry. He found the small latex kitten that he could handle. Gingerly, he lifted the toy into his mouth and scampered across to the door. Chloe eyed him with delight, as he turned and squeaked the toy in his mouth before disappearing down the hall.

Raleigh raced across the carpet, down the hall, and into the study, bounding up the back stairs into Ariel's room, squeaking the toy. The latex dog toy was very cumbersome, but the squirrel had amazing strength in his torso and mouth. He could hear Chloe barking furiously behind him. The dog loved the game. She could easily overtake him, but she carefully gave him a head start before pursuing the squirrel.

The house was quiet, as Chloe, intent on the game, stalked the squirrel. Silently he waited on the dresser, the toy clamped in his teeth. The toy had a strong odor of rubber and dog saliva that was not altogether unpleasant. When Chloe came into the room and peered onto the bed, he jumped down, scampering down the hall and downstairs into the living room. Chloe followed him, barking furiously. Raleigh hid the toy behind the door and waited by the fireplace, sitting on his haunches with apparent disinterest, grooming his coat. Chloe, her eyes bright, eyed him and sniffed the air and began searching for the toy. Within seconds, she had pushed the door back with her muzzle and retrieved the toy, squeaking it furiously, the signal for the squirrel to follow her. He chased her as she went into the den and hid the toy. Chloe stood panting beside the sofa, a dead giveaway that she had stuffed the toy under the tailored furniture skirt. Raleigh searched the room, pretending ignorance. Chloe watched him with curiosity, her bright eyes fixed on the squirrel as he searched the table-tops, the shelves, and the corners of the room. Finally, with a triumphant chatter, he dove under the sofa scampering toward the toy. Just as he reached for the toy, Chloe triumphantly snatched it from his reach and turned toward the kitchen, glancing over her shoulder toward Raleigh as she disappeared around the corner.

Raleigh followed her. Suddenly, the dog stopped abruptly in the kitchen and dropped the toy on the floor. The game forgotten, she began to sniff the air and whine softly. Then she lunged toward the dog door, barking and growling furiously. The dog door was locked.

Raleigh felt a prickly sensation, and his nerves were on fire.

Danger.

Chloe looked at him imploringly, willing him to slide back the dog door latch. Intuitively, he knew that he should not do it. He bounded over to the den window and peered out onto the verandah.

Nothing.

He ran back into the kitchen. Chloe had stopped barking, her head cocked with her tongue between her teeth. In the silence that followed, they heard the delicate scrape of the wrought-iron gate closing in the back-yard. The noise would have been imperceptible to a human but was loud enough for the heightened senses of an animal to detect.

Chloe looked at Raleigh knowingly, her bright expression now replaced with suspicion and anxiety.

The prowler was back.

Chapter XVIII

Raleigh and Chloe were lying by the back door when Ariel returned home from the cocktail party. She was accompanied by two of her friends, whom Raleigh recognized as the women Ariel called Emma and Krystal. Emma, the younger of the two, was in her late sixties with frothy yellow blonde hair. Raleigh noticed that she always trailed a heavy scent of roses. Ariel explained that it was an expensive perfume like the other scents women wore. Krystal, on the other hand, was quite elderly, with stooped shoulders, gnarled hands, and translucent crepe skin. The older woman had a sweet disposition and was fascinated with the squirrel.

"Here are your little friends, Ariel," Krystal sang as she came into the kitchen, leaning over to stroke Chloe's head. The dog arched her head back gratefully as Krystal stroked under her chin.

Raleigh could smell a pungent medicinal odor wafting down as she stroked the dog. Chloe seemed to smell it too, because her nose quivered. Ariel had explained to him that Krystal had been recovering from a serious illness. She had the scent that all infirm animals have at the end of their lives. It was the scent of death. This saddened him because he knew that Ariel considered Krystal her closest human friend.

"She is so beautiful, aren't you Chloe," Krystal crooned, stroking the dog's lustrous white coat. "Look at those gorgeous white eyelashes. Most women would kill for eyes like that."

Ariel poured each of the women a shot of brandy into three crystal glasses. "She is from an outstanding bloodline. Her father was one of the top stud dogs of his breed. They are pretty without sacrificing their sweet disposition. She has been a wonderful companion," Ariel replied, casting Chloe a loving glance.

Krystal strained down and touched Raleigh behind the ear, scratching him softly. "Delicate little man," she said as she grabbed onto the counter to straighten back up. "I always wanted a squirrel as a pet when I was a child. They seem to be such magical creatures, sailing across the oak trees. But, in Arkansas, people thought of them as hunting targets instead of pets." She shook her head with disapproval. "They are smart little animals. I don't know how anyone could shoot them."

Raleigh felt a shiver of fear going up his spine. He had seen a television show featuring hunters. The men talked about terrible things like killing the deer in the woods. In one scene, a beautiful female squirrel was sitting high in a pine tree, gnawing on a small cone, when a deafening sound suddenly knocked her from her perch onto the ground. A shorthaired hunting dog had retrieved the dead animal and happily brought it to a man with a rifle. The pointlessness of it all had reminded him of Kiki's death. Men were the cruelest of the predators, killing for sport instead of necessity.

Emma stood by the door, maintaining her distance from the animals. Both Chloe and Raleigh could sense her fear and distrust. "They seem to be the best of friends. I have never seen anything like it in my life. Usually, squirrels and dogs are archenemies. It is truly amazing."

"Chloe is very maternal, and they were raised together, so that makes a difference," Ariel replied, eying the dog door. "Ladies, I will meet you in the living room, but first I am going to let Chloe and Raleigh out."

Emma and Krystal carried the brandy and went into the other room to wait for their friend.

Ariel slid the door open. "You two can stay out as long as you like," she told them. Chloe bounded out like a rocket. Raleigh followed close behind, knowing that he would be safe with the dog, despite the fact that it was evening. All of their play activity had stimulated his kidneys and he needed the trip. Since he had moved in with the humans, he no longer had squirrel habits. In the wild, he would have been asleep, nestled in his tree, for hours. Instead, he was romping outside with a dog.

Chloe attended to her personal matters before inspecting the walkway around the gate. She lifted her large snout and sniffed the air. Unlike before, there were no telltale signs that the intruder had been present. There were no cigarette butts or footprints in the grass. But the odor was unmistakable. Chloe whined and anxiously gazed directly into her friend's eyes. Someone had been there inside the gate again.

There was something very wrong. This was the same prowler. The smell was the same.

Raleigh could feel the dog's restlessness and confusion. Warily, she sniffed the air again and padded quickly toward the house. She stopped short of the verandah and protectively nudged the squirrel with her muzzle, herding him toward the backdoor. The squirrel jumped onto the porch and slipped through the dog door. When Chloe came inside, he decisively pushed the sliding bolt into the locked position.

They lay down by the back door while Ariel entertained her guests. Patience did not come easily to the squirrel. Raleigh rested his head on Chloe's rear paw and tried to rest. But sleep evaded him.

He knew that something was not right. He needed to warn Ariel.

Raleigh did not have an opportunity to have a quiet moment with Ariel until the following afternoon before Rene came home from school. The weather had warmed into the seventies in advance of another winter storm. Ariel set up the iPad on the verandah to enjoy the mild afternoon. The sky was darkening overhead, and the air was heavy with moisture.

The grass was still green, and the azaleas were beginning to bloom, along with the tulips. Across the expanse of manicured lawn, Raleigh could see Kiki's little marble marker. Their small female pup ran across the lawn and buried a little treasure at the foot of a dormant crepe myrtle. Afterward, she bounded over to the verandah, begging for a few seeds and a piece of banana. Chloe nuzzled her affectionately. Before long, the little female lost interest and returned to the expanse of lawn. Overhead, another young male barked at them for attention and raced across the oak branches to the small feeder the gardener had installed by the rear wall.

Raleigh inhaled deeply. The fresh air and outside scents smelled delicious. He was beginning to forget how stale the inside air felt. It had a different smell inside too, like humans and their machines. He was grateful for the opportunity to sit outside again. He felt the urge to go over and explore the area by the fountain, scouting out the possibilities of a handout. But, he resisted the temptation. Ariel would worry now, and he could feel that his strong instincts were becoming dulled. He could never forget that he was still an animal of prey, despite the fact that he could read.

Ariel scowled at the sky. "It may rain on the parade tonight," she told the animals. Chloe cocked her head as if she had full comprehension of every word. "If the weather is not too bad, people will still go to the parades. It is amazing what people will do for a few beads. When my husband rode in Rex years ago, he would tell me all sorts of stories. But, I think even he would be surprised to know that people undressed for a few trinkets." She smiled in amusement and shook her head, her thoughts obviously in the past.

Raleigh sat miserably staring at the iPad. Today, he had tried without success to emphasize the danger he and Chloe had felt the night before. Ariel had refused to believe that there was anything to worry about.

"There are people milling around in the park all the time now. Students from the universities come over and walk down the side-walk. Some of them are just curious about the large houses and how the locals live." She had smiled reassuringly. Despite her age, Ariel still had beautiful teeth.

Today, Ariel's smile had failed to appease the squirrel. He felt an overwhelming sense of frustration with her blithe reaction. His heart pounded in his chest. Forcefully, he pawed the "No" at the edge of the screen. Then, he methodically, he tapped the electronic keyboard:

"D-a-n-g-e-r. "

Ariel sat looking pensively for a moment. "Well, your instincts about this are probably better than mine. Even Chloe has been stirred up."

Raleigh sat on his haunches, nodding his head. It made him dizzy, but Ariel had explained that this was the human way of agreement.

"Well, nothing has been stolen or damaged, and no one tried to come into the house. Maybe they were unrelated incidents."

Raleigh sat perfectly still staring into his friend's eyes. Why couldn't she feel the danger? There was something bad out there. He could feel it.

"I will call the security service again in a few minutes. They can watch for trespassers or loiterers when they patrol the area at night. I will trust your instincts. I really have not had this problem in a long time."

Raleigh felt a sense of relief. She was going to do something. He watched as his friend picked up the receiver from the portable phone and keyed in the number of the security company. Briefly, Ariel explained to the woman on the other end of the phone that they had recently experienced another intruder in the backyard. She faltered slightly when asked why she had not called the police, but explained that she had just hoped that they were not intruders. She said that someone had come in through the back gate on at least two occasions.

After she hung up, she turned to both animals. "They have promised to step up the security around the house. So, I think that will deter whomever it is. Besides, we do have a burglar alarm that will alert the police department immediately if someone were to break into the house."

Raleigh sat on his haunches and tapped the keyboard.

"G-o-o-d. S-a- f-e."

"Well, I am sure that will take care of it," Ariel replied matter-of-factly. "But let's not bother Rene with this. She is just a child, and I do not want her to be afraid when she is in the house. She is still very impressionable."

Raleigh nodded. After he snacked on a few sunflower seeds, he and Ariel played three rounds of checkers. His concentration was off today, and Ariel easily defeated him.

Rene raced into the study, giving her grandmother and Chloe a big hug. She stroked Raleigh behind the ears and then proudly displayed her latest piece of artwork. The children had melted colored candle wax into frosted brandy snifters decorated with glitter. Rene had selected purple wax and green and yellow glitter for the frosted glass.

"See! It's a Mardi Gras candle. We can burn it every night at dinner until Ash Wednesday," she told them breathlessly.

Ariel admired the candle and beamed at her great-granddaughter. "Let's put it in the breakfast room now. We can use it tonight."

Rene clapped her hands, and all four of them went into the breakfast room to set up the new masterpiece. "I can't wait until it gets dark, Granny Ariel."

"Well, we will turn down all of the lights and eat by candlelight. Won't that be fun?"

"Wonderful!" She studied Chloe and Raleigh for a moment. "Oh, I almost forgot! I have something for each of you!"

Rene raced upstairs to her room, lugging her backpack. In a few moments, she returned, having changed from her uniform into her corduroy pants and a shirt. She carried a wad of Mardi Gras trinkets in her hand.

"It looks like you racked up at the parade last night," observed Ariel.

The child placed the beads delicately on the table, along with three doubloons. She handed the doubloons and a set of delicate lavender glass beads to her grandmother.

"I know that purple is your favorite color, Granny Ariel. And it matches your purple dress today."

"Thank you, honey. They are lovely."

Rene fastened the clasp expertly for her grandmother. Then she pulled out two strands of beads that she strung together and wrapped around Chloe's neck. The dog patiently sat on her haunches and allowed the child to arrange the beads in the cloud of white fur. Finally, Rene doubled a bright red necklace and placed it around the squirrel's neck. Raleigh squirmed slightly. The beads felt odd. They were cool to the touch and amazingly light.

Rene sat back and beamed. "All of you look very glamorous. Now, we are dressed for dinner."

She left the room and returned with a hand mirror from the drawer in the powder room. Rene held up the mirror to show Raleigh his reflection. He stared in fascination, as the cheap beads glistened on his neck. For the child's sake, he resisted the temptation to pull them off.

"Well, homework time after your snack," said Ariel.

Rene returned the mirror to the powder room and went upstairs to study in her room. Dutifully, Chloe and Raleigh followed behind. Chloe would, as usual, take advantage of this time for a short nap. Raleigh would amuse himself with a book or the computer. The days in the park foraging and begging for food seemed long ago now.

As he pressed the start button on the computer, he pulled at the beads around his neck. With a start, he realized that he was finally and completely domesticated.

~

Mardi Gras day dawned clear and deliciously cool with temperatures in the high fifties. Claude picked them up promptly at eight. They were invited to an all-day party on First Avenue in the historic Garden District. The house was only a block off of St. Charles, and they could easily walk down to see the Rex Parade, while at the same time they were in close proximity to the restrooms and lunch.

Rene was dressed in her unicorn costume for the occasion. She had been reluctant to leave Chloe and Raleigh, but after much prodding, Brandy had finally convinced her that they would be fine at home.

"We're going to be around a lot of noise, and neither Chloe nor the little squirrel would like that. They can stay home with the dog door where they can go out if necessary or have a bite to eat. I promise that they will be fine," she had assured the child.

Finally, Rene agreed, and after embracing the animals, she left with Brandy and Granny Ariel. Traffic was already congested, and it took them nearly forty minutes to navigate through the crowds down to the Garden District. The two weeks of celebration culminated in the fabulous Rex Parade that left from downtown and progressed down St. Charles Avenue until Napoleon Avenue. The spectators were already lined up on the avenue, staking the best spots with ladders and lawn chairs. Cars loaded with food and drinks for hungry parade watchers coasted down toward the side streets in search of parking spots. Everywhere, children wore costumes. It was an amazing site. The city was virtually shutting down to accommodate the celebration of Fat Tuesday.

"The Duplantiers and several of their friends have a viewing stand," Claude told them as they watched a family unloading a step-ladder from an SUV.

"Thank God," replied Brandy. "Granny Ariel, Rene, and I can watch the parade without fear of getting trampled."

Brandy had worried about finding a safe place for herself and Rene for the parade. Generally, the crowds on St. Charles consisted of families and students. But there were also rough segments. The revelry on Canal Street consisted of a crush of tourists and adults. Celebration in the French Quarter was much more risqué. Women routinely bared their breasts for beads, and many of the scanty costumes left little to the imagination. Brandy wanted to celebrate the day in a wholesome environment for her child and grandmother. The Duplantiers' invitation had been perfect.

The Duplantiers lived in a three-story stone house surrounded by a nineteenth century cast-iron fence with a corn motif. Matching balconies were located on the front and rear of the structure. It was a beautiful house, listed on the historic register, and a must on any walking tour of the Garden District. Two years ago, it had been featured in *Architectural Digest*. The interior was elaborately decorated with a mélange of antiques from Europe interspersed with family heirlooms that literally shrieked prestige and money.

In direct contrast to her beautiful home, Alicia Duplantier and her husband, Mitchell, were conservative and understated. Alicia wore faded jeans with an oversized sweater. Her salt-and-pepper hair was pulled into a ponytail around her porcelain face that belied her thirty-nine years. Alicia and Mitchell were great sailing enthusiasts and kept a vacation house and yacht in Bahamas. Although the couple was slightly older than Brandy and Claude, the four of them had known each other for years.

Alicia gave them all a warm welcome. There was already a sizable crowd, despite the fact that it was not even 10:00 a.m. yet. Rene found a little friend from school and went into the den to play computer games until time to leave for the parade. A man in a white jacket served champagne and Mimosas to the adults. There was an elaborate brunch buffet in the dining room, and the four of them ate a hearty meal. Alicia had told them that later there would be barbeque chicken, hot dogs, and burgers.

After brunch, the four of them went down to the viewing stand to watch the parade. Their seats were high enough that Rene was nearly eye level with the men on the floats. It was a spectacular event and the most elaborate of all of the parades. Both Granny Ariel, Rene and Claude were acquainted with many of the men riding on the floats. Ariel's husband had been a member of the Krewe of Rex and Brandy, along with her mother and grandmother, had been a debutante presented at the Rex Ball. She had brought a large shopping bag for Rene to collect her beads. Brandy loved Mardi Gras. It was one of the things that she had missed most about New Orleans when she was living in the Caribbean.

It was mid-afternoon when the final float and band passed by the viewing stand. The four of them had not left the bleachers once during the event. Rene had a huge stash of beads and trinkets, including a Chinese paper umbrella, plastic drinking cups, and doubloons. When they returned to the Duplantiers, hot dogs and burgers were being grilled on the rear porch. A party tent had been installed on the rear lawn with tables and chairs for the kids near a moonwalk. It was a carnival atmosphere.

Rene found her friends and went outside to play while Brandy and Ariel mingled with the adults. The partiers spilled out onto the front terrace to further enjoy the beautiful afternoon. The expanse of revelers grew as they were joined by various neighbors and friends of the Duplantier family who were returning from the parade.

By four, Brandy was exhausted. Business at the shop over the past week had been hectic with tourists and downtown traffic. She had raced home every evening to take Rene out to the parades, and then worked late on her tax documents and inventory records she brought home in her briefcase. She realized with a little remorse, that tomorrow was a workday. She went inside and collapsed in a wrought-iron chair on the rear verandah, watching her daughter play with the other children on the moonwalk. Rene had removed her unicorn costume, which lay neatly folded in on a corner table.

Claude followed her out a few minutes later with two mugs of warm spiced wine.

"Here. I brought this for you," he said handing her one of the mugs. "It's getting cool out here in the shade. I don't know how these kids stand it."

Brandy gratefully accepted the steaming mug. "Youth. I remember that as a kid, I never needed a jacket. Of course, they are running around and we're sitting here like a couple of old fogies." She smiled warmly and brushed her russet hair back from her forehead.

Claude pulled up a chair beside her. "I have been looking for a chance to talk to you.. Do you think you could drop by the office after work tomorrow?"

Tomorrow was Ash Wednesday. Many of the tourists would be leaving, and she did not expect a big day. "Sure. I could get there about six thirty after the shop closes at six. Is that too late?

"Perfect."

She looked around to make sure they were alone. "What's up?"

"Alot. I had an interesting call from Recov's attorney yesterday morning. They have our most recent discovery responses. Of course, they are stunned about the value of the stones in your possession. The bottom line is that you have gotten to them. Before, they did not take you as a serious threat. They believed that in the worst-case scenario, they would pay you about $1 million or maybe even $2 million to go away. They would keep the rest. The journals and the emeralds have made you a really serious player in this. They can't ignore you any longer."

"What have they said about the journals?"

"Recov's attorney, Quinn Beazley, has implied that they might be a forgery. He wants them to be examined by a third party."

Brandy felt a flash of anger. "Can they do that? Those journals were written by my husband."

"We know that they are authentic, and we have an expert. They are so detailed that no court would ever think that they are not original."

"It just feels invasive. I never realized how aggravating a lawsuit could be. Can they force us to allow an examination?"

"They can file a motion and ask the court to appoint an independent party to evaluate them under controlled circumstances. In the meantime, I need you to get me some exemplars of Harris's handwriting like tax returns, cancelled checks, and letters. Can you do that?"

She sighed. "It is insulting to have to prove Harris's handwriting, but we can do it. I know that I have some files at home, like our tax returns and cancelled checks. Those should definitely prove that Harris wrote the journals."

He patted her hand. "Good. Try to bring whatever you can to my office tomorrow night. I want to get it to our forensics person right away."

"Every time I think about Thad's patronizing attitude after Harris's death, it makes my skin crawl. I am beginning to hate those people more than I ever thought possible."

Claude put gave her a gentle squeeze. "Easy. I know that it's hard, but you are in the driver's seat now. These are all positive developments. "

She closed her eyes momentarily and took a deep breath. "Life is never what you think it will be, is it?"

He leaned back in the chair. "No. Connie and I made a million plans together. Through sheer arrogance, we thought it would all be so easy. Life had progressed right on schedule until Connie died."

Brandy tried to repress the thoughts of her own problems temporarily. Claude rarely discussed Connie, and she was ready to listen as a friend. "What was she like?"

He was quiet for a moment, his expression revealing that he was delving into the past. "She was beautiful in a dark and exotic way. She was sleek, sophisticated, and confident-at ease in any crowd. I think that is one of the things that I liked most about her. Kids loved her. We had started seriously discussing our plans to have a baby and then she got pregnant. Sometimes, I think it may have been easier if we had had a child."

Brandy was quiet, nodding slightly with encouragement. He was right, of course. Having Rene had helped her through the pain of Harris's death. She still had someone to love. And also there was Ariel. Her family was different than she might have imagined, but she was fortunate enough to live with people she loved. Claude was clearly alone.

Claude continued. "I really could not believe it when it happened. I kept expecting to see her. Every once in a while, I would think that I needed to call her or would talk to her at night about something at work and then I would remember she was dead. So young and such a waste."

"How did it happen?" She knew he needed to talk about it. She had felt the same need to discuss the death of her parents and then Harris. Sudden death was extraordinarily painful and difficult to accept. How different a second or two could make in life.

"Connie was on her way home from work. It was late and a teenage driver and his friends were hopped up on drugs. The driver was looking for his cigarette lighter, and the car jumped the median and ran into Connie head-on. She was pinned in the car helplessly for thirty minutes before she died from internal hemorrhaging."

"I am so sorry."

"I had gone to a dinner party for a London client. The police were waiting for me when I went back to our condo in Georgetown. I had to identify the body." He drank his cider. "She had written me a note while she was in the car. Only Connie could have done that. She carried a pad to make notes and keep up with appointments. She had scribbled on the pad next to her in the seat. Only Connie would have been thinking of someone else at a time like that."

"Jesus."

"My emotions ran the gamut. I was initially in shock and then angry. Later, I was terribly depressed. All of the kids lived and walked away with barely a scratch. I tried to volunteer with the children's ward a few months after her death. I know that is what she would have wanted. But in the end, it was just too painful."

"I wish I had known her."

"You would have liked her. I am sure of it."

Brandy smiled. "I am sure of it, too. Such a terrible waste! It is impossible to tell why these things happen."

He drained his cider cup, placing it on the table between them. Rene and the other children were still playing noisily on the lawn. The sounds of a brass band could be heard in the distance, along with the cheering of parade revelers. Crowds of parade goers still milled around in crowds on the street.

"Brandy, if anyone knows how terrible you feel, I do. I wanted to die when Connie was killed and I wanted to personally put a bullet into the head of the little smart-ass punk who killed her. But I had to try to put that aside and focus on what Connie would have wanted. I wanted someone to pay, but I wanted to put the money to use for an important purpose. I wanted Connie's death to mean something and to help the kids that she loved. I did not want it all to be for nothing. I had to keep my eye on the ball."

"Sometimes it is hard to deal with all of the outrage," she replied simply.

"How well I know. This lawsuit will ultimately make you extremely wealthy. Your future and Rene's future will be secure. But maybe you might want to do something in Harris's memory—a contribution to a museum or to a school. I won't say that it will take away the pain, but it will be a tribute to his achievement. Harris accomplished something important, and he should be recognized."

She smiled. "That actually is a wonderful idea, Claude. I think that Harris would have liked that. Maybe we could fund a chair at the University of Miami or something at Tulane Law School's admiralty department. I think that trying to do something positive will make me feel better in the end. Maybe it will give me a true purpose other than just trying to get rich."

Just then, Alicia walked into the room, smiling radiantly at Brandy and Claude. "Taking refuge in the corner from all of the chaos? May I join you?"

Claude made room for Alicia on the small sofa on the verandah. The three of them chatted about Brandy's shop and the beautiful weather. Alicia told them that she and her husband were planning a trip to their summer home in the Bahamas.

"You must come down with us, Brandy. It would be wonderful. I think that Rene would enjoy it and it would do you both good. We should include Ariel, and of course, Claude, you would need to come too."

Claude grinned. "I've been waiting for another invitation down, Alicia. I enjoyed the trip last year immensely."

Alicia stood and smiled. "Well, it's settled then. We plan to go down in about two weeks. It is always more fun with a group."

"I could use a break," Claude replied. "We will look forward to the trip."

Alicia grinned with her easy confidence. "Well, it's been great, but I should get back to the rest of my guests." As she opened the door, she called back to Brandy. "I'll call you next week and we can select some dates. I can come by your shop and take you to lunch. Maybe you can even sell me something deliciously expensive. I still have a bare spot or two that I want to fill here."

Brandy turned back toward Claude. “She doesn’t take no for an answer, does she?”

“No, Alicia is accustomed to getting her way. It really is a beautiful place. I think it would do you good.”

“I really am not interested in a beach vacation right now with everything that has gone on. The psychological association reminds me of Harris and the Virgin Islands.”

Claude looked pensive. “Well, they have a great house in Beaver Creek also. Maybe you can convince them that you would prefer a skiing vacation. But you need to think of the shop and be pragmatic.”

“What do you mean?”

“She wants to buy something from you. Think of the trip as client development. You could use more customers like Alicia.”

Brandy giggled. “You’re too much, you know. Always thinking about the bottom line and business.”

He stood up and called toward the door. “Speaking of which business, you should think about all the prospective clients inside. I think we should go inside and mingle.”

“Do we have to?” she asked playfully.

He gave her a stern look. “Neither money nor friends grow on trees. They require careful cultivation.”

She rolled her eyes. “OK. You have made your point.”

Scanning the lawn, now brightly illuminated by floodlights, she saw that Rene was still playing contentedly with her new friends. Satisfied that all was well, she followed Claude into the house.

Chapter XIX

Ewan set the key in the top drawer of the oak desk in his spare bedroom for safekeeping. He had taken the key to the padlock of the rear garden gate one evening from the IBIX office while the receptionist was in the ladies' room. That same evening, he had two duplicates made for the key at a small Metairie shop before surreptitiously returning it to its rightful place in the office the next morning. The duplicate keys worked perfectly. The following evening after work, he changed into a black hoodie, jeans, and his old Nikes. He parked his car on Pine Street and walked several blocks to Walnut Street and crossed the park. There were no cars in the driveway, and most of the lights were out in the house. Quietly, Ewan had opened the gate and took time exploring accessibility to the house from the back garden. The back garden was tastefully illuminated with outdoor garden lights. Ewan was careful to stay in the shadows.

From his position crouched on the verandah, he could hear a dog barking fiercely in the interior of the house. The old woman had a big dog which was a problem. If he abducted the child from the interior of the house, he would need to kill the dog.

Maybe the best thing to do was to poison the dog beforehand. He had also heard that feeding a dog hamburger with ground glass was a sure way to kill the animal.

Ewan knew that he would have to deal with the dog sooner rather than later. He resolved to do some extensive Internet research into killing a dog. On the other hand, simple rat poison in hamburger meat would likely do the trick.

As he walked near the bank of windows leading toward the back door, he was disappointed to find that the house was equipped with a top-of-the-line-security system. All of the rear windows and doors were wired with alarms, and a security decal warning that the house was protected was posted on the backdoor. The glowing screen from the electronic panel from the security system, which was visible through the blinds, displayed that it was in activation mode. It would be impossible for him to break in to abduct the child in the night without setting off the alarm.

He sat on the stone bench in the shadow of a magnificent oak near the gate and enjoyed a few cigarettes. The fountain in the reflection pool had been turned off for the evening. The air was cool, and the rear garden was peaceful.

It was no wonder the old woman loved to sit outside.

He knew that abducting the child would be a challenge. He decided that he would return to the back garden to study their routine. This would require careful planning and execution. He had learned in the Marine Corps that studying habits and routines was important for any secret mission. He could not afford to be caught.

Of course, the older lady was a problem. She was frequently at home babysitting the little girl. He might need to deal with her as well. And he might need to sedate the child for some period of time.

As he considered the problem, he finally decided he would need to enlist Jimmy Thornton's help. He had spoken to him briefly a few days earlier, at Thad's suggestion, by telephone. Thornton—the loser—had already spent his share of the money they were paid to kill the diver, on drugs and cheap women. Thornton had needed work and he had contacted Thad. Ewan could use Thornton to help him ditch the car he would use to kidnap the kid. Afterward, he would kill Thornton. Ewan did not need any loose ends that could connect him to the kidnapping. He wanted a fresh start.

He sat at the table inside the gazebo for a while, staring inside and enjoying the evening. When he finally left, he carefully relocked the back gate and slipped into the dark shadows of the park. Across the street, he could see the security guard in his car reading a Kindle.

He did not encounter anyone else as he returned to his car on Pine Street. Most of the cars were parked on the street in this area. Most people would assume that he was there visiting a neighbor.

The engine sprang to life and he pulled away from the curb. Ewan checked his watch. He still had time to go by a home-and-garden center to check out the rat poison before going home. That might be just the thing to take care of the white dog.

Raleigh perched on the back of the Chippendale chair beside Rene's computer desk. He watched miserably as Rene organized her rolling canvas bag and packed her school supplies. The child had finished her homework for the day and had now embarked on a new project.

Chloe stretched out on the floor in the corner, snoring softly. Her ears, however, remained erect and her forepaws moved lightly as if she were running. Raleigh recognized the signs that the Samoyed was happily dreaming.

Rene stroked the floral brocade pattern of her new suitcase. "Isn't it beautiful, Raleigh? Mommy got it for me at Macy's. I just love it!"

The squirrel eyed the pattern stoically. Like Chloe, vivid colors appeared to be pastels to him, and he was unable to appreciate what Rene thought was so appealing about the bag.

"I just can't wait until the trip! Mommy said we leave this Friday afternoon," Rene chattered. Excitement and anticipation was evident in the child's face.

It was only three weeks after Mardi Gras, and the weather had suddenly turned sultry. Despite the fact that it was early April, Ariel had turned on the central air-conditioning unit to combat the damp, sticky weather. Raleigh had been glad of the cool respite from the unseasonable heat.

"We're going to go to the beach!" Rene continued, oblivious to his dark mood. "And tonight when Mommy comes home, we are going to the store to look for new bathing suits. Mommy said I have grown at least two inches since last year. My old suit won't fit anymore, so Mommy said we can get two or three new ones and some new play clothes!"

Raleigh listened patiently to the child's palaver. He watched her with interest as she organized and reorganized the little case. According to Ariel, they were going to the Bahamas, courtesy of the Duplantiers, for a long weekend. Although she had pointed out the location to Raleigh on the map, he was rather disinterested. Ariel had explained that it would be a nice trip for the three of them together. Despite the fact that Ariel did not particularly like to fly in airplanes, she had agreed to accompany them in the Duplantiers' private turbo-prop. Claude had also been invited along for the trip. Ariel had hired a dog sitter to stay over the weekend to care for Raleigh and Chloe.

Raleigh was already having separation anxiety. Since he had befriended Ariel, she had only left once when Harris Blake had died and she had flown down to see Brandy and Rene in the Virgin Islands. Other than that, he and Ariel had seen each other almost every day.

"And we are going in a private plane. Isn't that wonderful Raleigh? We'll have our own pilot and everything!"

Ariel had explained to him that it would be impossible for Chloe and Raleigh to join the group. She said something about customs that he could not completely understand. What he did get from her explanation was that animals could not freely come and go into the country without being subjected to a period of confinement. To a squirrel or a dog, that was an eternity. Given that alternative, he wanted to just stay home with Chloe. Also, he was afraid to fly. He had seen airplanes on television and sometimes he saw them high overhead when Ariel pointed out a mere speck in the sky trailing a pale spiral of smoke. Airplanes were like a lot of man-made things. They made him afraid.

The child finally ceremoniously zipped up the case, pulled out the plastic handle and rolled it over into the corner. She admired it momentarily and then turned back to the squirrel. The sudden activity startled Chloe, who woke up and gazed over toward them with a slightly dazed expression. She looked at the suitcase in the corner warily, obviously cognizant of its function. Satisfied that all was well at present, she lowered her muzzle to the floor and closed her dark eyes. With her white eyelashes, her lids were barely discernable slits in her brow. Even the squirrel admired her beauty.

"Well, that's all I can do for now. Why don't we go in the back yard? Or we can ask Granny Ariel if she will take us over to the park?"

Raleigh blinked at her, waiting for her decision.

The child obviously sensed his disappointment at being left behind. Suddenly, she leaned over and stroked him around his ears and under his chin with her tiny fingers. “I’m so sorry that you cannot go, Raleigh. I will miss you so much and I know that Granny Ariel will miss you. It does not seem fair that you and Chloe cannot go.” Then she lowered her voice and whispered surreptitiously. “But you know, Chloe hates getting dirty, and she hates the beach. Once we tried to take her to Lake Pontchartrain and Chloe hated it! So, if you could take care of her, it would be best,” she said importantly.

Raleigh tendered his right paw.

“So, you want to shake on it, Raleigh? Good boy,” she smiled. Gently, she took his little paw between her thumb and forefinger and gave it a delicate squeeze. “I don’t think there are too many good trees in the Bahamas other than palm trees,” she whispered conspiratorially. “And there might be lots of snakes, so it I don’t know how safe it would be anyway.”

The child was clearly playing to his fears. She obviously felt a lot of guilt that he would be left behind. He would miss them, but he really had no interest in traveling to the Bahamas. Tiring of the discussion, he hopped down onto the floor, disappeared under the bed, and located Chloe’s ball. He maneuvered it between the game boxes underneath and shoved it out from the bed. The ball rolled toward Chloe and hit her on the paw. Groggily, she looked up. Seeing the ball, with lightning speed, she picked it up between her tremendous jaws, leapt to her feet and sprang through the bedroom door. They could hear her nails clicking on the wooden floor between the Oriental rugs.

Rene giggled. “She’s got it. She wants to play now!”

Raleigh looked the child in the eyes and then scampered from the room, with Rene trailing behind. The squirrel took the front stairs through the entrance hall toward the door. Chloe was waiting for them by the backdoor with a bright expression on her face. As the two of them approached, she disappeared through the dog door into the rear yard.

Raleigh waited with Rene while she told Ariel that the three of them were going outside. They crossed the verandah and went out onto the wide expanse of grass behind the brick fountain. There was an effusion of blooming Pride of Mobile azaleas and light pink tulips that had turned the rear yard into a virtual fairyland. The late afternoon air under the oak canopy had cooled considerably and was now deliciously pleasant. Raleigh inhaled the fresh air into his lungs, once again glad to have emerged from the artificial environment of air-conditioning. The fragrant scent of the flowers pervaded the air. Chloe lifted her nose, sniffing the aroma of the flowers and freshly mowed grass before racing across the lawn. Chloe waited near the gazebo, panting heavily, the ball resting in the grass in front of her forepaws. This gesture signaled her clear challenge.

Rene crouched down and whispered conspiratorially to Raleigh as he stood on his hind legs in the grass, his tail curled behind him like a giant plume." You go one way, and I'll go the other."

Chloe gave them a knowing look of comprehension. Rene still did not appreciate the hearing range of the animals. The dog had obviously heard her whispers as clearly as if she had been standing next to her. Watching Rene's body language, she intuitively sensed that it was a strategy ploy. She flexed her front paws and danced beside the ball. Chloe's upturned lips and rosy tongue gave her a deliriously happy expression. It was the expression that was typical of the Samoyed-playful, independent, and yet gentle.

Without further warning, Rene dashed toward the left in a wide arc, suddenly turning toward the dog. Her eyes darted between Rene and Raleigh, who approached her from the other side. When they were dangerously close, Chloe grabbed the ball and dashed around the gazebo. Rene shrieked with laughter, calling to Raleigh, oblivious that Chloe would hear her now.

"Go around to the other side! We'll meet in the middle."

Chloe waited behind the gazebo with the ball in her mouth. As Rene approached, she darted to the right just out of reach as Rene grabbed for her collar and raced around.

"Go around the middle!" she instructed the squirrel.

The dog ran around the fountain, behind the trees, over to the verandah, and over to the gate. Rene and Raleigh followed close behind and stopped within a few feet of Chloe. The dog, sensitive that the child needed to win, set the ball down and bowed down on her rear legs playfully beckoning her with her eyes. Rene stood very still, making eye contact with the dog. Slowly, she lowered herself until she swiped the ball with her right hand and ran off toward the gazebo again. Chloe gave Raleigh a knowing glance as she watched the child run off. Chloe could easily overtake her, but she wanted Rene to have a chance with the ball. Raleigh bounded behind Chloe, pretending to try to struggle to catch Rene. The animals were, of course, much faster than a six-year-old girl. But out of affection for the child, they were very good at pretense.

They ran around for almost three quarters of an hour. Raleigh enjoyed the strenuous exercise. He had noticed, of late, that his more sedentary lifestyle made exercise more difficult. Obviously, his stamina had suffered. He was glad that the weather improved and that he could run outside again with the child.

Finally, their energy spent, the three of them collapsed in the grass by the fountain. Rene rested her head on Chloe's forepaws in the grass and stroked the animal's coat. Raleigh stretched out in the grass beside them, no longer offended by Chloe's pungent breath.

Overhead, an adolescent male squirrel chattered at them from his perch on the live oak. Raleigh decided that he must have claimed part of this territory as his own. The unknown squirrel stared at him curiously, as Raleigh lay on the grass beside the large dog and the child. Years ago, he would not have believed such a thing would have been possible himself. Now, it seemed the most natural thing in the world.

Raleigh stared at the enormous limbs of the oak canopy shielding them from the harsh sunlight. With a start, he realized that it had been ages since he had climbed a tree. It was odd that he had not really noticed that for some time. But then again, things were different now. He was loved, and he lived with those that he loved.

He was happy. And life seemed perfect.

~

The Beechcraft Kingair gently touched down on the runway just as the late afternoon sun edged behind a low stand of clouds to the west. There was a brisk crosswind as the pilot taxied toward the FBO for private aviation. It had been a beautiful flight across the Gulf of Mexico from New Orleans. The shallow water surrounding Eleuthera Island was a brilliant turquoise blue that glistened in the afternoon sun. A customs agent greeted them on the tarmac, wearing a pressed uniform with shorts. Recognizing Alicia and Mitchell, his scowling tanned face broke into a wide grin.

“Good afternoon Mr. and Mrs. Duplantier,” he said enthusiastically. “It is going to be a beautiful weekend. This will be wonderful weather just for you.” He patted the blond head of Alicia’s six-year-old daughter, Carey. “Still beautiful and growing up!” he crooned.

Alicia took the man’s hand and squeezed it warmly. Then she introduced him to everyone as Manuel. He gave Brandy an appreciative glance and smiled at Rene.

"You are a very beautiful little girl," he told her. "You will be a heartbreaker when you are a big girl."

Rene smiled shyly and squeezed her mother's hand. Brandy stroked her daughter's hair. "Thank you," she told Manuel. I am very proud of her."

Mitchell gave Manuel a friendly squeeze on the shoulder. "Be sure to drop by the house later. Alicia brought you and your family some pralines and beignet mix. I think that there is some frozen turtle soup in our case too."

Manuel smiled broadly, emphasizing the deep lines in his handsome face. "You are so kind to me. Maria will be so happy."

Brandy noticed that he did not make any pretense of trying to search the group. It was the result of having money and the right connections.

Manuel waited with the group as they unloaded their luggage and strolled across the apron toward the FBO. He chatted amiably with Claude as if they were old friends. The FBO was a modern, elegant stucco building landscaped with flowering tropical plants. Mitchell and Alicia greeted everyone inside as the group walked through the lobby. Outside, a limousine was waiting in the parking lot to drive them to the Duplantiers' beach house.

Claude chatted with Mitchell and Alicia in the middle seat. Brandy sat with Rene on her lap, watching the lovely coastal scenery unfold before them as the car wound around the two-lane roads. Impossibly blue water lapped at the pristine sand beside the hills. There was a gentle peacefulness in the late afternoon. It reminded her of her life with Harris. How she had loved those days when they had sat on their verandah sipping lemonade or wine staring at the brilliant water as the afternoon sank into evening. They had talked about little or nothing, sharing the beauty of the moment. That was, of course, before his overwhelming obsession with *BYZANTIUM*. With a pang, she remembered that those evenings on the verandah were few and far between in the year before his death.

Granny Ariel seemed to intuitively sense her anxiety. She patted Brandy on the hand and gave her a gentle squeeze. "Different than St. Thomas, isn't it? And much drier than Nassau. It shows you can still learn new things at eighty-five.

Brandy smiled despite her nostalgia. Granny was right, of course. This was not St. Thomas. "Peaceful," she said dreamily. "It is very relaxing after the bustle of New Orleans.

"It will be a wonderful weekend. I can just feel it," assured Granny Ariel.

Brandy smiled and continued to look out the window. It had been a stressful week. The forensic handwriting expert and document examiner had verified that Harris's journals were authentic and had not recently been fabricated. The documents had been numbered and turned over to the plaintiffs' attorneys. Thad and Recov had sent twelve bankers boxes of documents to Claude and the underwriters in support of their claim. They also had quite a bit of physical evidence that had been placed into the registry of the court, including emeralds, personal effects of the passengers and ship's artifacts, such as china and crystal from the dining room. They had stated their intent to exhibit some of the items that the insurers could not claim like the *RMST TITANIC* exhibit that had traveled the country. Claude and counsel representing the London insurers had arranged to photograph and view the items, with the salvage experts and a Harvard historian who they had retained. Depositions were scheduled to begin the end of next week in St. Thomas. The first round of depositions had been scheduled to begin the first week in April. Thad and Recov's attorneys notified Claude of their intent to depose Brandy the end of the month.

The nastiest surprise had occurred late Wednesday. Attorneys representing Thad and Recov had amended their complaint, posted a bond, and sought to arrest the *BYZANTIUM* hull. Their pleadings argued that the hull fragments of the vessel were easily accessible, lying on a shallow shelf under four hundred feet of water. Claude had assured her that it was unlikely that the motion would be granted. Claude, Dick Simpson, and Jeff Hastings were preparing a strenuous opposition in anticipation of the hearing date in two weeks. Claude had packed a briefcase and had carried his laptop on the Duplantiers' plane. He intended to travel from Eleuthera directly to St. Thomas instead of returning to New Orleans with them on Sunday. Chris Banks, a paralegal, and fifth-year associate would also meet him in St. Thomas on Monday. Brandy was scheduled to go down for the hearing in 20 days. She dreaded returning to St. Thomas, but Claude had told her that it was necessary.

"We need a client to be present," he said. "You will make a wonderful impression—the young mother and grieving widow against these entrepreneurs. Dick and Jeff have the difficult part because courts are seldom sympathetic to insurers."

"Will I have to testify?" she had asked.

"Maybe on a limited basis. We will review everything beforehand and it will be a breeze. "

"I will hold you to that, Mr. Parker," she had replied with an insouciance that belied her true feelings. In truth, she was terrified.

The recent flurry of activity had been emotionally stressful for her. She had begun to worry obsessively about the case. Her emotions wavered constantly.

Was she doing the right thing? The answers to plaintiffs' interrogatories had been very insulting. They had attacked her emotional stability and truthfulness. Was she just letting herself in for a major heartbreak and a public one at that? This was certain to be more unpleasant than she ever even realized.

She finally resolved that she would just have to trust her instincts. Harris had been a fighter, and he had sacrificed his life for something that he loved. She needed to stand up for him, no matter how difficult it was. She owed that to Rene.

The car finally pulled off onto a paved road, down the hillside. The Duplantier retreat was a two-story pink stucco colonnaded structure near the beach. There were deep verandahs on each floor overlooking the beach and an interior courtyard with a fountain. Brilliantly colored hibiscus bloomed in profusion. All seven bedrooms had an en suite bathroom. Brandy and Rene were going to share a room with twin beds with a fabulous view of the water.

After unpacking, Brandy and Rene changed into loose fitting cotton dress, sandals, and light cotton jacket. Downstairs Granny Ariel, Claude, Alicia and Mitchell were already enjoying chilled strawberry daiquiris and a platter of fruit the maid left in the refrigerator. Mitchell poured Brandy a drink. He also poured Rene a fruit drink.

"This is a Shirley Temple—without alcohol," he told her. "Carey's having one too. "

"I love strawberries! They are my favorite!" the child replied happily.

Brandy accepted a drink and leaned back in a brilliantly colored cotton chintz sofa. The French doors were open, and she could hear the crashing surf of the Atlantic in the darkness. The strain of the week had dissipated, and she was now relaxed.

"We'll go sailing tomorrow and do a little sport fishing in the morning," Mitchell told them. "Then we will go over to Harbor Island. They have a pink beach," he told her.

Brandy smiled. "I know that Rene has been looking forward to that, haven't you honey?"

Rene grinned happily. "I can't wait!"

Brandy realized a little guiltily that Rene had not had a real vacation since Harris's death eighteen months earlier. Brandy had been so self absorbed in Massenet and her own grief that she had overlooked what was really important. She would not let that happen again. She, Rene and Granny Ariel would take some weekend trips together. They could go to Natchez or the North Florida beaches. Maybe they could even drive up to the Smoky Mountains for a week at the end of the summer. She promised herself that she would make time.

"Well, you will love them honey," said Alicia. "It's one of our favorite places, isn't it Carey?"

Carey did not take her eyes off the video screen in the corner streaming a Netflix Disney movie." It's fun," she replied.

Shyly, Rene went over and sat by Carey and began watching the movie.

After the adults finished their drinks, they walked a few blocks to an elegant restaurant on the beach specializing in seafood dishes. Rene and Carey chattered together happily in the corner of the table. The child was having a wonderful time.

Brandy felt flushed from the wine with dinner and the light conversation. She noticed that Granny Ariel was completely enjoying herself. She was an enchanting old dame who charmed her companions with stories about her travels and life in the city. Although she had resisted the trip initially, Brandy was very glad that they had accepted the invitation from the Duplantiers. It was such a gift to spend time with her grandmother. Ariel had been the primary stabilizing force in her life, taking her in after her parents had died and then after Harris. How would she have done it without her? How many more years did they have together? She shuddered to think. Harris's death had taught her that life was short. She had to keep reminding herself that things never stayed the same, and she had to stop worrying about petty things and start enjoying life.

After dinner, the group returned to the house. It was slightly cool, and she was glad that she had insisted that Rene bring a light jacket. The adults continued their lively conversation on the ride back to the house. Rene promptly fell asleep in her mother's arms, exhausted from the excitement. Claude carried Rene upstairs and tenderly laid her on her bed for Ariel and Brandy.

"She's dead to the world," he commented to Ariel and Brandy as he walked to the bedroom door. "It is the sleep of the innocents. I wish I could sleep so soundly."

"She will wake up just enough to let us put on her gown before she falls asleep again," said Brandy. "Thanks again."

Claude smiled, exposing his perfect teeth. "Glad to help. Good night, ladies."

Granny Ariel closed the door behind Claude and helped Brandy put on Rene's nightgown. The child was groggy, but responded to light prodding from her mother. Brandy folded the little sundress and put it away in the little rolling canvas bag she had bought Rene.

She smiled at her grandmother and kissed her lightly on the cheek. “Thank you for helping and thanks for coming! It is so nice to be able to spend time with you away from the city.”

“Thank you for including an old lady like me.”

“When is the last time you took some time away? I remember when you traveled constantly.

Ariel sat in the chair by the window overlooking the water. The crashing surf was audible through the plantation blinds. “Well, it has less appeal for me now. I have my charity work and you and Rene. And, of course, I have Chloe, Raleigh, and Rene to look after. I am very lucky for an old woman. My life is very full.”

Brandy wanted to tell her that the silly squirrel and the dog were no substitute for her friends, but she held her tongue. Even Rene was completely wrapped up in the pets. Brandy decided that it was the receipt of unconditional love. She worried sometime what would happen if and when one of them died. Rene had suffered too much loss in her life up to this point.

“Well, you are everything to us, Granny Ariel. Without your help, I think I would have just stopped living.”

Ariel kissed her good-night and went to her room across the hall. It was after midnight by the time Brandy changed into her gown and washed her face, applying a light coat of moisturizer. Thoughts of her conversation with Ariel and the events of the last week swirled in her consciousness. She slept fitfully.

The next morning, Brandy and Rene woke up early and went out for a walk on the pink beach. The sky was a brilliant azure, dotted sparsely with a few fair-weather cumulous clouds overhead. Rene held her tiny collection of shells and starfish in a yellow plastic pail. The surf pounded the sand as the early morning tide rushed in.

"These shells are for Raleigh and Chloe, Mommy," Rene told her as they walked back to the house for breakfast.

"What will they do with them," she asked her child indulgently.

"Well, they can wear them like their Mardi Gras beads or just enjoy them," she replied authoritatively.

Brandy smiled. "That's nice, honey."

The squirrel and Chloe were extremely cooperative with the child. Undoubtedly, Rene tried to anthropomorphize them, projecting her own human emotions on the animals.

"I promised to bring them a present since they could not come," continued Rene.

"Then you need to bring them one!" Brandy replied, knowing that she had lost the logic game with the child.

They had breakfast on the large verandah overlooking the water. The maid had laid out fresh bread, cheese, jam, yogurt, juice, and sliced fresh fruit. There was a samovar of steaming strong coffee and tea. Ariel was already on the porch, chatting with the Duplantiers. Rene rushed up to show her grandmother and Carey her new possessions while Brandy fixed them both a plate of food. She had not realized that she was ravenous after the exercise and morning air.

After breakfast, they went sailing on Duplantiers' fifty-foot sailboat A LICIA II. Granny Ariel remained behind to read and enjoy the view from the safety of the verandah. After an hour or two, they brought down the sails, drifting lightly off of the coast on the Caribbean side of the island. Although it was only April, the midday sun was brutal. Mitchell and Claude caught a few fish for dinner. They brought the fish back to be placed on ice and then sailed over to Harbor Island at the northern tip of Eleuthera. The wooden buildings of the old settlement were painted in brilliant pastels. They toured the small town and then found a quiet casual restaurant with a shaded verandah overlooking the pink coral sand beach. The Atlantic surf vigorously pounded the sand as the waves broke over the beach.

After lunch, the children ran on the beach as the women watched from the comfort of a beach umbrella, buffeted by the brisk wind.

Finally Alicia sat up and brushed the sand off of her tanned legs. "Well, what do you say we go back? Mitchell will need to start cooking and cleaning these fish if we are going to have dinner at a reasonable time tonight."

"I am so relaxed, I can hardly move," said Brandy as she struggled to her feet. "This has been a fabulous day. Thank you so much for bringing us here."

"It has been our pleasure," said Alicia. "We enjoy having company on the weekends here."

Mitchell gathered Claude and the girls, and the group returned to the boat. They snacked on a few fresh vegetables and had a cool drink as they sailed back to the beach house. The housekeeper helped them off load the fish and refuse from the trip. While Mitchell and Claude cleaned up the boat, the two women and girls went inside to shower.

They dined on the terrace, feasting on the fish, fresh vegetables, rice, and caramel custard. Brandy had forgotten how wonderful life could be in a tropical environment. Rene and Ariel seemed relaxed too, going inside to watch Disney films and play games when the evening air chilled.

The following morning, Brandy and Rene went for another jaunt on the beach. After they cleaned up, the group went into town to a church service and to explore the tourist shops and open markets. Brandy bought Rene a large pottery piggy bank.

They ate a late lunch before returning to the airport to board the Kingair.

Brandy settled into her seat, quietly enjoying the turquoise expanse of water below them. From their height, she gradually watched the continental shelf abruptly disappear. An impressive line of thunderstorms loomed on the westerly horizon marking the leading edge of a late season cool front.

It was already dark by the time they landed at Lakefront Airport in New Orleans. A surly customs agent met their plane and chatted with Mitchell and the pilot briefly.

A feeling of dread overcame her as Brandy walked back to the car, wheeling two stackable suitcases behind her. Once again she would have to deal with the controversy surrounding *BYZANTIUM*. She hoped that she was up to the challenge.

At dusk, Ewan removed the hamburger meat from the refrigerator. The ground beef had been laced with rat poison he had purchased from Home Depot. He had been careful to use latex gloves to mix the poison with the hamburger meat earlier that day. He sat in the corner of his small patio and mixed the solution, careful to protect his hands and clothing. The packaging and labels were boldly marked with warnings that the poison was toxic to humans. As Ewan folded the poison into the ground hamburger, he noticed that it was colorless. The sales associate had assured him that it was the best vermin poison on the market.

"It attracts rats like you would not believe," the man in the orange Home Depot vest had told him. "I use it myself, and it is our number one selling product," he assured Ewan.

Ewan had carefully measured the poison necessary to kill a dog. He guessed that the white dog weighed about sixty pounds. Satisfied, he wrapped the meat loosely in tin foil.

He fortuitously learned the previous day that the old woman, the widow, and little girl were apparently out of town. He heard the house sitter telling a neighbor that she was staying until Sunday evening. Ewan knew that opportunities like this did not present themselves very often. He noticed when he returned later that evening that the woman really did not supervise the dog. She let her out in the back yard while she routinely stayed in the kitchen talking on her cell phone.

He had decided to make disposal of the dog a priority. A week ago, she had unexpectedly come through the dog door of the house and confronted him as he was gardening with the IBIX crew in the rear garden. The dog had growled and snapped as the old woman tugged her collar to lead her back into the house, apologizing profusely. It was as if the dog knew that he had been watching the house and had sneaked into the backyard. As Ewan had watched her going back inside, her fate was sealed. The dog was too wary, and she had a dislike for him. She was a problem he needed to quickly resolve. The dog would always be a buffer that he would need to deal with to access the kid.

He had been diligently working on a plan with military precision to abduct the child. After lengthy research, he had finally located an abandoned shack in one of the many swamps surrounding the city. The old building was probably an old fishing shack that had fallen into disrepair. It was the perfect place to secrete a child and was accessible only by water. There would be no possibility for the child to escape. The swamp was filled with water moccasins and large alligators. In fact, the first time that Ewan had pulled up in the boat, a six-foot alligator had been sunning on the sand and shell area near the shack.

It was dark by the time Ewan found a parking place near Loyola University. He carried the ground meat in a plastic bag. For safety, he wore two sets of latex gloves to protect himself.

The park was empty and he was easily able to glide through the shadows near the gate to the rear garden. Gingerly, he unwrapped the meat and tossed it over the fence.

Ewan waited by the azalea bank on the side of the house and waited. Within twenty minutes, the dog sitter had opened the rear door to let the dog into the back garden. The dog sniffed the air and then immediately found the hamburger meat. She was so intent on the food that she did not seem aware that Ewan was only thirty feet away. He watched with interest as she gingerly took the first few bites, before turning to leave.

He threw the gloves and the plastic wrap with tin foil into a garbage bin behind one of the buildings at Loyola. Then he carefully cleaned his hands with alcohol wipes and disposed of them in a dumpster behind one of the university buildings. Afterward, he drove to a small trendy neighborhood bar on Magazine Street. The night was still young and he might as well enjoy it.

Chapter XX

Brandy stood in the inner atrium of the federal courthouse in St. Thomas. She had hated to make the trip, but Chris and Claude had emphasized that it was necessary. Granny Ariel and Rene had been inconsolable since Chloe had died unexpectedly three weeks ago. The dog had been fine when they arrived home from the Bahamas. The next morning, she had been lying lifeless on the kitchen floor, her lustrous coat glowing in the morning light. They had buried Chloe in the back garden near the wall by a bed of pansies. It had been a devastating loss for Rene who was now refusing to go into the back garden. The house was not the same without Chloe. Brandy had resolved that, in time, she would arrange to get another Samoyed puppy for Granny Ariel. Chloe had been such an important part of their lives.

Nervously, she stood beside Chris, Claude, and Jeff Hastings. She watched as Thad and the Recov representative, Jack Hudson, walked together with their lead counsel, Quinn Beasley, across the hallway and entered the courtroom. A fleet of junior partners, associates, and two paralegals toting Bankers' Boxes and bulging briefcases followed close behind.

"Christ! That must be a $10,000-an-hour crew," whispered Jeff Hastings.

"Beasley is a real showman. He has a lot riding on today," replied Chris.

“From the look of those boxes and briefcases, we are going to be here for a month,” chimed in Simpson as he joined the group. “We are set up inside, so we may as well go in. The judge has asked that all counsel join him in chambers to set up the ground rules before we begin. The deputy will let us know when he is ready. He is still reviewing the briefs.”

Brandy, accompanied by Chris, followed Dick and Jeff into the courtroom. Their paralegal, Jenny, sat in the front row inside of the railing beside a Banker’s Box of documents. She was an attractive, heavyset blonde in her late thirties.

She smiled reassuringly when Brandy approached and then resumed her conversation with Simpson’s paralegal, Wendy. Wilson Staples, a Boudreaux Banks fifth-year associate, was removing documents from his briefcase at the defense table. Brandy sat at the table beside Chris, on the opposite end from Thad.

Chris had dark circles under his eyes. Both Wilson and Claude looked terribly sleep deprived. The three of them had been working frantically on a prehearing brief for the court. Apart from her meeting with Chris yesterday to go over her testimony, Brandy had barely seen her attorneys.

Brandy felt her hands sweating profusely, and the nervous tension was upsetting her stomach. She had slept less than three hours the night before worrying about the outcome of the hearing. St. Thomas was a terrible reminder of the life she had lost. The past two days had been very difficult. She had dreaded seeing Thad again after all this time. Despite her apprehension, she gazed over at Thad, who was smiling confidently at Quinn Beasley. When he noticed her staring in his direction, he waved unabashedly as if to let her know that he was completely at ease. Brandy turned her head away angrily and shifted in her seat, her eyes filling with tears.

Chris turned toward her and whispered in her ear. "What is the matter?"

"Thad just waved to me."

Chris leaned over and whispered again. "Just ignore him and try not to look in his direction. He is just trying to unnerve you. That is all part of his plan." He squeezed her hand.

She turned back and stared at the court reporter, seated at a table at the foot of the judge's bench, as she set up her equipment. The courtroom deputy concentrated on the computer screen at her station near the court reporter, typing furiously from notes in a large ledger.

Chris obtained a legal pad and pen from Jenny, placing them in front of Brandy on the defense table. "Take notes during the hearing," he instructed her.

The courtroom deputy interrupted her typing to answer the telephone and then stood at her station. "Judge Cornwell would like to see all counsel in his chambers before we begin this morning." She gazed authoritatively toward the attorneys. "Counsel, please follow me."

Chris leaned over toward Brandy. "Jenny and Wendy will take care of you. Just enjoy talking to them and ignore that jackass at the other table." He smiled and winked before joining the group heading toward the court's chambers.

Brandy pulled her chair toward Jenny and Wendy, carefully positioning the seat to place her back to Thad. The two women eagerly included her in their conversation, which was primarily focused on their young children. Both of them were single mothers and shared the same frustrations and fears that troubled Brandy. Within ten minutes, Thad and Jack Hudson left and went outside for a cigarette. Brandy heaved a sigh of relief when the group left the courtroom. She began to enjoy talking to the two women and discovered that she had finally relaxed.

Brandy finally checked her watch during a lull in the conversation and was surprised to find that over an hour had passed.

"What could be taking them so long?" Brandy asked the women.

"The same thing that happens at every court hearing," interjected Wendy. "The court talks to everyone about procedure and what to expect. He always asks about middle ground and tries to bring the parties toward mediation and settlement."

"It's always this way," said Jenny. "Hurry up and wait. There is always a lot of down time in court."

"So, everything is alright?"

"Yes," said Jenny. "I am sure that everything is fine. This is perfectly normal."

Twenty minutes later, the cluster of attorneys emerged from the court's chambers. Claude sat beside her and gave her a thumbs-up under the table.

Momentarily, the clerk walked into the room, announcing, "All rise. The United States District Court for the District of St. Thomas is now in session, Judge Jensen Cornwell presiding."

With his black robe sweeping behind him, Judge Cornwell took his seat on the judge's bench. He was much younger than Brandy had expected—probably only in his mid-forties. He was deeply tanned, and his thinning hair was bleached white from the sun.

Before the hearing, Chris had explained to Brandy that the president of the United States appoints federal judges for a life term. "They are generally great lawyers with a lot of political clout," he had told her. "His primary concern is to avoid getting reversed by the court of appeals. So, any minor local influence Thad might enjoy will not have any value."

"You mean we will not get home-towned?"

"Exactly," he had told her.

Everyone sat in rapt attention as Judge Cornwell cleared his throat. The clerk announced the caption and the cause number, and the attorneys for each side stood, introducing their respective clients. The court extended all parties a gracious welcome and then turned to the business at hand.

"Well, I have read all of the lengthy and erudite briefing that has been submitted to the court. I must say that this is really one of the more interesting cases of my career on the bench. I feel safe in commenting that most judges do not often see pure property salvage of a one-hundred-year old ship. We are here today on the plaintiffs' motion to arrest the wreckage and hull of the vessel *BYZANTIUM* that is lying under approximately four hundred feet of water on the high seas about fifty miles distant from St. Thomas. The vessel is not in the territorial seas of the United States and technically is in international waters in the Caribbean. Plaintiffs are seeking the exclusive rights for the continuing salvage of the hull. The defendants, various underwriters of Lloyd's of London and London Market companies and the defendant in intervention, Brandy Blake, individually and on behalf of the estate of Harris Blake, contest the motion." He paused, dramatically allowing his gaze to sweep the expanse of the courtroom before he continued. "Now, I understand there are several items that have been salvaged that are in the registry of the court."

Quinn Beasley stood. Beasley, a senior partner in an internationally prominent maritime firm based in New York, had been associated by Recov's local counsel in St. Thomas. He was a particularly unattractive man dressed in an obviously expensive hand-tailored suit. Beasley's measured speech patterns were mesmerizing, and he had a commanding presence. Brandy's heart sank realizing immediately that this man would be a worthy adversary.

"Yes, Your Honor," Beasley announced with importance. "My clients have tendered into the registry of the court a huge quantity of precious stones and various hull fragments. My understanding is that the defendant in intervention, Mrs. Blake, has also tendered a quantity of emeralds and hull fragments into the registry of the New Orleans court. As I am sure you are aware, there are two separate lawsuits pending in separate jurisdictions in this matter. All parties are paying the substantial costs of safekeeping the items pending a disposition by the court."

Chris stood. "That is correct, Your Honor. The distinction is that our client, Mrs. Blake, is only seeking a salvage award. Her husband, the decedent, was the primary salvor before his death."

"We disagree with that wholeheartedly, Your Honor," Beasley interrupted. "Mr. Blake's efforts—"

"The judge abruptly cut off Beasley. "We are not here today to hear the ultimate arguments of the case, Mr. Beasley. I have asked a simple question and you have answered it. We are going to take this in order, if you do not mind."

Brandy heaved a sigh of relief. Judge Cornwell was unquestionably in charge of the courtroom. He was not going to be pushed around by an attorney, regardless of his importance.

Judge Cornwell continued. "Now, I understand that your clients, Mr. Beasley, are asserting alternative relief in the form of ownership rights to the vessel and all of the emerald cargo under the law of finds or alternatively a salvage award of ninety percent of the value of the cargo and hull. Mr. Banks' client is seeking only a salvage award and has not asserted ownership rights under the law of finds. London Market Insurers recognize that a salvage award may be in order, but vigorously deny that the plaintiffs have a right to ownership under the law of finds. Also, Mrs. Blake is the plaintiff in the lawsuit pending in New Orleans. She has arrested the cargo of emeralds only and hull fragments in her action for Rule C and Rule E arrest." He stopped and allowed his gaze to drift from the plaintiff to defense table. "Is that correct, ladies and gentlemen?"

All lead counsel stood, parroting in unison, "Yes, Your Honor."

"Alright then," continued Cornwell. "Those are the ultimate issues to be determined at trial and we are not going to decide them today. What we are here to do today is to hear plaintiffs' motion for the vessel arrest. Mr. Beasley, you have the burden, and it is your motion. Are you prepared to put on testimony?"

Beasley stood, erect and obviously anxious to begin. "Yes, Your Honor. We have at least five witnesses in support of our motion."

Judge Cornwell scowled, dramatically furrowing his brow. "I do not know that we will need that many witnesses, Mr. Beasley. The court has other business this week. I hope that you can expedite this. Who is your first witness?"

"Plaintiffs would call Thad Stuart, your Honor."

Thad jauntily walked toward the witness box and paused before the clerk who administered the oath. Today, he wore a dark suit with a conservative tie in lieu of his usual tee shirt and shorts. Thad appeared to be the consummate businessman now.

After taking the oath, Thad ascended the witness box, folded his hands, and began responding to his attorney's questions. Brandy noticed that he seemed completely at ease in this situation. As he talked, he described his initial meeting with Harris, their search for the *BYZANTIUM*, and ultimately, Harris's death. During the course of the examination, the court constantly prodded Beasley, demanding that he limit the testimony to the matter in support of the motion. Beasley gradually steered the testimony to the present salvage operations of the ship. He described the expense and the tremendous effort involved in locating the hull fragments, cargo, possessions of the passengers, and additional precious stones. During the course of his testimony, he referred continually to several maps pinpointing the location of the *BYZANTIUM* as well as photographs of the salvage operation. Even Brandy had to admit that it was all well staged and impressive.

"It is a very time consuming process," he continued in response to Beasley's prompting. "*BYZANTIUM* sank during a hurricane. She broke apart during the storm and, over time, the currents have carried the hull fragments and the wreckage northeast. Some of the vessel was found almost one-sixteenth of a mile away. The depth of 450 feet in the open water prevents anyone from staying down very long."

"And is anyone else, to your knowledge, making any effort to raise or salvage the *BYZANTIUM* and its cargo?"

"No one," replied Thad emphatically. "Together with Recov, we are the only salvage operation for the vessel."

Judge Cornwell drummed his fingers on the bench and then typed furiously on his laptop computer stationed on the judge's bench. "Counsel, if you do not mind, I have a few questions of your client."

"Certainly, Your Honor," replied Beasley deferentially.

"Now Mr. Stuart, is it your testimony that the primary wreckage of the *BYZANTIUM* is located over fifty miles from St. Thomas in the open sea?"

"Yes."

"And it is not within twelve miles of any land mass, country or island, according to the coordinates you have given us and the maps your counsel has entered into evidence?"

"Yes, Your Honor," Thad replied confidently.

"And is it your testimony that the majority of the wreckage is still lying on the floor of the Caribbean Sea at a distance of more than twelve miles from any land mass, country, or island?"

"Yes."

"And currently there are no other salvage operations ongoing for this vessel?"

"That is correct," Thad replied.

"I have heard enough, Mr. Stuart. Unless counsel for the defendants has any further questions, I am prepared to hear oral argument on this question."

"Your Honor, we do have other testimony. We have flown down two experts at great expense," said Beasley, his voice suddenly taking on a whining quality that Brandy had not noticed before.

"That is certainly unfortunate that your client has incurred that expense, counsel. Do they plan to testify to anything other than what was contained in their declarations attached to the plaintiffs' brief?"

Beasley's shoulders stooped slightly. ."The declarations contain primarily—"

Judge Cornwell cut him off impatiently. "Well, I have thoroughly read their declarations. Their testimony is unnecessary at this time. Much of what they have to say is not pertinent to the ultimate facts before the court."

Quinn Beasley grimaced. "Your honor, for the record, we object. My clients have the right to have their—"

"Your objection is noted, counsel," said Judge Cornwell peremptorily. "Mr. Banks, any questions?"

Chris stood. "A few very brief questions, Your Honor."

Chris walked to the podium with a legal pad. His examination was efficient, lasting only about five minutes. He established that no one else was attempting to interfere with the salvage of the vessel. Also, he emphasized that the wreckage was in international waters that were constantly transited by cruise traffic and pleasure craft. There had been a number of scuba sightseers looking at the wreckage after all of the publicity, although no one had earnestly begun a salvage operation that interfered with Recov's efforts. Moreover, Thad reluctantly admitted that there were still hull fragments that no one had located to date. Brandy noticed that Judge Cornwell followed the examination with interest.

Chris finally turned the examination to Harris Blake's death. "And were you in charge of maintaining the diving equipment, including the tanks?"

"Yes."

"And you are familiar with the autopsy findings of the cause of death, aren't you, that Harris Blake died because of a contaminated oxygen tank?"

"Yes, I heard that," Thad replied reluctantly.

Quinn Beasley jumped to his feet with renewed vigor. "Your Honor, this examination is going beyond the scope of the motion today. We do not—"

"Thank you, Your Honor, I have nothing further. I tender the witness," Chris announced as he returned to the defense table.

Angrily, Beasley sat down in his seat. Brandy noticed that Thad's earlier confidence had dissipated with the last round of questions.

Judge Cornwell turned to the remaining defense counsel. "Mr. Simpson, Mr. Hastings. Any questions?

Simpson stood. "No, thank you, Your Honor. We do not have anything further at this juncture."

"Mr. Beasley. Any redirect?"

Quinn Beasley shifted in his seat uncomfortably and then stood before the plaintiffs' table. "No, not at this point, Your Honor. But the plaintiffs would like to object to the court's refusal to allow our remaining experts to testify."

"Objection noted and overruled. Mr. Stuart, you may be excused. Mr. Beasley, do you have any other witnesses?"

"No, Your Honor," Beasley replied, his face reddening with obvious anger. He was clearly irritated that the court had refused to allow his witnesses to testify.

Judge Cornwell shifted his gaze toward Chris, Claude, and Dick Simpson. "Do either the defendants or the Intervenor have anything further?"

"No, Your Honor," replied Simpson and Claude jointly."

"Good. Then I am prepared to rule, ladies and gentlemen."

Beasley lowered his significant frame into his seat as Thad descended the witness chair and returned to the plaintiffs' table. His face had taken on an ashen cast.

The court pulled out several pieces of paper from a manila folder and began reading aloud. Within moments, it became clear to Brandy that the court was going to rule in her favor on the motion.

"It is undisputed by all parties that the location of remaining hull and various fragments is in international waters. Although certain small pieces of the hull have been salvaged, and a significant amount of cargo, the principal hull rests in international waters where it has remained for the last one hundred years. There has not been any evidence to show that any other person or entity has made any effort or attempt to interfere with the salvage operation. This Court will follow the law of the Fourth Circuit in the recent *RMST* decision and the law of the United States Supreme Court in the *BROTHER JONATHAN*. Although the Court certainly has jurisdiction and authority over the wreckage and salvaged cargo within the jurisdiction, there is no jurisdiction or authority pursuant to Rule C of the Supplemental Rules for Admiralty and Maritime Claims or under the general maritime law for this Court to exercise authority over a wreck within international waters. It is therefore the Court's opinion that the plaintiffs' motion to arrest the vessel is without merit or factual support. Accordingly, the plaintiffs' motion for a Rule C and Rule E arrest and preliminary injunction against the world from interfering with the salvage operation is without merit or factual support and is hereby denied."

Quinn Beasley was on his feet like a leopard. "Your Honor, with all due respect, plaintiffs would like to move for reconsideration. Can the court grant us a time for oral argument?

Judge Cornwell closed his laptop and handed the opinion down to the clerk. "File your motion according to the Civil Rules. The Court will thereafter determine whether oral argument is necessary."

Beasley reluctantly sat down in his seat. His face bore the expression of one who had suffered a terrific defeat, although he quickly regained his composure. "Thank you, Your Honor."

The judge scanned the room. "Anything else, ladies and gentlemen?" He scanned the audience before announcing, "Then court is adjourned and you are dismissed." They all rose as the judge left the bench and disappeared through a concealed door behind the bench.

Beasley and his entourage quickly packed up and left the courtroom. Thad did not even glance in Brandy's direction as he accompanied the legal team out of the door.

"You were great," Brandy told Chris as he packed up his briefcase.

"Chris smiled. "Well, we had the law on our side. It is not always that easy. Anyway, we have Thad's deposition beginning on Wednesday, as well as the depositions of the two employees of Recov involved in the *BYZANTIUM* recovery. No rest for the weary."

"I feel greatly relieved," she told him.

He smiled. She noticed that he still looked very tired. "Hungry? I thought we would all go out for a celebratory lunch."

They returned to the hotel and ate a light lunch on the covered verandah overlooking the shimmering water. Conversation was light, and the atmosphere was relaxed. Jenny, Wendy and Wilson left promptly before dessert to go to the beach for a swim. Dick and Jeff went to play a short round of tennis to ease the tension before the work began anew.

Brandy stirred her coffee reflectively as Chris stared out over the water. "What was that today that you were asking Thad? What was the significance about the oxygen tanks?"

"I have wanted to talk to you about that, Brandy. I have just been waiting for the right time." He sat back in his seat and turned his attention to her. "We have studied Harris's journals pretty thoroughly by now. Most of the emeralds were found and salvaged in boxes more than two months before his death. So, we paid very little attention to the entries in the journals about three days before Harris died."

"Was there anything important in them? You just said all of the emeralds that were stored away were found and packaged about two months before he died."

Claude noticeably averted his gaze as Chris continued. "Well, that is what we thought. But we have tried to correlate the number of emeralds found as noted in the journals with the ones in storage. Some of them appear to have been missing."

"Missing? How?"

"Harris's last journal entries were made in a new volume. Only five or six pages were filled in, and the entries were cryptic. Wilson and Jenny were reading them last night after we finished working. They were the most intriguing pages."

"Why?"

He spoke slowly, as if he dreaded what he was about to say to her. "Harris and Thad had a bad argument a few days before Harris died. It turns out that Harris had all of the emeralds and Thad was not in possession of any of them. In fact, Thad discovered that Harris had recovered a significant amount of emerald cargo, or more than the handful of stones discovered half a year before, and he demanded that he was entitled to a share. Harris refused, claiming that it was all as a result of his effort. They argued about money."

"So you think that Thad took them from the storage area in the back of the house? I guess that is why I never could figure out why that space was empty when I showed the movers the area when I was going to move. It was the strangest thing, now that I think of it. Before Harris died, the storage shed was packed with boxes and crates. Afterward, they were all gone. I did not think it was of any consequence until now."

"Yes. Unfortunately for Thad, he did not know that Harris had stored additional cargo in the house."

She felt an epiphany. "So, that was another reason that Thad was so interested in getting the souvenir emeralds from me? He thought he had them all."

"It appears that way. Until you filed suit, they did not have any idea that Harris had stashed the remaining cargo in the house. It was a nasty surprise. Thad apparently cut a deal with Recov and thought he was on easy street."

"A liar and a thief," she said angrily. "So, is that everything?"

Chris ran his fingers through his hair. "No, the most damaging thing was in the last two pages. Harris accused Thad of intentionally contaminating the diving tanks. He was having headaches and feeling weak. Thad apparently threatened him and threatened to do something to you and Rene."

She felt bile rising in her throat. "Oh my God! You think—"

His voice was firm and even. "After reading the journals, it is all falling into place. I think that Harris may have been murdered."

CHAPTER XXI

Ewan briskly stepped toward the cash register and paid for his coffee and chocolate croissant pastry. He felt euphoric this morning after receiving confirmation the prior afternoon by text that $250,000 had been wired to his offshore account in the Cayman Islands. The balance of the $2 million dollar fee would be deposited after he had taken the child. The cashier gave him a bored, disinterested glance as he dropped his change in the tip bowl and strolled to his car parked a few blocks down on Carrollton Avenue.

Obviously, things had not gone well for Thad at the hearing this week. Thad had been uncontrollably angry with Brandy Blake and her attorneys. He was unquestionably greedy. There was certainly enough money to go around, and after splitting it, Thad would be wealthier than his wildest dreams. But, Thad was anxious to force Harris Blake's widow to enter into a nuisance-value settlement.

As he walked to his car, he began to review all of the preparations he had made. To date, he had already secured another vehicle for the job from a doper with a chop shop in Mississippi. The car was a nondescript GM sedan about nine years old with fading paint and an altered VIN with Mississippi plates. Despite its outwardly dilapidated appearance, the car was in excellent mechanical condition and was safe in a storage unit in Chalmette. He had visited the safe house again in the Honey Island Swamp to stock it with peanut butter, saltine crackers, Gatorade, and bottled water. He left an army surplus blanket and pillow on the dirty mattress in the corner, along with a flashlight, lighter, hurricane oil lantern, toilet paper, and some alcohol based cleaner. There was no electricity or running water. It was an isolated, dilapidated structure providing no hope of escape for the child. He would need to keep the child alive in case they wanted proof of life. After he received the ransom money, however, he would leave the child in the swamp and disappear into the expanse of waterways in South Louisiana toward freedom. Finally, Thornton would be arriving within the next 24 hours to help him with the second vehicle. After Thornton served his purpose, Ewan would kill him, making it appear that Thornton had kidnapped the little girl. Ewan smiled. The plan was certain to go off without a hitch.

Ewan quickened his step as he walked toward his car. It was going to be a busy day.

Detective Allen Conner's desktop was submerged in a sea of paperwork. A mound of filtered cigarette butts filled the cheap ashtray precariously balanced on the top of a stack of manila file folders. Despite the air-conditioning, the humidity caused the room to smell like damp concrete.

Brandy wiped her eyes again with a wad of dirty Kleenex, streaked with washable mascara. She felt bone-tired and drained. The barrage of detailed questions during the last two hours had caused her to relive the events following the news of Harris's death. Chris Banks sat in one of the wooden office chairs beside her.

Conner ran his fingers through the top of his thinning blonde hair, leaned back in his chair, and sighed. He looked more like an aging surfer than a detective.

"This was a real tragedy. I remember hearing about this when your husband's body was recovered. He was a nice guy. I met him once or twice. He was totally committed to the salvage operation. I never really took it seriously, but now I realize that he actually did it. What an amazing guy."

"He was very reserved about it. I did not even realize the magnitude of his discovery. Now, I think that he was trying to protect us." She wiped her eyes again. "So, what happens now?"

"So, I will need to look at the Coast Guard and autopsy reports again and have them reviewed by forensics in Miami. We do not have the manpower or capability for that here in St. Thomas. In the meantime, we are going to want to copy the journals, and to interview everyone involved in the operation, including Thad Stuart. Do you know where the diving equipment is?"

"No. I don't think under the circumstances that I ever asked. Maybe you could check with the Coast Guard."

"Did your husband have any sales slips for equipment, oxygen, and other expenses arising out of the salvage operation?"

"We have all of that very well documented. Harris was meticulous. We will see that you have copies of everything immediately."

Conner nodded and then furrowed his brow. "Mrs. Blake, you mentioned that Thad Stuart told you that Harris bought some secondhand diving equipment before he died to save money. Did you know anything about it?"

Brandy shook her head. "No, I did not. In fact, it seemed rather out of character for Harris, because he was a very serious diver. He was a scientist and he knew the risks, so he made sure that his equipment was the very best that he could afford. Also, now that you mention it, he had purchased new tanks and a regulator the year before. I think they are still packed in my grandmother's attic in New Orleans."

"Do you recall if the equipment is still operable?"

"I would have to look. But it looked to be in very good condition."

"How much equipment did he have?"

"Quite a bit, I think. There was additional diving equipment on the boat we owned."

The detective made a few notes on a legal pad placed across the mound of paperwork in front of him. "Are you a diver?"

"I have been certified, and I have been on a number of shallow dives with Harris. But when I was pregnant and after Rene, our daughter, was born, I did not want to take those risks, and I stopped going with him on his adventures, as he liked to call them. I think after that we actually started growing apart."

The detective shook his head. "Makes sense. Now, did you report your husband as missing the day he died?"

Brandy felt a pang of guilt. "Harris was seldom at home except the night before he died. When he was there, he locked himself into his study and worked. Sometimes, he stayed down at the boat and other times he stored things in our spare bedroom or in the storage shed behind the house. He was very involved in what he was doing. I had begun to think it was a pipedream. If he had only trusted me enough to let me know that he had succeeded." Her voice cracked and she dissolved into tears. Allen Conner waited patiently for her to finish crying.

Conner's voice was patient, and his eyes had a particularly sensitive quality. "Do you know who alerted the Coast Guard that he was not back?"

She dabbed her eyes again with Kleenex. "Thad, I think. He said a fishing boat had spotted their boat, the *CAPTAIN HOOK*, earlier that day. A few hours later when they returned in the mid-afternoon, they did not see Harris on board. They radioed Thad who called the Coast Guard. I am sure it will be in the report."

Conner was pensive for a moment. He jotted another note on his pad. "Did Harris customarily dive alone?"

"I know how dangerous it is, but yes, he was on a budget. I begged him to hire someone to go down with him. Usually, he had someone on board with him, but that person stopped working for Harris about a week before he died."

"What was his name?"

"Jimmy Thornton. He was a young kid, seeking thrills and adventure-just an itinerant moving from island to island."

"Do you know where he is now?"

"No. I think Harris said that he moved to Barbados, but I may be mistaken."

"Did you ever hear from him again?"

"No. Never," she said, shaking her head absently. "I never really cared for him. He seemed like a reckless doper to me."

"Do you have any employment records that might contain a Social Security number or other identifying information?"

"I have something in my office," Chris said. "We have looked for Thornton unsuccessfully. He is a material witness."

Detective Conner shook his head. "The government has resources, and we may have better luck. Just get me the information," he instructed Claude.

"We will have someone send it over this afternoon."

"Now, what about the outfit, Recov. Did you husband ever mention them to you?"

She shook her head. "Once or twice. He said that Thad was interested in working with them. They are a huge outfit, and Harris did not want them coming in on his work to locate *BYZANTIUM*."

Conner made another fastidious note. Brandy noticed that his print was even and clear. He sat back in his chair. "Have you had any problems since you have gone back to New Orleans?"

"What kinds of problems?"

"Prowlers? Anything?"

"Brandy's grandmother has complained that they found some mysterious cigarette butts in the backyard inside the wall. Then, about two weeks ago, her grandmother's dog was poisoned." Chris interjected.

"Did you report it?" Conner asked.

"Granny Ariel reported it to the police and the security service that patrols the neighborhood after the vet confirmed that Chloe had been poisoned. Chloe was a beautiful, gentle dog and I cannot imagine who would have done such a thing."

"I am glad she reported it to the authorities. It may be nothing, but better safe than sorry."

Brandy clenched the Kleenex in her right hand. "Do you think my husband was murdered?"

Conner sighed. "Mrs. Blake, I do not know the answer to that question. It may have been entirely innocent, but the circumstances look very suspicious. I want you to understand that having a suspicion and proof enough to charge someone are two different things. Right now, we don't really have a suspect, except perhaps Thad Stuart. He would have benefited the most from Harris' death. Then, we will need to talk to the folks at the dive shop. We will have a lot of work to do on this case. Right now, all we have is a diving accident. The man who reported the death allegedly threatened to hurt the victim or his family a few days before. The men had an argument over money—big money—before your husband's death. But we have almost no evidence. We will do our best. That is all that I can promise you now."

"Do you intend to talk to Thad Stuart soon?" Chris asked.

"I will get the Coast Guard reports and forensics faxed to me tomorrow. I will probably swing by and chat with him for a few moments tomorrow afternoon."

"We are deposing Stuart on Wednesday afternoon. It would be great if you could chat with him beforehand."

Conner grinned with a hint of malice. Obviously he was aware that if Thad were asked under oath about the interview during his deposition, he would have to admit that the authorities had questioned him about Harris's death. "I will try to catch him tomorrow morning first thing. I see his car there every morning."

"Do you think that Jimmy Thornton had anything to do with this?" Brandy asked.

Conner leaned back in his seat. "It's hard to say. But we are going to try to find out all about him and talk to him. We need those employment records."

Claude made a note on his legal pad. "I will have one of the paralegals look this up and fax a copy to you this afternoon."

Conner smiled warmly. "Thanks. That will be a good start."

Brandy stood up, noticing that her legs were weak from exhaustion. She shook Conner's hand and gave him a wan smile. "I hope that you can catch the person who did this. "

His expression sobered. "Mrs. Blake, if your husband was murdered, I certainly hope that we catch and convict his killer. But we really do not have anything at this point. Your husband died well over a year and a half ago, and the trail is very cold. We have a lot of suspicion and very little to indicate that he was murdered. The prosecutors need a case showing that the perpetrator was guilty beyond a reasonable doubt or beyond any reasonable hypothesis consistent with innocence. That is a heavy burden, and suspicion will not cut it. But I promise you that we will give this our very best shot. That is all I can say at this point."

She managed a smile. "I understand. Good luck."

He walked them to the front of the building into the warm, humid air. The glorious surroundings were suddenly at odds with the way she felt. She felt sobered by the conversation with Conner. She knew that he would give it his best shot. But it was impossible to ignore the import of what he was trying to tell her.

The odds were against them. Once again, Thad Stuart was going to come out ahead.

~

Brandy decided to stay an extra couple of days to attend the deposition of Thad Stuart. Natalie had assured her that she had things well under control. The tourist influx would continue into the early summer despite the terrific heat. Over the last week, Massenet had reaped the benefit of several large purchases, including an eighteenth century Chippendale bed, a French escritoire, three paintings, and a gorgeous Bombay chest with a marble top. Natalie had also sold a set of French Haviland china. Brandy would give her a hefty commission for her good work.

Granny Ariel had told her that Rene was safe and happy at home. The two of them had gone to a movie and downtown to shop and visit the aquarium. Rene's class had a field trip to the museum on Thursday afternoon. Brandy felt relieved that all was well. In fact, she realized, rather soberly, that she was hardly missed.

Tuesday morning, Brandy put on a simple cotton dress with sandals and met briefly with Chris, his associate, and the paralegals in the local counsel's office. Afterward, she went out for a stroll through the market and the shops, purchasing a few souvenirs for Granny Ariel, Rene, and Natalie. She had a light lunch and spent the remainder of the afternoon at the beach, trying to read a thriller on the best-seller list. Her attention roamed, and she felt unusually exhausted. In the end, she gave up and dozed under her hat. Later, she went for a long swim in the pool before going upstairs to shower and freshen up.

She met Chris, Claude, and their associate, along with Jeff Hastings and Dick Simpson, in the luxurious hotel dining room at seven.

"This is going to be a quick evening," Chris explained. "I still have lots to do before tomorrow."

She grinned. "I can entertain myself. I want you to earn your fee anyway. I would not feel right if you were enjoying yourself. Remember, my grandfather was an attorney. I know the drill."

He smiled, obviously pleased that she appreciated the situation. "Yes ma'am. I will make sure that I work my fingers to the bone," he replied with exaggerated obsequiousness.

Dinner was pleasant in the luxurious surroundings. They dined near an expanse of French doors overlooking the emerald Caribbean. A large verandah was decorated with stone urns carrying floral confections and bronze statuary that extended beyond the doors. Dinner was light with seafood, and no alcohol or dessert.

Brandy called Granny Ariel when she returned to the room. Rene was unfortunately already asleep. Brandy spent the remainder of the evening watching television and reading her Kindle. She slept fitfully and woke up groggy and exhausted. She knew that the stress was getting to her. Facing Thad again and knowing that he could have been responsible for Harris's death was almost more than she could stand. She felt an uncontrollable rage now. She had trusted him.

She met Chris and Claude downstairs for breakfast at seven thirty. Afterward, they took a cab to the office of Ziebart, Wicker, Copeland and Turnberry, a St. Thomas law firm. Local rules of the federal court in St. Thomas required that any out-of-town attorney associate local counsel for the case. Wally Ziebart had briefly attending the hearing on Monday. Unlike Boudreaux Banks, the Ziebart firm was being paid on an hourly basis at the hefty rate of $450 an hour. Chris assured her that despite the extraordinary expense, it was well worth the effort. Wally Ziebart, the grandson of the founder of the firm, was eminently successful and certainly the choice of local counsel. He obviously was well respected by the court. Brandy recalled meeting Wally briefly once at a party during the first year she and Harris lived in St. Thomas. After a while, when Harris had become completely focused on the *BYZANTIUM*, their social life had dwindled, and Brandy had nearly stopped attending parties.

The Ziebart office was located in a lovely two-story stucco building that screamed prestige. The spacious conference room overlooked the harbor and the towering thunderstorms overhead. Wally greeted them both warmly.

"The storm is terrible this morning. Good day to spend inside," he said with a smile as he extended his hand to her. "Nice to see you again."

Brandy shook his hand firmly and managed a polite smile. "It does look bad. How well I remember those days when the rain poured all day in sheets. But it rains pretty hard in New Orleans, too."

"Well, we had a brilliant day in court on Monday. And I know that you had a visit with Allen Conner. What a mess."

She felt her blood pressure rise and a pounding in her chest as she again contemplated the possibility that Thad had somehow been responsible for Harris's death. She struggled to maintain her equanimity. "It is incredible! And to think that I never even questioned Thad. I thought he was our friend."

"Betrayal is one of the worst discoveries," Wally told her. "Unfortunately, I see it more often than not in commercial litigation. But, Chris will knock them dead. He was one of my classmates at Harvard and graduated in the top five. You are in good hands."

She tried to smile in response to his warm assurances. "I have a lot of confidence in him."

Jenny and Wendy were setting up the exhibits in the conference room. A row of Banker's Boxes filled one wall. They showed her to a chair between Chris and Claude, directly across from where Thad would be seated. Two legal pads and three colored pens along with Post-it notes rested on the table in front of her seat.

Beasley and Thad arrived with their entourage a few minutes before nine. Beasley carried only a small briefcase. He and Thad smiled exuding an exaggerated confidence. Beasley asked to meet with Chris, Claude, Jeff, Wally, and Dick before the deposition. Brandy could hear Quinn Beasley's elevated voice though the walls in the adjoining conference room.

"What the fuck are you trying to prove? Don't think I don't know your tactic. I know that you and your client asked Alan Conner to pay my client a visit to scare us off. Thad Stuart is a prominent businessman in St. Thomas, and we won't allow you to smear his name."

Chris's reply was even but still audible to Brandy. "Your client is a small-time operator running an underinsured day sailing operation for tourists and nothing more. Based upon his tax returns for the last few years, he was barely holding on and almost lost his business. If there is a criminal investigation going on, I suggest that he cooperate. Everyone in this room knows that we cannot force a prosecution of anything. Now, I suggest that we get on with the deposition."

Brandy glanced over toward Thad whose face had turned a deep crimson. He returned her stare with unbridled hatred. She felt her pulse quicken again, and she took a few deep breaths to maintain her composure.

Chris, Claude, Dick, Jeff, and Beasley reemerged into the conference room with an air of solemnity. Dick Simpson began the questioning. Brandy admired his style. He was unfailingly polite but very direct. There was no question that he was in control of the process. The progress was arduous. Brandy never dreamed of how many foundation questions could be asked. By one-thirty, they had just begun to introduce the topic of the hunt for the *BYZANTIUM*.

"How did you get into business with Harris Blake?" Simpson finally asked.

Thad leaned back in his seat. "I used to see him all the time around the waterfront. Once in a while, we had a beer together or just chatted on the dock. One day, he confided to me about his project. He said he was running out of money. His wife, or the 'loan officer' as he called her, was tired of the project, and he asked me if I wanted to go in with him. His wife had a trust fund and she was funding his project. I got the impression that he and his wife did not really get along too well and that he had married her for her money." Thad cast a triumphant glance in Brandy's direction.

"Did you ever see or hear Brandy or Harris Blake argue?"

"No."

"Did you ever see or hear them physically fighting?"

Thad squirmed. "No. It was just an impression."

"So, is it fair to say that you don't have any facts to support your impression?"

"Just a feeling, based upon what he said."

Dick screwed up his face. "So, it was just your feeling then, is that correct?"

"Yes."

"You are badgering the witness, and your questions are inappropriate," interjected Beasley in a harsh tone. "You are wasting our time, counsel, and if we need to recess and contact the court, I will be happy to do so."

"Your client brought up the matter. Feel free to contact Judge Cornwell if you like, but you are just wasting time," Dick responded, unfazed by Beasley's threat.

"Just stick to the subject matter, counsel," Beasley grumbled, conceding the issue.

Dick folded his hands and continued the deposition with measured equanimity. "Was Brandy Blake ever rude to you?"

"No. She was always pretty civil."

"Did you consider the venture with Harris Blake a good business investment?"

"Sure."

"Tell me why."

"He was so committed."

"Wasn't there something else? He had at least ten twenty-carat emeralds that he had recovered by that point, didn't he?"

Thad looked over at his attorney.

"You don't need your attorney's consent to answer. Please answer the question. "Didn't Harris have several emeralds from the *BYZANTIUM* at the time he asked you to go into business with him?"

"Objection to the form," interjected Beasley.

"Yes," Thad said finally. "He had ten emeralds he had claimed he recovered from the *BYZANTIUM*."

"And that was before you were even in business with him."

Thad was quiet for a moment before he answered. Quinn Beasley's face was bright red. "Yes. It was before we formed our partnership."

Dick took a different tack. "Did the two of you ever seek advice from an attorney to draft a formal partnership agreement?"

"No. We really did not have the money."

"So, your understanding was oral?"

"Yes, it was."

"And what was the percentage you were going to divide the profits?"

"Fifty fifty."

"And you have read Harris Blake's journals, haven't you, Mr. Stuart?"

"Yes. "

"And are you aware that the journals say that the profits were to be divided seventy-five/twenty-five with Harris Blake retaining 75 percent of the profits?"

"Yes, I saw that, but it is not right."

"What other evidence do you have to support your assertion that you were entitled to 50 percent of the profits?"

"What do you mean evidence? I'm not a lawyer, so I don't understand," Thad replied in a hostile tone.

"Well, do you have any memos or other writings?"

"No."

"So, it is just your word."

"I guess it is."

"And Harris Blake is not here to contradict you on that?"

"No, he's not."

Brandy took another deep breath and stared openly at the man seated across from her. She was convinced now, more than ever, that he had been responsible for Harris's death.

"And would you agree that the only written evidence of your agreement is what was contained in Harris Blake's journals?"

"Yes," Thad replied reluctantly.

"And you are aware that Brandy Blake would contradict you?"

"Yes. I was told that."

"Did you contribute anything to this partnership?"

"Well, Harris needed a new boat, and I had my pulse on what was available in the area. He really could not afford the boat. He and his wife were living on her salary. She taught art or something like that."

"My question is, what, if anything, did you contribute to this partnership?"

"He bought a thirty-two-foot Bayliner. Harris sold his old Tollycraft and used that equity and a couple of thousand more to make up the difference. My maintenance man, Willie, made the repairs."

"Did you go out and dive with Harris Blake?"

"No, never did."

"Are you certified to dive?"

"No, he wanted to handle that part by himself. But later, we hired Jimmy Thornton to go out with him for safety and to help."

"How long did Thornton work for you?"

"About three months. He was just a young dive junkie moving around from island to island looking for adventure and thrills."

"How long ago did he leave?"

"A couple of weeks before Harris drowned."

"Do you know where he is today?"

"I don't have a clue."

"Why did he leave?"

"Bored with the gig. It was just time. He was just a kid."

"Have you talked to him since?"

Thad hesitated only imperceptibly. "No. One day he said he wanted to go and that afternoon was the last I ever talked to him."

"Who paid his salary in the informal arrangement?"

"Sometimes I did. Sometimes Harris did. It was a shoestring operation, and we were not getting any results."

"Did the operation recover any other emeralds?"

"One or two. Things were not going too well. I wanted to get a big outfit like Recov involved. The money was going to be good when we recovered all of the emeralds, even splitting the profit and we were not making any progress."

"Did Harris Blake agree?"

"No, he did not want some big outfit involved. He saw this as his baby."

Dick changed tactics. "Where were the emeralds that were recovered stored?"

Thad shifted in his seat. "I had the ones that were recovered when we were in partnership."

"What about the emeralds that were recovered before the partnership?

"I guess Harris had those."

"Now, of course, you are aware that a significant number of emeralds recovered by Harris Blake are in the registry of the court in New Orleans."

"I heard something about it."

"Do you know when those emeralds were recovered?"

"No."

"But as far as you know, Harris did not recover more than three or four emeralds while he was in partnership with you?"

"That's what he told me, unless he was concealing something–"

Beasley shot Thad an angry warning glance, and the witness stopped talking.

"How long after Harris died did you negotiate an agreement with Recov?"

"I don't really remember."

Dick handed Thad an agreement that had been premarked as a deposition exhibit. "Look at the bottom right-hand corner of this agreement. It shows that you signed it on November 4, exactly ten days after Harris Blake died, does it not?"

Thad stared at the document quietly before answering the question. "It says that I signed it then. I really don't remember when Harris Blake died."

"Did you contact Brandy Blake before you signed this agreement?"

"No."

"Do you know whether Brandy was given an opportunity to meet and confer with anyone from Recov?"

"No, I don't."

"So, as far as you know, she was in the dark about this thing?"

"I don't know what she did or did not know," Thad shot back defiantly.

Dick looked at his watch. "Well, it's after five now. I think we should recess until tomorrow. We have permission from the court to continue the deposition for two days as necessary since we are consolidating discovery between the two cases."

The group agreed to reconvene at eight-thirty the following morning. Wally drove Brandy, Chris, Wilson, and Claude back to the hotel. Dick, Jeff, and the paralegals wanted to go out for a walk to relax.

Chris, Claude, and Brandy went into the small hotel grill for an evening salad. Claude looked seemed pensive.

"Well, I hesitate to ask, but how did it go today?"

Chris grinned. "It went extremely well. Dick really kicked their ass. They have nothing to dispute the fact that the division of the profits was a 75/25 percent split. Also, the partnership did not show a profit, but Harris was in possession of a large quantity of emeralds. That makes you a real player. It also makes Recov and Thad look deceptive because no one consulted you before they signed the agreement, but they were trading on information developed by Harris. Hell, they even used partnership assets, and Thad lied to you about the boat. Technically, part of the boat was in Harris's estate, and you had an inchoate interest as a result of community property."

"So, it looks good?"

"There are never any guarantees, but things look really good. I would not be surprised if we could not reach a settlement. As I have been telling you all along, you are going to be an extremely wealthy woman."

"But he was probably responsible for Harris's death. I could feel it sitting across from him today. He ruined our lives. What consolation is money for that?" she said angrily. She realized that the stress was getting to her.

Chris looked at her with sober concern. "Brandy, I am so sorry about Harris. I am a typical lawyer, and I am getting carried away with the proof in the civil case. We are going to make sure that Harris's death is investigated as well as we can."

"What can we do?"

"Well, I can talk to Conner again. He may not object to us hiring another investigator to help with the investigation, like trying to locate Jimmy Thornton."

"Do you think we could find him?"

"I am not sure. But something tells me that he is a key witness in the criminal investigation, as well as the civil case. Thad and Recov may have paid him to go away. There is something strange about his disappearance. Conner thought so, too."

"How much would it cost?"

"Hourly rate plus expenses. Much cheaper than you would pay for an average attorney."

"Hire someone," she told him. "I want those bastards to pay."

Chapter XXII

Thad's deposition lasted another two full days. At times, Brandy found the process extraordinarily tedious. Both Dick and Chris arduously questioned Thad about all of the business records and events during his business relationship with Harris. Thad testified at great length about the diving equipment and the events immediately following Harris's death. As expected, all of the diving equipment had been ultimately discarded after Harris's body had been recovered. Some of Chris's questions had seemed almost pointless until he and Claude explained the process to her.

"We are laying the foundation for all of the important questions. Also, many of the documents individually may not be important. But they establish a pattern of conduct and course of dealing between Thad and Harris. Thad actually had very little to do with the salvage operation until after Harris's death. He has very little information about the day-to-day operations of the venture. It lends support to Harris's journals reflecting that the split of 75/25 percent," Chris explained the night after the second full day of testimony.

She attended the third day with a new appreciation for the deposition process and Claude's hard work. He was meticulous and well prepared. The stress was obviously taking its toll on Thad. She noticed that he had deep circles under his eyes and he looked haggard, probably from a lack of sleep. When the deposition concluded at six-thirty at the end of the third day, he seemed visibly relieved. Accompanied by Quinn Beasley, he quickly left Wally Ziebart's office, carefully avoiding eye contact with Brandy.

"How long will the Recov depositions last?" she asked Chris over their dinner salads in a waterside restaurant on the edge of the marketplace.

"Another two or three days at least. We have agreed to go through the weekend if necessary."

"I need to go back to the shop before then. Also, I miss Rene and Granny Ariel."

"There is no reason that you can't do that since Thad's deposition is over. Your presence while he testified had a great psychological effect. It was obvious he was becoming increasingly uncomfortable in your presence."

"It has been more difficult than I ever imagined. It is hard for me to be in the same room with the man who may have had something to do with Harris's death. I would like to reach across the conference room table and punch him in the nose. Being back here in St. Thomas has been extremely painful. It reminds me of what I lost."

Chris patted her arm. "I'm sorry, Brandy. I know this has been a really hard few days."

She wiped her eyes and managed a smile. "It's just stress. I'll be fine. Allen Conner left a message for me this morning. He would like to meet with me briefly before I go home tomorrow."

"Do you need one of us to go with you?" asked Chris.

"No, I think I can handle it."

"Of course you can. I just want you to know that one of us can be there for moral support if necessary."

She smiled warmly. "Both of you are a great legal team. But all of this has been tough for me. I think I need to decompress. She was tired and she wanted normalcy in her life again. "I think I will walk on the beach for a while. "

"I think I will hit the gym and then I need to review a few documents before the Recov depositions start," Chris told them. He nodded to Claude. "Why don't you and Brandy take a walk."

"I could use a break. I'll join you," Claude said.

They drove outside the city and stopped in a parking bay by a deserted beach. The sun was now just a bright orange disk hovering over the horizon casting a rose hue between the cumulous clouds. She kicked off her sandals and walked in her bare feet, relishing the feel of the sand between her toes. They walked and gathered a few sand dollars and starfish scattered along the beach. The crashing waves had a calming effect over her, and she returned to the car refreshed.

"You can spray paint these things with gold paint and use them as Christmas ornaments. Harris and I decorated our entire tree with shells, starfish and sand dollars tied with silver-and-gold ribbons," she told him in the car on the way back to the hotel. "Rene will be thrilled. It will give her a little project for after school."

"Oh, to be a child again," he replied. "Life's small pleasures are so exciting."

"I know," she said, settling back in her seat to admire the scenery. She was flooded with memories of her life with Harris in the early days in St. Thomas—evening walks on the beach, candlelit dinners on the veranda, and exploring the marketplace on Saturday mornings before a big breakfast of fresh fruit and waffles. It had been paradise before Harris's withdrawal and obsession with *BYZANTIUM.* Brandy briefly wondered about the small house she had sold to a retired couple within two weeks after Harris's death. She had resisted the temptation to drive by lest they had made any improvements. She wanted to remember things as they had been.

"Damn fool!" exclaimed Claude interrupting her reverie.

Brandy looked out of the front windshield in time to see a car slamming on its brakes in front of them. Skillfully, Claude pulled nearly to a stop and careened around the vehicle into the left lane. Suddenly, the car in front of them lurched forward and pulled to the left, trying to run Claude off the road. "I think this car has been following us," he told her as he finally managed to pull ahead, narrowly escaping a head-on collision with an oncoming vehicle.

Brandy turned in time to see the car with the crazed driver pull up close behind them, dangerously tailgating Claude's rental car. The lights were on the brightest setting, blinding her with their brilliance. She realized that in the darkness, she could not clearly see either the automobile or the driver. Suddenly, without warning, the passenger leaned out of the window and hurled a brick through the rear windshield. Glass shattered and showered Claude and Brandy with shards of glass. The car pulled forward again, and the passenger tossed another brick, aiming toward Claude's head. The brick fell just short, landing in the backseat.

"Get down!" Claude yelled at her.

Obediently, Brandy ducked down on the floorboard. Within seconds, another brick sailed across the front passenger headrest and smashed against the dashboard, missing her head by inches. If she had not stooped down, she would have suffered a severe head injury.

Claude stooped down in his seat and accelerated the car as another brick shattered the front windshield. Within another thirty seconds, the lights of the city greeted them. The car brakes behind them squealed and the driver slowed and made a U-turn in the street, disappearing into a side street.

Claude drove in the direction of their hotel. In the streetlight, Brandy noticed that he had a superficial scratch on his left cheek from a sailing brick that had lightly abraded his skin. His hair and clothes were coated in shattered glass.

"Are you alright?" He asked.

"I'm fine. We were lucky we weren't blinded from all of that glass or, worse yet, clubbed with a brick. Who do you think it was?"

"It could have been anyone—locals trying to rob a couple of tourists. Or—"

"Do you think it is related to Thad and this lawsuit?"

He looked at her with concern. "I don't know Brandy. Anything is possible."

He nosed the front of the rental car under the covered portico in the horseshoe drive in front of their hotel. The valet attendant rushed to open the door. Brandy's knees nearly buckled as she attempted to stand. Shards of glass rained down on the drive. She noticed that she had a few minor cuts on her hands and arms from the glass fragments. Her heart was racing wildly now as she realized what had happened. Within moments, the hotel manager, three housekeeping members, and Dick Simpson appeared. The local authorities were notified, and two officers were dispatched along with a general practitioner in the area. Brandy and Claude were ushered into a private reception area and given a glass of lemonade along with an antiseptic wash and cloths for their scratches while waiting for the hotel doctor on call. He arrived momentarily carrying a metal first-aid bag. He was a young Hispanic, looking barely old enough to have graduated from medical school, with a flowing ponytail clipped at the nape of his neck. Introducing himself as Dr. Carlo Lorca, he explained that he had just completed his residency in internal medicine at NYU and was spending time in the Virgin Islands before his fellowship began in San Francisco.

They were joined shortly by two uniformed officers. They briefly recounted the events of the evening to the officers and Dr. Lorca. The officers took a few perfunctory notes and promised to keep in touch, leaving them with the physician.

Dr. Lorca thoroughly examined their small cuts, washing them with antiseptic and expertly applying thin bandages. He dispensed some additional antibiotic cream and bandages with instructions for application for the next two days.

"I saw the car in the staff parking lot. You were lucky," he told them. "Especially you," he solemnly remarked to Brandy.

She shook her head. "I know. If Claude had not had the presence of mind to tell me to get my head down, I could have been seriously injured."

Dr. Lorca put his hand on her shoulder and monitored her pulse with the other hand. Brandy immediately felt the calming effect of a human touch. There was something about him that was surprisingly sexy. "You are trembling, and your pulse is racing," he told her. "I would like to prescribe a mild sedative to help you sleep. Tomorrow, you will put this all in perspective after a good night's sleep."

"I think I will be fine," she said stoically, knowing that in her state of mind, she would probably not sleep at all.

"My advice is that it is for the best. You have had a shock and what I understand is a stressful day. You are returning home tomorrow?"

"Yes," she replied.

"Then you want to arrive rested."

"I agree with Dr. Lorca," Claude interjected. "It has been a hard three days."

"What about him?" she said, nodding toward Claude.

The doctor laughed. "I think he has nerves of steel. He will be fine."

"I don't think I am half as tough as Brandy, but I need to put the finishing touches on my deposition preparation for tomorrow. It will take an hour or two. I am sure that I will sleep just fine after that," Claude said.

"Alright then," she acquiesced, accepting the sedative Dr. Lorca had given her, grateful that she would at least have a decent night's sleep.

Allen Conner came in just as Dr. Lorca wished them a good evening. It was almost ten o'clock, but he looked as fresh as if he had just showered and dressed. "I understand from the officers who were here a while ago that you have had an unpleasant experience with some of our locals," he said, lowering his thin frame into one of the luxurious sofas in the room. Brandy noticed that he had a concerned look on his face.

Claude briefly related what had happened. Allen listened assiduously, his small pad balanced on one knee. When Claude finished, he made a few notes.

"Sounds like you ruffled a few feathers around here," he said finally.

"Do you think it is related to the Recov suit?" Claude asked.

"Hard to say. We have a team of forensics looking at the car and going back to the site to see if anyone saw anything. That is a remote area—not too many houses and after dark, it is unlikely that we will find anyone. You said that there was one oncoming car. Do you know what kind of vehicle it was?"

"It was a light colored SUV—maybe a Chevrolet Suburban. I only saw it for a second in the rearview mirror when I looked back in time to see someone trying to throw another brick through the car window," Claude said.

"Well, we can try to look for a vehicle that generally meets that description. What about the car that was following you?"

"Looked like a plain sedan with at least two passengers, as best as I could tell."

Conner wrote another note on the pad.

"Have you had any luck in your attempt to talk to Thad?" Brandy asked when he finished writing.

"We have an appointment to talk briefly to him on Friday in the presence of his attorneys. I don't hold out much hope that we are going to get much. Quinn Beasley claims that he does not have any knowledge about the diving tanks used by Harris on the day of the accident. It does not hold out much promise at this point, but it is still too early to make a call about how it will turn out. The evidence is all cold and long since gone. The actual diving tanks were destroyed. "

Brandy squeezed her hands together, taking a deep breath to control her anger. "So, it looks like he is going to get away with it, is that what you are telling me?" she said, surprised at her own vehemence.

Conner remained nonplussed by her angry display. "No, not at all. I am telling you that we have an uphill battle, and no one but a clairvoyant can call this one. I did come with some promising news."

"We could use some good news about now," Claude replied, checking his watch. Brandy knew that he was counting the minutes until he could resume his deposition preparation.

"We're on Jimmy Thornton's trail. We found some of his friends in Barbados at the small hotel where he was tending bar. One of them said that he had mentioned that he had been involved in something heavy in St. Thomas and that he needed to leave in a hurry."

"Did he ever tell them what it was?"

"No," Conners replied.

"Have you found him?" Claude asked.

"About six months ago, he moved to Key West for about a month before he went home to Brownsville, Texas, where he was picked up for drunk driving and drug possession. His girlfriend is a small-time user and dealer. The local cops put the squeeze on her and she said that Jimmy has been telling her lately that he has a good friend whose 'ship has come in.' They are making plans to move to the Philippines, buy a shop, and live the good life."

"Any idea who the good friend could be?"

"We have located the wife of the former owner of the dive shop here in the Virgin Islands. The owner passed away in January of brain cancer. The wife occasionally worked in the shop. She remembers seeing Thornton out occasionally with one of their former shop employees, Ewan Donaldson. She thought it was odd because they seemed like two different people. Donaldson was an ex-military type, very serious and a hard worker. He left the Virgin Islands shortly after Mr. Blake was found. He told his bosses that he had 'island fever' and needed to get back to the mainland. It happens. She said that she was sorry to lose him."

"Do you know where Donaldson is?"

Allen shook his head. "We checked. He moved to Ft. Lauderdale and had a few dead-end jobs. The last record we have is that he worked waiting tables in a restaurant. The boss there liked Donaldson and said he was a good worker. He left last summer with no forwarding address."

"Do you think there is a connection with Harris's death?" Brandy asked the detective.

Allen Conner rubbed his brow and sighed. "We really do not know, Mrs. Blake. We are trying to run down every lead. At this point, he is a person of interest, and we would like to talk with him. He may have sold, or serviced, the diving equipment to your husband, but we do not know that. The dive shop has been closed for a long time, and many of the records were destroyed. VI Dive Adventures was a small shop. Some of the electronic records were backed up, but they were loose about record keeping. Some of the sales slips were simply old-fashioned paper tickets. Also, Janice, the widow of the VI Dive owner, had the computers wiped and resold. She needed money for her husband's medical bills."

Brandy felt her eyes welling in tears of frustration. "Will you try to find Donaldson?"

"We have an alert out," Conner told her. "And we will continue to look. He is another drifter, though, and it could take a while."

"Does Thornton's girlfriend have any explanation how a drifter like that could ever afford a shop or ticket out of the country?"asked Claude.

"Just that he was working on something that would be profitable. We know that it is not the stock-market, and Jimmy is a deadbeat. He does not have a bank account or even own a car."

"Has anyone tried to talk to him?" asked Brandy.

"They have already tried, but he has disappeared again," replied Conner. "He is now on our radar screen. It is a certainty that sooner or later a loser like that will be picked up again and then we will finally get some answers."

Brandy was unable to hide her disappointment. "So, in other words, my husband's killer is going to get away with his murder."

Allen Conner gave her a patient, but self-assured look. "I can guarantee you that if Jimmy Thornton had anything to do with your husband's death, Thornton was the little guy taking orders from someone else. He will not be able to stand the heat, and he will likely unload on the perps. It is just a matter of time before we talk to him again."

Ewan was pleased that the paint on the green Japanese sedan he had selected closely resembled Brandy's Honda. The red wig stowed in the duffle bag had been cut and styled in the same way that Brandy wore her hair. He had paid a dancer who performed at a transvestite bar near the airport $300 to teach him how to apply makeup to conceal his stubble and transform his bronzed complexion into the creamy skin of the redhead. Ewan had practiced with the makeup and wig until he was happy with the effect.

He had overheard the old lady talking in the backyard that afternoon that Brandy would be returning to New Orleans tomorrow, landing about 3:50 p.m. By the time she collected her luggage and drove home in the afternoon traffic, she would certainly not arrive before 4:30 or 5:00. The timing was perfect. He knew from months of monitoring their behavior that Rene came home early every Thursday afternoon. She usually spent every Thursday afternoon working on homework or painting on the back verandah or sitting in the gazebo. Monday and Wednesdays the child took piano lessons, and Tuesdays were her regularly scheduled ballet lessons. Ewan planned to park in the circular drive in front of the St. Charles house and abduct the child before her mother arrived in the back garden. Earlier in the day, he had left the lock to the rear garden open. Of course, he had the duplicate key in his pocket for safekeeping.

Ewan had some chloroform to keep the child sedated while he drove out of the city. Of course, he would have no trouble dealing with the old woman now that the dog was dead. He would stab her or slit her throat with the large hunting knife in his pocket. Anyone who happened to see him with the little girl would think that the child had gone with a woman. Ewan smiled, realizing that the police would be temporarily confused that any possible description of the abductor would match the description of the mother.

It was likely that the investigation would focus on the mother. Cops were predictable, and their heavy-handed investigation tactics were always the same. By the time they finally cleared the mother and began to look for another suspect in earnest, he would have over $2 million dollars.

It was a perfect plan.

~

Brandy took a hot bath in the jetted tub in her room before she took the sedative. She fell into a dreamless sleep and awoke the next morning at seven thirty. Hurriedly, she showered and dressed in a comfortable pair of slacks and flat-heeled shoes before going downstairs for breakfast. Chris and Claude were sitting in the dining room with Dick Simpson, drinking coffee.

"We've already eaten. But there is plenty of food at the buffet," Dick told her as she arrived. "I hope you have recovered from your evening last night."

"It was eventful, but no more so than raising a young child," she replied, flashing a convincing but insincere smile.

Claude eyed her clinically. "Sleep well?"

"Actually, I feel a little out of it—sort of like being in a bell jar. I think it is caused by the sedative. Coffee, though, should remedy this situation."

She ate a large breakfast, listening to the three men discussing the Recov depositions scheduled for nine o'clock that morning. After a full stomach and two cups of strong coffee, she began to feel like herself again.

"Whit Champlain is certainly one of the more unusual individuals in the cast of characters in this case," Dick told her. "Prestigious family, Brown undergrad, Wharton School of Business MBA, and then a dive junkie for a few years until he started a small salvage business. He shunned the usual vessel oil spill cleanup or prevention operations after a grounding or sinking which are viewed as the high ticket items. Instead, he gradually started focusing on the salvage of antiquities or older ships. He has fought a few losing battles because a number of the boats were declared to be the property of the adjoining state under the Submerged Shipwreck Act. Then he started focusing on taking over shoestring operations of smaller operators."

"Like Harris and Thad, you mean," Brandy replied stiffly.

Dick Simpson shifted in his seat, obviously eager to mollify Brandy. "Well, actually, from what our experts tell us, Harris had a reasonably focused operation. But there are a number of other ventures that are fly-by-night and, with his connections, Whit Champlain has been able to secure the financing and private investors in the corporation to take over these salvage operations with the right equipment. He has even had a few scientists on the payroll who have engineered a special submersible that has been patented to Recov and sold to other larger operations. Whit has small salvage operations all over the world, including the Dead Sea, South China Sea, and South Pacific. Today, at fifty, he operates a $500 million business. He mingles with the rich and famous and has been linked with a number of European starlets."

Brandy sipped her coffee. "How important is it to Recov to prevail in the *BYZANTIUM* case?"

"It is extremely important," Claude replied. "*BYZANTIUM* is an antiquity and has historical importance to the United States. Some of the artifacts undoubtedly belong at the Smithsonian. There is tremendous prestige associated with the discovery of the vessel. You know that yourself since the articles in the, *New York Times, Newsday* and *Wall Street Journal* appeared after the suit was filed. Whit Champlain is vying to become another Ballard, and *BYZANTIUM* will put him there. Then, of course, there is the issue of the money. The value of the emerald cargo is the one of the larger cargo salvage operation of antiquities to date. This would be Recov's largest profit yet, and possibly in the foreseeable future. Even if we prevail in the trial court, they are certain to appeal. There is too much at stake here. Also, there have been reports of Recov's financial problems. According to the forensic accountant we hired, the financial data we have obtained does not look very strong."

Her heart sank as she again realized the magnitude of the situation. It could be years. Imagine the cumulative stress of living with the painfully slow process of litigation. Of course, Chris had been warning her all along. She just had not really been listening to him. For her own sake, she needed to distance herself from this situation. She needed normalcy and her life with Rene and Ariel. That was all that was important.

"On that note, I guess I had better return to work to make a living. I need to finish packing and go out to the airport. I have a 10:40 flight to Miami and then on to New Orleans to arrive at 3:50," she announced cheerfully with a levity she did not feel.

Chris and Dick shook Brandy's hand wishing her safe travels. Claude rose from the table. "I'll walk you to the elevator. I have already paid the breakfast bill."

"Are you alright today?" he asked her as they stood in front of the elevator bank.

"I'm fine." She replied. "Actually, no, I am a little overwhelmed. Last night someone tried to hurt us, for God knows what reason. This morning it all finally hits me. We could be in litigation for the next ten years over this stupid boat. Harris died because of this boat. None of this is really worth it!" Her voice cracked, and she burst into tears. She felt embarrassed because she was usually capable of keeping her emotions in check.

His face clouded over with concern. "This has been a really hard week."

"Claude, I am just stressed. I am fine, really. I don't want to unnerve you before you and Chris depose Whit Champlain. There is something about being back down here that has brought it all back. I am just having a difficult morning. Sometimes, this all seems insurmountable, but when I find out what is involved, I realize that it is not and that I just need to take it all in stride." She dried her eyes quickly with the back of her hands.

"You are brave."

"Bullshit. I am just trying to do what is necessary. I want you to rip Whit Champlain a new one, as attorneys are fond of saying today."

He smiled, exposing his flawless teeth. "I'll call you tonight and give you all the blow-by-blow details."

"Call me tomorrow. I want to spend an evening uninterrupted with my family before I go back to work tomorrow. I am not going to let the *BYZANTIUM* take over my life."

"Safe trip and take care."

"Knock them dead," she called to him as she pushed the elevator button to her floor. She needed to go up to her room to pack, check out of the hotel, and fly to Miami. She could not wait to get home to see Rene and Granny Ariel.

CHAPTER XXIII

Raleigh munched on an apple crescent while waiting for Rene to finish her homework. As she wrote a few short sentences on her lined pad, he noticed that her penmanship had improved exponentially. Beyond the garden wall, gales of laughter could be heard from the gathering of college students over by the fountain in the park. Raleigh stretched, watching Rene write her sentences, and then set out for the limb of the live oak. The cadres of runners and walkers accompanied by their pets were out taking their daily exercise on the walking trail before sunset. Down the asphalt path, he could see a cluster of geese and ducks in the middle of the roadway studying the human walkers, hoping to be fed. He luxuriated in the scented air as he watched the activity below.

In the next tree, one of his pups chattered loudly to get his attention. He gave a friendly bark in return and wagged his tail in a half-hearted territorial claim.

He stretched again and ran up and down the tree again for exercise. Before long, he found a delicious strand of cambium hanging from a small branch of a live oak. Stopping to investigate, he severed the small hanging branch from the tree, furiously chewed on the fragrant, gummy cambium, savoring the green sap and the small pieces of bark. Fruit was delicious, but like all rodents, he needed something hard to wear down his teeth. They grew constantly, giving him the urge to gnaw.

The weather was perfect—warm without being hot and low humidity. He could feel the change, though. Soon, it would become stifling hot and so unbearable during the midday that all the squirrels would seek shelter in their nests until early evening.

Finally, surfeit from the cambium, he scampered across the oak branches at dizzying heights until he reached the wall to Ariel's house. With ease, he jumped down the six-foot-wall onto the soft grass and raced back up to the terrace. Ariel was sitting with Rene enjoying the drink they called lemonade.

Rene's tiny new electronic spelling aid was nearby on the table. The LCD screen burned brightly. The small keys were easy for him to use to communicate.

"There you are, sweetheart," Ariel called to him as he gracefully sailed across the lawn and sprang onto the verandah. "I was just telling Rene that Brandy will be home soon. The cooking service left a great meal to celebrate. I am sure that she will be exhausted."

Rene's eyes shined brightly with expectation. "I can't wait to see Mommy!" She grinned at Ariel and then Raleigh.

"I know that she will be glad to see you, too!" replied Ariel, stroking her granddaughter's red hair.

Raleigh sat on the table and selected a walnut from a dish. It had been partially cracked, and he efficiently removed the meat of the nut. Ariel seemed very sad these days. She desperately missed her companion, Chloe. But Ariel never mentioned Chloe in front of the child, explaining that she had suffered so much loss in the past. Raleigh missed the Samoyed as well. She had been such a gentle soul, but like Kiki, the world had taken her from him.

"Let's play checkers to make the time go faster," said Rene.

While Brandy had been away, Raleigh and Ariel had been teaching Rene to play hearts. But checkers was an easier game for the child, and the two of them wanted to keep her interested.

"Good idea!" replied Ariel. "Why don't you play Raleigh first and then I will play the winner."

Rene clapped her hands and then set up the board. As usual, she gave Raleigh the red pieces. Although he could easily have defeated her, he deliberately placed his pawns in unprotected positions, allowing Rene to make multiple jumps. Within minutes, Rene had jumped his last checker from the board with a final double jump. He carefully avoided Ariel's gaze. She would know that he was not trying. Raleigh was actually an expert checker player. Squirrels were inherently very good at strategy and assessing risks. That was one of the inherited talents from being on the lower level of the food chain.

Ariel and Rene played next. Ariel defeated Rene and then allowed Rene to defeat her. Raleigh watched and assessed each play, munching on walnut pieces and discarding the shell into a small porcelain saucer. During the third game, Ariel went in to answer her cell phone. Today, because of the glorious weather, the windows of the old house had been left open.

"Take over for me, will you, Raleigh?" Ariel said before she went into the house. "And give her a run for her money. We want her to be challenged."

Raleigh discarded the remainder of the walnut shells in the dish and began to focus. Before long, he had defeated Rene.

Like all young children, Rene hated to lose. She pouted slightly, checked her wristwatch and then brightened. She had learned to tell time two months ago and Brandy had presented her with a new

Little Mermaid watch. Rene's eyes shone brightly with expectation. "Mommy will be home in an hour," she told the squirrel.

Raleigh suddenly felt uneasy. He turned in time to see a woman with red hair walking briskly up the brick garden path toward the verandah. The woman carried a big purse and had something in her hand.

Something was wrong. The woman did not look exactly like Brandy. She was too big. Also, Brandy never entered the back gate. She always entered the house through the front or side door nearest the portico.

Suddenly, the woman bounded up the verandah steps. Rene, initially confused and captivated by the woman, leaned back in terror.

"You are not Mommy! You are a stranger. Go away!" she said firmly.

Raleigh became increasingly concerned. Rene was just a little girl. Unlike young squirrels, she was incapable of handling the threats of the world on her own. She would be at risk. He watched in horror as the woman suddenly grabbed Rene and covered her mouth with a cloth as the child struggled violently. Within seconds, Rene's body was limp. The woman carried the child into the house and put her in a chair in the study. A long string of drool spun like thread from Rene's mouth onto her tee shirt.

Raleigh sailed through the verandah window into the house. He sniffed the air intuitively recalling a familiar scent from the past. Then he remembered. It was the smell of the intruder!

He heard Ariel's muffled screams from the kitchen. The woman had Ariel in a death lock, gripping her from behind. Despite her age, Ariel was struggling violently, and her flailing legs pounded against the intruder. The barstools in front of the large kitchen island sailed across the room, and the dishes on the counter crashed to the floor. Raleigh watched helplessly as the intruder bludgeoned Ariel repeatedly in the face with her fist. Dazed, Ariel's body slowly collapsed, and the intruder released her grip. Ariel's limp body slid onto the kitchen floor in a heap. Raleigh, in shock, was unable to bark as the intruder pulled a large knife from the bag, plunging it into Ariel's back and side. He smelled the metallic scent of blood and helplessly watched it spill onto the white marble tiles of the kitchen floor. In her distress, Ariel caught the squirrel's gaze, staring at him intently. She seemed unable to speak.

The squirrel was helpless. The two people with whom he could communicate were incapacitated. They needed help and now. Sour bile rose to his throat.

Purposefully, the intruder abandoned Ariel in the kitchen and went back to the study, where Rene remained unconscious in the chair.

Danger! Danger! He could not let the man harm Rene. He could feel something terrible here. The man wanted to harm the child.

He stood up and began pawing at Rene's leg, but the child did not move. The intruder lifted the child gently into her arms and began to carry her out through the kitchen.

Raleigh was conflicted. Should he stay and help Ariel or go with Rene? As he went through the kitchen, Ariel was struggling to breathe.

She whispered softly to Raleigh. "Go with Rene."

The squirrel stared at his old friend in shock. Ariel had been his best friend in the world. She was dying, and he was helpless to do anything about it. He needed to protect Rene. The child was helpless. He gave Ariel a loving stare before bounding through the kitchen window. The intruder was parked in the driveway.

Fearing the worst, he bounded after Rene and the intruder. There was very little he could do. He was no match for this man, who could easily kill him with one stomp of his foot. If only Chloe were here! She could stop this.

He reached the intruder just as he tossed Rene into the trunk like a rag doll. On an impulse, Raleigh leapt in beside her, just barely slipping inside before the trunk snapped shut and locked. Rene lay on her side, oblivious to it all.

He knew that the two of them might die. Ariel was now possibly beyond hope, but he would do what he could to protect Rene.

Suddenly the engine roared to life. Within seconds, the car drove away.

∽

Brandy's flight had been delayed as a result of a terrific low front with towering thunderstorms in the Miami airport. She immediately noticed the police car and ambulance in front of the house as she pulled into the driveway and parked in garage. She threw the car into park, cut the engine, and raced inside the back. Jeanette, Ariel's next-door neighbor for more than twenty years, was standing in the kitchen, talking to a female detective. She had obviously been crying. Two uniformed officers were standing in the study beside an emergency medical technician.

Jeanette turned as Brandy walked into the foyer. She walked over and gave Brandy a firm embrace before dissolving into tears again.

"My God, what happened? Has something happened to Granny Ariel? Where is Rene?" She could see the concerned look on the young detective's face.

Jeanette released her and gave her a solemn look. "Brandy, I am so sorry, but someone has broken into the house and attacked Ariel. They have taken her to the hospital."

"How bad? I want to see her!" Brandy asked weakly. She knew that she was going into shock. It was the same terrible, gut-wrenching feeling that had overwhelmed her when she had been told that Harris was dead. She must remain in control. She had Rene to think about.

"Mrs. Blake, I am Detective Felecia Simon. Your grandmother is safe now and on her way to the hospital," she said in a reassuring voice.

"Attacked?" Brandy replied woodenly, oblivious to the tears running down her face.

"Yes," continued Detective Simon. "If it had not been for your neighbor, Mrs. Randall calling 911 when she heard Ariel scream, she would have died."

"Oh my God! I should have been here!"

"You need to sit down. We hope that she is going to be okay."

Detective Simon steered Brandy toward the study. A metallic odor wafted from the kitchen. In shock, she heard Jeannette tell the officers that she had called someone to clean up the kitchen.

"Mrs. Randall, first we need to have forensics study the scene and complete the photos," Detective Simon told Jeannette. Brandy was confused.

What was there to clean up?

Brandy became nearly hysterical. She was barely aware of Jeanette's lateral support as the torrent of tears poured down her cheeks. This could not be happening! She had seemed fine two days ago and last night when she had called. If only she had come home sooner.

"I need to go to the hospital to be with her," Brandy announced. "Jeanette, can you take care of Rene?"

She noticed an odd glance exchanged between Jeannette and Detective Simon. "She is at the hospital. You can get someone to drive you down there, honey," Jeannette told her.

"I will take you down in a bit," Detective Simon told Brandy, giving her shoulder a gentle squeeze. "Let's sit down first for a few minutes and go over a few things."

Still in shock, Brandy remained in the living room chair beside Jeannette. What if Granny Ariel died? She had always been there for her. She had been the backbone of her life. Why had she wasted her time pursuing a claim for *BYZANTIUM*? The only thing that was really important in life was family.

Jeannette left to make Brandy some herbal tea to help her calm down. Detective Simon told her that the uniformed officers would bring her luggage into the house.

Brandy gradually calmed down enough to talk as she sipped her tea.

"Where's Rene?" she asked Jeannette pointedly when she had regained her composure. She wiped her eyes with the back of her hands, oblivious to the streaks of mascara. "Is she okay?"

Detective Simon did not speak for a moment. Finally, after a long pause, she locked her gaze with Brandy. "Mrs. Blake, there is something we need to discuss about your daughter."

Brandy felt the blood pounding against her head. "Rene? Has something happened to Rene?"

Detective Simon gave her a compassionate look before she spoke again. "I am sorry, but Rene was kidnapped about an hour ago."

"Kidnapped? That is impossible!" she shrieked. This woman was crazy. Who would want to kidnap her daughter? There had been some mistake.

"I am sorry, Mrs. Blake. But we have an eyewitness. Two Loyola students saw a woman putting a young child into the trunk of a car. They took a cell phone video. We could not get the license plate except a partial letter, because it was smeared with grease."

"Nooooooo!" she shrieked. It could not be true! Not her baby.

Brandy felt the room spinning before she lost consciousness. The uniformed officer caught her before she hit the floor.

She was lying on the white damask sofa when she recovered. Jeannette had put a cool compress with ice on her forehead and covered her with a light cashmere blanket. Brandy began to uncontrollably shiver. This cannot be happening to me, she thought.

Jeannette kneeled beside her in a side chair and removed the compress. The woman gave her a hug. Jeannette, who was about sixty-five, was still wearing her loose clothing from hot yoga. Her silver gray hair was pulled in a ponytail displaying a kind, unlined face that belied her years. "The detective and the police need to talk to you. We need to find Rene."

Brandy wanted to resist. She wanted to be unconscious again where she could not feel the gut-wrenching pain that enveloped her. Rene had been kidnapped. How could this have happened? She never should have left! If only she had not gone back to St. Thomas, this would not have happened. Surely they were mistaken. It just could not be true.

There was silence in the room as she regained her composure.

"I am going to get all of us something to eat next door. I will be back momentarily," Jeannette told them.

"I can't even think about food," she said, barely aware of her surroundings. This could not be happening. Rene and even Granny Ariel.

"Mrs. Blake, you need to keep your strength up," the detective told her firmly. "Your daughter and your grandmother need you to be strong. We have work to do. I need you to be strong. I want you to eat something. Your neighbor has some cheese, crackers, and fruit. We can talk and take notes."

They were right. She had to be strong.

"Alright" she replied numbly.

As Jeannette brought in a platter, they were joined by several other plainclothes detectives. They introduced themselves and explained that they were going to set up a telephone tap in case there was a ransom demand.

Brandy ate without tasting the food. What had begun as a pleasant day had turned into the worst day imaginable. She did not want to live without Rene and Granny Ariel. Her life was over. She would have to be strong. She had to find Rene.

As she ate, Detective Simon related what had happened. Rene and Granny Ariel had been playing checkers on the back porch waiting for her to come home. Granny Ariel had been in the kitchen. Two Loyola students had been coming home from the library and were standing on the streetcar stop. The two of them saw a woman go in the back gate. A few minutes later, she came out carrying a child. They took a few photos of a red haired woman driving a dark green sedan and saw a passenger shove Rene into the trunk. Something else jumped in. It was small enough to be a squirrel, but she decided that it was just a small kitten. The girls called 911. Also, your neighbor thought she heard some screaming and came over to find your grandmother in the kitchen. She called 911 as well.

"Why would anyone want to kidnap Rene?" she finally asked Detective Simon.

"We don't know, but we are going to explore that," she replied softly. "I need you to be clear-headed, Mrs. Blake. I know that you are under a tremendous strain, but I need you to focus on what we have to do. You want us to find your little girl, don't you?"

Brandy began to cry again. "Oh God, yes!"

"Well, then stay with me," Detective Simon replied, squeezing Brandy's hand.

"Alright. I am trying."

"Now, you just came back from St. Thomas this evening, is that right?" The detective asked.

"Yes."

"Can I see your ticket please?"

" I had just gotten home. Surely you don't think that I had anything to do with—" She was incredulous. Surely she was not a suspect.

Detective Simon patted her on the arm. "Mrs. Blake, this is just police procedure. My supervisor will ask me to check out the whereabouts of every family member when this happened. It will be easy because you have a ticket. Someone at headquarters will double check with the airlines and eliminate you as a suspect. We do that in every case. What is very interesting is that the perp was trying to look like you, with a probable wig and dark car. It was likely a ploy to fool the child and confuse the investigating officers. We are here to help you. Please work with me." The detective stared at Brandy intently. Behind the soft demeanor were eyes of steel.

Brandy tried to pull herself together. "I parked in the long-term parking lot at the airport. The parking stub with the date and time that I left the lot is in my car. You are welcome to look in my car and search for anything you need there or in the house. All I want is my baby back."

"Thank you, Mrs. Blake." Detective Simon nodded toward the uniformed officer with her. She surrendered her car keys and he disappeared for a moment.

"Was there anything else that the students noticed that could be helpful?" Brandy asked.

The detective looked at her with new respect. "She said it appeared to be a darker colored Toyota Camry, maybe six years old. The only part of the tag she could make out was a partial letter that was probably "M". We are running the tags now to locate any vehicle fitting this description. The girls are down at the precinct now giving a written and videotaped statement."

That gave Brandy hope. They could at least identify the car.

"I want to meet them," she said firmly.

"Maybe at some point, but not right now. We need to work with the girls to get all of the information we can. Mrs. Randall gave us a picture of Rene, and the girls have identified her as the child that was placed into the trunk."

Brandy's heart sank as she heard the news. She had been nursing the impossible hope that this was all a big mistake. Now, there was no other explanation that she could embrace. The impossible had happened. Rene had been kidnapped.

"Mrs. Randall has been telling us about your lawsuit—*BYZANTIUM,* I think it is called in the Virgin Islands. She also told us that on a few occasions around Mardi Gras, you had an intruder in the back that was reported to the security service that patrols the neighborhood at night." Detective Simon looked at Brandy for confirmation.

She had known nothing about an intruder. Why had Granny Ariel kept this from her?

"Do you think that those things had anything to do with—"

"We don't know, Mrs. Blake. But we need to investigate every angle. Now, tell me about this litigation and what is at stake."

Brandy told the detectives everything about the lawsuits, including the suspicion that Harris had been murdered, her conversations with Detective Allen Connor, and the events last night with the car. She also told them about Jimmy Thornton. Detective Simon listened intently while another plainclothesman made notes on a small pad.

"Get in touch with Detective Conner in St. Thomas. No matter how late it is, get him," she told one of the other detectives that had just arrived. "Also, see what you can pull up on the NCIC about Jimmy Thornton and Ewan Donaldson. We need to tell the captain about this. I hate to say it, but we need to call in the feds on this one. Also, our kidnapping team will likely assume control of the investigation."

"I need to talk to my attorneys," Brandy told Detective Simon. "I need to tell him what happened."

"No, Mrs. Blake. We will get in touch with them. Right now, we just need you to stay close by and tell us whatever we can. Everyone else who is not in this room is a suspect."

"My attorneys would never do something like that."

"Mrs. Blake, from what you are telling me about this case, you and your daughter stand to get more money than most people can even dream about or count. You are a sitting duck and until everyone who is close to you is eliminated, they are a suspect. That includes your attorneys and every party and attorney involved."

She began to protest until Jeannette interrupted them. "It's the hospital, Brandy. Your grandmother has taken a turn for the worse. They want you to come now."

"We'll have a car drive you," Detective Simon said. "I'll follow you."

This time, she did not even bother to wipe the tears from her face. Stoically, she put her arm around Jeannette, and the two women walked out and got into the police car.

CHAPTER XXIV

Rene was inconsolable and terrified when she finally aroused from the drug-induced stupor. With every bloodcurdling scream, she thrust her small body over and over against the deep interior of the wall separating the trunk from the back seat.

"Let me OUT!" She shrieked. "LET ME OUT! I want to go home!"

Finally, realizing the futility of banging on the trunk, Rene eventually quieted down, curled into a ball, and moaned softly. Raleigh gave three low barks to signal to her before venturing over to her. It was pitch black in the trunk, and even the squirrel did not have any visual acuity.

"Raleigh?" Rene called quietly.

He replied with a low bark, their signal for yes.

"Come here, Raleigh! I'm soooo scared!" she cried.

He crawled over to her gingerly, not wanting to alarm the child further in her agitated state. He managed to locate her hands and delicately took two of her fingers between his tiny paws, rubbing them lightly. Satisfied that she would not hurt him, albeit unintentionally, he stood at full height and gently stroked her hair and her face with his paws, carefully retracting his nails to prevent scratching her. Rene's shoulders heaved as she began crying again.

The squirrel could smell the putrid scent of urine in the car. Rene had soiled herself. Rene's hands were covered in a sticky metallic scent. Blood. Like any wild animal, the child had tried to escape until she had bloodied her hands. The smell sickened him, but he continued to stroke her hair.

Raleigh continued to pet her shoulders and stroke her hair to calm her. After a time, Rene gently enfolded the squirrel into her arms, taking care not to crush him.

"I am so glad you are with me, Raleigh. How did you get in? Did you jump in after me? You are so brave."

He gave another low bark, letting her ramble.

"Where is the lady taking us? Do you think that she will bring us home? Will she hurt us?" She began crying again.

He barked twice for no, trying desperately to calm the child.

Danger!

He was afraid—as fearful as when Kiki had been injured all those months ago. Intuitively, he knew that they would probably die. This was a hopeless situation. He was no match for the woman, but he did not want to alarm the child. If there were any chance that they were to get out of this at all, he would have to keep his head.

His thoughts drifted to Ariel, lying in a pool of her own blood in the kitchen. He had felt her life force draining from her body. He had been helpless to assist her. But she had made it clear that she wanted him to go with Rene. Ariel did not want Rene to be alone.

The car had accelerated now and rocketed along the roadway without coming to a stop. The air in the trunk was now stale and extremely warm. He could smell the engine fumes and the noxious odor of lubricating oil on the tools against the wall. The trunk floor was covered in a thick carpet that badly needed to be shampooed. The heavy drumbeat accompanying the rap music on the car radio vibrated throughout the trunk. The car gently pitched and rolled along the uneven pavement. Despite the loud music coming from the interior of the car, Raleigh could now hear that other traffic on the road was nearly non-existent.

They had left the city. He could feel it.

Ariel had explained to him many times that New Orleans was essentially a city surrounded by water and swamps. The Mississippi River dissected the east and west banks of the city. The west bank stretched down the marshy lowland toward the flats and small towns that reached the Gulf of Mexico. To the north was Lake Pontchartrain, to the east and west, the marshy swamps and the rigolets. These areas were populated by dangerous predators, including poisonous snakes, hawks, coyotes, bobcats, raccoons, owls, and alligators. A squirrel would have little chance of survival in this wilderness, especially with a small child.

Still agitated, Rene began to cry again. "I'm hungry! I want to see my Mommy and Granny Ariel! I want to go home!" Her shoulders heaved, and she began trembling. He could smell the salt of her tears. He continued to stroke her hair and face, eternally vigilant, less she became uncontrollably anxious again. He knew that Rene would never intentionally hurt him. But like a wild animal, she was frightened and cornered and instinctively would try to escape for survival.

He was helpless. How could they get away? It was possible for him to run when the trunk opened. But, he would be in unfamiliar territory and extremely vulnerable. Death could be swift and unexpected in such circumstances. And he could not leave Rene. Ariel would never forgive him. He had to protect the child.

Was Ariel still alive? Were they looking for them yet? Maybe there was a possibility that they would be found. When Brandy came home, she would call the police.

Somehow he would have to try to protect Rene. He would have to keep them alive.

He snuggled next to Rene under her chin and lay on her chest. She folded him in her arms and softly stroked his fur and tail. He could feel her fluttering heart settle down.

It was working. Rene was starting to relax.

They lay there for what seemed to be a long time. Rene dozed, but Raleigh was wide-awake, trying to ignore the gnawing hunger in his stomach. He had not eaten now in several hours. Squirrels, like all little animals, needed to eat frequently.

He thought it was his imagination at first that the car was slowing down. Then he became aware of the crunch of gravel beneath them as the car roared to a stop. He heard the passenger door slam and the footsteps on the gravel. Then, he felt a welcome rush of fresh air as the trunk lid flipped open.

The institutional antiseptic smell made Brandy nauseous as she entered the hospital. Granny Ariel had been in emergency surgery and was now in the Recovery room. Detective Simon led Brandy and Jeannette onto the elevator and up to the Recovery room. The nurses ushered the women over to the bed nearest the nurses' station.

“She is still in a coma and has had a blood transfusion. The doctor will want to talk with you in a few minutes,” a young nurse told her.

Granny Ariel’s skin was still pasty white. Her eyelids were swollen to four times their natural size. The respirator attached to a tube down her throat regulated the steady rise and fall of her chest. Two IVs snaked up from her hands.

Brandy dissolved into tears again. “Oh God,” she cried, covering her face.

Jeannette stood beside her, tears running down her face. She and Brandy held hands.

“I’ll leave you two alone for a few minutes,” Detective Simon told them before walking toward the nurses’ station.

Brandy and Jeannette stared at Ariel in disbelief. Silently, Brandy began to pray for her grandmother’s life and the life of her child.

Why was God punishing her in this way? She was losing everyone who mattered in life.

The young nurse approached them again. “Dr. Kirkland would like to talk to you now,” she said softly. The woman had a gentle and concerned expression. Cynically, Brandy wondered whether her demeanor was sincere or just a practiced response honed by years of dealing with distraught families.

Dr. Kirkland was waiting for them in a small office behind the nurses’ station. There were several comfortable chairs and a large plain desk. He introduced himself and asked them to have a seat. Without exchanging many pleasantries, he began to talk.

"I am sorry to say that your grandmother is a very sick lady. Her stab wounds were severe and she has also had a significant heart attack. From what we can determine, she has a major blockage in the left descending carotid artery that stopped her heart. If she survives, we will need to insert some stents. We don't know if she has any brain activity. Tomorrow morning, the neurologist will perform an EEG. If she has brain activity, we will let her recover and then determine what steps are next. She would not survive the procedure in her current state and because of her advanced age. In the meantime, we will keep her on life support."

No brain activity. She may already have lost her. "What is the chance that she will recover?" Brandy asked shakily.

"It is difficult to say. She has had deep stab wounds that punctured one of her kidneys and a lung. She is elderly and has very little resilience. I think that there is a good possibility that she may not last the night. I am sorry. Depending upon the results of the neurological tests, we will need to address the question of continued life support."

Brandy felt the sting of the torrent of tears down her face. This could not be happening.

"Oh God!" she said quietly.

The physician put his hand gently on Brandy's arm. "I think the thing for you to do is to go home tonight and get a good night's sleep. I have heard about your daughter. Please let me know if there is anything I can do. I suggest that you go home. I will call you if you need to come back." His voice had the sound of practiced sincerity, but his face was dispassionate.

Brandy stared at him in shock. How could she leave her? Granny Ariel could be dying in the next room. She would not let her die alone without anyone like Harris. "I want to stay here," she told the doctor angrily. "I am not leaving."

Jeannette encircled her with her arms and stroked her hair. "Brandy, there is nothing else we can do here. These people are going to take good care of your grandmother. She needs rest and it is in God's hands now. We need to go home to help the police find Rene."

Brandy's shoulders heaved with her sobs. Rene. For a few moments she had nearly forgotten. Her heart ached to think that she may never spend time with her grandmother again. She had been the stabilizing force in her life. But, she would have to help find Rene. There was hope that the police could recover her child.

The nurse allowed her to see Granny Ariel once more before she left. Gently, she stroked her hands and shoulders, talking to her softly. She leaned over her and whispered. "Please come back to us, Granny Ariel. We can't live without you! Please! God bless you!"

Jeannette led her down the corridor, where they were met by Detective Simon. She and her partner, Detective Sanchez, drove the two women home.

There were two police cars and an unmarked police vehicle parked in front of Granny Ariel's house when they arrived home. The area near the fountain and the street had been roped off with yellow police tape, and a group of officers appeared to be scouring the scene. A traffic cop down the street waved the traffic around the area. A WDSU television news truck was parked near the fountain in the park. Nearby, a lovely black news reporter standing in a cylinder of brilliant light spoke into a microphone while staring straight ahead into the portable camera.

"They are working the crime scene—trying to preserve the evidence and find any details. They have been out there shortly after this was reported. You may not have noticed because of the situation with your grandmother," Detective Simon explained as she turned off the engine.

She felt a stab of pain in her stomach as she realized, once again, that Granny Ariel may not survive the night. "The news—"

"The press—get accustomed to seeing them there. We have drawn all the shades and drapes. Out of respect for you, they will keep their distance. We have withheld Rene's name and the name of the family, but eventually, we will release them, if necessary."

"If necessary?" Brandy asked the detective pointedly. "When do we know it is necessary? Who decides that? Is it when it is too late—beyond hope?" She felt herself losing control again. This could not be happening—not to Rene—not to her baby. Where was she now? Was she crying? Was she in pain? Was she cold or hungry? God, please let her be alive.

Detective Simon's face was filled with compassion. It was an odd contrast with the glint of steel in her eyes. She stopped and faced Brandy. "Mrs. Blake, I have two young children at home myself, and I cannot begin to imagine what you are going through. It is our job to help you. The hostage/ kidnapping division of the New Orleans Police Department is already working on this case. I need you to be strong and I do not want you to give up hope. We don't even know what happened here. We are going to take this one day at a time. We are going to do everything we can to find your daughter."

Brandy wiped her tears. "Call me Brandy. I am a widow."

"If this were not a professional situation, I would tell you to call me Felicia. But, we need to go by the book here. I am here to help you get through this and to work on this case. We are working together, and I need you to be strong."

Brandy felt herself sober. In spite of the situation, she liked this woman. "One day at a time," she heard herself reply.

Detective Simon led them into the house. Woodenly, Brandy walked beside the detective and Jeannette. None of this seemed real.

Several large electronic devices had been set up in the den, along with electronic tablets and a laptop. Two uniformed officers and two plainclothesmen were discussing the equipment. With slight alarm, Brandy realized that none of these men appeared older than thirty. Imagine. The fate of her child rested in the hands of these very young men.

Momentarily, two men appearing to be in their late forties entered the room. Both of them were fit and trim. The older of the two extended his hand. "Mrs. Blake, I am Agent Hebert from the FBI. I am going to be in charge of this investigation to locate your little girl. I understand from Detective Simon that the young women at the streetcar stop have given us a description of the child's clothing she was wearing today—turquoise blouse and slacks with white sandals. We have found some clothing fibers that appear to match this description. Also, we found some strands of hair that appear to belong to your daughter. We took some samples from the hairbrush on her dresser for comparative purposes."

She wanted to scream. What were these men doing, concentrating on hair and clothing fibers when her little girl was out there someplace frightened and alone.

"That is very interesting, but what are you doing to find my little girl?" she demanded.

"We are trying to secure clues—looking for anything that will link the perpetrators to the scene, so when we catch them, we can prosecute them," he replied levelly, obviously unaffected by her comments. "Please be assured, Mrs. Blake, that we are going to do everything we can to find your little girl. Let's sit down for a minute here, and I can explain the process to you."

Reluctantly, she found herself sitting on the sofa where she had sat so many times with Rene and Granny Ariel. Agent Hebert introduced the man with him as Agent Purvis. Patiently, he explained that the young men in the room were technical support who had set up equipment to trace and record all telephone calls. The officers would monitor all incoming and outgoing calls. Hopefully, they could trace the call. Right now, the telephone was Rene's only lifeline. They would also monitor Brandy's email and cellular telephone.

"Most kidnappers seeking ransom contact the victim's family within forty-eight hours," he explained. We will be ready. You are going to need to stay here, to answer the telephone."

"But my grandmother—"

Agent Hebert put his hand firmly on her arm. "Mrs. Blake, we need you here—especially now. Tomorrow, we will connect a cellular to your home phone so you can go to the hospital if necessary. Before then, you have to bear in mind that if this is a ransom situation, it is likely that someone is watching you and the house."

She looked at this man dully. "And if it is not as you say, a ransom situation? What then?"

She saw a shadow of concern coming over his face. "Let's just wait and see," he replied.

She nodded and leaned back against the plaid cushions. For now, there was nothing she could do but wait for the phone to ring.

⁂

Raleigh buried himself in Rene's arms as the trunk flew open. He suspected that the woman would take Rene out of the trunk now. He needed to go with her at all costs and he did not want to attract attention. The intruder had removed the red wig, wiped his face of the makeup, and now wore jeans and a tee shirt. Raleigh was surprised to see that the person he had believed was a woman was actually a man. The intruder peered inside the trunk. Raleigh noticed that they were parked on a shell parking lot near an abandoned country restaurant/bar that lay in the shadows. Across the way, a lone street light gave a diffusive glow.

Another man with disheveled blonde hair stood beside the intruder. Raleigh had never seen this man before. Raleigh sniffed the air and caught a medicinal smell. The blonde man appeared to be using drugs.

"Alright, we're changing cars here. I'm going to put this blindfold on you now. If you get out of control, I'm gonna tie you up and knock your fuckin' teeth out," the scruffy blonde man told Rene.

Raleigh felt Rene shiver.

"Look at this goddamn blood. You're getting it all over everything. What the fuck did you do, cut yourself?"

"I'll get a towel from the other trunk," the intruder said.

The blonde man roughly pulled Rene over and began wrapping a strip of cloth tightly around her head.

"What the fuck is that? What the hell is that thing in your arms?" he demanded, pulling her into the light.

Raleigh attempted to bury himself against Rene as tightly as possible. He extended his claws and grabbed onto her shirt. The fabric might tear, but he could not be separated from Rene.

"It's my pet, and you are not taking him away from me!" she shrieked.

"It's a fuckin' squirrel."

"Watch your language, man. Let her keep it, because it will keep her quiet," said the intruder.

The blonde man groaned, cursing under his breath.

"I'm going to change the plates now and wipe out the inside for prints before we torch it," the intruder said. "By the time the car is discovered, we'll be long gone. Put the kid and her pet into the trunk of the other car."

The blonde man grumbled again and then checked Rene's blindfold before lifting her and Raleigh out of the trunk, taking them across the lot and into a car parked behind the restaurant building. Once again, they were plunged into darkness.

CHAPTER XXV

Ewan felt a sense of relief wash over him as he climbed into the passenger seat of the blue Ford midsize sedan. He had driven all the way to the Atchafalaya Basin, about two hours west of New Orleans. It was unlikely that anyone would be looking for the child there. Thornton had met him with the new car at the abandoned catfish shack two miles off the main road.

Last night, he moved out of the apartment on Euterpe. Before he left, he had hired two different cleaning services to thoroughly clean the interior. Ewan had been careful to wipe the surfaces down that he had touched to destroy any prints. He had enjoyed living in the apartment in the Lower Garden District, but it was time for a change. Once he finished his tasks, he would be destined for better things.

Killing Thornton had been easy, and Ewan was glad to be rid of him. Thornton had gotten in touch with him a few weeks ago looking for a deal to make some money. Now, there would be no loose ends to tie him to the kidnapping. Over the last few days, Thornton had become as burdensome as an albatross. He had needed him initially to meet him with the other car, but afterward, Thornton was expendable and a liability. Thornton was weak, and since he had last seen him, had become heavily involved with drugs. Ewan, on the other hand, understood the necessity of discretion. It was well-known that too many criminals were damned by their own mouths. Cops were lazy and had limited resources. Too often, a cop made a case against a perp as a direct result of someone bragging afterward. There had never been any question in his mind that one day, he would need to kill Thornton.

After Thornton had put the kid in the trunk of the Ford sedan, Ewan had grabbed a brick in the parking lot and clubbed Thornton over the back of the head until he was bleeding and unconscious. Afterward, he shoved him into the backseat of the green sedan and poured lighter fuel all over the interior. The car had ignited easily and within moments was engulfed by flames, illuminating the night sky.

Ewan drove back to the main highway and turned the car east on Interstate 12 toward the safe house near the Honey Island Swamp near the Mississippi border. He had carefully selected a house strategically located in the opposite direction from the abduction car. Once the cops found Thornton's body, they would predictably focus their search on the Atchafalaya Basin area. The kid, of course, would be hidden over sixty miles away.

The Honey Island Swamp was an isolated preserve of wetlands that merged into the rigolets, lakes, channels, and rivers that covered South Louisiana and Mississippi. Except for an occasional tourist boat, the swamp was principally inhabited by a few sportsmen and locals who did not want any problems. The area was teaming with alligators and poisonous snakes. Even if the child miraculously escaped, she would never survive. The swamp was the perfect place to hide the child. Many of the local alligators in the area were at least twelve-feet long and would relish a young kid as a meal. It was the perfect solution.

Thad had insisted that he kill the kid's mother as well. It was a risk and he would need to lure her into the swamp and dispose of her body. Alligators were carrion-eaters, and they would easily consume a dead body. There would not be a trace of evidence to connect him to their deaths. The swamp was a perfect solution to protect him against discovery. Afterward, he could take a small boat over to Bay St. Louis, where he kept a car and had rented a small apartment. He had purchased a false passport and social security number in the name of Will North. Ewan would take the car and drive to Tennessee to wait a few weeks until it was safe to travel to the Philippines in pursuit of his new life and financial freedom.

~

Brandy lay awake in bed all night, unable to sleep. Agent Hebert had promised to wake her if there were anything to report. She could not hear any activity from downstairs. Felecia and Agent Hebert had explained that once the equipment installation was complete, the police would inconspicuously guard the house and monitor the telephones. The cars utilized by the force were unmarked sedans, and the officers were dressed in street clothes.

"We want to blend in. You are probably being watched. The department has a number of fancy cars forfeited in narcotics busts that fit into this neighborhood. We'll park them around and come and go. Some of these dapper young guys dress more like Saks or Brooks Brothers than Walmart now. Things are different now than when I started out."

At 4:00 a.m., she finally got up and called the hospital. The ICU nurse in the cardiac care ward assured her that Granny Ariel was stable. Visiting hours were still four hours away.

She was alive.

Brandy took a long hot shower and even shampooed her hair. Afterward, she pulled on a pair of fresh cotton slacks and a shirt and went downstairs to the kitchen. Agent Hebert was drinking coffee and talking to one of the other officers. Brandy grabbed a coffee pod and made herself a strong ten ounce cup of coffee.

The older of the two officers eyed her with concern. "Were you able to get any sleep at all?"

Brandy shook her head miserably. "All I can think of is Rene, afraid and alone, and Granny Ariel hooked up to those machines." She began to feel the all-too-familiar sting of hot wet tears on her cheeks.

The officers looked away in obvious discomfort. They were likely accustomed to dealing with hysterical victims.

"The hospital told me that my grandmother is stable," she announced once she had regained her composure. Brandy looked at Agent Hebert pointedly. "I've got to go to the hospital. This could be the last time, and I've got to see my grandmother. You need to make it happen and give me whatever electronic hookup you can, but I have to go," she said forcefully.

"We can arrange for your phone to be automatically forwarded to another line that we can monitor. You can take one of the phones with you, and we'll drive you down to the hospital."

"Thank you," she replied, praying that she would at least get to see her grandmother one more time. "And I will need to check on my shop with my assistant, Natalie. I need to let her know that I will not be coming in today. We will need to get in our emergency salesperson, Danielle. Natalie goes to school, and she needs to be relieved during the times she cannot be there."

"We'll arrange it," Agent Hebert told her. "We also need to check out these women, too."

"You don't think they could be involved, do you?" she replied indignantly.

"Mrs. Blake," he replied patiently, "we will turn over every rock until we find your daughter."

She nodded in assent and drank her cup of coffee. She wished that she could talk to Claude. Besides Granny Ariel, he was really her only other close friend at the moment.

After breakfast, a plainclothes FBI agent took Brandy down to the hospital in a powder blue 700 BMW. He was dressed expensively, resembling a stockbroker more than a law enforcement officer. Brandy had the police telephone in her purse. Her instructions were to answer it no matter what. All telephone calls would be recorded. Agent Hebert had also given her a notepad for any notes she might want to make. He encouraged her to let Granny Ariel's friends know that she was ill but cautioned her against openly discussing Rene's situation.

"This is a difficult situation here, but we don't want to compromise the investigation," he told her.

Granny Ariel was alert when Brandy came into the room. Her skin was unnaturally pallid and her eyes were still puffy. Brandy noticed the IV and a catheter that snaked around the mattress. Her expression was dazed, but she obviously recognized Brandy.

Brandy clasped her grandmother's hand and gave her a light squeeze and then kissed her cheek. "Granny Ariel, I am so glad that you are doing better! You gave us quite a fright!"

Her grandmother gave her a knowing look while Brandy tried to plump up the pillow and straighten the covers on the bed.

"I'm sorry," her grandmother mouthed silently. "I'm sorry."

Brandy noticed the fear and concern in her grandmother's eyes. She squeezed her hand softly. "Granny Ariel, it is not your fault. There are policemen working around the clock to find Rene. They are going to find her! It is not your fault! We need you! I need you to come back! I can't live there without you!"

A tear streamed across Granny Ariel's delicate cheek as she stared into her granddaughter's eyes.

"Raleigh," she mouthed.

"We think he's with Rene. A student saw him jump into the car after her. He's with her and she's not alone."

Granny Ariel nodded imperceptibly and closed her eyes. For reasons that Brandy could not understand, she seemed relieved. It was just a squirrel. Why was she concerned about the squirrel at a time like this?

Her grandmother opened her eyes again. This time, she saw a glimmer of hope and resolve. What was it about the squirrel that made her grandmother want to hold onto life?

Brandy smiled at her grandmother, clasping her hand. The room was silent, except for the constant sound of the ventilator. She was literally willing her grandmother to recover. All too soon, the officer came to get Brandy. Granny Ariel had another visitor.

One of Granny Ariel's friends, Corinne, had been visiting a sick relative in the ICU and discovered that Granny Ariel had suffered a heart attack. No doubt many of Granny Ariel's friends would come by in droves later. Corinne had promised to stay at the hospital with Granny Ariel. Brandy knew that it was the only possible solution. If she could not stay with Granny Ariel, Corinne was the next best person. She did not want her grandmother to be alone in the hospital. Tears welled in her eyes as she thought of leaving her in the ICU. She was torn between her love for her grandmother and her daughter, but she needed to go home to help find Rene. Every hour that she was gone made it less likely that she would return.

Brandy returned to the ICU cubicle to see Granny Ariel one last time. Her skin was still pasty and it was obvious that everything was a struggle.

Brandy gave Granny Ariel a gentle hug before she left the ICU. She had a deep sense of foreboding that she would not see Granny Ariel again. Everything that had ever meant anything to her had been taken away and her life was in shambles.

∽

Agent Hebert was waiting for her in the parking garage. As they drove home, he gave her the latest news. The police had found the charred shell of a car on behind a bar outside a deserted bar near the Atchafalaya Basin. The interior was still smoldering, and an unidentified man's remains were inside. Fibers, hair, and blood in the vicinity of the automobile were en route for testing at the police lab. One of the hair samples was a long strand of red hair intermingled with what appeared to be animal fur. There were smatterings of what appeared to be human blood on the shell surface of the lot near the automobile. There was no sign of any other occupants.

"The license plate had partially melted, but the car appears to have been the car used to abduct your daughter. There were fragments of green paint found in the area. The fire department believes that the accelerant used was lighter fuel. When the gas in the fuel tank ignited, there was a huge explosion, and much of the useful evidence was destroyed. Fortunately, the fire was discovered quickly when a trucker traveling to a nearby all-night diner reported the fire to the authorities," he told her.

Brandy listened dully with an increasing sense of dread. Now there could be murder involved? That gave very little hope for Rene. Her baby could be killed. "What does this mean?" she asked Agent Hebert, her voice cracking with tension.

He stared straight ahead, negotiating the traffic on St. Charles Avenue. Momentarily, when he finally stopped at the light on Jefferson Avenue, he looked over at her and began to explain the situation.

"We know from the witnesses' statements that there was one person in the car that abducted Rene. The driver appeared to be a woman dressed like you. Apparently, the abductor had an accomplice meet him or her at abandoned catfish restaurant. For whatever reason, more than likely, one killed the other—maybe even to cover the perp's tracks. It may point to the involvement of a third person. On the other hand, someone could have happened up and seen them, and the perp took his car and decided to dispose of the body. Only time will tell. The body has been sent to the crime lab. We may be able to identify the male from dental records." He began driving again when the light changed.

"Either way, the person who has my daughter is a killer. Isn't that what you are really trying to tell me? I need to know the unvarnished truth. Don't feed me any crap! In the last two and a half years, I have either lost or come close to losing everyone important to me. Lying to me or protecting my feelings will not make it any easier. I want the goddamn truth for once!"

He paused only slightly, avoiding her gaze and appearing to concentrate on the traffic again. "It is beginning to look that way, but we don't know the situation. These could be amateurs, or this could have been a highly organized event. At any rate, it points more and more to a ransom situation. These people probably want something from you—like a huge sum of money. On a positive note, I think we can now rule out a deranged serial killer or child rapist. This is a serious kidnapping situation with a motive. The stakes are obviously very high. Someone either did not want any witnesses or wants a bigger share for himself or herself. It is hard to tell at this point."

"Do you think it is connected to my potential recovery in the *BYZANTIUM* suit? Could Thad Stuart or Recov be involved?" she asked, slightly mollified that he was at least being forthright.

"No one can tell you right now. The publicity has been in the paper. Someone could have seen it and targeted you and your daughter. Also, you live in an extremely affluent segment of New Orleans. You obviously come from money. It could just as easily be someone that you do not know. Or, it could be a workman or delivery person who has been to your house over the last year. It could be someone who habitually frequents the park. We will not know until you get the first call demanding money."

"How will you ever be able to figure out who did this and who to look for?"

"First, we are following up every lead, including interviewing every single delivery worker and workman who has been here over the last few months. We are checking with the lawn service and cleaning service, as well as the security service, to find out if there are any new workers or whether one of the workers has left. Apparently, the gardening service had someone quit last week. We are getting the employment records. We have officers conducting interviews and searches. There is also a team working the park, speaking to the regulars."

"Regulars?" She asked. How could they possibly pick out the regulars in the park?

"Generally, they are elderly retired people with pets or those people who go to feed the animals. There are the people who exercise early in the morning. Many of them notice things. We have many statements already. Then we will talk to the neighbors and canvas the neighborhood. Finally, we will wait for the call. It has been sixteen hours now. The calls generally come within the first twenty-four to forty-eight hours. That gives the kidnappers time to find a safe location and avoid scrutiny. Also, there is a psychological effect. Most kidnappers intuitively sense that most parents or caretakers are frantic at that point. They are desperate, and they want news."

"So I may have another twenty-four hours of this before we know anything?"

He looked at her sympathetically. He was painfully accustomed to dealing with helpless and overwrought people. "Maybe even forty-eight hours. Sometimes, it is even seventy-two hours, but that is the exception. Generally, they do not want the parents to go to the police. But let's just take this as it comes. There is no way to predict what these people are trying to do. Every case is different. I have that point brought home to me every time."

"How will I know what to do when the call comes?"

"We will go over that now. That is why we wanted you to come home. We are in the window of time now that most calls come in. We will want you to try to stall and get as much information as you can. Ask to speak to Rene. We want you to be very insistent that you talk to her or have proof that she is alive. Try to find out exactly what they want. The longer you stay on the line, the easier it will be to trace the call. The trick is that they will be aware of that fact, so they will be rushing you. The kidnapper will want to be in control and keep you off balance. You are going to need to assume control. There are certain tricks of the trade that my agents are going to teach you."

She nodded her head and wiped away the tears that were welling in her eyes again. It was all in her hands. What if she made a mistake? Rene may never come home. Oh God, don't let her die. She had to be strong. She would not let her little girl die.

"Agent Hebert, I promise that I will be the quickest study that you have ever seen in maintaining control. If it is the last thing I do, I am going to get my daughter back."

He gave her an appreciative glance. "Good. That is what it will take."

Agent Hebert parked the car in the drive. Without another word, they went into the house to wait for the call.

~

Raleigh curled up next to Rene in the trunk. This car smelled cleaner than the first one. It was probably newer. The man drove this car for a long time, before stopping for a few minutes. Their captor opened the trunk just long enough to give the child a packet of cupcakes, an apple, and a bottle of water before he slammed the lid. He and Rene had shared the food and the water. Finally, the child had fallen asleep from exhaustion and stress.

Raleigh knew that something had happened after they had changed cars. He had smelled the acrid scent of smoke before they had driven off. There was silence now in the front seat. The intruder was alone again.

For a time, the car had returned to the highway. Raleigh could hear the tires singing lightly over the roadway. The car occasionally pitched as it encountered uneven pavement. They were traveling slower now, and he could hear the crackle of shells on what he assumed was the roadbed. Rene stirred slightly. His nostrils filled with the scent of damp earth and water. It was incredibly warm, humid, and quiet.

Was he going to hurt them? What did he want?

Raleigh wondered what time it was. His body told him that it was early morning. Ariel and Brandy would be frantic by now with worry. He thought about Chloe. If only she were here. The squirrel felt a little sick. He needed more to eat than just the apple. He needed cambium or a pine cone. How he would love to have some sunflower seeds.

Suddenly, the car careened to a stop.

Rene awoke. "I need to go potty bad," she told Raleigh, her voice groggy.

The squirrel scampered over to the child. Her breath smelled sour, and she had the scent of fear. Gently, he stroked her hair with his paws and curled beneath her chin. She snuggled with him, and he could feel her calm down.

He heard the car door open followed by the pounding of footsteps on the soft earth. He felt Rene's body go rigid next to him. Momentarily, the trunk was flooded with early morning light and a rush of warm, humid air. Overhead were the branches of large cypress trees decorated with Spanish moss against a slate sky. There was the smell of mud and water everywhere. He peered over Rene's arm and looked at the intruder, who now wore a mask.

"Cover your eyes with your hands and turn around," the man demanded.

Rene lifted her hands to her eyes. Roughly, the man cinched a bandana around her head and tied it in the back. "Don't ever try to look at me," he instructed.

"I need to go potty, please!" cried Rene. "I'm going to wet my pants."

"Okay, I am going to let you out and you can squat by the car. I'll turn around. We are in the middle of the swamp, and there is no place for you to run. This place is crawling with alligators and water moccasins, and you'll be dead before you know it."

Raleigh felt Rene shiver. "Okay," she replied meekly.

The man lifted them from the trunk and set her on the soft earth. "Take a leak here, kid. I'm not looking."

Raleigh also took the opportunity to relieve himself. After Rene finished, he jumped back into her arms when she called to him. The man took Rene's arm.

"Watch your step. We are going inside now."

Rene allowed the man to lead her down the drive to a wooden pier that extended out over the dark water. Algae, reeds and cattails grew in the water along the banks. The cypress trees soared overhead, blocking the light. There was an eerie beauty about the place.

This must be the swamp.

They trudged along the pier to a primitive house built over the water on stilts. The back of the house bordered a strand of black water. A porch surrounded the shack on three sides. Raleigh felt a stab of fear as he noticed what appeared to be a ten-foot alligator resting on a log near the bank. Overhead, a red-tailed hawk screeched and soared. A raccoon climbed along the tree branch of a gnarled oak. For a squirrel and small child, this felt like a place of death. He knew that there was very little chance of escape.

He caught the man's scent again and involuntarily shuddered.

It was the scent of danger. This scent belonged to the person who had poisoned Chloe.

The cypress timber shack smelled musty inside. Raleigh caught a predatory scent. In the corner, he noticed what appeared to be a sloughed snake skin. There was also the scent of rats and nutria. If a snake or rat came into the shack at night, he could easily be killed. Rene seemed oblivious to the danger awaiting them now.

The man quietly led Rene to an interior, windowless room inside the shack. He nudged Rene inside and remained outside of the door.

The room had a bed with a blanket in the corner. An old fruit stand held a camping flashlight. There was a small blackboard with colored chalk on the blanket along with a small stack of ratty children's books and some oversized tee shirts. A metal tub and pitcher with two towels and facecloths rested in the middle of the floor beside a jug.

The man came into the room. "Can you read?" he barked.

"Yes," she replied timidly.

"From here on out, write what you want on this board. When I want to come in, I will knock. You will immediately turn around and hide your face. You are not to look at me again. If you try, I am going to kill your little pet or hurt him so bad you will want him to die. We are not going to talk anymore unless I tell you. I will write on this chalkboard to tell you what I want you to do." His voice had a hard edge. There was very little doubt that he meant what he said.

Rene began to cry. "I understand. Please don't hurt Raleigh. I love him so much! I won't try to look! I promise."

"Okay. I am going to take off the scarf now. You stand there and don't move until I shut the door. From then on, we will be silent," he demanded.

Roughly, the man removed the scarf. Then he walked across the room and shut the door. Once again, the two of them were alone.

CHAPTER XXVI

Detective Simon was waiting inside with Agent Plauche when Brandy returned from the hospital. She reported that the preliminary DNA studies had confirmed that the long red hair found at the site of the burned car belonged to Rene. Agent Herbert explained that they would now review what to do when the kidnappers contacted Brandy. Agent Plauche had brewed them each a cup of coffee. Woodenly, Brandy retrieved a plate of pastries from the crisper and placed it on the center of the breakfast room table. Brandy could not help but notice that the wireless telephone was placed prominently on the table closest to her seat.

Silently, Brandy drank the coffee and nibbled on a pastry. She felt a groaning in the pit of her stomach and was suddenly overcome with exhaustion. Although she knew that she was hungry, she was unable to taste the pastry that she ordinarily loved.

How much difference a day could make! Less than twenty-four hours ago, she was happily returning from Miami, eagerly awaiting a warm welcome from her daughter and grandmother. How could she ever have imagined the horror that awaited her? The most important people in the world to her were Rene and Granny Ariel. She could barely think of losing both of them. Her life would be completely over at that point.

"Mrs. Blake, we think we should begin reviewing the protocol now. I can only imagine how difficult this is for you, but you will have our full support," Agent Plauche said.

"No, I actually do not think you can even imagine how difficult this is," she snapped. "I was widowed almost two years ago. Yesterday, my entire life was destroyed in a matter of two hours. My daughter and grandmother are all I have."

She glared at him and he returned her gaze in silence. She estimated that he was only a year or two older than she was. His one-eighth-inch haircut and arrogant self-confidence suggested that he had a military background. Despite her barbed comment, he had a no-nonsense air of compassion about him. He was used to this, of course—dealing with overwrought individuals. Her rage was probably fairly predictable.

She felt Detective Simon put her hand softly on her arm. She gave her a squeeze. It brought her back to reality. These people were trying to help. She did not need to insult them. She needed to listen.

She attempted to compose herself and shoved her hair back from her forehead. "Look, I am sorry that I appear to be taking this out on you. I just feel so afraid! My daughter is out there alone, and my grandmother could be dying, and I don't know what to do! They are all that I have and there is absolutely no way that you could know what I am feeling now." A flood of tears streamed down her cheeks and her hands began to tremble.

"Mrs. Blake," Agent Plauche said softly as he put his hands on her shoulder.

"Call me Brandy," she told them, wiping her eyes. "I know. I need to be strong. This is just the stress. I am determined to get my daughter back, and I am ready to listen. Agent Hebert and I have been discussing this in the car on the way back from the hospital. I understand how important this will be." She managed a slight smile as if to confirm that the hysterical outburst was over. She had to be strong. No matter what she had to be strong.

"Law enforcement officers in St. Martin, Iberville and St. Landry Parish are all on a high alert for your daughter in the area. The green sedan was located outside Henderson, and it is probable that your daughter is in the vicinity."

"That area borders on a massive swampland. It is a desolate area, and some of the Cajun houses in the swamp would be ideal for holding a child."

Brandy tried to resist the temptation to scream. A child could never escape from the swamp.

"There is a massive manhunt underway," Agent Plauche interjected. "We are doing everything we can."

Brandy shook her head and contemplated the situation in silence. She could sense that finding Rene was a long shot. The Atchafalaya Basin was a vast wilderness area. It would be easy to conceal a child for a few days or dispose of her body in the swamp. As much as she did not want to admit it, it was quite possible that Rene was not coming back.

Agent Plauche set his coffee cup on the sideboard and pulled out a diagram along with a laminated piece of paper containing a list of instructions. If he had been insulted by her outburst, he concealed it well. He also had a legal pad with two pens. He gave Brandy a pen and paper.

"Now, as Agent Herbert has already explained to you, most telephone calls from abductors occur within the first seventy-two hours. I want you to understand that this is not a hard-and-fast rule. The individuals we are dealing with seem to have a definite agenda that is likely a large sum of money. They are not afraid to take risks, and there is probably very little trust between them."

"I thought that at least one of them could be dead. How do you know that there is another one?" Brandy asked.

"We don't," Agent Plauche replied. "But we suspect that a second person brought the newer car near the Atchafalaya Basin, unless the perp high-jacked a car from an innocent third party. Besides, in most cases, we have discovered that there are at least two and sometimes three people involved. More often than not, a man and a woman are involved in this type of case. It is certainly less suspicious to see a man and a woman with a young child. They look like a family to everyone in the outside world. We cannot confirm yet that a woman is involved in this case, but it is a good possibility."

"That is one of the things that you can help us find out," Agent Herbert interjected. "Agent Plauche has a list of things here on these sheets. They have been posted by every telephone in the house along with a pad and pen. All of the telephones are now equipped with recording devices, and we are going to try to trace any call that you receive."

"When a call comes in, we want you to take a deep breath and focus. The first telephone call will generally set the tone for our dealing with these people. I know that it will be incredibly difficult for you, but it is necessary. We need information, and you are the one person who can get it for us. There are a lot of subtle comments and questions you can ask that are designed to elicit important information. So, we need to go over that. We do not want anyone calling before you have a chance to digest this information."

"Alright." Brandy felt more determined now. Finally, she would be able to do something.

"Now, the first thing is that you want immediate confirmation from the kidnapper that your daughter is alive and well. Ask to speak to her. If the caller tries to avoid this, insist upon it. If the caller tells you that Rene is not there, ask where she is. Ask whether she is alone. Tell the caller that Rene is afraid of the dark. Ask when the last time she had eaten and whether she has had a bath. Tell the caller that you need to confirm that Rene has not been harmed and that she is not afraid. If we can find out that she is not alone, but she is not close by, then it is likely that there is another accomplice. You need to be firm and assertive without alienating the caller. This will take concentration and finesse."

Brandy nodded, inviting him to continue.

"Now, according to you, Rene has a pet squirrel from the park. The witnesses said that she noticed Rene because a squirrel was playing chase with her, and she believes that she saw the squirrel jump into the trunk before it closed. Now, what is the squirrel's name?"

"Raleigh."

"Alright, ask the caller if Raleigh is with Rene. Don't mention that Raleigh is a squirrel. Instead, what we want you to do is to get the caller to confirm that Rene has or did have a squirrel with her. If the squirrel is alive, then Rene is probably fine. Does the squirrel need to eat anything special?"

"Sunflower seeds, birdseed, and fruit, I think. He is really more of my grandmother's pet. I have never actually fed Raleigh myself."

"Alright, be sure to tell the caller that. Insist that the caller buy some seeds and emphasize how important the squirrel is to Rene and to your grandmother. Create whatever story you want, but persist. It may result in information that we might not otherwise have. Remember, you need to be in control and to call the shots. Next, ask the caller if he or she has a camera and ask that he or she send you a digital picture of Rene from an Internet café. If the caller indicates that there is nothing like that close by, we may be able to determine that they are far out of the city."

"Alright," she replied weakly. "I can do that."

"Next, try to pin down exactly what the caller wants. Find out if it is money. Don't let the caller rush you. Ask the caller to repeat whatever he or she says more than once. Tell him that you need to write any instructions down. Emphasize that you will not go to the police about the call unless they refuse to cooperate with you. The news media has been reporting the abduction of a little girl from Audubon Park. If the caller does not mention the news story, the caller may not have watched television or looked at a paper. This is unlikely, but it may indicate that they are in a remote spot. Then, ask about Rene again. Tell the caller that you have to know that she is well and alive. Ask if she has the right clothes. Don't be afraid to be assertive. The caller wants something from you, and you have every right to demand a quid pro quo. The caller will tell you that you will have to have trust him. Don't be afraid to say that is bullshit. Tell the caller that this is just a business deal—pure and simple. You need answers."

Brandy made a note on her pad.

"As difficult as it is, I want you to focus and try to stay controlled. You want to avoid the sound of hysteria or fear in your voice. It will only empower the kidnapper. Be logical, clear and firm. Speak slowly and clearly. Focus on getting information. Remember, the kidnapper wants something from you, and you can only give it to them on your terms."

"I am afraid that I will cry," Brandy replied.

"Just do the best that you can," Agent Hebert interjected in a sympathetic tone. "The caller may expect some tears, but try to steel yourself and still be assertive. This is a poker game now."

"The caller will likely insist that you leave the city and make a money drop, just like all of the television shows. If the caller presses you, mention what happened to your grandmother as a result of this stress. Emphasize that you have other responsibilities here and that she is gravely ill. Tell the caller that you cannot leave at the drop of a hat now. It may fluster the caller and buy us additional time. You need to be close by. What this means is that you are going to try to draw the caller back into the city. And, you want to see Rene immediately. What we want to avoid is dropping off money and then not having access to Rene. You are a business-woman, and I am sure that you understand that you want to bargain for an even trade."

Agent Plauche paused and looked at her intently, as if to gauge whether she was up to the task. Brandy realized that he approached everything with clipped military precision, in comparison to Agent Hebert's gentle compassionate disposition. Her resolve must have been apparent, because he quickly continued.

"Finally, just remember that we want you to draw out the telephone conversation as long as possible. Time is our friend here."

Detective Simon answered her cell phone. She made a few notes on her legal pad before giving the caller a few instructions and hanging up. "Good news," she announced principally to Agent Herbert. "Allen Conner called from St. Thomas. It looks like Jimmy Thornton made a trip to the dentist when he lived in the Virgin Islands. The x-rays are being flown up overnight."

"Do you think that Jimmy had something to do with Rene's disappearance?" Brandy asked incredulously.

Agent Herbert folded his beefy hands on the table. "Mrs. Blake, Allen Conner suspects that Jimmy Thornton either was directly or indirectly involved in your husband's murder. If he was not involved he had information or a suspicion of what happened. Secondly, he meets the description of the man who abducted your daughter. According to the college student, the abductor was at least six three, appeared to be healthy and muscular."

"That's about how I would describe Jimmy," Brandy said quietly with the sick realization that he may have attempted to harm her little girl.

"Let's just wait and see what the dental records show," Agent Herbert told her. "But if the body is Jimmy Thornton, then we have just gotten a big break in this case."

"Do you have any idea who the second person would be," she asked.

"Thornton had a friend in a dive shop—Donaldson—who left the Virgin Islands and moved to Ft. Lauderdale. After that, his trail went cold. We don't know if he was involved. There is another man who worked for your gardening service. He quit his job a couple of weeks ago and left without a forwarding address. He was living on Euterpe, but stiffed the landlord and left town. He had a small bank account that was cleaned out the day before. It may be coincidence, but we are checking this out," Agent Hebert told her.

"I just can't believe that Jimmy would have tried to hurt Rene," Brandy said. "He always seemed so gentle. He actually seemed to like children the few times that I saw him."

"There are millions at stake in the *BYZANTIUM* civil case, right, Mrs. Blake?" Agent Herbert said. "That amount of money makes people do crazy things. We don't know what he was promised by Thad Stuart. To a beach bum type like Thornton, who has had very little motivation to earn a living, a cut of a few million dollars looks like easy street for the rest of his life."

"Are you telling me that Thad Stuart may have had something to do with the disappearance of my little girl?"

Detective Simon put her hand on her arm again as if to reassure her. "We don't know. But there is obviously a connection between

Stuart and Thornton. We are going to know a lot more when the caller contacts you and when we determine whether this was Thornton's body in that car. In the meantime, Allen Connor is trying to interview Thad Stuart. This is a dynamic situation. Twenty four hours from now, we hopefully will have much more information."

Brandy nodded her head and let the information gradually sink in. As she sipped her coffee, the phone rang, its shrill sound piercing the silence. The time had come. She looked at Agent Plauche and took a deep breath to strengthen her resolve. With a trembling hand, she lifted the receiver and pushed the button to answer the call.

~

After a time, their eyes adjusted to the darkness. Raleigh's night vision was far superior to the child's sight. The broken slats near the ceiling allowed the only light into the room. They began exploring the small room and found a metal box on the bed filled with chips, cookies, three apples, a jar of peanut butter, and a loaf of bread. The squirrel realized that they would need to ration the food. He could eat part of the sandwich and apple. There was very little indication of how long they would be left without more food. They found two bottles of water resting on the small crate near the bed, along with a rough rag, hand towel and a plastic container of antibiotic wipes. There was also a high-beam flashlight, a broom, a rusty can opener, and a butt end fragment of a rod-and-reel fishing pole. A large heavy clay pot in the corner reeking of urine was obviously the makeshift toilet.

"It smells bad in here," Rene said out loud.

Raleigh barked once in reply.

Rene tugged at the blanket folded at the foot of the bare stained mattress.

"There aren't any sheets!" she said, her voice shaky with tears. "How can we sleep like this?"

Raleigh barked and jumping on the bed, burrowed into the mattress. He peeked out from under the blanket and barked again, trying to entertain the child.

She seemed to relax watching his antics and climbed onto the bed. Some of the boards from the wall behind them had parted high overhead, and a thin shaft of sunlight fell across the mattress, illuminating a sliver of the darkness. "Like camping, I guess."

He went over to the chalkboard and chattered. It was far too big for him to lift. It would be their only means of communication. Rene lifted the small board and the box of chalk, bringing it over to the bed.

"We can write on this," she told Raleigh. Extracting a piece of chalk from the box, she broke off a tiny piece and handed it to Raleigh. The squirrel wrestled with the chalk and wrote: "Okay?"

"I am scared," she told him. "I miss Mommy! How are we going to get away?"

He tapped the tablet with his paw and scampered over to the wall. Fortunately, the walls were made of rough wood. His claws would easily hold him into place. With ease, he climbed the wall and peeked out of the shack through the thin chinks in the wood above them. There was a ribbon of shell-and-dirt road that extended through the swamp. On either side, he could see black water with cypress trees draped with bearded Spanish moss. He could feel the intense heat and smell the acrid water. From his position, he could just make out the snout of the alligator dozing on a sun-drenched log. He was almost perfectly camouflaged by the dark-brown wood. Raleigh felt a bone-chilling fear in his chest. Alligators could run quickly for short distances on land. He was not certain that he could outrun one even if it were completely safe to run down the road. He heard some unfamiliar screeching and decided that it probably emanated from the birds. Red-shouldered hawks were plentiful in this region, according to the swamp documentaries on the Discovery Channel.

"What do you see?" Rene asked him from below.

He gave a low bark and continued to gaze out through the small hole in the wall. He was tiring rapidly, though. He had underestimated the texture of the wood, which was just smooth enough to make it difficult for him to hold on very long.

"Could we run away?" Rene asked.

Raleigh replied with a soft moan. They had no way to determine how long the road was leading out of the swamp, or whether the connecting main road was well traveled enough to attract the attention of a passing motorist. Then there was the danger from the alligators and snakes. Rene was still a very tiny child. She tired easily and would likely be a delectable meal to an alligator. It was unlikely that she could carry him out. They were likely miles away from civilization or rescue. He knew that it was unlikely that he could venture out alone. An unprotected squirrel would quickly attract the attention of a raptor. A hawk's vision was several times better than his and would be able to follow his movements from an undetectable height. He would not last half an hour. The cattails, branches and bushes trailing alongside of the road were also off limits. They would be covered with snakes, raccoons and nutria, lying in wait for an unsuspecting squirrel. He would be ambushed and killed within seconds. Assuming he survived, what would a lone squirrel do when he reached the road? No one would think a squirrel running alongside the road was out of the ordinary. No passing motorist would stop for him. He was a wild animal. Someone might even decide to kill and eat him. They were in the backcountry, and even for humans, he was a prospective meal.

It was hopeless. But he had to remain calm. He did not want to frighten Rene. He just needed to think. There had to be a way out.

He descended back down the wall and hopped onto the bare mattress with Rene. He sat on his haunches and tapped his head with his forepaw. It was their signal that he needed to think. Rene watched him pensively. He could see the exhaustion from the ordeal in her face.

Picking up the chalk, he drew a grid on the board. He gathered a small stick in the corner and nibbled it into pieces and colored half of them with chalk, arranging them on the chalk board like a checkers game. He positioned the board in the crevice of light slipping through the broken boards. Then he planted his paw on the makeshift pawn and slid it forward, careful not to erase the chalk lines. Rene's eyes lit up with delight. It was a welcome diversion from their terrible stress. They played several rounds until Rene leaned back and slipped under the blanket.

"I am just going to close my eyes for a few minutes," she assured Raleigh. Momentarily, the child was asleep.

Raleigh stayed awake, holding vigil over Rene and the room. He was afraid—with a fear unlike anything he had ever felt in his life. He had a terrible feeling that neither one of them would ever leave this God-forsaken place.

Claude's sunny voice greeted Brandy on the other end of the telephone receiver. He was apparently oblivious to the events over the last few hours. Brandy felt both a sense of relief and disappointment that the kidnapper was not on the other end of the phone.

"I bet you are really glad to be home! I am still here and things are going well. We are finishing up tomorrow, and then I will come back to New Orleans," he told her.

"Claude," she replied sharply. "Granny Ariel was attacked by a burglar late yesterday. She was stabbed and then had a heart attack. She is in the hospital." She glanced over at Agent Herbert, who signaled to her not to mention Rene's disappearance. He traced his hand horizontally over the base of his throat, indicating that she should quickly wrap up the call.

"Oh my God, Brandy! I am so sorry. How is she?"

"She was better today but she is still in the intensive care unit on a respirator. I am actually on my way out, Claude, to go back to the cardiac care unit. I came home to shower."

"Is there anything I can do now? I can come home," he said, the concern evident in his voice.

She slightly faltered. "No, Claude, stay and finish your work. Granny Ariel's friends are helping me."

"I'll be home late tomorrow night."

"Thank you Claude. We'll see you then. I need to run."

"Take care, Brandy. Tell Granny Ariel that I am thinking of her."

"Good-bye."

She hung up and placed the receiver prominently on the table in front of her. Within seconds of removing her hand from the receiver, the telephone rang again.

"Hello."

"Do you miss your little girl, Rene?" The man's voice was surprisingly soft and almost friendly. She was sure that it was no one that she had ever spoken with before.

Brandy steeled herself and tried to focus. "Of course I miss her. Please let me talk to her."

"It's impossible," he replied matter-of-factly.

"Why?"

"Because she is not here. She is someplace safe."

"What do you consider safe?"

"She's not here."

"Has she eaten? Is someone with her? I need to know that she is alive!"

"She's not starving."

"Rene is afraid of being alone. Do you have someone with her?"

"Look, I know that you are trying to drag this out. Listen carefully, or I will hang up."

She felt a surge of anger. "Tell me what you want."

"Five million dollars cash in unmarked bills in seventy-two hours."

"I don't have that kind of money."

"Then get it," the caller replied before hanging up.

"But it is impossible." She screamed.

She listened to the dial tone on the other end of the receiver. She had lost control, and the negotiations had just begun.

"I'm sorry—I tried," she told the officers at the table.

She could see the disappointment in Agent Hebert's face. He gave her a practiced smile. "Based upon what he said, we think that Rene is being held at another location. There are likely at least two abductors, and they have a specific demand. We think the call came from a cell. The man who called is obviously the negotiator."

"Will he call back?" she asked.

"Of course. He wants money, and he is already mentally spending it."

"What do we do now?"

"We wait for him to call back."

CHAPTER XXVII

He awoke with a start. Something was terribly wrong. He could feel it.

Danger!

He listened intently to the faint noise coming from the other side of the room.

Something or someone was in the room with them!

He needed the flashlight. The sliver of moonlight coming through a chink above them lit up the crate beside the bed.

All clear on the top of the crate.

He leapt up onto the top of the crate behind the flashlight. It was extremely heavy. With a violent shove, he slid the rocker switch forward. Suddenly, the room was partially illuminated by a brilliant shaft of light. The cone of yellow light was too high, though. Whatever was in the room was down on the floor. Rene was still sleeping soundly in the bed beside him. He shoved with all of his strength against the flashlight, moving it toward the edge of the crate. Part of the floor came into view from the yellow light. He felt his breath catch in his throat.

It was a snake.

The snake lay across the floor not ten feet from the bed. Raleigh wondered how it possibly could have gotten into the room. It was unlikely that it had crawled through the chink in the wall above them. It probably had come in through a gap in the floor where it crudely adjoined the wall.

Could it smell him? Had it come for him?

Mesmerized, he stared at the snake again. It was no longer moving and appeared to be basking in the golden light of the flashlight. It was not very large—maybe about two feet in length. It was the color of muddy soil with the distinctly triangular head of the pit viper.

Water moccasin. They were territorial and aggressive—one of the more deadly poisonous snakes. It would be easy for the snake to kill and eat him. Rene would easily be bitten. Without medical attention, she could die. He had to do something.

He began to bark and jumped on the bed with Rene. Groggily, she tried to shove the squirrel aside. He continued to bark until the child opened her eyes and sat up.

"Raleigh, what is the light doing on?"

Raleigh continued to bark, leaping over onto the crate and back on the bed. Rene sat up slowly, and her eyes moved over to the shaft of light on the floor and then let out a blood curdling scream. Raleigh signaled to the chalkboard.

"What are we going to do, Raleigh," the child wailed.

The squirrel continued to bark until she moved the chalkboard onto the bed. Rene handed him a piece of chalk.

"K-i-l-l." He wrote.

"How?" she asked helplessly.

Raleigh scanned the room. The flashlight was heavy enough to throw on the snake, but it would likely break. It they could not kill him, they would be trapped in the dark with an angry snake. Maybe Rene could toss the crate on top of the snake, but it was heavy and it was unlikely that she could get close enough and not get bitten. Then his eyes rested on the butt end of the fishing pole fragment. It was about four and one-half feet in length and was of partially metal construction. Maybe Rene could beat it to death. His mind raced, and he realized the improbability of that scenario. The snake could easily wrap around the pole and bite the child. That would be certain death for both of them.

He glanced over at the reptile again. It was beginning to stir. They would have to act fast! The snake could try to crawl onto the bed with them.

There was no safe place in this tiny room.

Then the idea hit him as Raleigh positioned his chalk between his paws to write another message. It was a long shot, but it was one of their few options, and they were running out of time. He would need Rene's help. He could not do it alone.

He scribbled as quickly as possible. The chalk was unwieldy and his writing was nearly illegible. "Move crate on floor—smash S. R cut head."

Rene stared at him with fear in her eyes. "Oh no, Raleigh! I am too scared!"

Tears began to run down her cheeks.

He watched the snake stir again. There was so little time.

Raleigh printed furiously with the chalk. "Yes. Slow! R help!"

"I'm too scared! I hate snakes!" Rene wailed, working herself into a frenzy. Her hair was a tangled mess and her skin smelled sour. Her clothes were filthy and stained with dirt.

Frustrated, Raleigh grabbed the chalk again and erased the prior writing. "Now! No time!" He chattered and barked, giving her his most pleading gaze.

"Nooooo," she cried.

"Crate safe. Push to S," he wrote.

Rene looked at him with the first glimmer of understanding and began to calm down as she glanced over at the snake. He noticed a resolve and glint of steel in her eyes. The child was a survivor, and she did not want to get hurt.

"I'll try, Raleigh," she promised him.

"S-l-o-w," he scrawled. "Not scare."

Rene nodded, wiped her face and then moved to the head of the bed nearest the crate. Carefully, she began moving things from the top of the crate and transferring them onto the bed. Raleigh watched her with relief as she took the flashlight and carefully positioned it onto the bed so that it illuminated a pathway from the crate to the bed. She reached over and gently shoved the crate away from the wall. As he had hoped, the back of the crate was open. It was the perfect human shield. If she could get close enough to the snake, they could shove the crate over on top of it.

Gently, Rene lowered herself onto the floor behind the crate. Raleigh picked up the heavy church key can opener and shoved it into the opening of the crate. The triangular end was sharp, and although small, it could still be lethal. Rene slowly began to slide the crate over the floor in the direction of the snake. The reptile, feeling the vibrations, began to stir. Rene continued to shove the crate gently toward the snake. When they were within four feet of the reptile, he became agitated. Rapidly, he coiled his body and raised his head into the striking position. Raleigh could see the snake's forked tongue flickering in the air. He smelled the child and the squirrel. He was hungry. Raleigh could feel it.

Raleigh barked once to Rene to stop. He froze and stared at the snake through the wooden slats of the crate. Rene remained still. Raleigh could feel her pounding pulse as she stroked him for comfort while hiding behind the crate. They stood there for what seemed to be an eternity. Finally, the snake uncoiled and slowly slithered to the edge of the light before disappearing into the dark corner of the room.

Raleigh and Rene bounded back onto the bed, trying to locate the snake with the cone of light. Finally, they found it again, lying by the heavy makeshift toilet pot. Rene adjusted the light again, propping it on the bed so that it would shine on the snake. It was now about ten feet away. Raleigh knew that they needed to get closer to the snake. Maybe they could stand behind the crate and Rene could beat it with the metal fishing pole fragment until they could get close enough to shove the crate over on the snake. It was risky, but it was their only choice. The snake was hungry and it was mad.

Raleigh picked up the chalk again in his mouth and wrote: "Move crate—beat S pole—smash."

"OK."

"S-l-o-w. S feel us move." He willed her to understand that a snake felt vibrations and smelled its prey. This would be a difficult concept for a child to understand because she perceived the world so differently.

They waited a few minutes for the snake to relax and then descended behind the crate again, gently sliding it across the floor toward the reptile. The child tried to lift the crate off the floor, but it was too heavy. She braced the fishing pole fragment on top of the crate and began to slide the crate across the wooden planks. Rene walked slower now, pausing several minutes between steps to allow the snake to relax. Intuitively, she seemed to understand that the snake could feel their vibrations on the floor. It was a painstaking process, but they made progress, slowly narrowing the gap between them and the wary reptile on the floor.

Raleigh noticed the large swamp rat when they were within two feet of the snake. The water moccasin had partially coiled again, sniffing the air hungrily. The rat seemed completely unafraid of Rene, scurrying around the room outside the perimeter of the light. One of the sandwiches had fallen off the bed, and the rat had dragged it off near the wall and was furiously gnawing through the plastic wrap.

The snake's forked tongue began wildly flickering in the air. It seemed confused by the scent of the girl and the squirrel behind the crate, and the rat with the peanut butter and jelly sandwich. With incredible agility, the snake coiled into the striking position. Raleigh watched intently, his heart pounding savagely in his chest. The reptile was capable of extremely fast movement. Coiled, he could strike with lightning speed. Both he and Rene ducked behind the crate.

Could he strike and grab them through the wooden slats of the crate? Raleigh was not sure. Silently, he prayed that Rene would not panic and run from the safety of the crate. A water moccasin, like most snakes, could strike a distance of at least twice its length. If Rene tried to move from behind the crate, the snake could easily bite her and then bite the squirrel. Raleigh gently stroked Rene's fingers with his paw to reassure her. He felt the trembling of her hands and the quickening of her pulse. The child was also terrified.

The deafening silence in the room was only interrupted by the gentle rustle of the plastic wrap as the rat voraciously ate the sandwich. Raleigh morbidly marveled at the length of the huge rat. It was cordovan in color and nearly twice Raleigh's size, with prominent teeth. Of course, it was not just a swamp rat, he realized. It was a young nutria, a type of swamp rodent. It was an omnivore and would easily try to kill a squirrel. Rene could also be in danger because a nutria was aggressive and had a nasty bite. The nutria seemed oblivious of everything but the remains of the sandwich that he had devoured. Fastidiously, it licked the peanut butter from the inside of the plastic wrap, fascinated with the unique object.

The snake's head wavered both in the direction of the nutria and toward the crate. The squirrel realized that their lives hung in the balance.

Suddenly, without warning, the snake sprang toward the nutria, biting it on the flank. It happened so quickly that the snake's body seemed a mere blur in the air. The reptile recoiled and then struck again, burying its fangs deep into the neck of the nutria. The startled rodent abandoned the plastic and screamed in pain. Rene covered her ears, and tears began to pour down her cheeks. Raleigh's body went rigid with fear. After the initial shock, he regained his senses.

He had to control Rene. The worst thing that could happen is that she could panic and leave the safety of the crate. They needed to act quickly while the snake was distracted.

Raleigh stroked Rene's hands and then tapped her wrist insistently. He locked her gaze, willing her to understand.

They had to act now.

Raleigh gave a low, soft bark and shoved against the crate with his paws. He stared intently at Rene again. The child seemed to understand. Not bothering to wipe her face, she gently grabbed the fishing pole fragment that rested precariously on top of the crate and gently slid the crate toward the snake. The reptile was focused on the dying nutria, who was struggling toward the perceived safety of the wall. Its flank was paralyzed now, and the nutria reeled dizzily from the poison injected into its neck. Without warning, the snake struck again, catching the nutria in the thoracic region of its spine. Within less than a minute, the nutria collapsed in violent seizures. White foam spewed from its mouth. The snake's tongue licked the air hungrily as it watched the nutria.

Raleigh felt that he was watching one of the most evil things on earth as he and Rene crept toward the snake. The reptile seemed oblivious to them now, intent on its meal of the young, dying nutria.

Together, they narrowed the gap again between the back of the crate and the snake. Conscious that time was of the essence, Rene moved stealthily and as quickly as the circumstances would allow without upsetting the snake. Raleigh hopped beside Rene, intently watching the horrible creature as it unhinged its jaws and began to devour the hapless nutria, head first into the chasm of its yawning mouth. Raleigh was sickened by the horrific sight, realizing that but for the sudden presence of the nutria, he would have suffered the same fate.

He steeled himself and tapped Rene on the hand again, staring at her intently. He shoved his paws in the air, signaling that the time had arrived. The snake could not bite them now with a full mouth.

They had to act now.

The crate was now positioned one foot from the snake who was busily devouring its prey. It eyed them over the spine of the nutria.

Silently, Rene set the pole fragment on the floor behind her. Raleigh removed the church key from the crate and stood by the pole. He could feel the blood pounding in his head.

What if they were unsuccessful? He could not imagine anything worse than being eaten by the snake. They had to kill it now.

With a force that amazed the squirrel, Rene shoved the crate down on the snake's body. Her aim was precise and perfect. Only about three inches of the snake had escaped the blow. Rene stood in the crate, grabbed the fishing pole fragment and began to pound the snake's head with the blunt end.

"Bad, ugly, evil creature!" she shrieked. "I HATE YOU! I HATE YOU! You killed that little rat."

Furious, the snake tried to writhe beneath the crate, but Rene's weight was centered in the middle of the crate, preventing it from wobbling back and forth. Blood from the battered snake and the dead nutria covered the floor as Rene relentlessly pounded the snake on the head and neck. The water moccasin spat out the head of the nutria and began to hiss, furiously biting at the pole. Rene had blinded the snake in one eye. With the next blow, she crushed the reptile's right jaw. Rene continued to jab at the head, sometimes only managing to pound the floor.

Suddenly, without warning, the pole broke and fell on the floor, and the largest segment rolled five feet from the crate. The remaining fragment nearest the crate was less than six inches long. The child would have to bend over very close to the snake. One wrong move and the snake could bite her hand. Despite its injuries, it was still quick. Rene looked startled and turned to Raleigh for guidance. Tears streamed down her cheek from her hysterical outburst while battering the snake.

"Raleigh, what can we do?" she cried.

His mind raced for a solution. The snake was still lethal, despite its injuries. He signaled to Rene to remain in the crate. He grabbed the church key.

It was the only way. If he did not succeed, it would mean certain death. What choice did they have? They were alone, and there was no one to help them. He had to succeed.

The church key was heavy and unwieldy, constructed of stainless steel at either end with a yellow plastic handle. The can opener segment was still sharp.

He would have to be precise. He could not miss!

Purposefully, he hopped around the crate, dragging the can opener until he was face to face with the water moccasin. Rene remained in the crate above him, balancing her full weight on the snake.

"Be careful, Raleigh! Please don't get hurt!" she called.

The squirrel tried to obliterate everything else from his mind but killing the snake. He ignored the sickening smell of death, poison, and the acrid odor of damp fur mixed with peanut butter. The squirrel began to focus with all of his concentration.

He grabbed the plastic that was coated with saliva and a few residual streaks of peanut butter and jelly. It obviously had been a fine last meal for the nutria. Careful to avoid the snake's eye, he dropped the plastic over the snake's head.

He would have to do it now! Could the snake bite through the plastic? Of course it could. But maybe it would confuse him.

Raleigh took a deep breath and moved as close to the snake's head as possible. His chest pounded furiously as he watched the snake's tongue dart out of its mouth licking its mouth.

It smelled him, and it was still hungry.

The snake was gently swaying its head back and forth, hissing softly. The weight of the crate on its body and Rene's beating was taking its toll. The snake seemed dazed by the plastic now. Slowly, Raleigh lifted the church key into the air and then with all of the force he could muster, brought the sharp end of the church key down toward the serpent. With a strength that surprised even him, he impaled the serpent's neck to the floor with the church key.

Raleigh hopped back. The can opener was perpendicular to the floor, perfectly severing the center of the snake's throat. The water moccasin writhed slightly, but was hampered by the plastic. With morbid fascination, Raleigh watched the snake die. The snake's struggle awakened a primitive survival instinct deep within him.

So, this is what it was like to be a predator and to enjoy watching animals die. He was actually enjoying watching the snake as its life-force weakened.

Rene was singing and cheering above him, but he did hear her. Instead, he watched the life drain slowly away from the snake. The reptile's eyes were glazed, and it was still. Blood pooled on the floor from the nutria and the snake.

Raleigh looked at the snake with satisfaction and then glanced at Rene expectantly. She laughed with glee, stepped out of the box, and scooped him into her arms.

"We did it! We did it! We killed that monster!" she sang, dancing around on the dusty floorboards.

The immediate danger was over. Now, they could relax, if only for a few hours.

~

Feeling too wired to sleep after the thrill of their victory, Raleigh and Rene quenched their thirst from the water bottle. They ignored the remains of the dead snake and nutria in the corner. Raleigh noticed that he was beginning to feel weak. He had not eaten in a few hours, and he was ravenous from their activity. The two of them shared half of the remaining peanut butter sandwich. The squirrel longed for sweet seeds and the juicy cambium of a young oak. If they ran out of food, he would have to venture outside of the safety the cabin to find something to eat. It was only a matter of time before he would have to assume that risk. It was a distinct possibility that the man might never come back, and the two of them could be trapped in the shack.

Suddenly, he felt a tightening of the chest. Were they really safe in the shack? The snake and the rat had come in. What was to stop some other predator from coming in? Next time, they might not be so lucky. Next time, they could die. They would have to inspect every inch of the floor and try to plug the holes. He had been a fool to relax, even for a second. They could still be in danger. They would have to find the holes before the flashlight batteries were worn down. If not, they might not see the next snake that came in. How could he have been so cavalier?

He hopped over to the chalkboard, picked up the chalk and began to scribble furiously. It was a nearly impossible task. The chalk was difficult for him to use. He kept erasing many of the letters with his tail.

Rene sat beside him, singing softly, oblivious to his concern. The child was exhausted, but he could not let her sleep. There was still work to do. They would have to stop up the holes. The food and the two of them were emitting an unusual smell that would attract predators and their prey. The dead bodies of the nutria and the snake would also attract predators or scavengers. They would need to do something now.

Finally finished writing, he moved away from the chalk board to let her read his message.

"F-i-n-d h-o-l-e-s. N-o s-n-a-k-e-s."

Rene read the message and then stared into the squirrel's eyes. The fear had returned to her face. She understood. They were not safe.

"Do you think there will be more, Raleigh?" she asked, deferring to his judgment with a child's trusting nature about all things in the wild.

The squirrel barked once for yes.

Rene did not waste any time. She got up from the bed and lifted the flashlight in her hands. It was heavy, primarily used for camping, and much too heavy for a six-year-old child. She began to slide it along the floor. The squirrel scampered behind her as they inspected each floor board and segment of the wall as it met the floor. There were only a few small chinks that were perhaps large enough to allow a small snake to come into the room. Raleigh got the chalk and they marked the location of each hole on the floor. They worked around the carcasses of the nutria and the snake. Raleigh squeezed next to the wall, but he did not notice any other holes nearby.

They worked their way around the room. He noticed through the chink in the wall over the bed that the sun had come up, but they still needed the flashlight in the room. He sniffed the air. It was stifling hot today and very humid. They would be miserable in the shack.

Finally, they had completed three walls of the structure. The only thing left was the area behind the bed. It was a plain old iron bed with a patina of rust and grime. Obviously, it had been a cheap piece of furniture even when it was new. It was too heavy for a mere child and a squirrel to lift. Raleigh began to notice that their light had slightly weakened. The battery must be running down.

Rene looked exhausted, but she persevered with a determination he had never seen her exhibit before. Wearily, she shoved the flashlight under the bed, exposing a gaping hole nearly eight inches in diameter.

So the snake and the rat had entered the room underneath them as they had soundly slept on the mattress above. They could have easily been killed.

"Oh no, Raleigh! We will have to stop up that hole! It is big enough for an alligator to come through!" Rene wailed. "How will we do it?"

Raleigh stared at the hole in silence, racking his brain for a solution. Then it hit him. They would plug the hole with the mattress stuffing. Rene might even be able to break apart the crate and use one or two of the slats. Of course, that would deprive them of their shield in the event that another snake managed to break through the barrier, but it would have to be done. They would also need to move the bodies of the young nutria and the snake through the hole to prevent attracting other predators.

Rene watched him in wonder as he hopped up onto the mattress and began gnawing the mattress ticking on the cover. Within moments, the squirrel's sharp teeth had gnawed a large hole in the foot of the mattress. It felt wonderful to gnaw. He realized that his teeth had been bothering him.

"Raleigh, what are you doing?" Rene asked him.

The squirrel reached in and pulled out a plug of the crude stuffing from the thin mattress.

"You are right!" Rene cried with relief. "We could use that."

Raleigh grabbed the slate again and wrote out the plan. Rene would shove the snake and nutria carcasses through the hole with the long end of the pole. It would certainly bloody the floor, but it could not be helped. They would try to use a slat or two from the crate. If not, they would plug the holes with the mattress stuffing and shove the partially empty mattress on the floor. Then, if at all possible, they would have to shove the bed on its side, allowing the rusty coils to form a crude barrier in front of the hole. It was not an optimal solution, but it was their only option now.

The two of them began working. Rene carried the mattress stuffing over to the spots marked along the wall, and Raleigh began tamping the stuffing into the crevices. His tiny paws were well suited to the work.

Finally, Rene assumed the nasty task of shoving the rat and snake through the hole with the fishing pole. A narrow trail of blood formed a thin burgundy river across the dirty floor. Raleigh signaled to Rene not to touch the animals with her fingers. Nutria were dirty and probably carried diseases. They could get sick.

They stopped briefly to share a little water. The squirrel's fur was damp, and Rene was sweating profusely. The squirrel noticed that she had rings of black dirt under her nails. Rene's hair, which was usually meticulously combed into a cognac-hued pony-tail cascading down her back, hung limply and carelessly in tangles around her face. If Rene was conscious of her appearance, she did not seem to notice.

After they had plugged all the small holes, they turned their attention to the large hole under the bed. It was certain that the two of them could not move the bed. Whatever they did, they would have to crawl under it to patch the hole in the floor.

Raleigh watched as Rene desperately tugged at the wooden slats of the crate. The nails held in place. After a few tries, she grabbed the end of the fishing pole and banged on the side without success. Her face became distorted with frustration and tears began to fall down her cheeks.

Raleigh watched her anxiously. The child was too weak to break the crate. He certainly could not do it himself. Maybe it was not such a bad thing, though. Maybe there was a way to keep the crate. The bed was tall enough that they could turn the crate on its side and slide it under the bed as a barrier in front of the mattress stuffing. It was not ideal, but it was a partial solution. On the other hand, maybe they could slide the mattress onto the floor under the bed so that it blocked access from a larger animal. Then they could keep the crate. Of course, the mattress would not stop a snake. Everyone knew that snakes and rats could slide between incredibly narrow spaces to enter homes. Besides, maybe they could use the hole. It was definitely large enough for him to pass through. If he gnawed around it, maybe he could enlarge the hole to allow Rene to slide through also. After last night, he knew that the cabin was not really safe. And who knew what their captors had in mind? They had probably killed one man. What would stop them from killing him and Rene. He would trust his gut instinct. They needed to escape at any cost.

The squirrel gave a sharp, high-pitched bark. Rene turned and looked at him. The child was clearly exhausted and he noticed that she was developing blisters on her hands.

"I'm trying Raleigh. I am really trying!" she exclaimed before dissolving into tears. "I can't do it!" She buried her face in her tiny hands, and her shoulders heaved with sobs.

Raleigh leapt onto the crate and began gently stroking Rene's hair, clucking softly. After a few moments, the child began to visibly relax from the soothing motion of the squirrel's paws on the crown of her head. She wiped her eyes with the back of her hand and blew her nose into her shirt. As soon as she was composed, Raleigh hopped down and shoved the chalkboard into the shaft of light from the wall high overhead. The battery in the flashlight was dimming, and they would need to conserve the light. There was no assurance that another predator might not try to come in later, in which case they would need the flashlight. He flicked the rocker switch on the flashlight and, once again, their only illumination was from the crevice above. He knew that the light deprivation was more difficult for the child. Squirrels could see reasonably well in dim light, which was one of the ways that they were superior to humans.

He began writing on the chalk board. "M-a-t-t-r-e-s-s—o-n—f-l-o-o-r---p-l-u-g---h-o-l-e. C-r-a-t-e—f-r-o-n-t."

Rene studied the chalkboard carefully. Raleigh could see the comprehension register in her face. She gave him a faint smile.

"That might work Raleigh. I can try to push it off the bed and against the wall. It's not too heavy."

Raleigh barked once for yes.

Her face clouded. "But what if something squeezes through the hole?"

"U-s-e—h-o-l-e—e-s-c-a-p-e."

She read the slate. "I'm too big for the hole," she replied matter-of-factly.

Raleigh erased the slate with his paw and wrote furiously: "R—g-n-a-w—b-i-g-g-e-r."

"We can run away Do you think we can do it?" she asked, her face suddenly becoming somber again.

He had to be confident. They might easily die trying, but he had to be strong for the child. He could never let her know that the odds were against them.

He barked once for yes and began hopping up and down from the floor to the crate. It was their signal for excitement.

His enthusiasm was infectious. Rene brightened for the first time in two days. "We can run away and go home to my Mommy and Granny Ariel. Yes!"

Raleigh barked once for yes again. It would take time and patience, but it was their only chance. He could feel the danger deep inside from the stranger. He intended to kill them or hurt them badly. It was their only option.

"Good plan, Raleigh. You are so smart!" she remarked as she stroked the squirrel's back.

With renewed hope, she began to focus on their plan. Rene fastidiously erased the chalkboard and laid it down on the floor, humming softly to herself. Afterward, she cleared off the bed and began to purposefully shove the mattress onto the floor.

~

Brandy went back to the hospital with Agent Hebert to check on her grandmother. Granny Ariel's condition had deteriorated again thirty-six hours after the attack. The night before, she had yet another blood transfusion and had been bleeding internally. The physicians had explained that Granny Ariel's heart was still very weak, and her prospects were dismal. Reluctantly, Brandy left with the officer to return home to wait to hear from the kidnappers.

Brandy made a few calls to check with Natalie about the shop. She lied and said that she had a touch of the flu. Natalie assured her that everything was under control. Natalie did not want her to worry. They had sold a Chippendale table yesterday with eighteen chairs to a dentist from Montreal. Ordinarily, Brandy would have been thrilled with the news of another large sale, but she no longer cared. All she could think about was her daughter and Granny Ariel.

Brandy checked her voice messages on her cell phone while Agent Hebert drove them back down St. Charles Avenue. Both of the messages were from Claude. Thad wanted to settle with her. They were offering her $7.5 million from the sale of the emeralds to dismiss her claim with prejudice. Claude carefully noted that he was not recommending the settlement, but he had an ethical obligation to convey the settlement. He was coming home later in the day and would drop by that evening to report the substance of the first half of the Recov depositions. They would be resumed again in a month in St. Thomas.

"That's odd," she told Agent Hebert. "Thad and Recov have offered me a settlement of $7.5 million."

Agent Hebert's eyes never left the road. "I don't really know anything about civil work. But that seems like an insulting offer to me. The value of your claim is almost $300 million. I would tell them to take a hike, but do whatever your lawyer recommends."

"I can't even think about it right now. I just want my little girl back and my grandmother to live," she replied as she folded the cell phone in half and slid it into her purse.

"Do you trust your attorneys?"

"Chris Banks is a very ethical and highly rated attorney. And Claude is an old friend. I trust him implicitly."

"Forgive my skepticism, but it just seems odd that they make you an offer just when you need $5 million and there is enough there to pay a hefty attorneys' fee. Just an observation that could be critical to your daughter's kidnapping."

Before she could reply, Agent Hebert answered his cell phone. It was an extended conversation. She ignored him and thought about the potential settlement. Agent Hebert was right. The timing was odd. There could be a connection.

Agent Hebert talked until they pulled up into the drive. Once in the kitchen, Brandy poured them both a cup of strong coffee.

Two new FBI agents were waiting in the study with Agent Plauche. They identified themselves as Agent Weller and Agent Radosky. The men explained that it was likely that the conspiracy to kidnap Rene likely crossed state lines. It had become a federal matter. The FBI would coordinate the investigation with the members of the New Orleans Police and Detective Conner in St. Thomas.

Agent Plauche reported the latest developments as he and Brandy sat in the den. He explained that the dental records clearly identified the burned body in the trunk of the car a few miles away from Henderson as that of Jimmy Thornton. The car was reported stolen by a Loyola University college student ten days earlier. It had been crudely repainted before the abduction, and the tags had been switched. The tag on the car belonged to a Chevy Blazer from the projects in the Ninth Ward. According to Thornton's sister, who had been interviewed earlier that morning, Thornton had recently moved here from Texas to stay with his sister for a few weeks, and made a few trips recently to a small hotel outside of Pass Christian to meet some of Thornton's business associates. The sister, a sometimes waitress in a gentleman's' club, claimed that she never was allowed to attend the meetings, but she was sure that Jimmy was meeting with a man about thirty-five years old.

"Do you believe her?" Brandy asked. "Do you think she knew?"

"We believe she knew something—probably enough to make her a conspirator. She is still being interviewed, and we are getting a wiretap order to allow us to tap her phone. We have also informed her that she may be charged with conspiracy to commit kidnapping and murder. She has every incentive now to cooperate. A search warrant has been issued to search Thornton's apartment and car. We are getting his telephone and cell records for the last year and are interviewing his acquaintances and employer. We will find out something."

Her blood ran cold. Jimmy Thornton had probably helped to kidnap her little girl. She had trusted him. Jimmy had worked for Harris. Why was this happening?

“Is all of this going to help find my little girl?” she managed. We have forty-eight hours left before they kill her! And you people keep changing the officers in charge as frequently as I change my shoes.” She glanced over at Agent Plauche and Agent Herbert, neither of whom acknowledged her gaze.

Agent Radosky intervened. “Mrs. Blake, I am sure that it feels like there is no coordination in this investigation, but I can assure you that is not true. The officers in St. Thomas, Key West, and New Orleans have done an outstanding job and we are coordinating our efforts to work as a team. None of these officers will be off the case. I assure you that we are working together.” He met her angry gaze straight on with a look of compassionate professionalism. “We want to find your little girl and to punish the people who took her. That is our job. We are also looking into your husband’s death.”

“The federal government has tremendous resources. Having additional officers work on this case is a good development, Brandy,” Agent Herbert assured her. Agent Plauche and I will still be here with you 100 percent of the way.”

She shoved her hair back from her face and sighed. “Alright. What choice do I have but to trust you people.”

“We are going to find your daughter, Mrs. Blake,” Agent Radosky told her.

She leaned back in the chair and took a sip of the coffee that Agent Plauche had poured for them when they returned from the hospital. “Does this mean that Jimmy Thornton probably had something to do with Harris’s death?”

“At this point, it would appear that all of these things may be connected. Thad may have hired Thornton to kill your husband. That would explain his lifestyle when he first moved to Texas. He and his girlfriend spent it all, however, on a nice apartment, drugs, and parties. He knew about the suit and knew how much money you stood to gain from *BYZANTIUM* and probably decided to shake you down," Agent Weller explained.

"Do you think Thad had anything to do with Rene's disappearance?" she asked.

"Maybe he wanted to force you into settling your claim quickly. Agent Hebert told me that your lawyer is bringing home a settlement offer. If you accepted, Thad could recover the money when you pay the ransom. Then, he keeps most of the money, and he pays the kidnappers or has them killed. If that is the scheme, it is actually brilliant. He would not be out-of-pocket much money, and he becomes richer than in his wildest dreams. We need to make our investigation and let the evidence develop."

Brandy looked at Agent Weller with surprise. It all fit together like a neat package. If that were the case, was Claude involved? Once again, had she been too trusting? Had he set this all in motion, coincidentally coming into the shop and encouraging her to file a claim? Did he know? And how could anyone think she would settle such a large claim for a pittance? Agent Hebert was right. Had she been a fool?

She felt a surge of adrenaline. She needed to stay in control and focus. Thad had taken away her husband. She could not let him take away her little girl.

She gave Agent Weller a steely gaze. "Just tell me what you want me to do. I intend to help you bring my daughter home."

Chapter XXVIII

Ewan spent the night in a Motel 6 in Slidell. He had checked in about 10:00 p.m. and paid in advance. There was a short blurb on the local news about a break in and stabbing near Audubon Park, but the names had not been released.

He would need to be very careful. Obviously, law enforcement was on high alert.

Ewan set the alarm on his cell phone for 5:00 a.m., and was asleep before 11:00 p.m. He left before daylight, after a hot shower, shave, and change of clothes. Afterward, he stopped at the nearby Denny's for a huge breakfast of eggs, toast, bacon, grits, juice, and coffee. He was annoyed by the bleached blonde middle-aged waitress who fluttered around his booth, anxious to flirt with the handsome man sitting by himself. The sun was just coming up as he left a generous tip for the woman. Refreshed, he went to a nearby Walmart to buy a cheap tape recorder and a small notebook.

The conversation with the mother had not gone well the day before. She would need to be motivated. He needed proof of life that the little girl was alive.

Ewan sat in the car in the Walmart parking lot preparing the statement he would have the little girl read. He took his time composing the child's statement for the ransom demand. It could not be too long and needed to be forceful. He would need the child's cooperation, and as inducement, he had purchased a bag of small candy bars and a bag of cookies. A hysterical child would not be any help to him.

As he drove toward the swamp, he considered the events of the last two days. He felt no real remorse about Jimmy Thornton. Unfortunately, Jimmy had been unable to live with the fact that they had adulterated the diver's tank. Over the last two years, he had spent all of his money and was using meth. At some point, Jimmy would have been arrested and predictably, he would have used information about Ewan and the diver's death as a bargaining chip. Jimmy's death had been necessary, he told himself.

He wondered how long it had taken the old woman to die. She had always been kind to the IBIX team, leaving fresh lemonade in those hot months and occasionally cookies. It was a shame that she had to die, but she was old and in his way. Despite her age, the old lady had fought like a tiger, drawing blood on his arms with her nails, and stomping on his feet as he gripped her from behind. She had fought so hard, it had been impossible for him to grip her neck to strangle her or slit her throat without suffering wounds himself. As a last resort, he had slugged her in the face inflicted vicious stab wounds with a kitchen knife to disable her. From the amount of blood, it was clear that she would be dead within the hour.

He felt slightly uneasy about kidnapping the kid. It was one thing to harm an adult but quite another to kidnap a kid and kill the mother. His negotiations with Thad to take this on had been bitter and protracted. Thad was not very solvent at the moment, but somehow he had managed to wire $250,000 to an offshore account as a down payment. An amount like that, however, was not nearly sufficient to induce Ewan to kidnap a kid. Ewan had his eye on the ball. He intended to live the good life now in a way that he would not have to worry. A job like this would require intense planning to succeed.

Ewan did not plan to take any risk that would cause him to spend the rest of his life in prison.

Finally, he and Thad agreed that Ewan would keep $2.5 million of the ransom money. In order to do that, he would need to entice the mother to drop the money off in the swamp. Afterward, Ewan would kill her and any trailing law enforcement officers secretly watching the drop off with the assault rifle he had purchased in Texas. He would keep all of the ransom money.

He smiled. It would not be too long before his future was secure.

࿐

The sun was hovering over the horizon in the mid-afternoon when Raleigh heard the distinctive crunch of shells from a car coming down the road toward the cabin. Rene was taking a nap on what remained of the mattress. The child was exhausted from the events of the last eighteen hours since they had killed the snake. Raleigh stopped gnawing on the hole in the wall and sniffed the air.

He was coming back. They could not let him know that they were trying to escape. Otherwise, the man might kill them. He would have to warn Rene.

He gave a sharp bark and the child's eyes fluttered open. Immediately vigilant now, she sat up and listened.

"He is coming!" she whispered. The look of terror returned to her face and her hands began to tremble. "What if he takes us away and we cannot leave?"

They did not have a moment to lose. He could not let the child panic now.

Raleigh pushed the air with his paws, signaling Rene to shove the mattress against the wall. They had made tremendous progress during the day enlarging the hole under the bed. The squirrel systematically gnawed splinters of wood until they were weak enough for Rene to pull away from the wall. It was tedious work, but by some time the next day, the hole would certainly be large enough for Rene to slip through and escape the confines of the cabin.

Rene strained and lifted the corner of the mattress and shoved it to cover the hole. The mattress was now perpendicular to the wall and the empty bed frame. Now, at least half of the mattress was exposed, jutting out from under the bed. Rene leaned against the bed frame, and grabbed the chalkboard, which she placed near the door for her captors. Raleigh had insisted that she use some water from the jug to completely erase their various exchanges on the board. Consistent with their plan, she sat with her back to the cabin door, pretending to read one of the elementary children's' books that the captor had left in the weak slivers of light from above. The illustrated book she selected featured a herd of elephants in a game park in Africa.

Raleigh climbed up the wall and concealed himself in the tiny crawl space over the door jam inside of the wall. He had explained to Rene that it would be better if the kidnapper could not terrorize Rene by threatening to kill the squirrel. Intuitively, Raleigh felt that the man would love nothing more than to kill him just to hurt the child. He was one of those humans who enjoyed killing for sport. But he needed Rene now. He was not sure why, but Raleigh knew that the man would not kill Rene until it was necessary. Raleigh had coached Rene over and over that she was not to beg to go home. He sensed that it would be devastating if Rene were hard to handle. Rene had agreed to be pliable and obedient. It was probably the only way she would stay alive another day.

Raleigh tucked his tail underneath him and tried to remain calm. His jaws ached from the constant gnawing of the cabin walls throughout the day. A sliver of wood had punctured his gum, but Rene had easily extracted it for him with her tiny hands. It had bled slightly, but then the bleeding stopped, and he had washed his mouth out with a long drink of water. As he heard the car door slam outside, he allowed himself to wonder about Ariel and Chloe.

He worried about Ariel. Had she survived? That would be a miracle. He wanted to get back to his home. He had to bring Rene home.

He heard the heavy footfalls of the man ascending the stoop. Rene still pretended to read, her back dutifully to the door. Raleigh could smell her fear. The key in the lock turned and the door flew open, emitting a wave of fresh, heavy and humid air. The man who had locked them up in the cabin about thirty-six hours ago still wore a face mask.

The man had a small black rectangle in his hand. He partially closed the door behind him and flipped on a floodlight. Raleigh noticed that the man wore clean pressed clothes and smelled faintly of soap and aftershave.

He handed Rene a bag of bite-sized Snickers candy bars and a separate bag of cookies. She gripped the bags and laid them down on the mattress beside her.

"Thank you," she said softly, looking down.

"I need you to say a few words into the recorder," the man instructed Rene. "I need you to say exactly what is written on this paper. Can you do that?" His voice and tone were soothing and gentle today.

Raleigh felt a shiver down his spine. Thirty-six hours ago, the man did not want to talk in front of Rene. He had obviously worried about being identified.

Something had changed. He did not care whether Rene heard him anymore. He intended to kill her. That much was clear. Oh God, let her have at least another day. Don't let him kill her today.

"Yes," she replied, careful not to look in the man's direction.

"Good," he said, handing her a folded sheet of paper with print. "Now, read this aloud for me. Then we are going to record your voice."

"Alright", Rene replied obediently.

Torrents of tears streamed down her cheeks as Rene stared at the block print on the paper.

"Read it aloud," the man coaxed. "There is no reason to be upset. You are just telling your mother to pay me some money and then I will let you go. But you have to convince her that this is serious. If she thinks we are not serious, she will not pay me."

The child nodded her head in comprehension. Rene's voice cracked as she began to read the words on the paper. "Mommy, this is Rene. Today is April 24th, and I am alive and okay. Pay the money now or I will die."

The man insisted that Rene practice three times. Then he recorded the message twice. Finally satisfied, the man turned off the recorder and turned to leave.

"I will be back late tomorrow or the next day," he told Rene as he shut the door.

Raleigh heard the key engage the dead bolt. He waited as the man walked down the drive.

Raleigh felt his heart grow cold. He planned to kill Rene. They would have to leave soon—even if it meant working all night. The odds of survival were against them in the swamp, but they would have to try now. There was no choice.

He waited until he heard the car drive away before he came out of hiding. He was hungry, and they would need to eat to keep their strength up. They would have to work all night. Their situation was urgent now. They would need to leave the cabin by morning.

~

Rene and Raleigh shared two peanut butter sandwiches. They were both ravenously hungry, but decided to save the rest for later. After they left the cabin, it would be impossible to know when they would eat again. Rene cleaned up with the jug of water, liquid soap, and alcohol wipes left by the man. Raleigh helped her tie her hair back into a ponytail with the rubber band that secured the packet of alcohol wipes. Rene took the blanket and created a makeshift pack that she would tie around her neck when they left.

Together, they worked on the opening until Rene could easily slip through the hole. Afterward, Raleigh stood guard while Rene took a short nap. The child was clearly exhausted, but she had worked purposefully until almost midnight. He knew that he would have to allow her a brief respite before their escape.

He could not let her panic. She needed to be strong. Who knew what terror waited for them outside the cabin? Would they survive? He did not know, but they would have to try.

Raleigh guessed that it was about three hours before dawn when he woke Rene up. She washed the sleep from her eyes with water and wiped her hands and face with the alcohol wipes. Each of them took a large drink of water from the jug. Raleigh encouraged her to drink as much as she could stand. It was impossible to know when they might find water again. Rene was capable of carrying only a small bottle, some candy, the sandwiches, and a few alcohol wipes in the makeshift pack.

About two hours before dawn, Raleigh slipped through the hole in the wall. Satisfied that the coast was clear, he barked for Rene to follow. There was a full moon overhead lighting the cypress trees in eerie spikes across the sky. The moon lit the white shell roadway that extended back toward the main road from the cabin.

Rene climbed through the hole onto a porch that extended around the shack on three sides. With the curiosity of a child, she walked around the porch, surveying the tiny cabin. The back of the shack appeared to be built on stilts extending into the shallow swamp water. Heavy vines and Spanish-moss covered cypress draped down toward the dark water. The moonbeams glistened on the dark scales of a tremendous alligator resting on a log. It was rigidly still, but Raleigh could feel it surreptitiously watching them.

Raleigh barked sharply. Large segments of the deck were dry and rotten. Rene needed to take care lest she fall through.

If she were injured and fell into the water, she could be devoured by the alligator. Moreover, if she could not walk, their captor would certainly find them and kill them. She had to be careful.

Ebullient to finally be free of the shack, Rene danced around the deck, ignoring Raleigh's obvious signal for caution.

"We're out! We are out of that terrible place! We can go home now!" she sang with a childish optimism. She skipped over to the back deck nearest the water. "Raleigh! Look! A little boat! Come and see!"

Cautiously, the squirrel lightly sailed across the deck, after scanning the area for predators. Satisfied that the area was clear, he ventured toward the ledge. A rickety dock less than four feet long extended from the rear porch. A small bass boat was concealed in the bushes, loosely tethered to a nearby tree with an old rope. He scanned the interior for predators. The hull was very dark, but it seemed to be dry. A single oar with a partially broken handle lay inside. The outboard motor was gone. It was just a metal shell about ten feet long with two bench seats. In order to reach the boat, they would have to climb onto the tree and lower themselves into the water.

Where had this come from? It was a miracle that the man had not noticed the old Bass boat.

"I'm going to get the flashlight," Rene announced. Before he could stop her, Rene had returned to the cabin, emerging with the new flashlight left by their captor. She descended the single stair on the dock until she reached the edge of the boat. Carefully, she scanned the interior of the boat, illuminating every surface with the brilliant cone of light.

All was dry and there were no predators, including snakes, rats, or alligators. The alligator on the log several yards away continued to eye them both with interest.

"Let's take the boat!" Rene urged! We can float away and they cannot find us!"

He felt a sickness in the pit of his stomach. Squirrels hated water. And they would both be defenseless against predators. If the boat turned over or sank, it would mean certain death for both of them. What if a snake from a branch above dropped into the boat? They would not stand a chance. Of course, they would also be easy victims to predators on dry land. On the other hand, the boat could keep them safe until they reached land far away. The water was calm, and they could lie down and sleep for a while. They could also carry water, a cup, the flashlight and the sandwiches. Perhaps Rene was right.

He barked once for "yes."

Rene smiled. "Let's get some supplies to take with us."

They crawled through the small hole back into their former prison. Rene gathered everything they could conceivably use, including the church key, the flashlight, the broken fishing pole, the jug of water, the blanket, food, a plastic glass, the soap, and alcohol wipes. They even took the slate and two pieces of chalk.

"I wish we could take our crate," she told Raleigh as she shoved their supplies through the hole. "At least, we can eat and drink now."

Rene clumsily carried all of their supplies down to the dock. Raleigh searched the cabin for one last time for anything else that would conceivably be of use. He began to focus and felt purposeful.

They might actually survive this.

Rene also searched the far side of the deck on the other side of the shack. She came back with a packet of kitchen matches and a partially burned candle sealed in a plastic bag.

"Look, Raleigh! Where do you think these things came from?" she asked as she displayed the bag. With the clumsiness of a child, she pulled apart the seal and extracted the candle and the matches. She shook the box. "The box is full. We might need the candle," she said matter-of-factly.

She took the matches and candle and placed them on the dock. She began the process of climbing onto the tree to ferry their possessions into the boat. When they finished, Raleigh began to test the rope. It was relatively loose, and he felt certain that he could easily untie it. He waited patiently in the boat for Rene. He picked up the scent of dried blood in the boat. He could not tell whether it was the blood of a fish or a human. The smell made him slightly nauseous. The moonlight was waning now. Dawn was not far away. He could feel it. In the distance, he could hear the soft calling of an owl. It reminded him of Kiki.

An owl or a hawk could easily rip him from the confines of the boat, killing him within seconds. He would have to use great care. Perhaps he could make a little tent of the blanket Rene had brought to partially conceal himself. During the day, he would be easy prey for a predatory bird.

Rene dropped the candle wrapped in the plastic bag into the boat. She held onto the box of matches and gave Raleigh a solemn look.

They were wasting time. They needed to be far away from this place. Who knew when their captor would return?

He made a series of sharp barks to hurry Rene along. The alligator several yards away shifted its position, obviously excited by the noise.

"I want to light the matches and burn the shack down, Raleigh," she announced.

Raleigh responded with a shrill bark.

"No! I am not leaving before we set it on fire. They will think we died. Then they may not look for us! Yes! Yes! Yes!" Rene insisted stubbornly. "I hate this place! I want to start a fire!"

He hated fire. It was yet another one of those things that could cause instant death to a squirrel. But she might be right. The captor might think that Rene had perished in the fire. It could have been caused by lightning. He had seen lightning set a tree on fire in the park when he was a mere pup. The mattress would probably burn very easily, and the shack wood was dry and brittle. Rene was right.

Raleigh responded with one quiet bark for yes.

They returned to the shack one last time. Raleigh pulled out a wad of stuffing and placed it on the floor. Rene lit it with a match. Momentarily, it caught fire and burned furiously. Together they pulled out additional wads of mattress stuffing, laying them on top of the mattress. Rene sequentially lit five small piles on the mattress with a match. The room was already becoming smoky. Raleigh barked for Rene to leave the room and crawled through the hole into the fresh air. Rene followed him and then peeked through the hole in the wall, admiring her work. Suddenly, there was a large whoosh and the entire mattress was engulfed in flames. They could feel the heat through the hole in the wall.

They would have to leave quickly!

They raced across the deck, across the tree limb, and hopped into the boat. Rene tugged at the rope, loosening the knot and casting away from the dock with a hard push. The two of them sat in the center of the craft. The boat drifted out in the still water and came to rest about twenty feet from the cabin perimeter. The alligator jumped off of the log, disappearing into the dark water below them. The boat was not very stable and rocked very easily. Slowly, Rene took the broken oar and from her position on the bench, softly paddled the water to navigate between the trees.

The outer wall of the cabin suddenly erupted into flames as then floated more than seventy-five feet away from the shack. They could feel the intense heat as the flames licked the rotted wood. Mesmerized, they watched for several minutes until the roof collapsed in a wall of fire and the decks and old dock disappeared. The flames soared into the sky, lighting the darkened swamp with near daylight. Several of the flames jumped over to a cypress branch, igniting the tree which smoldered and burst into a sunflower of flames. They could hear a loud crackle and roar from the fire.

The fire was spreading in the swamp. They needed to seek safety now. They did not want to be visible if the kidnapper returned. He certainly had a gun. They could still be shot.

Gently, he touched Rene's hand and barked softly, signaling to her that they needed to leave. She seemed hypnotized by the sight.

She studied the incredible sight of the immense flames. The trees surrounding the cabin now burned as brightly as stars in the heavens. There was a heavy smell of smoke in the air.

"You're right, Raleigh. We should go. We can't let the fire catch up with us."

Reluctantly, she picked up the broken oar and began to paddle into the bowels of the swamp out of the path of the fire. Within minutes, they escaped the light and slipped into the darkness of the pre-dawn morning.

Claude called Brandy about nine o'clock that evening when he arrived home from St. Thomas. Agent Weller and Agent Hebert instructed her to invite Claude to come by to discuss the settlement. They wanted to observe Claude's demeanor. If he was involved in the kidnapping as a sham, he might become nervous or make a mistake. It was a long shot, but they wanted to observe him just the same.

After Claude arrived, he and Brandy went into the living room to talk privately for a time. Claude had been devastated about Rene's disappearance. After Brandy gave him the details she turned the conversation to the precipitous offer from Quinn Beasley. Claude adamantly attempted to dissuade her from accepting the settlement offer.

"It is an insulting offer—one made just to test the waters. Dick and the London Underwriters also want you to reject the offer," he told her. "The real settlement value of the case is about one hundred times that much. They are just trying to find a threshold for settlement, hoping that you are weak. The Recov depositions have gone very well so far. Quinn Beasley knows that they have problems with their case. He just hopes that you are sick of it. Ethically, I have a responsibility to report all settlement offers to you. But my advice is that you should reject this one."

"I need the money now," she told him. "Things have changed—with Rene," she replied, trying to stymie her tears. "I just want my daughter back! She covered her face as her shoulders heaved with sobs.

Claude reached over and held her in his arms, stroking her hair. "It's going to be alright, Brandy. I am going to do everything I can to help you get Rene back," he promised.

Before he left, Brandy heard Claude talking softly to Agent Weller and Agent Herbert in the kitchen. The three of them were discussing the possibility of Quinn Beazley's involvement in the kidnapping. Ignoring them, Brandy called the hospital and spoke with the head nurse in the ICU. There was no change in Granny Ariel's condition. She was still weak and on the respirator.

That evening, Brandy slept fitfully, battling night sweats and disturbing dreams. She got up at 4:00 a.m., showered, washed her hair, and changed into a comfortable pair of turquoise slacks, matching cotton blouse, and flats. She pulled her hair into a thick ponytail with a turquoise clasp in the back.

The hospital called about 5:00 a.m. Granny Ariel had developed severe hemorrhaging and was being taken to emergency surgery. Agent Hebert drove her to the hospital.

The investigative team had forwarded her home telephone calls to a new cell phone with a speaker phone capacity and recording device attached. This way, Brandy was available if the kidnappers called.

She waited with Jeannette and a few of Granny Ariel's friends in the waiting room. Claude arrived a few minutes later, already dressed in a navy business suit for work. He explained that he had a federal court conference later that morning.

"Thank you for coming," Brandy told him.

"Ladies, let's go downstairs to get a bite to eat. It is my treat," he told Brandy and the two older women.

"I'm not really hungry, but I suppose that I should eat something to keep up my strength. I am certainly not able to sleep," she said reluctantly.

Claude and Brandy went down to the hospital cafeteria. Brandy suddenly realized that she was ravenously hungry. Soon her tray was loaded with scrambled eggs, bacon, grits, and dry toast. They found a table in the corner and at in silence. The cafeteria was relatively crowded and noisy despite the early hour. Agent Weller and Agent Hebert joined them after a few minutes.

Claude wiped his mouth and signaled for the cafeteria attendant to pick up his tray when they finished breakfast. "I had a long talk with Agent Weller and Agent Hebert last night. They agree that you should not settle the case. All of us agree that it is awfully strange that this settlement offer has come on the heels of Rene's disappearance. We all question whether even Quinn Beazley is involved."

"What choice do I have, Claude? I have to get the money for Rene's ransom. I don't have any other way to get that kind of money," she said almost angrily.

"I have access to that much money that was disbursed from my trust fund when I reached my thirty-fourth birthday. I want to put up Rene's ransom," he told her. "I have talked to Agent Weller and Agent Hebert, and we have started the wheels in motion."

"Brandy looked at him with surprise. How could she ever have doubted Claude? How could she have believed that he had been mixed up in this? "Oh my God, Claude! Thank you so much! But I can never repay you—until we win the lawsuit, that is."

Agent Weller intervened. "The money will be marked, and the wire transfers are being sent now. The money will be traceable. We need to use the money as bait to get your daughter back. That's all."

"Won't it be just that simple? We pay and they hand her over?" she asked.

Agent Weller hesitated and looked down momentarily. She saw a cloud of doubt pass across his face. "We certainly hope that it is that simple. We need to appeal to their greed and we will need to maintain control over this situation. Quid pro quo—an even exchange—the money for Rene."

Tears of anger welled in her eyes again. "You think she's dead, don't you? You think my little girl is dead!" she spat.

Agent Weller's gaze did not waver, and he maintained his equanimity. "We do not have any reason to believe that now, Mrs. Blake." He cleared his throat. "Now, against my better judgment, I should also tell you that late last night, a federal judge issued a wiretap order to tap the phones of Thad Stuart and the CEO of

Recov on the basis of the settlement offer and the identity of Jimmy Thornton's body. We hope that we can find evidence linking them all together as conspirators for Rene's disappearance and your husband's death."

Brandy felt a sense of relief. "That is great news."

"We have also placed them under surveillance as suspects. If there is a connection, hopefully, we will find evidence that will lead us to your little girl, even before the ransom deadline. We have also obtained their telephone, fax, and cell phone records and have placed a mail cover to monitor their mail. We are also going to look into their banking records," he continued. "From now on, they won't make a move that we don't know about it."

"This is a very positive development," Agent Hebert told her. "Identifying Jimmy Thornton's body was a big break. The Feds in Texas are still interviewing his girlfriend and Thornton's friends. His banking records reflected that he had a large amount of cash for a drifter—fifty thousand dollars in a checking account under a pseudonym in a local branch that was spent quickly. We are now trying to trace the money back to Stuart and/or Recov. Once we determine the source of the money, we can bring them in."

"Do you think that money was a payoff for my husband's death? Do you think that Jimmy Thornton killed Harris?" She asked.

"It is beginning to look that way," Agent Hebert told her. "Now, we just have to gather enough evidence to catch them."

~

Granny Ariel was in the Recovery room by the time that Brandy, Claude, Agent Weller and Agent Hebert arrived back in the surgery waiting room. The surgeon, Dr. Gordon, had been highly recommended by

Dr. Kirkland. Dr. Gordon came out to see Brandy a few minutes after nine. She tried to read something in his expression as he walked into the room.

Please God, let her be alive!

Dr. Gordon sat across from her. He seemed very relaxed. "Mrs. Massenet is a real trooper. Unfortunately, we had to remove one of her kidneys because of the damage from the assault. While we were there, we put a stent in three of her arteries." He took out a pen and began to draw a crude outline of the heart and arteries. "We placed the stents in the left ascending and descending arteries and the right ascending artery. Already her color is better, and she is resting in the cardiac wing of the recovery room. She will need to stay here for at least another ten days. At some point, we will need to get her up and around and on a low-impact exercise regimen. It is not good for older people to lie around in the hospital. There is a high risk of pneumonia and bacteriological infections, so we want her out of here as soon as possible. I suggest that she go to a rehabilitation center before she returns home. She will need nurses to assist her for several weeks after she returns home."

"Then she is alright?"

"She has had a severe injury, and her arteries were occluded. I have to be guarded, of course. We are not out of the woods, but she tolerated the procedure very well and from all indication, it is possible that she may recover. She is elderly and complications can arise," he replied. "I cannot make any promises."

Brandy shook his hand numbly. "Thank you, Can we see her?"

"Barring anything unforeseen, she should be out of recovery this afternoon and back in the ICU. I think there is a visitation at four o'clock."

Brandy gave a deep sigh. Hopefully, Granny Ariel would pull through this trauma. She thanked Dr. Gordon again before leaving with Agent Hebert to go back home to wait for the kidnapper to call.

Chapter XXIX

Claude followed Brandy, Agent Hebert and Agent Weller to the hospital parking lot with plans to return to his office to prepare for the federal settlement conference in another pending case. He told Agent Weller that after the federal conference he would go to his office to participate in a scheduled telephone call with Quinn Beasley concerning Recov's recent settlement offer. An FBI agent had been assigned to monitor the call. They were looking for information substantiating any correlation between Recov's settlement offer and the ransom demand. Claude had assured them that it was unlikely that an attorney of Quinn Beasley's stature in the legal community would risk his livelihood and freedom by conspiring to kidnap Rene. Agent Weller, however, was very skeptical, and Claude agreed to provide them with his full cooperation. He promised to come by later that evening for moral support.

By the time Claude left, he had received confirmation that the wire transfer to pay the ransom demand had been made to the FBI. The agency would work with the Secret Service in obtaining marked bills with sequential serial numbers that were easily traceable. The money would also be packed with indelible orange dye packets utilized by banks. Unless the kidnappers knew what to look for, they would be indelibly stained with the dye and the money would not be usable. There was a risk, of course, that the kidnappers were more sophisticated than anyone had imagined and that they might kill Rene in retaliation.

Brandy sat in the den drinking a glass of lemonade, unsuccessfully attempting to concentrate on the inventory that Natalie had messengered over early that morning. The television was muted, and Brandy noticed yet another photograph of the Audubon Park fountain on the screen. The small group of reporters that had clustered in the park immediately after Rene's disappearance had long since disbanded. Like the newspaper, the television continued to report an unidentified child's abduction from a residence near the park. Rene's identity, however, was withheld. Nothing had been released to the press about the ransom demand, the details of the kidnapping, or the involvement of the FBI. Similarly, the identification of the burned remains inside of the charred vehicle as Jimmy Thornton had not been released to the press nor had the connection to *BYZANTIUM*, Thad Stuart, Recov or the pending litigation been mentioned. There was no mention of any other collateral investigation. To the rest of the world, an unidentified child was gone and there were no leads.

It had been about fifty-five hours since the first telephone call. Morbidly, Brandy wondered if he would call again or if Rene was even alive.

Agent Herbert gave her a nod of encouragement when the phone rang. Brandy pressed the hands free key. The telephone was connected to a digital recording device and automatically accessible by both the police department and the FBI for tracing purposes.

She had to focus. She had to be strong.

Rene's timid voice filled the room, relaying the ransom demand. Brandy listened in horror as her little girl told her that the man would kill her if he was not paid.

Rene was alive! Today was April 24. There was hope.

"Do you have the money, yet?" asked the caller.

"Has Rene eaten? Are you taking good care of her?" she insisted as she had been instructed. Suppressing all her instincts, she omitted every reference to Jimmy Thornton. Agent Weller had warned her that this knowledge might spook the kidnappers. There was no guarantee that fear of being caught might not cause them to abandon their plan and possibly kill Rene.

"She is alive. Now do you have the money?"

"Yes, I have it now," she replied simply.

The caller sounded pleased. "I will be in touch with the instructions," he said as he disconnected the call.

Panicked, she looked over at Agent Weller expectantly. Hopefully, they had come up with something.

Agent Weller ignored her gaze. He was engaged in animated conversation with someone on his cell phone. After a few moments, he hung up his cell phone, looking very pleased. "They have located the GPS on the cell phone. The call was coming from a parking lot of a gas station near Bayou Manchac. The officers downtown are notifying local law enforcement officers in the area now to try to take down the caller." He dialed another number on his cell phone and went into the breakfast room where the other officers and agents were gathered with their equipment.

"I'm going out to Lakefront Airport," Agent Radosky announced as he stood and gathered his briefcase. He nodded to Brandy and Agent Hebert before leaving the room.

"Agent Radosky is going to go on a helicopter to work with the other local officers. I will wait here for the drop instructions while they are scouring the area," Agent Weller told her when he returned from the kitchen.

Agent Hebert spoke briefly with an officer in the hall while Brandy waited in the den, replaying the call in her mind. Rene sounded afraid. She could feel it. Agent Weller ignored her, talking on his cell phone again and making notes.

"My men tell me that Agent Plauche and Detective Simon are going to join in the search. We are also dispatching a S.W.A.T. team to the area. It is a remote location with a very few law enforcement officers. They are going to need all the backup that they can get," Agent Hebert said when he came back into the room.

"Do you think they are going to find him now?" she asked Agent Hebert.

He looked slightly troubled. "It is hard to know. The caller knows from the news that a law enforcement investigation is ongoing and that you are probably cooperating with the police. It was unavoidable. The perp expects that we are trying to locate him from the call. But investigators may find someone who remembers him, or can identify the license plate, or give a description of the perp. Many of the service stations and convenience stores now have security cameras because of robberies. We may just get lucky and get him today."

It was all based on luck. There were no guarantees. "Do you think that Rene is with them?"

"In all likelihood, Rene is probably within a radius of no greater than ten or fifteen miles," Agent Hebert explained.

"How can you be sure?" Brandy asked, still trying very hard to suppress her panic that they would not be able to recover Rene in time. The child was alone now and certainly afraid.

"Well, it is likely that he has her concealed someplace. It is improbable that the kidnapper would bring Rene in the car with all of the publicity. Of course, they may have dyed and cut her hair to change her appearance, but she is still old enough to cause a stir in public trying to go home. It is also a big risk for him to be out and about with the child because they could more easily be caught. She is either drugged or in hiding someplace. The kidnapper will not want to be too far away from Rene to make this work. He will need to keep her close enough to get to her and move her if necessary."

Tears began to well in Brandy's eyes again. Her baby was alone and at the mercy of sadists. She might well never see her again.

"It is a good sign that Rene has given today's date. He may just simply want the money. Also, we have leads here. Sometimes, we have nothing at all. We also hope to obtain information from the wiretap on Thad Stuart's phone."

Brandy's hands trembled, and her heart continued to pound from the shock of it all. Probably was not enough. Why couldn't they be sure that she was alright? Didn't they handle cases like this all the time? She wanted to scream.

"She sounded so afraid," she said woodenly.

Agent Hebert looked at Brandy with compassion. "We need to focus on the fact that your little girl is alive. This man's primary interest is in the money. He has obviously planned this very well. Ewan Donaldson is an ex-marine who has held a number of dead-end jobs. If he is involved, he simply wants the money."

She wiped her face again with a Kleenex from the box that had been permanently placed on the coffee table.

Agent Weller returned from the kitchen and sat down with them in the den. He balanced a glass of lemonade and two cookies in one hand and his cell phone in the other. He set his glass down on the coffee table. "Mrs. Blake we are now at the critical juncture. You have done an outstanding job of holding up under this pressure. I just need you to hold on a little while longer."

"Of course I am going to hold on. Surely you don't think that I am going to stop cooperating here. This is my child—my flesh and blood," she replied sarcastically.

Brandy tried to stymie her anger. She really did not like Agent Weller personally. He seemed cold and aloof—unlike Agent Hebert who seemed to embrace Rene's disappearance as if she were a member of his own family. She just hoped that Agent Weller was competent enough to find her little girl.

Agent Weller studied her intensely for a second or two. "Look, I went at this all wrong. I am sorry. What I am trying to say is that this is one of the most critical phases of this investigation. We have put out the hook now. The caller knows that you will have the money. Now he is going to give you the drop-off instructions soon—certainly within the next twenty-four hours."

"So, exactly how will this be any different than what we have done up to this point?" she asked.

"First, as he demanded, you will need to be accessible. I need you to stay here until the caller gives you the drop-off instructions for the money," he replied.

"That is not a problem."

"This could be a life-or-death decision affecting your daughter," he replied pointedly, looking into her eyes. "I am sorry. The kidnapper probably will not give you much time to react. He may want you to leave immediately. We need to have our tracing equipment with us. This is critical. I need you to bear with me."

She looked over at Agent Hebert for support. "I will do everything I can to save my daughter."

Agent Hebert patted her hand again and gave her an encouraging look. "The caller smells the bait. He will want the money, and the call should come within twenty-four to thirty-six hours. Your reaction time will need to be very quick."

"Will he want me to deliver the money?" she asked, understanding the problem for the first time.

"It is very likely," Agent Weller replied, visibly relieved that Brandy was now focusing on the task.

"Will I get Rene back then?"

"Well, we want you to bargain for that. We want Rene to be close by," he said.

"Bargain for that?" she asked incredulously. "Why would he want to keep her if he has the money?"

"Realistically, he would not," Agent Hebert interjected. "But once they have the money, they would have no reason to try to help. They want the money and while you have it, you cannot give it up until you have some assurance about Rene's whereabouts."

"How am I going to do that?" she asked.

"We are going to work on that. By the time the call comes in, you will know what to do," he assured her.

~

The air was intensely humid in the swamp. With the exception of the soft croaking of the bullfrogs, it was completely silent. The towering cypress trees with their sprawling limbs decorated with Spanish moss provided a respite from the relentless sun. Overhead through the soaring branches, Raleigh occasionally caught a glimpse of an azure cloudless sky. The water beneath them was still and placid. The swamp had a distinct beauty all its own.

The tiny vessel floated aimlessly in the ebony swamp. Earlier in the day, the craft had become lodged on a huge cypress knee. Rene had managed to shove them off again with the broken oar, and the raft continued to float without further incident.

They had almost become accustomed to the sight of the occasional alligator floating listlessly in the water or the water moccasins draped across low-hanging branches that extended over the black depths. Around midday, a curious alligator had bumped against the boat with its nose, gently shoving the boat in a circular motion. Rene had screamed and grabbed the oar, paddling them away from immediate peril. The alligator continued to float in the water, and fortunately, had not pursued them.

Raleigh wondered if the giant reptile regarded the contents of the boat as a food source. Alligators had a very long life-span—over seven times the lifespan of a squirrel. Many of the larger alligators lived sixty or seventy years. What they lacked in intelligence, they learned through experience.

Was the alligator trying to turn the boat over? Or was the reptile just curious? Had it been fed scraps of fish from a boat by fishermen? Once in the water, death would be swift and certain. They would need to be extremely cautious.

Raleigh took a sip of water that Rene had poured into the bottle cap. He sat under the bench beneath the confines of a little makeshift tent that Rene had constructed out of the corner of the blanket they had managed to rip off. The cloth had a dirty, musty odor and was frayed at the edges. But Raleigh was glad for the protection it afforded him from predators. The primary danger to the squirrel in these circumstances was an owl or a hawk. Birds of prey had incredible vision, far superior to that of a human or a squirrel. They could sail through the air and surprise prey on the ground with near silence. He needed the camouflage to avoid being suddenly snatched from the vessel by a winged predator. It was unlikely that a bird would seek him out under the bench and beneath the dark blanket, although that was a risk.

Raleigh stood watch from his position under the bench. He had taken a short nap after they had drifted to safety from the burning shack. He had been too afraid to sleep very long. Cautiously, he scanned the area around them for danger. He could only see overhead or large obstructions looming in front of the bow of the vessel. Rene slept soundly, curled in the bottom of the bass boat, her head propped on her arm. She had several welts on her legs now from the relentless mosquitoes that infested the swamp. The insects fortunately had ignored him as he crouched under the bench partially concealed by the blanket remnant.

He allowed his mind to ramble, thinking about Ariel and Chloe. He wished Chloe were here with them and had not died. If only she had been with them. But Chloe was no match for an alligator or a snake. An alligator could easily kill a dog or even a child.

They were extremely vulnerable now. What if the vessel turned over? Death would be inevitable. They had only enough food for two days, if strictly rationed. Eventually, in three or four days, they would starve. How big was the swamp? Would someone else find them? Could their captor easily find them? Would they eventually run into a road or the ocean? But what choice did they have? They could not have stayed in the shack. Death would have been certain. At least now they had a chance at life.

The sun gradually waned as Rene continued to sleep. After she woke up, he would take another short nap before nightfall. They had the flashlight with them, but they could not use it all night long. The batteries had been nearly exhausted on one light. They would be at their most vulnerable at night and would need to be eternally vigilant when darkness fell.

Rene finally stirred and woke up. She stretched and wiped the sleep from her eyes. They shared some more water and one of the remaining peanut butter sandwiches that they had rationed. There was only one more sandwich left and another bottle of water. He doubted that they could drink the swamp water. It very likely was diseased. Without a constant source of water, he knew that he would die. His metabolism was much faster than the child's metabolism.

As she ate, Raleigh watched a large alligator as it rested on a fallen branch, lazily eying a nutria busily gnawing on the stubs of a cypress knee nearby. He noticed in fascination that the reptile was nearly camouflaged on the dark branch. Momentarily, the giant creature silently slid into the water and glided toward the unsuspecting nutria. Raleigh averted his gaze.

Death was all around them. How he longed for the safety of the park and the afternoons in Ariel's garden.

"I feel better," Rene told him brightly after they had eaten. "The air feels fresh out here—better than that yucky old shack." She smiled with a child's ignorance of lurking danger and scanned the natural ceiling of soaring limbs above them.

Raleigh clucked softly in agreement, not wanting to alert predators of his presence.

Rene sat on the bench and grabbed the chalkboard. "Come and sit in my lap, Raleigh. I will protect you from those birds, and we can play hangman before it gets dark."

She lifted the squirrel up onto her lap. He noticed that Rene now had the odor of grime, sweat, smoke, and peanut butter. Raleigh snuggled against her chest. The chalkboard was balanced on her knees. Each of them had a small piece of colored chalk.

They played in earnest, spelling every word longer than five letters that were in Rene's vocabulary. It was a nice diversion. Rene drew a small box in the upper left hand corner of the chalkboard. Oblivious to any possible danger to them, the child giggled in delight every time she stumped the squirrel. Her laughter pierced the silence in the waning afternoon light. He sensed that they were alone—probably for miles. He was glad for the company and glad that he had followed Rene. By now, she likely would have been dead.

After an hour or so, Raleigh was overtaken with exhaustion. He slept in Rene's lap as she stared out in fascination at the swamp. He slept deeply, dreaming of a little girl who was shot and consumed in a fire.

He woke suddenly at the sound of Rene's piercing scream. The light was dimmer now in the approaching twilight of the day.

"Raleigh, help!" she shrieked. The boat was rocking violently as Rene balanced on the bench. He crouched on the bench as Rene cried wildly. "Don't let him bite us!"

Raleigh felt a jolt of terror when he saw the source of her fear. A water moccasin had fallen into the boat.

Chapter XXX

Agent Weller and Agent Hebert spent the remainder of the afternoon coaching Brandy on her response to the next call from the abductor. Just like the other two calls, this call would also be taped and would transmit to a speakerphone in the kitchen. They coached Brandy to ask the kidnapper to slowly repeat the instructions for the drop-off of the ransom. She would insist that Rene be nearby to the drop-off. Otherwise, once the money changed hands, Brandy would have very little leverage. They had been adamant that Brandy would not be allowed to participate in the drop-off.

"It is too dangerous," Agent Weller told her. "We have an agent who will wear a wig, and our makeup artists will create a striking resemblance of you. Even you will be surprised. That agent will wear a wire, and the bag will contain transponders so we can track the perp and his location."

"What if he discovers that the agent is not really me? Then what?" she had demanded. "Won't he be wary of the cops? This man specifically picked out my child and must know me. We don't want the abductor to panic. You have said it yourself fifty times over the last few days. If he realizes it is not me, he may get spooked. I have to deliver the money. It is the only way," she replied pointedly. "I have a college education. How hard can this be? This is my child, and I will do whatever I can to protect her, even if it means losing my life. You teach me what to do! That is your job!" She crossed her arms and glared at Agent Weller pointedly.

"No. It is out of the question," he replied with a slightly bored stare. Obviously, he was accustomed to these demands from distraught parents.

"I am making the drop-off. I refuse to allow you to jeopardize my child's life because of some hidebound FBI protocol," she snapped, glaring at him in the long silence that followed.

"Alright," Agent Weller replied in exasperation. "I will have to get approval. We would follow you with a S.W.A.T. team. But you need to follow the rules, whether you agree with them or not."

"I will do whatever you tell me to do. I just want to be the one who makes the drop-off because any risk that Rene could be killed is too great for me. I would lay down my life for my child."

Agent Hebert looked at her with renewed respect. "Well, then, we had better get started teaching you what to do."

They spent the rest of the afternoon and early evening discussing strategy and protocol. Brandy agreed to wear a wire that transmitted sound to a receiving device in a nearby vehicle. The range was only line of sight, so there was a danger that they would lose the transmission. She would also wear a small transponder and carry a stun gun for protection. They spent some time role-playing and going over the equipment. It was a good distraction.

෴

The nurses in the ICU reported that Granny Ariel's condition continued to improve throughout the day. Dr. Gordon called a few minutes after seven.

"I have just finished my evening rounds," he told Brandy. "Your grandmother is doing extremely well—better than any of us expected. I am very encouraged by her progress."

"I am so relieved," Brandy replied. "Thank you so much for everything. I don't know if I could take anything else." Her voice cracked, and she began to cry softly.

"Mrs. Blake," Dr. Gordon responded gently, "I cannot imagine what you are going through right now with your little girl. But rest assured that we are going to take excellent care of your grandmother so you can concentrate on what you need to do. I have left orders with the nurses to call you immediately if anything comes up tonight."

She managed to regain her composure. "Thank you, Dr. Gordon. I appreciate this more than you know."

She hung up, feeling more hopeful about Granny Ariel than she had in the last three days. Sleep evaded her, so she continued to peruse the records Natalie had sent over earlier in the day.

Claude came by around eight. He brought a half dozen oyster and shrimp sandwiches from the Acme in the French Quarter, a gallon of crawfish bisque, and chocolate ice cream. "I thought you might all be hungry," he told Agent Weller as he unpacked the food in the kitchen.

"Claude, that is very sweet. I know that the officers will appreciate this," Brandy told him. "But I barely have an appetite tonight."

Claude ignored her comment and continued to unpack the food. "I told Quinn Beasley this afternoon that we were rejecting the settlement offer and that we were ready to go to trial. I am sure that you already have the 302 report from Agent Sorenson," he said to Agent Weller. Claude was referring to the official report prepared by the field agent after the call.

"Was he surprised?" Agent Hebert asked.

"Not really, or he is a very good actor. He indicated that he did not really think that we would accept it, but that ethically, he was duty bound to convey the offer as instructed by his client," Claude replied as he set part of a sandwich and a cup of bisque in front of Brandy.

"He may not be involved. But then again, money and greed do strange things to people," Agent Weller observed. "We will see how his clients react to the news. We may pick up something on the wire. Did he mention Rene?"

"Not a word," Claude replied soberly.

Brandy listened desultorily and shoved the sandwich toward the middle of the table. She was not hungry. All she could do was think about Rene. Was she cold or afraid? Was she still alive? Did the man kill her after she read the ransom note?

"You need to eat," Agent Hebert told her. "The critical stage is coming up, and we need you to be clear-headed."

Brandy nodded her head and gave them a weak smile. Despite her depression, she managed to eat half of a shrimp po'boy and a small cup of the bisque. Afterward, she and Claude returned to the den. She dozed lightly on the sofa while Claude worked on some documents he had in his briefcase.

She was jolted awake by the sound of Agent Hebert's cell phone about 11:30 p.m. He retired to the kitchen to take the call. She could hear the muffled conversation between Agent Hebert and Agent Weller in the kitchen. Claude continued to concentrate on his documents. Brandy yawned and stretched. She had been dreaming that they were all in Eleuthera again. In the dream, she and Rene were playing in the shallow waves along the beach until suddenly, without warning, the tide had swept Rene into the deep water. The child was surrounded by sharks and Brandy could not reach her. She had tried to scream for help, but she could not use her voice. She had awakened just as Rene's head had disappeared under the water.

Her body felt stone-heavy, and she was suddenly aware of her acute exhaustion from sleeplessness and stress over the past few days. She noticed that despite the air-conditioning, she had begun to sweat. The minor cuts on her hands and shoulders from the windshield glass resulting from their accident in St. Thomas had begun to scab over.

The trip to St. Thomas seemed like a million years ago. It was hard to believe that she had only been home for three days. In that short time, her entire life had changed. They had all been so happy, and now her family was torn apart again.

Claude's hair was slightly mussed, and his eyes were bloodshot. He was making fastidious notes on a legal pad as he perused a deposition transcript, marking the critical passages with a yellow highlighter. He looked equally exhausted. It was surprising because Claude usually had boundless energy.

"It's late," she told Claude. "Aren't you tired?"

He closed the manila folder and inserted it, along with a legal pad, into the pocket of his soft leather briefcase. "Yeah, I am a little tired. But I don't want to leave you under these circumstances."

"I am fine. I have all the police protection a lady would need."

"Do you want me to go?"

She gave him a thin smile. "You can stay in one of the guest rooms. I need moral support now. I feel so strange with Granny Ariel and Rene gone and all of these strangers in the house."

"Good. That is what I hoped. I brought a change of clothes in my car. I just don't want to leave you under these circumstances," he told her.

"Thank you, Claude," she said simply. Brandy sat up and drank a sip of the lemonade resting on the coaster. The ice had long since melted, and the liquid was now room temperature. Her mouth was dry, and the lemonade felt good in her throat.

Agent Hebert and Agent Weller returned to the room a few minutes later. Agent Weller gave her the news. "Well, we have received a report from our officers working in Bayou Manchac. The gas station is a small operation and is not affiliated with a major oil company with a convenience store. There was no surveillance system. The attendant is a twenty-year-old male who sells gas and runs the small maintenance operation. He recalls seeing a male in a baseball cap driving a dark blue Ford parked in the lot for a few minutes. He is sure that it had a Louisiana tag, but he does not remember the number. The car was traveling east."

"The DMV ran all the blue Ford sedans in the state. A white Ford sedan was stolen from a Kroger parking lot in Baton Rouge about a week ago," Agent Hebert interjected. "It may have been the car, and an APB had been put out on it in the region. It was located abandoned in a parking lot earlier this evening. It is being dusted for prints, hair, and fibers. It may be our perp, but then again, it could have just been some kids taking it out for a joy ride."

Brandy felt a huge sense of disappointment. All of the leads were just dead-ends. She knew that the forensic evidence was important, but they needed to actually find Rene's abductor. Agent Hebert had explained to her that unless the perpetrator had been arrested, served in the military, or been in an occupation that required that his finger prints were on file, they would not know his identity even if they obtained a usable print. She wanted to scream.

"Are you getting any more information from the wiretap on Thad's phone?" she asked Agent Weller suddenly.

"Our agents in St. Thomas have been working with Detective Conner. All is quiet now, but the real tip-off may come after the drop-off. In the meantime, we are paying Mr. Stuart a visit right about now to try to break something loose. That may get some conversation started with Recov or the abductor."

"What will that accomplish?" she asked.

"We are hoping that the abductors will contact Thad Stuart if there is a connection," Agent Weller continued.

"And in the meantime?" she asked.

"We continue to wait."

~

The bass boat lurched wildly from port to starboard as Rene balanced on the bench. A stream of ebony swamp water sluiced in small rivulets into the bottom of the small craft. Raleigh dug his nails into the wood, hoping that he would not be pitched over the side. A few feet away, he could see the gleaming eyes of an alligator, betraying its submerged body under the pitch black water.

The snake crouched on the floor of the boat, hissing angrily. Slowly, its rubbery body began to coil into a striking position. It was twice the size of the snake that had invaded the shack. Raleigh guessed that it was about three and one-half feet long. Its triangular head confirmed that it was certainly lethal. The reptile gave another aggressive hiss.

Raleigh felt a surge of adrenaline coursing through his body. He had to stop Rene. She would turn the boat over, and they would be hopelessly lost. There was no land anywhere in sight. Their only hope would be to climb a tree if they could avoid one of the large predators. But they could never out-swim the alligator floating a few feet away. One of them would certainly die. He had to keep the boat afloat at all costs. What could he do?

The squirrel caught a glimpse of the broken oar. Only the very tip of the handle had broken and was jagged with long splinters. But the oar itself was still several feet long and certainly longer than the snake. The paddle edge was wide.

It could be a lethal weapon. Without a barrier, though, Rene would likely get bitten this time if she tried to club the snake to death. This snake was not distracted, and it was capable of moving with lightning speed. But, maybe Rene could scoop the snake out with a paddle. The snake was feeling threatened, and there was a good chance that it might welcome the escape.

He began scolding Rene furiously. He tugged on her sandals and barked sharply. The child eventually stopped rocking and looked down at him. Her face was red and even in the reduced light he could clearly see the tears falling down her cheeks. The natural movement of the hard rocking motion still caused the boat to sway gently from port to starboard.

Raleigh jumped on the paddle and with his forepaws made a scooping motion in the air as if he were lifting the snake over the side. He tried not to direct her gaze in the direction of the alligator. He did not want her to panic.

Rene gave him a fearful glance and then a look of comprehension. “Over the side? I don’t know if I can do it,” she told him.

Raleigh barked, oblivious to the fact that he was obviously calling attention to himself to winged predators. She had to act now. They could not stay with the snake in the boat. Sooner or later, one of them would get bitten. She had to try.

She studied the snake momentarily and looked at Raleigh soberly. "Well, we got rid of the other one. Okay, Raleigh. I'm gonna try."

He barked again sharply. It was a danger bark that Rene had learned to understand.

"I will do it slowly," she replied with comprehension. "We just want it out of the boat."

Rene slowly stepped off the bench and lifted the oar. She moved the oar near the head of the snake. Angrily, he hissed and struck at the wooden oar.

Rene stood still, ignoring the snake. She held the oar in place waiting for what seemed to be an eternity until it settled down. After a while, the snake began to relax again. Minutes went by as Rene stayed in position. Then, very slowly, she lowered the oar down underneath the snake. The reptile eyed her cautiously. Finally, with one hard swoop, she shoved the oar under the snake and lifted it over toward the side.

Suddenly, the snake fell off the oar, landing on the side of the boat. Raleigh felt his heart lurch. Rene did not panic. With a determination that she had only acquired over the last two days, he watched in amazement as Rene brought the oar down on the snake's head with a loud "whop!" She continued to pound the snake with the edge of the oar until it fell into the water. The paddle end of the oar was covered with the snake's blood. Rene immediately dipped the oar into the water and paddled away furiously.

Dazed and severely injured, the snake struggled in the water. As Rene and Raleigh watched, they saw the giant alligator shoot out of the still, dark water and grab the snake in its mouth. The giant reptile thrashed mightily in the water as it clamped its jaws around the snake and disappeared into the depths of the swamp. The power of the fearsome creature was a frightening sight.

Rene sucked in her breath deeply. "Oh no!" she cried.

Raleigh hopped into the safety of Rene's lap and stroked her hair. The child gave him a brief kiss on the top of his head as she held onto the oar with her left hand.

It would be night soon. What protection would they have against the predators then? Would another snake drop into the boat that night? They might not notice until it was too late. Could an alligator turn them over in the water? Would they survive the night?

He snuggled closer to the child and focused on the darkening shadows ahead. Together, they remained in gloomy silence as the little bass boat drifted farther into the darkening swamp.

∽

From his position on the shell walk, the remnants of the charred shack appeared as a cluster of broken sticks against the twilight sky. Lightning had no doubt set the tinder-box of dry wood on fire. The heat from the fire had been so intense that the stilts and dock had burned down to the waterline. There was no sign of the kid's remains.

He was careful to watch his step on the shell drive to avoid poisonous snakes. During the early evening and at night, snakes stretched out on nearby roadbeds and the shell lanes that still radiated the warmth from the afternoons. The swamp area was densely populated with poisonous snakes. Although the venom could kill a child, the worst problem was necrosis of the flesh, often resulting in gangrene and loss of an appendage from the venom.

When he walked toward the southeastern edge of the deck, he noticed that the old abandoned bass boat that had been tied to a tree about ten feet from the edge of the dock was gone. Of course, it could have been completely consumed by the fire, but that seemed unlikely. It seemed odd that there was nothing left of the boat. The water was shallow here—only two or three feet deep or so and littered with tree stumps. There was no sign of a rope or even the charred remains of the boat.

Instinctively he knew that the kid had taken the boat. Somehow, she had escaped the fire and was out in the swamp. A thin smile played across his lips as he considered the problem. Even Ewan had to admire her guts and ingenuity. But a young kid all alone could not travel far in this wilderness. The swamp was a death-trap for the inexperienced. He was confident that she would not last the night. If she was still alive tomorrow, he would find her. He would be equipped with military night vision goggles and tracking devices. Ewan had a high-powered scope on the 50-caliber military sniper rifle he had purchased on the black market that he planned to use to kill the red-head. During his stint in Iraq, Ewan had finely honed his skills as an expert marksman. The shallow-hulled boat he had stolen was equipped with a 200-horsepower outboard motor and would quickly close the distance between him and the kid.

She would be easy prey.

~

The ransom money had been transferred to a safe downtown at the local FBI headquarters. It had been marked and numbered, and equipped with dye packs. Two transponders were placed in the bottom of the duffle bag.

Brandy woke up early. The officers had repeatedly warned her that the kidnappers would not give her much time to make the drop-off after the call came in.

"He will press you to your limits," Agent Hebert had told her. "It is his way of maintaining control and giving you less opportunity for law enforcement to become involved. After the drop-off call comes in, he will likely want you to leave immediately."

She showered and shampooed her hair. Afterward, she changed into a clean pair of slacks and a pullover cotton shirt and pulled her hair back into a clip at the base of her neck. Despite the last few sleepless nights, she felt incredibly alert and wired. She was going to focus. She was going to get Rene back. Today was *the day.*

Claude was already sitting in the kitchen when she went downstairs. He had showered and changed clothes from the previous night. His hair was still damp. "The hospital called. Your grandmother had a good night last night."

Brandy smiled with relief. "Thank God. I am just so thankful that she is getting better."

She drank a cup of coffee, nibbled on a fresh peach, and drank a tall glass of orange juice. Claude continued to work on the same file he had been reading the night before. Agent Weller was in the den, talking to a cadre of new officers that had appeared during the night. Agent Hebert was on a secure landline that had been installed during the operation, making notes on his small pad. After a while, Agent Weller returned to the kitchen and emptied the remaining coffee in his cup before rinsing it and placing it in the dishwasher. He sat down at the breakfast room table with them, reading a field report on his laptop.

"I found something," Claude announced suddenly after Agent Hebert hung up the phone and returned to the kitchen. "I knew that it was in his deposition somewhere." He folded the pages back and shoved the volume of the transcript across the table toward Brandy and Agent Hebert. "Read this."

Brandy looked at the large print scrawled across the page that Claude had highlighted. It was an unofficial, first draft, unedited transcript of the deposition of Thad Stuart. Essentially, this consisted of daily copies obtained from the court reporter. The cost had been shared with Underwriters' attorneys. Claude had assured Brandy that the benefit was well worth the cost. He explained that the official transcript would be given to them later after Thad had an opportunity to review, correct, and sign the transcript.

"Thad admitted that he contributed to Jimmy Thornton's salary," Claude told them. "He also admitted that he had loaned him money once or twice." He folded the pages back to another passage that he had marked. "Remember, we subpoenaed a copy of all of Thad's business records and personal records for the deposition. There were a number of cash withdrawals from an account within a period of three months totaling almost $100,000. These withdrawals occurred about the time Thad entered into his contract with Recov. Thad claimed that this money was used as salvage expenses. He could not be specific, no matter how hard we pressed him. But, the Recov contract did not require Thad to invest any more of his own money. In exchange for his information and cooperation, he would receive 50 percent of the salvage award. So, Recov would have borne those daily expenses."

Agent Weller looked up from his notes and began listening intently.

"How much did you tell me that the upper limits of the salvage award would possibly be?" Agent Hebert asked.

"Best estimate---about three hundred fifty million dollars," Claude replied.

"Enough money to fight over," Lt. Herbert said pensively. He turned and gave Agent Weller a knowing gaze.

"So one-half of the cash withdrawals are the equivalent of the total amount of money Jimmy Thornton had in his account in Key West—fifty grand," Agent Weller interjected. Where do you think he spent the other fifty thousand?"

"Maybe he paid Ewan Donaldson?" suggested Claude.

"So, here is our connection," said Agent Hebert. "You were getting too close this week. No wonder those hoods in St. Thomas were trying to kill you or at least scare you. The two of you were getting too close to the truth."

"Exactly!" said Claude.

"What about Recov?" Agent Hebert asked. He looked toward Brandy. "Explain to me again why your husband did not want them in on this deal."

"He thought they were a sleazy outfit and that they would end up cheating him and Thad out of the money and, I suppose, the glory and credit of the find. Recov is an international operation. They really did not need Thad or Harris. My husband was worried about getting shoved out and cheated by the big guys."

"Makes sense," Agent Hebert agreed.

"He tried to convince Thad that they should stick it out on their own. It created a real strain on their relationship. Thad did not have the money to keep investing, and Harris had almost depleted my inheritance from my parents. Salvage work is expensive and high tech now. We were living on my salary as an art teacher. Things were getting tight, and Harris was nervous. He never told me how many emeralds that he found, though. If he had only told me—Harris was worried all of the time and he was obsessed with *BYZANTIUM.* He and Thad had begun to argue. Harris was secretive, and he spent all his time working. He told me that he was not going to allow Recov to come in and shove them out of a project that had taken five years of their lives. He refused to even consider cutting a deal with Recov."

"But of course, once Thad had talked to Recov about the salvage operation, the cat was out of the bag. There was nothing to keep Recov from conducting their own operation and seeking a court order giving them either exclusive or partial salvage rights to this operation," Claude explained.

"So, in other words, Recov had them both over a barrel," observed Agent Hebert.

"Well, they were faced with significant expenses in the manner of legal fees. Eventually, Recov and its attorney would try to get exclusive rights to the operation, and whatever Thad and Harris recovered would be eaten up by their legal expenses and salvage costs. They were in a no-win situation. Recov can afford to litigate with high-powered lawyers like Quinn Beasley indefinitely. The costs themselves of a suit like this are enough to break most people," Claude explained.

"And the insurers in London—aren't they entitled to a piece of this?" Agent Hebert asked.

"Eventually, they will get a recovery for the cargo and vessel fragments that will reimburse them for the cost of their insurance payments over a hundred years ago, with interest. Also, they technically had ownership rights in the cargo and the ship. Once they reimbursed the owners for the ship and emeralds, the syndicates technically purchased the property and had title despite the fact that it was at the bottom of the sea. Any recovery they make will certainly reimburse their attorneys. The problem is that it takes special skill and money for salvage so, in cases like this, the salvors like Harris, Thad, and Recov stand to gain the most. The London syndicates, however, could recover as much as one hundred fifty million out of this. Given other similar cases, the court probably will not allow them to have much more, because essentially other people, like Thad and Harris, have done all of the work."

"So, Thad Stuart saw his interest diminishing, and he just wanted Harris out of the way because he refused to cooperate with Recov. He saw this as his only option," said Agent Weller.

"Probably. That is the only rational explanation," replied Claude.

"He tried to take the few emeralds that I knew about from me after Harris died," Brandy told them. "He said that they were worthless and that nothing much would come of the *BYZANTIUM* find. He said he wanted to display them in his day sailing business for notoriety. He testified, though, that three days after Harris's funeral, he signed an agreement with Recov."

"He wanted all of the evidence of your husband's involvement, so you would not have the right to make a claim later," observed Agent Hebert.

"Well, I really thought that was all there was until I found the boxes loaded with emeralds in the attic over a year later."

Agent Weller stroked his brow and made a few more notes. "What is really bothering me is that where would a low-life with a day sailing business like Thad Stuart get $50,000 to pay Jimmy Thornton to murder your husband? With that kind of money, he would need help from someone like Recov. Also, Thornton was not the brightest bulb. He probably had help."

"How exactly did your husband die?" asked Agent Hobert.

"The tanks he was using were old. Harris had purchased them second-hand. The oxygen content of the Nitrox I mixture was likely compromised, and he became disoriented and drowned," she said.

Did Thornton have access to these tanks?" Agent Weller asked.

"I am not sure. Harris had a couple sets of tanks that he maintained in a storeroom area on Thad's property. These were just back-up, and I don't know if Harris had ever even used them before. Anyway, I thought that Jimmy left about a week before Harris died," she said.

"Did Jimmy have a key to the storeroom?"

She shrugged. "I really don't know. I would assume he did. Harris also used a dive shop, but the shop is closed now according to Detective Conner."

"So, that gives both Thad and Jimmy motive and opportunity," said Weller. "Ewan Donaldson was the worker at the dive shop. A waiter from a nearby restaurant recalls that he worked at the shop. Apparently, he was friendly with Jimmy. We have confirmed with your gardening service that a man named James Weeks fitting Donaldson's general description quit work two weeks ago. According to the ID badge from IBIX, Donaldson has a shaved head now. His address was listed in the Lower Garden District on Euterpe, but he skipped town."

"Any leads on where he might have gone?"

"We are looking into it, but don't have anything definite yet. This could be a dead-end and but we think that Weeks is the same man as Donaldson.

"Thad is very smooth. After Harris died, he spoke and sent flowers to the memorial service. My God, he is a monster."

"Killers do some odd things. It is also possible that Thornton could have told some of his friends and they could have decided to kidnap Rene to run their own sting operation," said Agent Hebert. "The two things may not be connected. In other words, Thad could have had your husband murdered, but he may not have anything to do with your daughter's kidnapping."

Agent Weller rose and walked over to the secure landline in the kitchen. "I am going to contact our agents in St. Thomas and email these deposition pages. They can liaise with Detective Conner and put Thad Stuart on the hot seat during the interrogation. If he knows anything about your daughter's kidnapping, we will find out now. We will get a warrant for his business records, computers, tablets and cell phones, and a search warrant for his home. They will meet with the prosecuting attorney. Over the course of the day, we will likely have enough circumstantial evidence to charge him with murder for hire. In the meantime, I think we should switch to plan B."

"What do you mean?" Brandy asked.

"I think it is too dangerous for you to make the drop-off. We don't know if Stuart is connected to your daughter's kidnapping. If he is connected, he will have every reason to have you killed. If both you and your daughter disappear, both his problems and Recov's problems are over. It is too dangerous," Agent Weller responded.

"I have to make the drop-off. They expect me! They probably have been watching the house. They know what I look like! If they are watching the drop-off, they just might be able to tell the difference!"

"They have every incentive to kill you! Without you and Rene, Thad and Recov can easily settle this case with the London insurers and there are no complications," he insisted.

"I am going to make the drop-off. This is just a theory! You cannot be certain if there is a connection between Rene's disappearance and Thad Stuart. This is my little girl and I am going, no matter what!" she demanded, raising her voice and casting Agent Weller a defiant look. "This is just a case to you. When this is over, you will go home to your family and friends. This is my child and I am going to do whatever it takes to bring her home!"

"I think he will try to kill you," Agent Weller said in the overly rational tone of someone dealing with a distraught individual. "There is more here than a kidnapping. We cannot give you the protection that you need, other than to give you a bullet-proof vest and wire."

"I am making the drop-off no matter what the risk because any risk that the kidnappers will get spooked could make the difference between whether Rene is dead or alive," she replied looking toward Claude for support.

"She's right," Claude said softly, giving Brandy's hand a squeeze.

Agent Weller studied her critically. "Alright, have it your way," he said with exasperation. "I am going to email this to St. Thomas."

Brandy sat back in her chair and gave Claude and Agent Hebert a triumphant gaze. Now, all there was to do was to wait for the call.

CHAPTER XXXI

Raleigh and Rene shared the last peanut butter sandwich shortly after sunrise. Rene carefully rationed the water, offering Raleigh a cap of the tepid liquid to quench his thirst. A low overcast of deep slate blue clouds obscured the sky, and the scent of ozone was pervasive. The still air was heavy with humidity, and a brisk breeze stirred the cypress limbs overhead.

Raleigh was thankful when dawn had approached. The batteries on the flashlight that the kidnapper had left behind had finally failed during the night, and the two of them had sat huddled together, forced to survive the night in the bleak darkness of the swamp. Occasionally, the small boat had made a hard thump as it drifted into a tree and then gradually floated aimlessly away. Raleigh had become accustomed to the hooting of the owls as they pursued their nocturnal hunt. He had steeled himself to ignore his vulnerable feelings caused by the disconcerting calls, realizing that it was unlikely that an owl would try to rip him from Rene's grasp.

Raleigh did what he could to soothe the child in the dark of night. Despite their precarious position, Raleigh and Rene had each managed to sleep a few hours curled on the floor of the boat and the night had otherwise been uneventful.

Raleigh chewed on the delicate bark and cambium of a cypress limb that Rene had snagged for him from a low branch that had stretched overhead. It felt wonderful to gnaw again, and he enjoyed the sweet cambium of the tender young branch. When he had sated his appetite with the branch, he relaxed and sniffed the air from the safety of his small tent under the bench. He could smell the approaching storm in the distance. He was afraid that a hard rain would fill the bottom of the boat with water, making the vessel unstable and likely to tip over. Moreover, a brisk wind could flip the boat, dumping both of them into the water. He looked around at the array of supplies Rene had taken from the shack. They could use one of the empty-bottles to bail water, if necessary. They could also fill up their existing water bottles with fresh rainwater. He knew that a squirrel could live for a while with a source of fresh water and cambium. He was concerned about Rene.

Could the child eat cambium? He was not sure.

A breeze ruffled his fur, and the temperature was slightly cooler now as he cuddled next to Rene's leg. Today, she had not been interested in games, and she had ignored Raleigh's antics to entice her to play. Instead, the child sat on the bench with the oar draped across her legs gazing watchfully out at the swamp. She had begun to ignore the occasional water moccasin that slid through the still black pool, or the clusters of alligators suspended just beneath the surface of the water. Raleigh noticed that Rene had taken on an air of watchfulness, stoicism, and confidence that she did not have several days ago. She was a survivor now, and it was as if the kidnapper had stolen her innocence.

He had become weary of the sameness of the swamp. The squirrel knew that they were hopelessly lost. He could not hear any human sounds of cars or voices. There was no sign of even a clump of dry land anywhere. They were stranded and alone in the bleak wilderness.

When did the swamp end? Had they been going in circles? How many miles must they travel before they were discovered? Would they die in this watery wilderness? He could not think like that. He had to be strong for Rene. He had to protect the child. He would do it for Ariel. The squirrel could not imagine how devastated she would be if she had lost her grandchild.

Rene hummed softly to herself. Raleigh recognized it as a French song about Napoleon that she had learned at school this year. He tried to enjoy the music as he stared into the looming cypress branches. Occasionally, he noticed what he thought was a squirrel or bird nest high overhead. He did not see any squirrels or birds, though. They were also afraid of the predators. This was a place of great danger for small animals.

Suddenly, a strong gust of wind shoved the branches forcefully against the blackening sky. The light had become flat, and the surrounding swamp was clothed in dark shadows. Within moments, Raleigh felt the first large droplets of rain. It would be a bad storm. He could feel it.

The squirrel stepped back under the bench for protection. Feeling a sudden chill of water under his toes, he inspected the bottom of the boat. He noticed a small river of water that was slowly accumulating under the bench.

He realized what had happened immediately. The boat had sprung a leak.

Brandy was sitting at a stool at the kitchen island with Agent Weller and Agent Hebert when the telephone call finally came nearly four hours later. The older man gave her an encouraging nod as she lifted the phone to her ear.

"Do you have the money?"

Brandy steeled her resolve as she recognized the kidnapper's voice. She felt a morbid sense of relief because she had actually begun to worry that he would not call back. Today, she could sense a nervous quality in his voice that she had not heard before. "I have it," she replied simply. "I just want my daughter back."

"Then follow my instructions to the letter. I am only going to say this once. You have four hours. No cops—no FBI—just you."

Brandy listened as he gave her the drop-off instructions. He wanted her to take I-10 east to Highway 90 to a designated exit where she would double back onto a dirt road leading to the edge of the swamp. From that point, she was instructed to take a small bass boat and drop the money off at a certain location in the swamp. The kidnapper told her that there would be a map with further instructions in the boat. Brandy listened intently, not bothering to write anything down. She had been assured that the call was taped, and the kidnapper's directions were being transcribed by an FBI agent.

"What about Rene?" she cried, trying to squelch the mounting hysteria in her voice.

"No cops," the caller demanded as he abruptly disconnected the call.

Brandy looked over toward Agent Hebert for reassurance. Her eyes brimmed with tears and nervous anticipation, but she was ready to make the drop-off. "What do you think?" she asked them.

"We don't have much time. Four hours is a tight schedule," Agent Hebert replied. "You need to get out on I-10 east before the afternoon traffic begins to build.

"He is trying to maintain control by keeping you on his schedule," Agent Weller interjected.

"I am ready," she announced with steely resolve.

Brandy realized that this was something she would have to do alone. She had declined Claude's invitation to accompany her on the drop-off or to sit with her until the kidnapper called. Instead, she had asked him to visit Granny Ariel for her until the ordeal was over. Besides, she needed to focus completely on getting Rene back. That was the only thing that mattered now.

A female FBI agent assisted her in putting on a bulletproof vest which was concealed under a baggy cotton shirt that buttoned up the front and a pair of cotton slacks. The vest was equipped with a transponder that would transmit Brandy's location to the field agents.

"It will protect your vital organs, but your head will still be exposed," the woman had told her.

The vest felt slightly heavy and alien under her clothing, but her breathing and movement were not impaired. Brandy had refused to wear a helmet and instead selected a baseball cap, pulling her red hair through the opening in the back. She was concerned that a helmet would immediately alert the kidnappers that she was not alone. Agent Weller had explained that field agents would be in vicinity monitoring her location, and three snipers would be air-lifted into the swamp. The goal was to apprehend the perpetrator when he came to pick up the money.

Brandy was concerned about the presence of the snipers because of the possibility that the kidnapper would spot them. "Are you sure that he will not get angry and kill Rene when he finds out about the snipers?"

"These men are accustomed to moving with stealth in dangerous areas," Agent Weller told her. "He will never know that they are there. Besides, it is for your protection. If you are alone, there is nothing to stop him from killing you and your little girl. We are not taking that risk."

"As long as you are sure they are not going to compromise the plan," she replied.

"Most perpetrators are apprehended after the drop-off," he had told her. "That seems to be the time they take the greatest risks to get the money. That is what they have been working toward and they are not about to let it get away. It is our greatest opportunity to grab him, take him into custody, and locate Rene."

"But if they kill him, we may never find Rene."

"They may wound him, but they will not kill him before we find your little girl."

Brandy was determined to help them find the kidnapper. She wanted her daughter back—at any cost. Over the last few days, she had long since stopped thinking about herself.

Brandy slipped on a pair of bulky cotton socks and her Nike Air running shoes before grabbing a large canvas tote bag containing a cell phone, mace, and a two-way radio. She also had a can of mosquito repellent and a rain jacket with a hood. The two purple canvas duffle bags filled with money and a transponder had already been stowed in the car. A GPS with a military tracker had been inserted into the lining of each bag and clipped inside two of the paper bands holding the money together.

A field agent handed her two maps, one of which was hand drawn. The other map was very detailed displaying the local roads off the interstate, and the route had been highlighted. Additionally, there was a narrative with explicit instructions. Finally, they had programmed a portable GPS on her car console. She was amazed at their efficiency. She was not sure she could have found the drop off-point if she had been alone.

She climbed into her car alone and drove toward the I-10 entrance ramp downtown. Brandy could see both unmarked cars traveling a safe distance behind her. Agents Weller and Radosky would travel in the helicopter that had been sent to the small uncontrolled airfield in Slidell on the north shore of Lake Pontchartrain. It had begun to rain softly, and as she drove up the interstate ramp, she noticed the black clouds looming over the westerly horizon. Brandy clenched the steering wheel and tried to breathe deeply. Within forty-five minutes, she had negotiated the early afternoon traffic and had driven over the intercostal canal bridge. By the time she reached the seven-mile-long bridge across Lake Pontchartrain, traffic had thinned significantly. She checked the rear-view mirror, noticing that the two unmarked cars were still behind her.

Brandy shifted in the seat, accelerated the car and set the cruise control. She placed the maps prominently on the console. It had begun to rain harder now, and she increased the speed of the windshield wipers. Ignoring the pounding in her chest, she tried to focus on the road ahead as the car sped in the direction of the darkening sky.

~

Thunder pounded overhead, and the swamp was bathed in a brilliant light as a bolt of lightning struck a cluster of trees nearby. A towering cypress tree effortlessly felled by the lightning strike crashed about twenty feet from the boat sending a circle of surging waves through the swamp. The limbs stood high out of the shallow water propped on a stand of cypress knees, blocking the path of the boat.

Raleigh felt the heavy, cold raindrops pelting his head and back. Rene's exposed arms and legs were covered with raised goose bumps from the chilly rain and wind. She crouched with him on the floor of the vessel, shoving her head under the bench. The small boat pitched feverishly as it floated aimlessly on the churning dark water. It was leaking vigorously now, as a continuous fountain of swamp water sprouted from the bottom of the boat. The wooden hull had a small puncture wound, probably from scraping a cypress knee in the shallow water.

Raleigh worked feverishly, trying to plug the hole with a piece of gnawed cypress. It was only a partial solution, merely stymieing the water to a slow drip. He could tell the hull was partially rotten. As he worked, the wood splintered and shattered into a fine powder. The rain water had mingled with the stream from the leak and collected in the square stern of the boat.

Soon, they would have to bail the water. If only he had something sticky to put around the small cypress branch temporarily until they could reach safety.

Rene shivered as she huddled under the bench. "It's so cold, Raleigh," she complained. Tears welled in her eyes. "I am scared, and I just want to go home," she sobbed.

Raleigh leaned over and tried to comfort her. He stroked her wet hair and caressed her cheek with the furry side of his paw. The child continued to cry, her sobs muffled by the pounding rain. As he stroked her cheek, he noticed several pieces of dried gum stuck under the seat of the boat.

It might be possible to use it to plug the leak.

He patted Rene's cheek and went over to inspect the gum. They were hard, solid masses that could have been there for years. Raleigh gnawed the gum away from the bench and shoved it on the hull floor where it was pounded by rain. Rene calmed down and watched him with interest. After a time, the gum began to soften from the water, and Rene was able to knead it between her small fingers. It had very little elasticity, but it could provide them with some relief. When it became pliable enough, Raleigh managed to tamp it around the wood as a sealant, closing the leak. It was only a temporary solution, but it would plug the hole for a short time.

Relieved that the immediate danger was over, the two of them huddled together under the bench, seeking respite from the pouring rain. Within an hour, the storm had waned, and the rain slacked to a steady light drizzle. The sky was still black, signaling the approach of another thunderstorm.

They had managed to collect some fresh rain water in one of the empty bottles. Rene turned the cap and set the full bottle in the bow of the little boat. She used the other empty bottle to bail the rainwater from the stern. It was deeper now—nearly two inches—and the boat rode slightly lower in the water in the stern. The baling was hard work and Rene began to work up a sweat. After thirty minutes of hard bailing, she had barely made a dent in the pool of water that sloshed around in the boat. Exhausted and breathing heavily, Rene moved to the bow of the boat and drained nearly half of the bottle of fresh rainwater. Afterward, she sat with her back propped against the little boat with Raleigh on her lap.

"I'm hungry, Raleigh," she complained. "We're all out of food."

Would the cambium in the cypress make her sick, or would it help alleviate her hunger? He decided that he should only suggest it as a last resort. He realized now that it was unlikely that they would ever make it out of the swamp unless they reached land soon.

Within the hour, the rain began again in earnest. Raleigh and Rene stared at the ever-increasing pool of water in the stern of the boat. The water rapidly crept toward the bow, lifting the oar from its resting place on the hull.

There was no sign that the rain would let up, and the small lake in the hull of the vessel was increasing at a frightening rate. Something was wrong.

Raleigh waded through the water to inspect the area he had plugged earlier. He felt a jolt of sheer panic as he realized that the plug had failed. Although the sticks were still partially in place, the gum had floated to the far wall of the stern, settling on the hull floor. He hopped through the water and tried to repatch the hole with the gum. The gum had lost all of its elasticity, and soon he realized that it was hopeless.

Suddenly, he felt a hard jolt that sent him sailing through the air and crashing against the stern wall.

The boat had stopped moving. They were stuck.

Rene screamed and grabbed the oar. "We're stuck and something has broken the boat!" she wailed.

Raleigh sloshed through the water toward Rene. Something under the water, probably a cypress knee, had ruptured the hull of the boat. He saw the knobby surface of the wood as it pierced the smooth wooden surface of the boat. Water began to pour through the hole.

Within minutes they would sink. He had to do something!

Rene grabbed the oar and began trying to shove off the stump by pushing the oar against a nearby tree. Raleigh watched her helplessly from the safety of the bench. The boat rocked wildly from side to side. He noticed the cruel eyes of a large alligator nearby as it glided by the boat, surveying them with interest. He obviously knew that they were in danger. Like all predators, he was only waiting for an opportunity for a meal.

They would have to abandon the boat. Could they climb to safety in a tree? It was their only hope.

Within seconds, he felt the boat lurch hard to the port side. Suddenly, Raleigh and Rene were flying through the air. Within seconds, he realized that the boat had turned over. He felt a sharp chill as he fell into the water and sank into the blackness of the swamp.

~

Brandy drove another hour after she left the interstate through the back roads until she reached an unmarked shell road that was partially overgrown with scrub brush. The land had given way to a marsh populated by cattails and red-winged blackbirds. She had thirty minutes left to find the small skiff and make the drop-off.

A hard rain pelted the car, and she could hear the deep booming of thunder in the distance.

She was nearing the swamp. Was Rene in the swamp? How could a child survive in this environment?

The shell road was less than three-fourths of a mile long. Brandy parked at the end of the road and put on her rain parka. She grabbed her tote and the two duffle bags containing the money and trudged through the rain toward a small homemade dock. The dock was dilapidated with missing crossties. She carefully stepped across the missing planks until she reached a small skiff.

She tossed the bags into the boat. There was standing water from the rain in the hull. A sealed baggy containing a crude map for the drop-off floated in the water. Satisfied that there were no snakes inside the boat, she lowered f the bags and then herself into the skiff. She untied the new nylon rope that tethered the skiff to the dock.

The small craft was equipped with a relatively powerful outboard motor. Much to Brandy's surprise, the motor easily roared to life. Heaving a sigh of relief, she placed the drop-off instructions and a compass on her lap and steered the vessel away from the dock toward the bowels of the swamp.

CHAPTER XXXII

Raleigh began to swim furiously toward the dimly lighted surface. His heart pounded in his chest, and he felt a sense of sheer panic. Through the murky black wilderness, he could see churning water and large clawed feet less than four feet away.

Was it the alligator? Had it grabbed Rene?

As Raleigh burst through the surface, he noticed Rene perched on the bottom of the inverted hull. She was drenched with swamp water and her long hair was pasted to her face. The port side of the small boat was propped precariously on a stand of cypress knees above the swamp. Rene lay flat on her stomach clinging to the hull. Raleigh could see the snout of the alligator a few feet away nudging the side of the boat, his powerful tail slowly churning the black water in rhythmic strokes. From what he could determine, it was a huge animal—probably at least twelve feet long. In fact, from the tip of its nose to the end of its tail, it was probably longer than the boat. His jaw appeared to be at least a foot across. Morbidly, he realized that Rene could easily fit into the creature's mouth. The reptile expelled a loud hiss as it continued to nudge the boat.

The predator was interested in Rene. Intuitively, it could sense her vulnerability. The reptile instinctively viewed Rene as a meal.

"Raleigh! Come on! The alligator is right there!" she screamed hysterically. "Don't let him get you, Raleigh! Please!"

He surveyed the situation carefully as he slowly glided toward the boat. Fortunately, the boat was constructed of wood, and he could easily grip the surface and climb to safety. He inched to the side of the boat.

The alligator was too close. He would never make it before being caught and killed. There had to be another way.

Suddenly, the alligator clenched his powerful jaws around the inverted starboard side of the vessel and shook it vigorously. Rene shrieked and gripped the hull of the boat with her hands. She flattened herself against the hull, clinging to the rim of the bow that stood high out of the water. The vessel lurched wildly back and forth. The creature grunted and eyed Rene intently.

He was trying to dislodge her from her perch and throw her into the water.

Raleigh had seen the television shows depicting what alligators did with their prey. Alligators were carrion eaters. The giant reptiles thrashed about drowning their victims before bringing them to the bottom of the swamp where they guarded them ferociously. After a time, they would consume their prey with relish. If Rene were unlucky enough to fall into the water again, death would be swift and certain.

He could not let that happen. He needed to reach Rene, if nothing more than for moral support. They could climb to safety later—maybe even high in a cypress tree. He could not let Rene die such a horrible death.

Thus far, the alligator did not appear to be aware of the squirrel's presence in the water. Could it smell him? He was not sure, so he would need to be cautious. He suddenly felt the brush of something against his leg in the water. He steeled himself and remained motionless in the water.

Was it a snake or a fish? Some of the species of fish in the swamp were large enough to consume a squirrel.

He tried to remain very still, feeling the relentless pounding of his heart in his chest. If he were bitten by a water moccasin, he would be dead within minutes. Drawing on his instincts, he continued to remain motionless. Snakes were color-blind, but they were drawn to movement and had a keen sense of smell. He would have to hope that the reptile would ignore him. Seconds dragged on and nothing brushed against him again. Finally, convinced that it had only been a fish, he slowly began to close the gap between him and the upended boat. Careful not to stir up the black water unnecessarily, he inched toward the amidships and surveyed the possibilities of escape.

He studied the boat, propped out of the water on the cypress knees. It rose abruptly, soaring about six feet in the air. The water here was likely very shallow—no more than three or four feet. He could still see the alligator, gently nudging the boat now. Raleigh tried to block out the sounds of Rene's screams and to focus. His heart continued to pound in his chest. The longer he stayed in the water, the more likely that he would not survive.

He had to get out of the water.

The alligator still remained stationed watchfully at the upended stern of the boat, blocking an easy access to the spine of the inverted hull. The vessel was at a very sharp angle, and it would be impossible for him to jump up onto the hull from his location in the water. Then he had an idea. He decided to swim underneath the boat and climb onto one of the cypress knees. From there, he could crawl onto the underside of the boat, grip the side, and crawl over the top.

It was certainly possible since he had the uncanny ability to hang upside down. There was always a danger that the alligator would shake him off. It was a dangerous plan, but, he would have to try. From there, the two of them could possibly reach the sturdy trunk of the nearby cypress tree and climb to safety. Of course, snakes could climb up cypress trees, but hopefully, they would remain at the lower elevations. It was a risk, but clearly, they needed to abandon the boat.

Raleigh made his way through the water under the boat. Rene still shrieked above him. He wondered briefly how much time he had been in the water. Probably less than a minute, but he could not afford to wait any longer.

Slowly, he paddled through the water, creating tiny ripples as he moved. Then, with a sudden push, he sprang onto one of the cypress knees. Without bothering to shake off his coat, he lunged over and gripped the bottom of the wooden hull with his sharp nails, hanging partially upside down. Fortunately, it felt perfectly natural because Raleigh, like all squirrels, was equipped with an incredible equilibrium. As he hung there, calculating his next move to reach the topside of the boat, he noticed a large water moccasin gliding effortlessly across the water. Obviously, it had been eyeing him as he had been studying a way to hop on the boat.

Raleigh gripped the boat tightly as the alligator gave the boat another violent lurch with his snout. Raleigh felt the boat shake as the reptile tried to crawl on the makeshift ramp created by the inverted boat to grab Rene. The child continued to scream from her precarious perch. Raleigh could smell the odor of fear that her body emitted. He knew that the alligator could probably smell it, too. In fact, the odor of fear had probably aroused the reptile into a frenzied state.

He would have to get her under control. The alligator probably weighed at least a thousand pounds. If he managed to climb up onto the boat any farther, his sheer weight would topple the craft. It was their only chance.

Raleigh gave a series of sharp barks to signal to Rene that he was alive from the safety of the underside of the boat. Within seconds, her crying and screaming subsided. He barked sharply again as he laboriously crawled under the boat, grabbing a purchase onto the bow of the boat and pulling himself up onto the inverted bow. He dug his nails in hard. The underside of the boat was slick with slime and algae, and his paws felt unstable as he made his way across the surface to Rene. He could see a small trail where the slime had been partially cleared from the underside of the boat as Rene struggled to maintain her purchase. He nuzzled her tear-covered face. Over her shoulder, he could see the cavernous jaws and lethal teeth of the alligator as it rested on the vessel, studying their every movement with his hard gaze. A male blue heron watched the entire drama unfold from the safety of a nearby cypress branch.

Gradually, Rene began to calm down as Raleigh snuggled against her face. "Oh Raleigh!" she cried. "I thought you were dead! I love you so much!"

The child was filthy dirty, and the tips of her hair were coated with the green slime from the swamp. He tried to ignore the alligator stationed watchfully several feet below them. Raleigh lifted one paw toward a huge cypress branch overhead. If Rene could manage to rise up and stand on her knees, she could grab the branch and climb to safety. Raleigh could hold onto her until she reached the branch.

He barked sharply three times and stared at Rene intently. Her eyes were desperate now, and he sensed that she was bordering on hysteria. But as she caught sight of the branch above them, she returned the squirrel's gaze with understanding.

"Think we can make it?" she asked him.

He barked sharply and motioned upward with his paw. Rene tried to rise up onto her knees. Her left hand firmly gripped the left port side of the boat. Fortunately, the child was not heavy, and her movements did not seem to affect the stability of the boat. Suddenly, her knees began to slide, and she screamed.

"I can't! I will slip and fall into the alligator's mouth!" she shrieked.

Raleigh gave her a moment to recover before he motioned up again. He looked at her with encouragement, his eyes blinking hard because of the steady rain. Within a minute, she regained her composure and successfully lifted herself onto her knees and grabbed onto the branch overhead. Raleigh hopped onto her back, digging his nails into the cotton fabric of Rene's shirt as she pulled herself onto the branch. Raleigh hopped off her and scampered along the branch toward the trunk, barking at Rene to follow him. Rene paused a moment to watch the defeated alligator, deprived of its prey, shove off the boat and float suspended in the water. After a time, she managed to turn around and scooted over to join Raleigh near the safety of the trunk. Shaking but relieved, the two of them sat huddled in the crotch of the tree, as the alligator continued to wait below.

Brandy steered the boat across the marsh in a steady rain that pitted the smooth surface of the water. A wide channel of brown water bordered on either side by a wilderness of reeds stretched across the horizon. Dense fog hung low over the watery, flat landscape. From her current position, she could barely see a stand of cypress trees in the distance to the south. She was uncertain how much fuel she had onboard the little boat. There were two oars lying on the floor of the hull. She was determined to make it to the drop-off point, even if she had to paddle through the swamp.

A harsh wind whipped the water into choppy waves, causing the little boat to bounce across the water. The temperature was surprisingly cool over the water, despite the fact that it was late April. The water was probably shallow here—no more than five to ten feet in the marsh. Overhead, a cluster of red-winged blackbirds flew toward the northeast, probably seeking shelter from the storm. Undeterred by the weather, a snowy egret hovered over the swamp grass searching for a meal. From a distance, she saw two fishermen sitting in a small bass boat anchored near the marsh grasses. She waved, slowed down as a courtesy, and steered the craft over to the other side of the channel. Neither man gave any indication that he thought it was unusual for a woman to be traveling alone in the marsh.

As she motored along, she caught sight of a juvenile alligator as it breached the surface of the water with a large nutria in its mouth. The rodents were not originally indigenous to the area, but provided adequate food for the predators in the region. She felt a sudden chill as she morbidly watched the animal devour the nutria in one gulp. An alligator, even a juvenile one, could easily kill a human. They had nearly been hunted to extinction at one time until they had become environmentally protected. Today, the dangerous creatures proliferated in the area.

She was clearly out of her element here. Obviously, humans were not at the top of the food chain in this marshland.

She looked down at the map of the area that had been highlighted by the field agent. From here, the marshland stretched down into the Honey Island Swamp, a national wildlife refuge area, to the south. Mississippi lay to the east beyond the Pearl River, where fresh water in the vast marshlands became brackish, connecting through the rigolets to Lake Saint Catherine and Lake Borgne to the Mississippi Sound and ultimately the Gulf of Mexico. The region was a hunter's and fisherman's paradise and was often frequented by sportsmen in small boats. NASA also had an installation near the Mississippi Gulf

Coast, utilizing the Pearl River as a route to ship rocket parts down to the Port of New Orleans.

She did not see any other vessels in the area as she motored toward the horizon of trees ahead. The occasional fishing shacks on stilts that she had seen as she traveled to the boat had all disappeared.

She was alone and an open target for the kidnapper.

Brandy wondered about the field agents who were tracking her movements. Were they up ahead in the swamp, having traveled a different route to intercept the kidnappers when they tried to recover the money? Had the snipers arrived? She realized how vulnerable she was in the open marshland. Anyone with a high-powered rifle and scope could easily kill her from a distance and take the money. She recalled Agent Weller's cautionary words that Thad and Recov would profit greatly with Rene and Brandy's death. She had no heirs, other than Granny Ariel, and Recov would be entitled to the majority of the salvage award. Morbidly, she realized that Rene could likely be dead. After all, how could a child survive in this environment? It would be impossible.

Was this just a deathtrap? Was Rene dead and was she next? No, she could not think like that. She had to be strong. She had to focus. Rene was the most important thing in her life. She had to get her back.

She checked her watch again as the bass boat drew nearer to the stand of cypress trees that signaled the outskirts of the Honey Island Swamp. She had only forty minutes to reach the drop-off point.

The rain continued to pepper the water in a steady downpour. Lightning flashed, and the thunder roared from the west across the marsh. The relentless rain was loud as it hammered the marsh water.

Brandy noticed that her pants and jacket were now soaked. She felt chilled, despite the extra layer of the bulletproof vest. The baseball cap was saturated, but the bill provided slight protection for her face from the blinding storm.

The stands of cypress and tupelo trees offered some protection from the rain as she steered the vessel into the swamp. It was a both an eerie and mesmerizingly beautiful place with beards of Spanish moss draped across the leafy cypress trees. Except for the pattering rain, the water appeared calm and still. Algae and something that looked like green slime floated in occasional colonies on the black water. She was forced to slow her speed to avoid the random stands of trees. Cypress knees stood out of the water, and thick vines sometimes blocked her path. She noticed several water moccasins perched on the overhanging cypress branches, as well as a red-shouldered hawk overhead. A colorful red, yellow, and black snake slithered through the water near the boat. She decided that it was a plain water snake rather than a coral snake, but just in case, she gave him a wide berth. A large snapping turtle fell off a downed cypress branch as she motored past. Except for the sound of the motor and an occasional hooting of an owl or bullfrog, the area had a peaceful quality.

She continued onward in accordance with the compass heading she had been given by the kidnapper. She now had less than twenty minutes to make it to the drop-off point. She checked the compass and the map again. She felt lost in the sameness of her alien surroundings. The caller had instructed her to look for a large cypress that had been marked with green paint. She was to leave the money on the cypress knees nearby.

She felt a sense of panic as she realized that a landmark like this would be easy to miss. The swamp covered a huge area. What if she could not find it? Could she just leave the money nearby? Was the caller watching her?

Suddenly, the deafening sound of a rifle shot pierced the silence of the swamp. With horror, Brandy saw that the bullet had felled a large cypress branch that crashed into the water behind the boat.

Someone was shooting at her!

She increased her speed and ducked down into the boat, trying to stay out of sight. As the boat lurched forward, she heard another shot behind her as she continued her search for the drop-off point.

Resting in Rene's arms, Raleigh gave a shiver when he caught sight of the large red-shouldered hawk watching him from a high branch in an opposing tree. The creature's ruthless, dark eyes stared at him hungrily, waiting for an opportunity to grab him from Rene's clutches. The squirrel leaned against Rene, flattening himself down in her arms for safety.

Would the hawk attack Rene and attempt to wrench him from her arms? He was not sure. A hawk was equipped with a sharp beak and razor sharp claws. He could easily hurt the child and kill him. Raleigh could not leave the safety of Rene's arms or climb further up the tree until the hawk abandoned the pursuit.

They were perched in the lower crotch of the tree about six feet above the water's surface. Their situation appeared hopeless now. They were stranded in the tree without food or water and no means of escape. The nearest trees were too far away for Rene to safely jump into without the risk of falling into the water. The monstrous alligator, ever vigilant, was still suspended in the water below them. Raleigh estimated that he had remained at his stationary point for the greater part of an hour.

The rain had begun to subside and had slowed to a mere drizzle now. He could tell that Rene was uncomfortable as she shifted her position on the branch.

How could the child possibly sleep in the tree? She would likely fall out, and there was nothing he could do to stop it. He could easily perch in the tree and safely rest for several hours. But, there were the predators like the hawk or an errant snake, so he could never be safe in the trees without Rene shielding him.

Finally, after a time, the hawk recognized the futility of its endeavor and flew away, leaving Raleigh and Rene alone in the tree. Rene, oblivious to the danger presented by the hawk, stroked Raleigh's fur, humming to herself and absently looking out at the swamp. The child was obviously exhausted by her ordeal with the alligator.

"He's still waiting for us," she finally whispered to Raleigh, pointing down at the mammoth alligator below. He had propped his snout and front legs on the inverted hull again and his eyes were partially closed. To any casual bystander, the predator would have appeared to be asleep. But like all cold blooded animals, the reptile was capable of moving at tremendous speed for short periods. This was a finely honed skill utilized to surprise its prey.

Raleigh tapped her hand with his paw gently once for "yes." For the moment, the alligator was the least of his worries. His primary concern now was the possibility of being captured by a hawk or bitten by a snake.

"He's not giving up, but we are safe now in the tree," she continued, stroking the squirrel's fur more fervently now. "We can just wait here until someone comes to get us," she said.

Raleigh felt heartsick at her childish optimism. Except for their captor, they had not seen another person in nearly three days. It was unlikely that there would be anyone who would ever discover them until long after they were dead. Their situation was more hopeless than ever now. They were stuck, without a means to leave the swamp. Their only hope had been the boat. Should they have tried to go down the shell road instead? Could they have found safety? They would never know.

Suddenly, two loud rifle shots pierced the silence in rapid succession, followed by a third. Raleigh felt panic welling within him again. The sound appeared to be not even a hundred yards from their tree.

Danger! Was it a hunter? Or had their kidnapper found them? They would need to hide immediately. He only knew to do what all squirrels do to avoid danger. They would need to climb higher in the tree out of sight of the predator below.

"A gunshot!" Rene whispered to him. "Is someone trying to get us? We need to hide! I don't want them to get us again!"

Raleigh gave her a low, sharp bark. It was a signal that Rene had come to understand meant danger. Ignoring any danger from any arboreal predators, he sprang from her arms onto the trunk of the cypress tree. He barked again and began to climb the tree, signaling the child to follow.

~

Ewan had moored his small watercraft near a stand of cypress knees. He was concealed in a hunter's blind perched eight feet above the water across the sprawling limbs of a majestic cypress tree. The wooden stand had a sturdy overhang supported by two walls that served both to conceal the occupant and provide shelter from the elements. The abandoned shelter had no doubt been utilized by alligator poachers. Since the reptiles had been declared a protected species, their hides brought a hefty sum on the black market. As always, there was an ever-increasing demand for alligator shoes, belts, and purses. He had precipitously discovered the stand two months earlier when he was on a reconnoitering mission in preparation for the kidnapping operation.

He reloaded the sniper rifle, draping it across his legs. A military assault rifle with a scope was positioned nearby in easy reach. He had also purchased three live hand grenades on the black market in Texas. With the aid of his field binoculars, he could easily watch Brandy's boat in the distance, despite the waning light and relentless rain. Wearing camouflage hunter's pants and jacket, Ewan was satisfied that he was well concealed in the blind.

Ewan was exhilarated by the deadly game of cat and mouse that he was playing with the redhead. He was amused by the wild careening of the boat as he fired a shot in close range just to jolt her nerves. Ewan, an expert marksman, could have easily killed her with a strategically placed shot to the head. She was certainly wearing a bullet-proof vest, and a head shot from the sniper rifle would mean certain death. But, beforehand, he wanted to scare her and force any S.W.A.T. team in the area to reveal themselves. Not a half hour earlier, a helicopter hovering over the area had made a strategic drop of three snipers into the swamp. One of them packed something that looked like a camouflaged inflatable raft. Ewan had anticipated the presence of cops and was lying in wait prepared to kill them. He had a general sense of their location as they were lowered separately into the wilderness below. Unlike Ewan, however, the men did not have the protection of the hunter's blind to shield them from view. Ewan would be a worthy match for them because he had seen combat. He had done a stint in Iraq and had spent three years in Afghanistan.

Of course, Ewan would not kill the woman before she made the drop-off of the ransom money. He wanted her reasonably close to him so he could transfer the money to the empty duffle bag resting on the floor. It was a certainty that the cops had inserted a transponder into the widow's money bags and that the bags contained dye designed to stain his hands with indelible stain. Ewan had anticipated those cheap tricks and wore latex gloves and arm covers. After he transferred the money, he would drop the original bags in the swamp a mile or so from the drop-off point to confuse the cops. He would then hide the money for a few weeks in a storage facility he had rented in Pascagoula until he shipped it to himself in California by common carrier.

With the assistance of the high-range military binoculars, he noticed movement in a tree. The little girl and her pet squirrel seemed to be stuck in the tree. His fingers delicately caressed the barrel of the sniper rifle as he debated killing her immediately. There would be plenty of time for that after he killed her mother. The kid could not go far. He decided to wait before ending her life. He needed to do things in the logical progression military style. First, he would kill the assault team, then the mother, and then the kid. It was the only proper plan of action.

Some distance from the kid, Ewan observed a camouflaged sniper with a rifle trained in his direction. From his strategic vantage point, Ewan noticed that the sniper was aiming southwest of his position. Ewan knew that from this direction, he was completely concealed by the blind. He cradled the sniper rifle in his arms and aimed, oblivious to the recoil as he fired. Ewan watched in satisfaction as the sniper's head exploded into a beautiful red cloud before he fell into the swamp below.

Behind him a thunderous shot blew off the northeast corner of the blind overhang. Ever cool under pressure, Ewan located the assailant with the scope and fired. It was another perfect shot. He could not resist smiling as the second sniper tumbled into the water spouting a fountain of blood from what had been the upper half of the man's head. As he lowered the scope, he watched an alligator grab the body, thrashing violently in a churning motion to instinctively drown its victim.

Things were going as planned.

Peering over the bow of the bass boat, Brandy sped through the swamp, turning the boat wildly to avoid hitting the trees in her path. She heard a third shot crack behind her as she wheeled the vessel abruptly south under a large vine hanging like a swag between two cypress trees. Her heart hammered against the walls of her chest.

It was a set-up. The kidnapper intended to kill her and then take the money from the boat. There was never supposed to be a drop-off. It was a deathtrap, and she had foolishly walked into it.

She began to regret that she had declined use of the helmet. Would it have made a difference in the case of such a high-powered weapon? She was not sure. In fact, she did not know whether the bullet-proof vest was strong enough to protect her vital organs in the event that she was shot. She knew that her only hope of remaining alive was to hide in the swamp. Abandoning the boat was out of the question. It was unlikely that a human could survive for very long in the swamp without the protection of a boat.

The small boat careened around a thick cluster of trees, pitching to starboard so hard that the boat nearly turned over. Brandy lost her grip on the steering rod and was thrown through the air, landing against the gunwales of the small vessel. She felt winded momentarily from the hard fall. Somehow, she managed to grab the steering rod again just in time to prevent the boat from crashing headlong into a huge cypress. Suddenly, Brandy felt the bow of the boat knock harshly against the cypress knees that protruded from the water.

Was her pursuer in a hunting stand or was he also in a boat? If she shut the engine down, how long would it take him to find her? Was there more than one? Was the killer intentionally forcing her deeper into the interior of the swamp where she would ambushed by a second killer? She could not be sure. The only thing she knew at this point was that there was definitely a link between Rene's kidnapping and the *BYZANTIUM* lawsuit. Thad and Recov wanted her out of the way so they could make a meager settlement with her estate and take the majority of the salvage award.

As she spun the steering rod to a hard left, she wondered whether the field agents dropped by the helicopter would be able to save her. Perhaps the kidnapper had ambushed and murdered them. It seemed unlikely that anyone could save her now. She would have to outrun them in the small boat, if that were even possible.

Because of the danger of the cypress knees, she could no longer keep her head below the bow of the boat. The small vessel sides obstructed her vision unless she sat on the small bench that stretched across the area nearest to the stern. She knew that if she ran into a cypress knee at such a high speed, it could cause the boat to flip over in the air. There was also a danger that a collision at this speed could throw her from the boat. She would have to be as careful as possible under the circumstances.

The trees became thicker and thicker until she reached an area that appeared to be a channel. Evidence of a gentle current rippled across the surface. Brandy studied the area momentarily. On the one hand, she would be more exposed to the killer, but on the other hand, she could gain speed if she stayed near the trees. She elected to take the risk, increasing the boat to top speed as she sped through the water.

She heard the sputter of the engine before the outboard motor died. Brandy knew immediately that the little boat was out of gas. Unlike many bass boats, this one was not equipped with a gas can on board for just such an eventuality.

She was stranded.

Brandy grabbed one of the oars and began to paddle through the channel. Without the boat's speed, speed, she would need to return to the safety of the trees. She paddled as hard as possible, ignoring the ache in her arms. The boat was too wide to use both oars at the same time. Therefore, it was necessary for her to paddle on one side and then the other to steer the boat. Despite the persistent rain, she felt herself beginning to sweat underneath her jacket. She would need to remove the jacket. It was bright yellow, which was a color that stood out in the swamp. Underneath, she had on a soft-green cotton shirt. The color would be less noticeable from a distance.

She heard the crack of another rifle shot as she began to unzip the jacket. Brandy's left arm began to sting, and she saw a burgundy plume of blood that began to cover her jacket sleeve. The fabric on the sleeve had been shredded and hung loosely on her arm.

Had she been shot? She only felt a slight stinging sensation. Was she badly hurt? She needed to get out of the open! It was her only hope.

With lightning speed, she ripped off the jacket and tossed it into the water. It was noticeable enough that she could not afford to keep it in the boat. She realized that her arm was bleeding from the bullet.

Had she driven toward the killer instead of away from him? Her only hope was to get into the trees.

Ignoring the pain in her arm, she lifted the oar to paddle the boat into the trees. As she dipped the oar into the water, she turned just in time to see a large alligator, sniffing the bloody fabric of her jacket. Stimulated by the smell of blood, the large reptile clenched its jaws around her jacket and towed it under the surface. Ignoring her trembling hands and the pain in her arm, Brandy turned away from the reptile and furiously paddled in the direction of the stand of cypress trees. Within less than a minute, she was camouflaged by the stands of towering cypress trees. Desperately, she continued to paddle the small boat into the interior of the swamp.

CHAPTER XXXIII

Her back was peppered by rain as Brandy frantically oared her way through the swamp. Within minutes, she was nestled again among the trees. Pain shot through her arms while she furiously paddled the boat. After what had seemed hours, she finally took refuge among a tight cluster of cypress trees that formed a small natural enclosure, slipping the boat into the small haven. She could hear her ragged breath over the din of the rain.

Was she concealed? She could not be sure. The killer had the advantage of binoculars. At the very least, he could probably locate her with the rifle scope. She had to be well concealed or she would certainly not survive.

Brandy ignored the large water moccasin that coiled around a branch overhead that stretched out over the swamp water. She would not allow herself to think about what would happen if it dropped into the boat. Under ordinary circumstances, she would have given the snake a wide berth. Now, she did not have that luxury, and she was forced to share the small territory with the reptile.

Out of habit, she checked her watch. Over twenty minutes had passed since she had tossed her jacket into the swamp. She had clearly missed the drop-off deadline, as if it really mattered. Brandy leaned down inside of the boat, curling up into a fetal position. She was vaguely aware that tears poured down her cheeks, mixing with the relentless rain. Feeling a numbness settle over her chest, she allowed herself to think about Rene as she huddled down inside of the boat.

Surely her baby was dead. It seemed impossible, really. Had she suffered? Oh, please God, let it have been quick. Now, she was alone. Maybe she should just let them shoot her. She had nothing to live for now. Without Rene, Brandy's life was over.

She tried to rest, ignoring the stinging of her left arm. The area where the bullet had grazed her had left a deep flesh wound, likely affecting the musculature of her arm. If she survived, she would need to get immediate medical attention and fresh water, lest a severe infection set in. She had only a single bottle of water with her which contained less than a cup of water. Careful not to waste any of the fluid, Brandy inverted the bottle and gently washed the wound. It had bled profusely, and the wound was crusted with blood. Gently, she dabbed the wound with the edge of her shirt.

Brandy surveyed the damage to her arm. She had been lucky this time, but next time she might not survive. It would be necessary to cover her arm. Insects, and especially mosquitoes, that lived around the fetid swamp water carried dangerous infections. Laboriously, she managed to rip a piece of her shirt and wrap it around her arm with her right hand. The fabric was wet from the rain, allowing her to tie a rather taunt knot around her upper arm. It was only a temporary solution, but it would have to work for now.

There had been no more gunshots. Was he close by? Could he see her? Was he in a boat? She did not hear another motor.

As she crouched in the boat, she noticed that the light was waning. According to her watch, it was a little after six forty-five. It would be pitch-dark in less than an hour. Given the dark shadows in the swamp, long-range visibility would be impaired within thirty minutes. Unless the kidnapper had military night vision goggles, the darkness would even the playing field. If she could stay successfully hidden just a little longer, she could leave the area during the night and hopefully reach safety. She flattened herself against the side of the little boat and continued to wait in silence.

∾

Ewan searched the swamp with the scope shoved through the narrow opening of the blind. The woman was about one hundred yards away, partially concealed in a thicket of cypress trees. Fortunately, she had stopped running and had decided to remain stationary. He had easily located the kid who had miraculously ascended the heights of the cypress. Her new position now made her a perfect target. He decided to kill her immediately after he shot the last sniper. The operation had stalled. He knew instinctively from his military experience that time in this situation could often be an enemy.

Again, he scanned the horizon, searching for the remaining sniper in the trees. Ever vigilant, he searched the swamp below for a sign of the small dingy. As the twilight faded, he switched to his night vision goggles. With fastidious precision, he studied the surrounding trees for any sign of the last sniper.

Ewan knew that he needed to be highly vigilant. The last sniper may have pinpointed his location in the blind based upon the range of the shots he had fired at the other snipers.

He could hear what sounded like an approaching helicopter in the distance. They were likely bringing in reinforcements. This was an unwelcome development.

He saw the movement from the stand of cypress knees about twenty feet away in his peripheral vision. As he turned to aim, he was suddenly knocked down by a powerful blow. The bullet-proof vest had protected him from the gunshot, although the force of the shot had thrown him down on the wooden platform. Ewan immediately lifted his weapon and aimed at the sniper below him. He was partially shielded by the hunting blind and clearly had the advantage. The man was moving across the cypress knees coming toward him with his weapon pointed toward the blind.

Ewan heard a deafening noise from below him as he prepared to pull the trigger. The bullet shattered the cypress platform beneath him and spiraled into the back of his head. For a few seconds, he marveled at the kaleidoscope of colorful light before his skull exploded, raining brain matter into the swamp.

And then there was darkness.

~

Raleigh and Rene perched at least forty feet overhead on a limb of the cypress tree in the waning light. The rain had subsided into a gentle spray, and night was beginning to fall. Rene was barefoot, having abandoned her leather-soled sandals that had hindered her ability to climb the tree.

They were safe temporarily. The gunshots had stopped again. With the exception of the dripping water from the trees and the fine rain, the swamp was silent again.

A cacophony of bullfrogs sang in the gathering darkness below them. Raleigh lapped some rain-water from an indentation in the branch and chewed on the cambium of a new cypress branch. He felt exhausted and weak. Neither he nor Rene had had anything to eat since morning. He had given Rene a small branch to chew on as a distraction to take her mind off her hunger. Rene had not said a word in over an hour. The child clasped to the tree like a young monkey, silently gnawing on the cypress branch.

He would have to convince her to move down the tree for the nightfall where she could lie in the crotch of the tree. If Rene fell out of the tree from this height, she would certainly be killed. They would have to be watchful of predators.

Raleigh made a soft, gentle clucking noise to Rene to signal to her that they had to go down the tree. She nodded and attempted to follow the agile squirrel as he expertly climbed down the tree trunk toward the water. He watched from a nearby limb as Rene struggled to climb down the tree. It was more difficult for a child who had a healthy fear of heights.

Within minutes, Rene had finally climbed down from her perch to the crotch of the tree, where three large branches converged. The tree provided an area where Rene could comfortably stretch her legs over a branch and safely lean against the tree trunk. Raleigh hopped into the child's arms, and together they took a nap, cradled in the crotch of the tree as darkness fell.

~

He awoke with a start. He had dreamed about Gerald Morris, the old man again, cradling his limp granddaughter in his arms. She was a beautiful child with golden curls and an angelic face. The gunshot had shattered her skull and the old man was screaming her name.

Jenny was her name. He remembered now! He had loved her so much!. She had looked so much like her mother, Mindy. How did he know so much about this old man? How did he know his name? It was the same dream that had plagued him for years. He knew that the man's life had ended when the child had died. A few years later, Morris had died of a heart attack. Did he ever know this man? How was that possible since he had been dead for many years? Had he once been human? Had he in fact been Gerald Morris? And was Rene really Jenny? It was so odd the way he could see her beautiful face, even though she had died nearly half a century earlier. He was unsure of what had happened, but he knew that he had been living for this moment! He could not let anything happen to Rene. Rene and Granny Ariel were his entire life and he loved them more than life itself.

Raleigh listened carefully. He could hear the familiar sound of a paddle as it dipped into the water below.

Was it the kidnapper?

He froze and instinctively wagged his tail for the danger signal. Rene heard the sound also. She jerked awake and leaned against the tree. He could feel her heart pounding in her chest. He wagged his tail furiously to signal to Rene to be silent. He dare not bark or he would alert the killer.

The rain had stopped, and the sky had partially cleared. Light from a half-moon shone overhead. In the half-light, he could barely make out a lone figure below paddling a small boat only on the right. The metallic smell of fresh and crusted blood wafted up from the boat. Whoever it was had been injured.

Rene wiped her eyes and stared in disbelief. "Mommy!" she cried plaintively.

Raleigh saw the startled figure in the boat look up just as another gunshot rang out from behind them.

~

"Don't move, Rene!" Brandy whispered as she caught sight of them on the branch. "Duck down, baby," she instructed her daughter.

Brandy lay down flat in the bottom of the boat in the dark shadows.

Rene trembled on the branch beside him. She cried softly, her shoulders heaving. “I want Mommy!” she told Raleigh.

Before he could stop her Rene, began climbing down the tree toward the little boat and her mother. Raleigh watched helplessly as she hung from the side of the trunk, attempting to scoot over low enough to jump onto an adjoining cypress knee. It was a long distance, and he wondered whether the child would make it.

Her best chance was to be still. If she fell into the water, she could easily die before her mother could reach her.

A large helicopter suddenly appeared overhead, shining a blinding cone of light that illuminated the swamp around them. Brandy was clearly visible in the tiny boat below. Noisily, the helicopter hovered directly overhead, blowing the tops of the cypress trees. “Stay where you are!” a loud voice amplified from a loudspeaker told them. “The kidnapper is dead. Someone will come and get you.”

Rene continued her climb down the tree toward her mother. As Rene lowered herself down to the lowest branch, Raleigh saw the water moccasin languidly eying Rene several feet away. He watched helplessly as Rene, oblivious to the danger, grabbed the branch and attempted to lower herself down to a cypress knee to reach her mother. The snake began to slither toward the child’s hands. Suddenly, Rene became aware of the snake and began to scream.

He had to do something! This was a very large snake and probably venomous enough to kill a child. He had to save her even if it cost him his life.

Raleigh sprang from the trunk across to the branch, landing on the back of the snake with his long claws. He bit the snake hard on the back to distract it and attempted to shove it from the branch. His teeth were not really sharp enough to do any major damage, although they were blunt enough to draw blood. With lightning speed, the snake turned and bit him on the nape of the neck. At the same time, Raleigh shoved the snake with all of his might partially off the branch and tangled together, both of them fell into the water.

Raleigh felt a numbness envelope his body immediately. Oddly, it was not painful. He was vaguely aware of being hoisted from the water in a fishing net. He could feel Rene's gentle hands stroking his coat as she cradled him in her arms against her chest.

"He saved me, Mommy! Raleigh saved me!" Rene cried. "I love him so much! I do not want him to die!" she sobbed.

"I know, honey. I saw Raleigh attack the snake. It was very brave," Brandy said as she held Rene in her arms. Tears of relief were running down her face.

Raleigh felt strangely calm as he lay immobilized against Rene. It was more difficult to breathe now. He savored the gentle stroking of his little friend's hands as he closed his eyes.

He had saved her. She was alive against incredible odds. It made everything alright.

He wanted to comfort Rene, but he found that he could not move. As the poison coursed through his veins, he felt strangely warm and peaceful. He was happy now, safe in Rene's arms. He had not been able to save Jenny all those years ago, but he had saved Rene. He surrendered to the sense of peacefulness that calmed him as he lay quietly in her arms. He wanted to tell her not to cry. He had lived two full lives—once as a human and then as a squirrel.

Nothing else mattered now that Rene was alive. Rene and her mother would be saved now and they would lead a happy life. He felt himself begin to float on a soft cloud, and he could feel Jenny's presence. Rene's voice was distant now, as he began peacefully to move toward the beautiful light.

Epilogue

TWO YEARS LATER

Brandy took a shower and changed into a green dress and matching high-heels. This afternoon, she was taking Rene and four of her friends to see the stage production of the *Lion King* to celebrate Rene's birthday, followed by an early dinner at Commander's Palace. Ginger, the mother of Rene's best friend Molly, had agreed to join them to help with the kids at dinner.

As she left her room, she glanced over toward the door to Granny Ariel's room which now remained closed. Today, as was often her habit, Brandy opened the door to remember her grandmother. Nothing had been changed in the room since her death six months ago. Granny Ariel had recovered nicely from the surgery two years ago and had lived a full life until last October when she had died peacefully in her sleep. Brandy and Rene had not had the heart to change one thing in the room or to disturb her grandmother's clothes. Somehow, keeping her room the same had kept her alive in Brandy's mind just a little bit longer.

Brandy's eyes rested on the tiny antique doll bed where Granny Ariel had kept her pet squirrel. Of course, they had all been surely exaggerating Raleigh's talents. Remarkably, though, he had been ferociously protective of Rene and had sacrificed his own life to save her from the water moccasin. They had buried the squirrel under a small marble marker in the back-yard near the gazebo where he had sat with Granny Ariel so many times. Granny Ariel and Rene had been devastated by the loss of their little pet. Rene and Granny Ariel had made friends with some of the other squirrels in the park, but they assured Brandy that "it was not the same." Rene told her every day now that she was sure that Raleigh and Granny Ariel were in heaven together playing checkers.

Thad Stuart, Whit Champlain, and Quinn Beazley were indicted for conspiracy to commit kidnapping of Rene and the murder of Harris Blake. The New Orleans District Attorney also indicted the men with counts for intimidation of a witness, obstruction of justice, perjury, and the felony murder of two law enforcement officers. The three men pleaded guilty to life without parole to avoid the death sentence, and their state and federal sentences were set to run consecutively. Thad, Whit Champlain, and Recov all relinquished their rights to the salvage operation or cargo from BYZANTIUM as a bargaining tool to escape the death sentence.

Twenty months ago, Brandy and the London Underwriters subscribing to the BYZANTIUM hull and cargo slips had easily reached a settlement agreement, equally dividing the proceeds from the sale of the emeralds. The firm of Boudreaux Banks had recovered a large fee. Chris bought a second home in the south of France with his settlement and partially retired. Claude's career had flourished as a result of his mere involvement in the case, which provided him with an international reputation in the field. The amount of his referral work had increased tenfold and, as a result, the size of the boutique firm had nearly tripled.

Brandy received $200 million dollars as her portion of the settlement. She endowed a marine biology chair in Harris's name at Tulane University. A few of the largest emeralds and hull fragments were donated in Harris's name to the Smithsonian and the British Museum. Brandy established a large trust for Rene and expanded

Massenet. The two of them did not have any financial worries for the rest of their lives.

Most importantly, though, the two of them were alive. Rene had some counseling after her ordeal, but the therapists had assured Brandy that the child was remarkably unscathed. This assurance was worth more than any of the money she received in the settlement. Brandy could not believe that so many people had died out of greed.

She took one last look around Granny Ariel's room before closing the door. One day, she knew that she would need to clean out the room and store her grandmother's things. But for now, she would keep the status quo as a bittersweet reminder of her grandmother's life.

Made in the USA
Middletown, DE
25 August 2017